The White Elephant Kneels

By Roxana Gillett

GPS, Write Direction Publishing
Las Cruces, N.M.

THE WHITE ELEPHANT KNEELS

GPS, Write Direction Publishing
Las Cruces, N.M. 88011

ISBN-13:978-0-615-98342-4
ISBN-10:0615983421

Cover design by Mengyuan Xue

Manufactured in the United States of America
First printing March 2014

DEDICATION

To the best friend I've ever had. Without you, Darwin, "The White Elephant Kneels" would have been nothing more than an unexpressed thought . . . as would my life.

To the animals that have touched my heart and on occasion raised the hairs on my neck, I'm forever grateful for us being in the same place at the same time. To Marine World Africa USA and all the people who worked there; you are at the core of who I am.

ACKNOWLEDEGMENTS

To the gang of six in Gig Harbor, Washington, thanks for your support and critiques. Teri, a special thanks to you for "everything;" for the courage you instilled in me, the time you so generously gave; and for the hard, (ouch!) hard push to keep writing. To Larry, who always encouraged and untangled my computer frustration, more than once. To Cheryl, Barb and Brent who labored though page after page of early drafts. To Colleen Slater (Gig Harbor News), the first of my editors, thanks for not laughing too loud, at all the errors and for educating me on when, where and how to use a comma...still confusing.

To Lori Handelman, PhD, at Clear Voice Editing. This story could never have been told with such clarity, without your detailed story edits, I owe you big time. Ditto goes for Rob Bignell, for his expert editing, formatting and pulling "The White Elephant Kneels" together and getting it online. And to the last piece in the publishing puzzle, Mengyuan Xue, thanks for the cover.

Chapter 1
The First Ten

The Sunday morning before my tenth birthday, I sat at our kitchen table looking out the window, watching a dozen or so sunbirds sip nectar from the tulip tree blossoms. The tree was over 30 feet tall and grew at the edge of our yard. During the morning it cast a wide shadow all the way to the covered front porch. Our house was large, one-story wood-sided and painted white, with a sturdy tin roof. It didn't fit Africa's uncomplicated backdrop. It looked as out of place among the thatched roof huts of Ndogo as I felt.

Nanta, the African woman who had raised me since birth, stood behind my chair, her strong fingers weaving my wild auburn hair into a tight French braid. My own fingers were busy arranging little bits of toast crumbs into a small circle on the table top. Nanta was as tall and thin, as most Maasai men, and dressed in a slip dress dyed blue. It hung loose on her thin frame, her shoulders and arms bare, and her skin so dark it glistened even in the shade. There were two chairs at the table; one was dad's and one was mine.

The ceiling fan was still. The smells of morning eggs and burnt toast lingered in the confines of the kitchen's soft butter-colored walls. The dishes sat in the sink. Outside, the morning breeze sat quiet, bashful, not unlike the question I was gathering the courage to ask. I looked down at my circle of crumbs, swallowed, chewed on my lower lip, released it and swallowed again.

"Nanta, where is my mother buried?" I asked. My heartbeat quickened when I turned to glance at her, then plummeted when I caught the stern look on her face.

"Why do you want to know such a thing?"

"Because dad's taking me to Mbali tomorrow, and I've heard there's voodoo there."

"Who told you there was voodoo in Mbali?" She gathered another bunch of my hair in her hands, as I nudged the crumbs into the shape of a box.

"Nobody, I just heard," I said and pushed the crumbs back into a circle.

"Don't believe everything you hear, Lill. Your father is taking you to Mbali for your birthday because you asked to see the elephants."

"But the villagers whisper things when they think I'm not listening and I heard them say my mother was a witchdoctor. So, I thought if there is voodoo in Mbali, then maybe that's where she's—"

Her tongue hit sharp against the roof of her mouth. "*Click-click.* Enough. Your mother died after giving birth to you. She was holding you in her arms when she took her last breath. No voodoo...no voodoo burial in Mbali. The people who talk of such things, of *machawis* and witchdoctors, shouldn't be talking about them. We are Christians here in Ndogo. Your father would not approve of such gossip."

"My mother held me?"

"Hush child, I've said too much. You know your father doesn't want us talking about her."

"Why not?

"That's between him and his God."

"Everything is between him and God," I snapped. I felt bad as soon as I said it and chewed on my thumbnail waiting for Nanta to scold me for being disrespectful. When she didn't, I mumbled, "Well, wherever her grave is, I should be able to go see it. What's the big secret?"

"You know not to ask me these questions. Where your mother is...is not my place to say. You need to ask your father." Nanta tucked the last bit of my hair in place. "There. We're finished. Now go get your father and hurry him up or he'll be late for church." She patted my head and sent me on my way.

Dad, the reverend John Francis Drake, was the minister of our small village. I remember him always wearing black. Except for the pure white of his clerical collar that shone out from under his clean shaven chin, there was nothing he wore that wasn't serious and black. His pale Irish face was as somber as his clothes. The only thing about him that was out of place was his unruly red hair. No matter how many times he pushed it back, a thing he did both unconsciously and consciously all day long, it instantly sprang back to where it wanted to be. My own hair was just as unmanageable but darker, a blend of my African mother's hair and his.

Dad sat behind the big wooden desk in his office, writing. *The Book of Sermons* was opened next to his notepad. He scribbled with furious dedication across a writing pad illuminated by the brass lamp on his desk. I stopped and waited in the doorway for him to finish and notice me. The familiar smell of leather, shoe polish, and clove-scented pipe tobacco waited with me. A narrow shaft of morning light slipped between the drawn curtain panels behind him and marched, without any hesitation, into the room.

Dad finally set his pen down, closed his eyes and leaned back in his chair. He drew on his pipe. I straightened my shoulders but didn't move from the doorway.

"Dad?" My timid voice tripped over itself as it fell across the room.

"Come on in, Lill. I'm finished." His fingers beckoned me into his dimly lit office. He closed *The Book of Sermons* as his eyes scanned over what he had just written. He caught something that needed correcting, picked up his pen and added a quick notation.

My nervous legs carried me to the edge of his desk where I ran my fingers back and forth across its smooth wood as my teeth and tongue worried my lower lip.

"Lill?" His brows arched. He placed his pipe on the china dish next to the lamp and switched off the light. He pushed his chair back, stood, came around the desk and lifted me in his arms with a smile and a hug.

"Dad, Nanta said I should ask you where my mother is buried." The words burst out before I lost my courage and changed my mind.

Dad's lips closed into a thin tight line then parted. "Nanta said this?"

"Yes," I replied in a quiet little voice.

Frowning, dad carried me to the rocking chair in the corner of the room next to the big grandfather clock and sat me down in it. I didn't look at him. Instead I focused my attention on the chair. The chair was covered in a light-brown-leather, the same color as me; we blended. I studied the pattern of my green Sunday dress and smoothed the fabric. My legs were bare and my feet wore white socks and black Sunday school shoes. I tapped my shoes together, keeping time to the big clock's relentless tick-tocking, picked at the stitching in the chair and waited for Dad to answer.

The back of his smooth hand reached down and stroked my cheek. His fingers slipped under my chin and gently held it; with the thumb of his other hand he marked the sign of the cross on my forehead. He removed his hands and I watched, broken-hearted, as his black shoes carried him toward the door. My unanswered question spilled down my cheeks along with the tears.

When he reached the office door he stopped. Hopeful, I wiped my face dry. "Your mother is living in..." He spoke without facing me, his voice dragged down by the undertow of emotion. He sighed, ran his fingers through his hair then turned in my direction. "She's living in heaven with God. Let it be, Lill. Let her be."

Except for his Sunday sermons, dad never talked loudly. Even his hard-soled shoes walked him around on hushed whispers. On Sunday he wore a black cassock over his black suit. A thin black stole hung around his shoulders, each end embroidered with a large gold cross.

Dad's sermons began when he brought his fingertips to the tip of his nose and made a pointy church steeple. His penetrating blue eyes dared every member of the congregation to admit they hadn't sinned. When he was satisfied he had their attention, he closed his eyes. Reverent and humble he offered the morning-prayer, asking God for their salvation as well his own. And mine, too. With the "Amen," he stretched his arms wide as his eyes cast out a threatening look over his flock. Then dad took up his Bible and bounded from behind the pulpit to the center of the stage.

"God's power." His deep voice thundered as his foot stomped the floor and his hand shook the Bible high over his head. His warning glare cautioned the congregation to remain silent. Ten rows of wooden pews on either side of the aisle were filled with the faithful. Some blotted their faces as the temperature rose inside the tiny church. Others squirmed in their seats, ill at ease. Very few sat pious and free of sin.

"God's power will cast the wicked into hell!" His voice was filled with foreboding, ominous and disapproving. Mothers, fathers, children and grandparents clutched their hands tightly around Bibles and each other. I sat alone in the front pew; my own Bible untouched on the bench beside me.

Dad leaned toward the congregation and whispered a warning. "God watches you when you sin and he hears you when you lie; he knows your darkest secrets." His stout finger pointed randomly around the room.

In a raised voice he scolded, "God holds you accountable for your transgression." He waited a moment for effect then added, "But God forgives you. Praise the Lord!" He slapped his hand against his Bible, stomped his foot then reached to the heaven he believed in and shouted, "Praise the Lord, praise the Lord. Hallelujah! Praise the Lord."

I was amazed and frightened that Dad's God had the power to change Dad so completely. Later, I came to understand this was the only time and place he actually felt safe and protected by the God he worshiped.

I didn't believe God knew my secret. I bowed my head when Dad said to but I never prayed—I was afraid God might somehow change me, too.

Dad carried me in his warm arms that night to my bedroom. After he tucked me in and leaned over to give me a goodnight kiss, he sat on my bed. When his eyes met mine, his head snapped aside as if to free himself from what he saw in them. I'd seen dad do this before, but tonight his reaction was so strong he didn't have time to hide it. This frightened me more than the fear I felt when I looked at my eyes in a mirror.

"Dad, what's...?"

He gently pressed his fingertips to my lips, to stop further inquiry, closed his eyes and bent forward. He kissed my forehead. He moved his lips to my ear and whispered, "Got to rub the kiss in, Lill, so God will keep you safe." I could feel the sign of the cross his thumb made on my brow and I felt his lips continue to move in a silent and secret prayer. When he finished, he kissed the top of my head, stood, then walked to the door and switched off the light. "Goodnight, Lill. Sweet dreams," he whispered in the dark, closing the door behind him.

Alone, I stared at the ceiling and wondered what he saw in my eyes and wouldn't tell me.

I puffed out an angry breath of air, pursed my lips, rolled on my side, hugged my pillow and started counting imaginary elephant people waving their trunks at me as they moved through the green mist of the Mbali jungle. Sleep nudged my eyelids closed.

"You promised." A woman's harsh whisper cut through the screen of my open window.

My eyes sprang wide. Clutching the blanket, I sat up in bed. I turned my head to the left then to the right, trying to hear more. Everything was quiet but the sound of my racing heart. I took a deep breath to calm it and listened more intensely. A minute passed, then two. My eyes grew heavy. I stifled a yawn. A nightmare? No, it must have been a dream, just a dream. I yawned and stretched then scooted down in bed, pulled the cover up to my chin and fell asleep.

"You promised me." The woman's voice stabbed the midnight air and flew across the room to the edge of my bed.

I jerked into a sitting position and pressed my back against the wall beside my bed. Pulling my legs under me, I turned an ear toward the window, rubbed my sleep-bound eyes awake and strained to hear what she was saying. Above my bed, the rough wooden cross tied to a circle of intertwined twigs listened with me.

"Goddamn you. It's not right!" Dad's angry voice shattered the moonless sky. I had never heard Dad take the Lord's name in vain. Not once, not ever. And the very idea he had, forced me tighter to the wall.

"Don't damn me. You agreed to this. You gave your oath...you swore to it in your God's name."

"I'll damn you if I want! I'll damn you and your voodoo soul!"

"If she fails, you can have her back. But we both need to know what she is capable of. This will be settled tomorrow. It was never up to us. It was out of my hands and yours from the beginning. Just bring her to Mbali."

Who did this woman want dad to take with us to Mbali? I

gathered the blanket in my hands and covered my ears, so I could think. Their leftover echoes rumbled around in my head, but nothing they said made any sense. I gave up and lowered the blanket to hear more but their shouting had stopped. The night was quiet, too still, and the odd silence scared me more than their angry voices.

The back door opened and closed. Dad came in the house and I listened to his weary footsteps take him to his bedroom. He pulled his door shut with a soft click.

In a tree outside my window an owl asked, "Whooo-whoo?"

My shoulders relaxed and I took a deep breath as the soothing night voices of Africa returned. The animals were talking again. There was nothing to be afraid of.

A dog in the village barked…another answered.

The high screech of the night bird sliced through the darkness as it took flight, bringing the flutter of soft wings past my window in the pursuit of prey.

Kooee-kooee, a crowned eagle chimed from a distant treetop.

I glanced at the cross above my head and realized it was the animals that made me feel safe. I trusted them more than I trusted dad's God. I wiggled down under the bed covers, rolled onto my side, and closed my eyes. I fell asleep to the happy sounds of chattering animals and the tranquil sighs of Africa.

The wind woke me. Its thunderous gale rattled and pounded on the front door, demanding entrance. I pulled the blanket over my head and hid. The wind slammed and pushed the wood door, battering it with ruthless determination, until it finally gave way. The steel doorknob crashed against the living room wall and the wind blasted down the hall and banged against my door, then suddenly stopped. I froze, held rigid by the unspeakable quiet, by the un-breathable emptiness that followed. A feral sound cracked through the void and convulsed down the hall on heavy angry paws. I curled into a tight ball, held my breath and waited. Outside my bedroom the feet paced back and forth like a caged animal. I sucked in a determined gulp of air then cursed myself for making such a loud noise, but I went ahead and lifted the covers. My heart ran wild when I saw the fractured vapor of a red-black light crawl through the slit beneath my door.

"Nooo!" dad screamed, hitting the door with the full force of his body.

"Daddy, please..." I whispered, too frightened to shout, too afraid to move.

I could hear dad gasp for air as he fought with the unseen terror; as he tugged and pulled at the glowing red fog to keep it from clawing its way further into my room. A hate-filled snarl spit hot embers through the slim opening, sending red sparks skittering across the floor all the way to the edge of my bed. I pulled my knees to my chest and held them tight against me. My body shook. Tears tumbled down my face. I clenched my teeth and sucked in a sob.

I listened to dad's fists slam into flesh: one, two, three times, more. The red-black vapor flashed bright then grew dimmer with each punch. A nightmarish howl filled the house and the unearthly red vapor vanished. I heard dad race toward the front door, bound down the front steps and out into the yard...and then...I heard nothing more.

I unwrapped myself in inches, bit by bit. The faint smell of charred wood clung to the motionless air that had overtaken my room. Nothing moved, inside or out. Then the air shifted, and the hellish sound of paws running toward my window quickened my heartbeat. A demented red vapor smashed into the screen as fierce white fangs ripped into the mesh.

"Leave her alone!" dad screamed from afar. The creature hissed and snarled. The red glow flashed bright then quickly vanished. I blinked into the darkness it left behind.

"Whooo?" the night owl asked.

Dad ran up the back porch steps.

"Tok-tok," answered the crow.

The back door opened and shut.

The low *kooee-kooee* from a crowned eagle settled the night.

"Lill." Dad tapped on my door, opened it, and walked hurriedly across the room. He sat on my bed and pulled me onto his lap.

"Dad, what happened?" I asked, as his arms held me to his chest.

"There was a leopard in the village, Lill." Dad brushed some strands of hair from my face then tucked them behind my ear and kissed the top of my head, before he continued. "He got in the house. He's gone now. Are you okay, sweetheart?"

"I'm okay. A leopard? But I saw a red light and sparks."

"No sparks, just my flashlight. That's all it was, my flashlight and a very confused leopard. Nothing more. I chased him away, you're safe now."

"Did he hurt you?"

"No. I'm okay. Everything is taken care of. There's nothing for you to be afraid of."

"You were yelling at a woman, Dad. She said—"

"A woman from another village; she was having a problem. I'm sorry our disagreement woke you."

"You said something about voodoo, and she said something about Mbali."

"Ah, Lill, she'd been drinking. It was the drink talking. Now get some sleep. It's your birthday tomorrow, a big day for you. We're going to find out if that mist and those elephant- people you talk about seeing are real. "

"Dad, I know there are no elephant people waving at me from the mist. It's just something I like to pretend. But there are elephants in Mbali...and I really do want to see them." I didn't say I'd heard there was voodoo in Mbali, too, because I knew he wouldn't talk about it; he never did.

With a quick kiss, dad rolled me back in bed and pulled up

the cover. He stood and walked to the door.

"But I do see the mist," I said.

"Tomorrow we'll find out what you can see and what you can't. Goodnight, Lill, sweet dreams.

Chapter 2

Dawn-gray light shadowed my room. In the distance I heard a pack of *fisi* (hyena) laughing. Today was my tenth birthday so I pretended the hyenas were singing a happy birthday song just for me. And with each ghoulish giggle they were lighting another candle on my birthday cake.

Joining the hyena's macabre melody, a female *Bongo*, hidden in the thick brush beyond our house, emitted a long, weak *moo* after each and every ghastly cackle. This was followed by the strange snort-snuffle-honk of wild hogs. A spotted eagle added a high-pitched screech to their primitive song as they gathered their voices together, singing the best animal version of happy birthday ever sung.

I waited for their song to fade, then slid bravely from my single bed and walked twelve short steps across the wood floor to the window. I sat in the wooden chair next to the sill, hesitated for just a second, then reached up and touched the torn screen. My heartbeat quickened as I ran my fingers over the mesh. I thought about the wind and the leopard. The wind must have frightened the big cat as much at it frightened me and sent him running into the house.

During the day, I sometimes sat in the hard-backed chair and watched the mystical green mist quiver along the rim of the Mbali jungle. I imagined enchanted elephant people stepping out of the fuzzy haze and waving; beckoning me to come inside their secret emerald forest and play. I leaned forward and rested my elbows on the windowsill and watched *Jua*, the Lady Sun, getting ready to wake the day. I was mesmerized by *Jua's* magic, how she embraced the dawn's ashen veil and wove the sky into a purplish steel color. How she set the treetops of the Mbali

Jungle alight with her sun fire, long before she poked her hot round face over the edge of the earth. *Jua's* sunlight would color the green-mist of Mbali with her golden warmth and it would sparkle-like jewels.

Anxious for my birthday to begin, I wiggled in my seat. The instant I saw her golden head, I'd spin in the chair and check the clock on my nightstand. The time had to be right; it just had to be. I knew so little about my birth, but I did know what time I was born.

Jua's head popped up. I rotated in my seat and looked at the clock; it read 5:55, the exact moment of my birth. My stomach fluttered as if a dozen tree frogs were hopping around inside it. Something special was going to happen today; I just knew it.

The time of my birth was something I overheard Nanta and Senento, her son, whispering about when they didn't know I was listening. They talked about the numbers adding up.

"It's a sign," Nanta told him. "Three tens."

Senento said, "Ten is a strong number. But three of them..."

Nanta clicked her tongue, "It can't be questioned. 5:55 was the time of Lillian's birth. The first two fives in the time add up to ten. The last five and the day she was born, the second ten. October is the tenth month and the third ten."

I didn't understand why the time of my birth was such a big secret and could only be talked about in whispers. But I believed dad when he said my tenth birthday, more than all the others, was going to be the best one ever—he was taking me to Mbali to see the elephants. So I pushed aside my questions and turned to watch the enchantment outside. *Jua* was filling the sky with her orange brilliance. I breathed in deep, hoping to catch the magical colors of her sunrise inside me. Warmth filled us...the sky, the earth, and me. I was one with Mother Earth; she was the only mother I had ever known.

A soft knock on my bedroom door interrupted my thoughts. Nanta opened it and stepped inside.

"*Click-click,*" the sound of Nanta's African tongue hitting the roof of her mouth was followed by, "watching the sunrise; it is a good way to start your birthday." She closed the door behind her and stood still like a tall tree, her thin arms crossed under her small breasts. She lowered them and strode into the room on quick bare feet. "Come, I have a surprise for you."

She turned my back toward her then rapidly and with much pulling and tugging raked her strong slender fingers through my morning hair. Untangling the long strands and parting the unruly curls away from my face, Nanta gathered the whole mess at the back of my head. She hung onto it when I tilted my head back and asked, "Nanta, did you hear the wind last night? Did you see the leopard?"

"Child, where did you come up with this? Wind? There was no wind. Your father told me about the cat. It was unusual but nothing more." With a flick of her wrist three long strings of shiny silver and gold beads slipped into her hand. "Now turn around and hold still." Nanta promptly started to braid one of the strands into my hair.

"But, Nanta, the wind blew the front door open. It banged so loud the doorknob must have smashed a hole in the wall."

"*Click-click,*" Nanta's tongue scolded. "There is no hole in the wall."

"But—"

"Stop, child, enough of your foolishness. No wind, no hole, just a frightened leopard. Nothing more."

"And there was shouting outside my window. Dad was yelling and he—"

"Stop. No more talk," she chided as she wove in the last string of beads. "Now take a look," she said as she guided me to the long mirror beside my dresser. Nanta spun me around and put the hand mirror, from on top the dresser, in my hand.

I avoided looking at my eyes in either mirror as I studied Nanta's handy work. I didn't like my eyes, as they weren't normal. They were mostly brown, but there were three little blue pie-shaped wedges in each eye that never held still. Each blue-triangle was rimmed with gold. When these edges flashed, the blue parts shrank away and were overtaken by gold dagger-shaped lights. I hated my eyes. Actually, I didn't hate them...I was afraid of them. But, like always, I had to take a peek. I focused on my eyes in the hand mirror. Today the gold dagger lights were brighter and more defined then I'd ever seen them. The blue wedges were half their normal size. Startled, I squinted my eyelids shut, opened them and took another look. The daggers flared and heat flooded my eyes. My throat tightened. I blinked and swallowed then glanced in the mirror again. The gold dagger lights were gone.

In the long mirror behind me, I caught Nanta watching. Our eyes met in the glass. Her dark-brown eyes had turned cat green. Nanta quickly lowered her lids, hooding her eyes under a blanket of dark secrets. I had learned something just then but I wasn't sure what it was. Embarrassed to be caught staring, I turned my head to the side and inspected the sparkling beads one more time. "Thank you, Nanta. They're very beautiful," I whispered.

"Happy birthday, Lill." Nanta stepped close behind me, reached around and closed my eyelids with a soft brush of her thumbs then she covered them with her hands. She took in a determined breath and let it out before letting go.

"There are some things I promised your mother I would tell you on your tenth birthday." She rested her hands firmly on my shoulders. "Listen carefully. I will only tell you these things once. Ten, in your mother's...aah...religion is the age of passage. Every ten years, on your birthday, you will be tested."

"Tested for what?" I shrugged off her hands and set the hand mirror back on the dresser. I glanced up, trying to catch her eyes again but she looked away.

"*Click-click*," her tongue snapped. "No questions Lill, just listen." Nanta turned me toward the bed, "See the cross?" She pointed above my bed. "That cross was not made by the people of this village, like your father was told. It was made by a *Machawi-shaitani.*"

"A witchdoctor? Yesterday you told me there was no such thing as witchdoctors and voodoo."

"Witchdoctor and voodoo are the words your father would use, because he is too afraid to understand the truth. A *Machawi-shaitani* is much more than a witchdoctor. Now, pay close attention to what I tell you next. Lill, look at the cross."

"Nanta—"

"The horizontal arm of the cross represents the earth's plane. The vertical arm is the path to the two spirit worlds; heaven and hell. In the center of the cross there is a gate, your father thinks this gate is a voodoo superstition, but it's not. It is the gate to the spirit world that keeps our souls safe. If you can see the soul's light, you will be able to open this gate."

"Dad says when people die their souls go to heaven and live with God. You shouldn't be talking to me about witchdoctors and voodoo superstitions. Dad wouldn't want you to."

"Lill, please, you must pay attention. This is important." Nanta grabbed my hand and pulled me next to her as she sat on the bed. "There is another story I promised your mother I would tell you today."

"I thought dad didn't want you talking about my mother. Sunday, yesterday, in the kitchen, you said you couldn't talk about her," I challenged.

"Yesterday was yesterday and today is today. Things have changed and you're not the one who's talking, you are listening. Today is your tenth birthday and it is no longer about what your father wants. It's about what your mother wanted. It's not only the elephants and mist that attract you to Mbali. Inside Mbali, just beyond an old arch, there is an ancient city called Ona."

"Ona means to see."

"Yes."

"So, why do I want to go to Ona?"

"To see if you can see the lights of souls. It is a very special gift, Lill. Today you will find out if you have such a gift."

"But, Nanta..." Confusion briefly caught my throat. "What's...that got to do with going to Mbali? And—"

Her hand squeezed mine to stop me from asking more questions.

"Your father and his God consider the gift to see souls, evil, but he is wrong. To be able to see the light of a human soul is a very special and very important gift...Your father believes being able to do this is voodoo, and he's afraid of it."

"Voodoo is black magic. Dad said it's the work of the devil."

"Hush, child. Not all voodoo is black magic and involves the devil. Voodoo can also be white magic and good. Your mother wanted you to know another thing, the elephant holds the key. The elephant will protect you if you get into trouble." Nanta released my hand, stood, and gave me a stern look, "Say nothing to your father about our talk."

"Why is it—?"

"No more questions. Now, hurry and get dressed. It's a long drive. Once you are inside Mbali, if you see the arch you will find Ona and your destiny will be out of our hands."

"I won't go. I won't go anywhere, unless you tell me why it's so important to find some stupid arch in some stupid old city and see lights of some dead souls that shouldn't be here on earth, anyway. They should be in heaven with God."

"*Click-click*," her tongue cautioned. Nanta's thumb and finger pulled at her chin while she thought, then she asked, "Did you ask your father where your mother was buried?"

"Yes."

"Did he tell you?" She crossed her arms and cocked her head, knowing what my answer would be.

"No. He only told me she was in heaven...with God."

"Your father couldn't tell you where she is...ah...buried, because he doesn't know. He doesn't know where she was...ah...taken...after she gave birth to you. If you want to see your mother's grave you must go to Mbali and find the ancient city of Ona. There is no other way." She turned briskly and walked out of my room without saying another word.

I sat very still on my bed and I knew I wanted to find my mother's grave, more than I wanted to see the elephants. Seeing where she was buried would make her more real. But I didn't understand what seeing souls had to do with it. I got up and went to the mirror. My eyes stared back at me; the gold dagger-shapes danced and flashed as if they were bursting to get out. I closed and rubbed my eyes hard, trying to make them be still. When I looked in the mirror again, if anything, they were more active and more frightening than before. I looked away and went to the closet.

I opened the bedroom door, tucked my pink T-shirt into my jeans and stepped into the hall; the morning smell of burnt toast filled my nose. The sound of eggs being cracked into the hot brown butter in Nanta's black skillet spattered into my ears as I entered the kitchen. Seeing me, Nanta cocked her head and tilted her chin toward the table instructing me to hurry and sit. Then she turned back to the stove to scramble my eggs.

Dad's back was to me. He was hunched forward eating, the sound of his fork clicked against the white stoneware as he ate. His hair was plastered down and wavy-wet from his morning shower. Wide comb marks split his hair into rows across his head. The ends of his hair were dry and sprung free around his head like a red halo.

I tiptoed between dad, the old black stove and Nanta in her corn-flower-colored apron and sat down opposite him. Nanta's tongue gave a sharp *click-click* and a stern finger went to her lips, warning me not to mention our talk of voodoo to my dad.

I hooked my thumbs through the front belt loops of my jeans and wove my fingers together: every-other, every-other. I huffed out a quick breath from my nose then pressed my lips together the ends turned up in a tight smile. My fingers tapped up and down on my knuckles as the seconds ticked by, waiting for Dad to stop eating and reading his Bible and to wish me a happy birthday.

When he finally looked up, he ignored my smiling face; instead he closed his Bible, his thumb holding his place, leaned sideways and looked under the table at my bare feet dangling inches above the floor. He straightened, set his bible upside down on the table and grabbed his blue coffee mug in his left hand. He bumped it against his plate then lifted it to his lips with a nod to my shoeless feet. He said nothing but his fingernail tapped the rim of the coffee mug twice, then he took a sip and set it down. He re-opened his Bible and continued to read. Shoes, he was always wanting me to wear shoes.

Nanta sat a plateful of eggs and toast in front of me. I released my fingers, picked up the cloth napkin next to my plate and placed it on my lap. I glanced across the table at dad, smiled with my lips smashed together, and waited.

Dad put a marker in his Bible then pushed it next to the church newsletter and raised his coffee cup to his lips. His eyes peered at me over the rim. Steam fogged his reading glasses. He removed them, tipped the cup up and slurped in coffee. He swallowed and smacked his lips with a loud pop and gave me a playful grin.

Surprised and astonished at dad's silliness—he was rarely silly—I looked closely at his face. His eyes refused to meet mine but they crinkled in the corners in a happy-resigned kind of way. Then he slurped his coffee again and smacked his lips with an even louder *pop-pop*.

I slurped my juice and smacked my lips in response. We both giggled.

Dad put his cup down, brushed the hair away from his face with one hand, and with the other he pushed a small, white, flat box to the center of the table. It must have been hidden under the church newsletter the whole time.

"Happy Birthday, Lill." His voice was flat and soft, neither sad nor happy. "Go ahead, open it," he encouraged and shoved the little box closer, then quickly removed his hand and placed it on top of his Bible. "It's okay. It won't bite. Open it."

I pulled the box in front of me and lifted the lid. I looked over at dad, and he nodded. I peeled aside the thin blue tissue paper exposing the most beautiful gold necklace I'd ever seen. Ten gold elephants, each one linked trunk to tail, trunk to tail and in the middle, a single white elephant carved of ivory. I slipped the gold chain over my head. When it came to rest, around my neck, it felt warm, almost as if it were a living thing, not cold like metal.

"Dad, the elephants, they're so beautiful, and the white one, she's the most beautiful of all. I love it. Thank you." I leapt from my chair, ran around the table, threw my arms around his neck and kissed his cheek. He gave me a quick hug and sent me back to my chair with a flick of his hand and an uneasy grin. As I ate, dad once again opened his Bible and began to read. And I wished, selfishly, he would spend as much time with me as he spent with God.

When he finished eating, dad rolled his head from side to side to stretch his neck, stood, wiped his hands on the napkin, then set it on the table. He gathered up his Bible and the church newsletter and headed for the back door.

"Hurry up, Lill. We have a long trip ahead of us. And you'll need shoes for walking." He stepped outside and the door shut softly behind him. I ate quickly, picked up my breakfast dishes and set them next to the sink. Nanta surprised me when she wrapped her arms around me and pulled me tight against her.

"Lill, pay close attention to everything you see today. Now go put your shoes on."

The church's old brown Jeep had no roof, so from the back porch it was easy for Nanta and me to see dad sitting in the passenger seat, reading. His shoulders were pitched forward, and he wore a black baseball cap on his head. His red hair sprang wildly around the brim.

"Nanta, how will I find my mother's grave?"

"Keep your eyes open. If you can see the soul lights your journey to her will begin. If not, you will have a nice birthday; eat lots of cake and come back home. You will be just like every other little girl in Ndogo."

"I won't have a mother."

"No, no, you won't have a mother, but you have a father who loves you very much."

"I just wish everything about her wasn't so mysterious, that's all." I looked up to catch her eyes but she turned away and focused on the Jeep.

"They're waiting for you. Here." She handed me my red sweater. "It could be cold in Mbali."

I took it then followed her gaze and headed off across the dry dirt.

Nanta's two sons are by the driver's side door talking and laughing. They were dressed alike with light-brown pants, white long-sleeved shirts rolled to their elbows and opened to the middle of their chests. Neither brother wore shoes. I had on my sensible walking shoes and socks.

Semoi, the oldest and tallest of the two brothers was somewhat shy, and like Nanta he averted his eyes whenever he spoke to me. As I got closer I could see he had one foot on the running board ready to start today's adventure the minute dad gave the word. When Semoi saw me approaching, he waved, flicking his long fingers in my direction but continued talking.

"Jumbo, Semoi!" I shouted in answer to his wave but not expecting him to answer.

Senento twisted his body in my direction, "Jumbo, Lill," his deep voice was strong and his gap-tooth smile wide. He gave me a quick wave before returning to finish his conversation with Semoi.

"Jumbo, Senento," I greeted when I reached the Jeep then climbed into the back seat behind dad and tapped him on the shoulder, "I'm ready, Dad."

"Then I guess we are, too. Let's go, Semoi." Dad, closed his Bible with a snap, removed his cap, put his reading glasses in his shirt pocket and rubbed his eyes. He ran his fingers through his unruly hair and put the cap back on his head before he turned and faced Semoi.

"Nanta gave you directions to get us to Mbali?" he asked Semoi.

"Yes."

"Good. Then I think I'll take a nap. It was a long night last night. Wake me if you need me." He tugged the bill of his cap over his eyes and got comfortable in the seat.

Senento jumped in the back with me and set a woven reed basket between us. Nanta had packed it with our lunch. I laid my sweater next to it, kicked off my shoes, pulled off my socks and wiggled my toes.

"Happy Birthday, Lill." Senento winked and gave the basket a loving pat with his large hand. A grin filled his face, "Nanta packed a cake. Yes, it is to be your birthday cake. Ten years old today. Very special, yes, ten is a very special number." If possible, his grin grew wider.

Semoi turned in the driver's seat and not taking his eyes off the basket he said, "Happy birthday, Lill. That cake will be very good, indeed. We will eat a lot of that cake." He shifted his attention back to front and tugged on the Jeep door until it groaned shut in protest. Semoi gave the key a quick twist and the engine sputtered to life. He ground the gears and we took off with a bumpy jerk. It's going to be a happy birthday, I thought to myself, as we pulled away from Ndogo. I'm off to Mbali to find my mother's grave. Seeing the elephants had become less important.

"Senento, how will we know when we reach Mbali?" I asked.

"Nanta has told us how to get there and where to find the three baobab trees. It will be easy. There will be a cross. A wooden cross tied to a circle of twigs, nailed to the center tree. It signals the entrance into Mbali."

"I have a cross like that in my bedroom, Nanta said it..." Senento wagged his finger and pointed at my dad. I knew better than to say anything more.

When *Jua* was perched straight above us and cast no shadows, Semoi skillfully guided the Jeep through a tight cluster of trees. He brought it to a halt under a canopy of soft green light filtered through the wide leaves of three very old and very tall baobab trees. Nailed to the center tree was the wooden cross. We were at the entrance of the Mbali jungle.

My stomach jumped with excitement and nervousness. To the right of the Jeep, a gentle breeze pushed feathery branches of lime-colored ferns in our direction. Each frond a thin finger begging me to come inside and play, just like the elephant people I pretended to see. But the air under the trees wasn't right.

"Dad, there's no mist."

He removed his ball cap and shifted in his seat to face me. "Lill, it's the air and the reflection of the green jungle plants mixing together, playing tricks on your eyes. There is no mist."

"Okay...I guess...but I'll bet once we get inside Mbali, on the other side of those trees, I bet it'll be filled with a ton of mist."

With an understanding smile he opened his door and stepped down onto the thick bed of leaves that had fallen from the trees overhead. The instant his feet were planted, a howling gust of wind whipped the leaves into a whirlwind, trapping him inside a leaf-spinning funnel.

Senento, Semoi and I jumped out of the Jeep at the same time and ran to help, shouting against the noise of the twister, hollering for it to stop.

"Dad, what's happening?" I reached out, slapping the leaves, but Senento pulled my hands away.

"Pastor Drake, what should we do?" Senento yelled.

Semoi had taken off his shirt and was beating the wind and leaves as they blew past him, trying, but unable, to break them apart.

"Help him," I begged, snapping my head from one brother to the other.

"I'm warning you. I'll take her home right now," Dad bellowed from inside the twister. The wind slowed, but the funnel continued to hold him.

"Dad, who are you talking to?" I yelled.

"Not now, Lill!" he shouted over the noise of the wind, then raised his fists into the air. "I brought her here just like you wanted. You don't need to do this."

A swooshing sound blasted our ears and the leaves crashed to the ground, formed a sharp flat wedge, lifted up and slid through the branches of the trees, upsetting a family of vervet monkeys on its way. It blew out the top and sped away.

I wrenched free from Senento's grasp and rushed to dad's side, throwing my arms around his waist. "Are you okay? What made the leaves do that?"

"Lill—" Overhead the baby vervets screamed out harsh gargles of panic, their urgent cries interrupting him. We turned our attention to the middle of the tree and watched their mother pull them into a cluster and hide them from our view. When we looked away we noticed the leaves on the tree's branches, the bushes, even the finger ferns had stopped moving. I squeezed my arms tighter around dad's waist and glanced up at him. He turned away from my gaze and directed his attention to Semoi and Senento, his eyes questioning them with concern.

"Dad...?" I let go of his waist and tugged on his hand, "What's happening?" I was afraid something really, really bad was going on and it felt more like black magic than white.

"Dad, take me home. I don't care about seeing the elephants or finding my—"

"Lill," Senento cut me off before I said more and gave me a warning glare.

Dad's eyes quizzed Senento then me. His eyes were very blue and half closed with worry. He pulled me close to his side, cradled my head with his soft hand then gently tucked some wild stands of my hair behind my ear. His fingers stopped long enough to mark the sign of the cross on my cheek. He looked out beyond the trees. "Please, God, don't make me do this," he begged, then knelt in front of me. He focused his eyes on mine and this time he didn't turn away. "Lill, I'm so sorry. This isn't easy for me. It's not easy to explain...Your eyes are very gold today. More like your mother's than mine, I'm afraid."

"What?" I felt a warmth flood into them and I knew the gold daggers were flashing. "My mother had lights in her eyes, too?"

"Yes, Lill, she had the lights." Dad reached for the gold chain of elephants around my neck. He tenderly slipped his fingers under the links and closed them. "This was hers."

"My mother's?"

"Yes. She wanted me to tell you, if you can see the lights, and I pray to God you can't, not to be afraid. I don't want any of this to be true. Oh, God. I don't want this, Lill. Whatever happens, remember I love you and God loves you. And I swear, as God is my witness, there is no such thing as voodoo, and today will prove it. There will be no lights, and this will be the end of it."

He let go of the chain, shifted his balance, placed one knee on the ground then he reached up and held my face between his hands and drank in the color of my eyes. When he kissed my forehead, my lips trembled and he drew the sign of the cross on them, too. "I wish I could stop this, but I can't." Defeated, dad dropped his left hand to his side.

"Stop what?"

His right hand stroked the edge of my eye then came to a rest on my temple, "Your mother believed in voodoo. She wrongly believed she could see the souls of the dead." He lowered his hand. His thumb brushed across the white elephant in the center of my necklace before it reached the ground. He sighed, gathered up a hand full of dirt then let it go.

"Nanta said seeing the light of souls is a very special gift..."

"I promised your mother I'd bring you here on your tenth birthday, but I'm only doing it to prove to her and to the people who believe in voodoo that they're wrong. To prove, once and for all, that God, my God, that our Christian God, is stronger than your mother's misguided beliefs. She believed her blood held the magic, and it would be passed on to you. Half of your blood is hers, but the other half is mine. Blood is blood, Lill, there can be no difference. No magic in one and not the other." Dad drew the sign of the cross in the dirt then gathered it in his hand and held it. He opened his fingers and let it sift out between them. His eyes studied mine then he brushed my cheek with the back of his hand. "Lill, you must believe me when I tell you these lights are not souls; they are a trick, a sleight of hand to fool people and make them believe in voodoo. I guarantee you won't see any soul lights. But if you think you do, remember, they are not real and there is no special magic inside you that will help you see them. It's the witchdoctors, Lill, they do it. The voodoo witchdoctors who practice black magic; they make the lights with their smoke and mirrors. They do it to deceive and control people."

"Nanta said there's white magic, too."

"There is no such thing as white magic. If there is any magic at all in Mbali, it belongs to Satan." He surprised me when he scooped me up in his arms as he stood. "But you're not going.

You're not going to see any lights; I won't risk it."

With sudden determined steps, he carried me back to the Jeep. When we reached it, Dad's lifted his face to the heavens and spoke out in his church voice, "God, please forgive me. I promised in your name to bring her here today, but this is one promise I'm not going to keep." He motioned to Senento and Semoi.

"Semoi, get in the Jeep, Senento, you, too. We're getting out of here."

The hellish wind blew out of nowhere. It was tangled and pricked with wickedness. It bit the branches of the trees. It hacked up clouds of dust green phlegm and sent them tumbling in every direction.

I screamed and clung to dad when a flash of black-red light exploded in the tree over our heads. The blast severed a huge branch from the trunk and sent it hurtling down toward us, and before I heard it crash, everything went black.

Chapter 3

Zzdz-dzzd. A loud buzz rattled my brain. My pulse quickened, and I spun in the direction of the noise.

Zzdz-dzzd. The metallic sound of the Goliath beetle clattered again. I focused my attention to a nubby limb half way up the marula tree. At five inches long the beetle was easy to spot. He rubbed his hard wings together producing another sharp, *Zzdz-dzzd.* He stopped and scraped a gob of tree sap from each corner of his mouth, then chipped loose a chunk of bark, spun it around, took aim, and pitched it over the edge. It landed next to my feet and split open with a loud crack. An orange colored, jell like goo spilled out. It shook violently and burst into a swarming pool of ants. They had my feet circled in seconds, holding me hostage like Indians around a wagon train.

"Dad...?" Not daring to move my toes, afraid the slightest motion would entice the ants to bite. I pivoted my head this-way-and-that, searching for any signs of him. "Dad, can you hear me? Please, I need help."

Zzdz-dzzd. The beetle's wings hammered and picked up speed, emitting a much louder and longer, *Zzdz-dzz-dzz, zzzdzz-zz.* Then the Goliath stilled his wings, rotated his jaw and bit off a small piece of bark. He chewed it for a second and with a quick snap of his head, spit. I raised my hands and leaned to the right to avoid being hit. The wet chunk of wood whizzed pass and plopped with a thump into the ring of circling ants. The ants sizzled like Nanta's bacon frying in her frying pan. An orange steam rose up from the ants and dissolved into an empty wet puddle.

Zzdz-dzzd. The beetle stretched his wings and flew away.

"Dad? Senento? Semoi?" I squeaked out a desperate plea for

help, inched away from the tree and started looking for dad and the Jeep. Thoughts of black magic and voodoo stuffed my head so full it began to ache. My lungs constricted and overflowed with despair; this place didn't feel like a trick, it felt real. One minute the four of us were together watching a branch fall from the baobab tree then a second later I'm alone, standing next to a marula tree watching a beetle eat bark.

I pulled my teeth across my lower lip and dug my toes into the earth and continued to search for dad. I strained to remember everything Nanta had told me and wondered if I had somehow entered Mbali by mistake. The rich soil embraced my toes, but did little to calm my fears or stop me from worrying about what had happened to dad and Nanta's two sons. I drug one foot and then the other through the glove-soft dirt. My heart thumped with its familiarity. It felt like I'd been here before but I knew that wasn't possible. I wiggled my toes in the soil again to feel its warmth but the ground beneath them had turned unexpectedly cold. Heat washed over my eyes and an odd unsettling gnawed its way to the surface of my skin and made me shudder.

"Aaah!" I screamed.

Senento's left hand had clasped down on my shoulder. In his other hand he held out my sweater. "Are you cold, Lill?" His slow calculated voice asked as he released his grip on me.

"You're here." I smiled, relieved, then looked behind him. "Where's dad? Where's Semoi?"

"They're not here. They are on the other side."

"Are we in Mbali?"

"Yes."

"How did we get in here? How did..." And then I stopped talking and just stared at him. Senento had changed. He was shirtless. A tattered and torn animal skin clung to his waist and hung in jagged lines to his knees. It was held in place by three red, moldy-green strands of animal entrails. A stringy piece of animal bowel was cinched flat against his forehead and knotted above his left ear. Two finger-wide streaks of red paint ran from under each eye down to his jaw. His shoulders and chest were powdered with white dust. His skin was blemished with copper and green scabs.

Senento, behaving as though nothing about him was different, helped me put on my sweater. I asked, sounding more courageous than I felt. "Why are you dressed like that?"

"It's hard to explain, Lill." Senento's lips quivered at the corners. "If you find Ona, you will begin to understand. Ona is a place where *machawi* see things that normal people can't." Senento's smile thins, "Ten. It is a very important number. Every ten years, it could be very dangerous for you...or not. Some people are gifted and can see souls. Your mother could see them...so...maybe you can, too. But you have only half her blood and that may be a problem. We'll see whose blood is stronger; perhaps your father's, yes?" He licked his lips and chuckled.

"Senento, stop talking like that. You need to get us out of here."

"Like the lights, Lill, things are not always what they seem." He wiped the back of his hand across his wet lips and continued. "Souls are the size of human hearts, did Nanta tell you that? And these lights of the dead, they are not always so nice," his cold voice warned.

"Senento, please stop talking. Take me back to dad and the Jeep."

"Your father hides the truth from you. He hopes you won't be able to see the souls. No matter how today ends...no matter, how it ends, his God will keep him in the dark. A sad thing, really, his God is so limiting. The *Machawi-shaitani*...their voodoo is very powerful and there are few limits to what they can see...and do.

"Senento, stop it, you're scaring me." My lips parted, and I stared, paralyzed, as the red lines under his eyes turned to liquid and ran down his neck onto his chest then circled his waist like a bleeding snake; and dripped red.

"If you see the lights, Lill, choose carefully. One bad choice, and even the elephant won't be able to help you. The elephant and the souls will die."

"What do you mean the elephant and the souls will die? Souls go to Heaven and live with God. Don't you listen to dad's sermons? Stop twisting the truth. Get me out of here." I reached out and pushed his arm, "Get me out of here right now!"

Senento slapped me hard across the face. "Don't tell me what to do, little girl. You are nothing if you can't see the souls. You are nothing but a half-breed annoyance. You cannot succeed."

Shocked, I pressed my right hand to the sting Senento's slap left on my cheek. Hot pain seared through my eyes. My stomach clenched, a dozen gold daggers shot from my eyes and into Senento's face. He screamed and tried to pull out the little darts but they kept coming. They pinned his hands to his face and devoured them; turning them into a grotesque mask of burning flesh.

"Things are not what they seem," Senento's voice choked from the melted ruin of his face. He collapsed to his knees. The earth opened, and Senento and the scorched air surrounding him were gone.

There was no sound. The light in the forest throbbed then blurred. Everything inside Mbali and in my life had changed. I pressed my fingertips to my eyes. They were warm but no longer hot, and I was more afraid of them than I had ever been.

The muffled crunch of tense footsteps resonated from behind a nearby tree. My heart jumped and sent a jolt of fear to steal air from my lungs. I backed up and glanced to each side of the tree's trunk. The ground was littered with dry twigs and pointy thick leaves but no one was there. I crossed my fingers and inched closer, hoping I wouldn't see Senento, hoping to see dad. But if it was Senento, or whatever he had become, I was ready to run. I looked beyond the tree, cupped my hands over my mouth and breathed into them, "Is someone back there? Dad?"

On the left of the trunk a pile of brittle twigs lifted and the leaves on top of them shifted. My eyes zeroed in on the cluster of sharp-edged leaves. They buckled up and fell apart. Senento! I tried to run, but my feet wouldn't move. The leaves gave another heave and the small branches under them tumbled aside. My heart constricted and sent another bolt of panic slamming into my lungs.

A lazy blue lizard, about half the size of a slender-snouted crocodile, popped his large head through the disheveled leaves then stretched his neck and stepped out, one scaly foot at a time. He skittered to the trunk of the tree, placed a foot on the large root exposed at the bottom then stopped. His bulging eyes swiveled around and penetrated mine then rotated back to the limb above his head. He jumped on the root, his feet clinging effortlessly to the bark as he climbed up the tree. When he was half the way up, he rounded a limb and I could no longer see him but I heard the rattle of the leaves as he pushed his way between them.

I walked slowly to the root, sat down and leaned against the trunk. I picked up a leaf, turned it over and over in my hand, careful not to cut myself on its razor-sharp edges. While my mind churned in circles of confusion I raised the leaf to my eyes and caught the smell of its crusty skin. I sneezed, accidently grabbed it, and sliced my hand. Blood oozed from the base of my middle finger to the bottom of my palm. I wiped it off on my sweater then inspected the cut. Only a small pink scar remained. I rubbed the scar with my thumb, it didn't open or bleed. I buttoned my sweater up to my neck.

My tenth birthday wasn't turning out to be much fun. I was lost in a place with strange-behaving animals. I hadn't seen one single elephant, hadn't found the city of Ona, my mother's grave, or come across any mysterious soul lights. I didn't know where Dad was and my friend Senento is, was, a witch or some sort of voodoo black magic thing. And I killed him with tiny golden daggers that came shooting out of my eyes. I pressed my fingers to my temples. My heart ached. It ached with longing so strong I had to call out her name.

"Mother." The word was barely audible; trapped inside the green-velvet coffin that had become the Mbali jungle. "Mother," I tried again. This time it evaporated, leaving nothing but a lime-colored vapor hanging from my lips. "Mother," my voice croaked. Time dragged in silence as I waited for a response. Slowly, my hope gave way to anger. "Forget it. I don't care if I ever find you. I don't want to know where you're buried. I don't care about you anymore." Tears filled my eyes, "Do you hear me? I don't care about you or finding your stupid grave. I want out of here. I want dad, and I want to go home."

I wiped my tears dry with the back of my hand and stood. I moved away from the tree, checking the dirt for footprints, hoping to find my way back to the entrance of Mbali, dad, and the Jeep. My stomach tightened, and I pressed my hand against it. It rumbled, pleading for food. Nanta's basket was in the Jeep. I reached in the pockets of my sweater hoping to find a forgotten piece of candy or maybe some nuts and found a small red apple instead. I bounced it in my hand and wondered why I hadn't noticed it before. I thought about dad teaching the book of Genesis, how the devil had enticed Adam and Eve to eat the apple. I worried that maybe God was testing me, or worse, that the black magic that had overtaken Senento was tempting me to join forces with the devil.

I polished the apple on the bottom edge of my sweater. My mouth watered, begging me to take a bite. I was hungry, but I was more than a little worried about where the apple had come from and if I should risk eating it.

My stomach gave a loud grumble. Nanta had to have put the apple in my pocket, I reasoned. After all, she was the one who suggested I bring it. I glanced over my shoulder, right then left, closed my eyes and bit down. The apple's flesh crunched between my teeth. I savored its sweet juice, rolling it around with my tongue. I thought about Adam and Eve and held the flesh and juice in my mouth then I thought of Nanta handing me the sweater and swallowed. The air dulled to an acid yellow. What had I done?

My hand trembled. I released the uneaten portion of the apple and let it drop to the ground. I kicked dirt over it, tamped it down with my foot then added another layer of dirt. Frantic to be rid of the thing, I got down on my hand and knees and buried it under even more dirt. But the panic I felt wouldn't go away. Shaken and defeated, I sank down on my calves and covered my face with my hands. I was lost and didn't know what to do. I snorted out a breath, lowered my hands and studied the forest in front of me. I had to get out of here and find dad. I got up and glanced back at the marula tree. An old arch, at least twelve feet tall and built of stacked stones stood in its place. It was tilted sideways like an old man's crooked smile. The arch groaned, bent, and folded over me before I had time to run.

The ancient huts were covered with gray dust; their walls, broken and crumbling piles of stones, three and four feet tall. The thatched roofs, that had once kept out the sun and rain lay decaying on the ground, waiting for time to claim what was left. I walked along the earth path from one ruin to the next hunting for clues, clues that would tell me where to go, or where I was. I came to a part in the path where it split into a Y; I hesitated, shrugged and stepped to the left. An African pygmy mouse loped out from under one of the rotting roofs and bound down the trail on the right then ran behind the last hut on the path. He seemed to know where he was going, so I changed directions and followed him.

He waited at the edge of the forest cleaning his whiskers.

His triangular ears twitched, and his beady brown eyes sparkled. He hopped straight up in the air, landed on all four feet and started to spin. He spun so fast and in such a tight circle he looked like a tiny red-brick marble. He continued to gain speed until he flew apart in a massive explosion of deep-blue sparks. The air and the forest were instantly saturated in blue light. Everything was silent except for the faint beating of my heart.

In front of me, a shimmering gold and silver ball, the size of a human heart, pulsed against the indigo backdrop of the cobalt jungle. A burst of sparks shot from the center of the ball and I raised my hand to shield my face from the flying embers. When the sparks subsided I heard, for the first time, the faint th-thump, th-thump...th-thump, th-thump, coming from the orb. The sphere's pulsating rhythm played perfectly with the beat of my own heart. Maybe I wouldn't find my mother's grave, but maybe this light was her soul and maybe that was what Nanta had been trying to tell me all along.

I was both scared and hopeful when I whispered, "Mother, is that you?" The opalescent soul flashed with colors of gold and silver matching the beads in my hair. And I knew it was Nanta's way of letting me know that this soul was my mother's.

The orb drew nearer. It hovered within inches of my face, like it was looking for something in my eyes. Timid, I reached out with both hands to touch it. The soul's light surrounded them and clasped them tight together. My breathing quickened. I struggled to pull free, but I couldn't. The earth behind me shook and before I could turn my head to look, my hands were ablaze with phosphorescent flames. I screamed. The fire climbed up my arms then shot over my shoulders with ear-wrenching speed and slammed into the ground behind me. I twisted around, as best I could, and watched the sparks and hot embers assault the earth. The ground wrenched up but the fire and flames beat it back down. The earth hushed and lay quiet. The sphere released my hands and as quickly as my mother's soul came, it vanished. I stared at the burnt earth she'd left behind and shivered.

Dark bands of blue air whipped around my legs and the scorched earth cracked apart in chunks. I hugged my arms across my chest. My eyes grew wider as I waited for what lay underneath. I had no place to go. Senento's words haunted me: "Choose carefully, Lill. Not all the souls are nice." But I believed the soul that had come to my rescue was my mother's...her sparks matched Nanta's beads.

A deep and menacing growl erupted from beneath the earth and spit out a sickening stench. Mute horror pressed down on my lungs and held my breath. A huge black leopard slunk out of the lightless hole, its ebony skin quivering in the eerie blue light. Two hellish eyes blazed hazel green then dissolved into the wickedness of its glistening coat. Panic cut into my lungs and released my breath. The cat curled his lips and snarled. His honed teeth snapped a sharp warning before they were licked wet and swallowed back into his ebony face. The beast's threat was unquestionably murderous. When the leopard opened his eyes again they were no longer hazel; they had turned blood red.

"Mother, please help me," I begged through terror-dried lips, but it appeared my mother's soul had abandoned me...or was it just smoke and mirrors? Had I been deceived?

Smelling my fear, the sleek-coated feline advanced, slinking forward like a dark satanic shadow, each movement calculated and deadly. His thick rough tongue licked across murderous white teeth. His ears flattened on top his head. The leopard's breath was sour with the smell of hate. I silently bid the cat to look at my eyes, hoping the heat and the darts would return and save me, but nothing happened.

"Mother, why did you want me to come to Mbali and find Ona, if you were just going to let me die?"

The cat snarled and hissed. He was impatient, anxious for the taste of death. His black-lashed lids closed to half mast, making him look more evil than Lucifer himself. The cat lowered his head, unwavering, getting ready to attack. His lower lip curled under. His powerful muscles twitched with nervous hunger. I dared to inch backwards.

White hot sparks exploded before my eyes. My mother's gold and silver sphere had returned and stopped directly above the treacherous black cat. Her pulsating soul light dropped down over him like a net. Undaunted, the big cat kept advancing, dragging her soul with him. The leopard let loose an insane growl that carried his rank breath, once again, to my nose. My mother's soul rose up, hovered above me, and delivered a blinding blast of light down on the horrid creature. The flash haloed the ground beneath him. The leopard's front claws pierced through her light and the dug into the black dirt. He hunched and sprung. His weight slammed me backward and pinned me to the earth. His hot breath clung to my face and death looked into my eyes.

White light from my mother's soul tore into the leopard's black skin and flashed across his eyes and into mine.

"Mother...please, help me," I pleaded.

My vision blurred and my mother's soul dropped to my side. The cat lifted his head but didn't relinquish his hold on me. He snarled, threw his head back and screamed his message of death and victory into the indigo colored sky; the same cry I heard outside my bedroom window. The beast snarled and growled. The power of his hate was so strong I feared it would overtake my mother's soul and I would die.

The demon flexed his muscles. The weight of his body on my chest stifled the beating of my heart. With the last bit of strength I had, I struggled to take a breath, but couldn't. I was losing consciousness. I barely felt his teeth rip the elephant chain from my neck then toss it aside with a quick shake of his head. My mother's soul wedged its light between the massive cat and me, shielding my eyes from seeing my own death. Knowing she could not protect me, I waited for death to walk its final last steps. With no air in my lungs, my lips hardly moved but I managed a voiceless plea. My lips didn't ask for my Mother's help, instead they trembled, "Dad...Dad...help me."

My mother's iridescent soul light rushed into my mouth, suffocating the words. A small breath of air was returned to me, and I cried out, "Dad." My mother's light spilled out along with his name.

When I opened my eyes, it was night. Stars dotted the sky. Hours had passed. Dad was sitting on the ground holding me in his lap. "Dad, you're okay." I tried to smile, but I cried instead.

"Hush," his eyes crinkled, "I'm okay. And now, you're okay." He made the sign of the cross on my forehead then kissed the spot he marked. My chest hurt when I took a breath, but I needed to tell him what had happened. "Dad, a black leopard tried to kill me and I saw my mother's—"

"Bayamchawi," Senento said and cut off the rest of my story.

Senento? Senento's alive? Blackness overcame me and I floated in and out of consciousness on fractured shades of sight and sound.

Somewhere in this strange darkness I heard dad's voice but his words were garbled and misshapen like a hippo talking underwater. "Bay...ama...chawi?" I think I heard him ask.

"The devil..." Senento's muffled and disjointed voice explained.

"Black magic. Bad voodoo," Semoi's words were less than a whisper and laced with fear.

"Dad?" I struggled to ask, wanting to know what they were talking about.

"Don't talk, Lill. Take it easy. You're tough, but you've taken a beating. Thank God nothing was broken and you're alive. Now, let's get you in the Jeep. We've got to get you out of Africa as soon as we can, we must—"

"Leaving...Afr...ca?" My sluggish tongue worked to get the words out.

Dad's voice started to fade, "can't stay here. Pray...he doesn't fol..."

"He'll want her back," Semoi's veiled words mumbled.

"He'll have to take me first," Dad said. I fought to grasp the meaning of his words but my brain was dull and losing the battle to stay awake.

I was vaguely aware of dad laying me down in the back seat of the Jeep, cradling my head against his shoulder and stroking my face. When the Jeep's engine turned over and I forced my eyes open. Senento had shifted in the front passenger seat and was facing me. The headlights bounced ghostly reflections off the trees, sending broken lines crisscrossing his face.

"Don't be afraid, Lill. Things are not what they seem." Semoi engaged the engine and as we headed away from Mbali my mind gave way to nothingness.

Chapter 4
The Second Ten

We moved to a house in Sacramento, California. It had been dad's parents' house. I had grandparents. Well, not living grandparents; they had been killed in a car crash on Highway 90, before I was born. In the living room was an 8x10 photo of them, Emma and George. Dad's father had red hair and looked just like him. They'd left their house to him, and he'd lived in it before he got the calling to become a missionary and moved to Africa. It was a 1930s two-story stucco Spanish Victorian. It had been well maintained but empty for the last 12 years. Dad said someday the house would be mine.

Two weeks after we arrived, dad was assigned to a perfectly churchy-church in downtown Sacramento in which to preach.

"Our lives will be normal now," he told me that first Sunday morning as we drove to his new church. I had thought it was normal when we lived in Africa. Well, normal until my tenth birthday. However, it was obvious that dad's normal was the ruling one, and I had no choice but to adjust. What happened in Ona was discussed only once.

We had finished eating dinner. Dad and I sat next to each other on our new sofa. The living room was small but the ceiling was high. Across one entire wall, floor to ceiling, shelves held most of dad's books, some of mine, and the television. My grandparents' picture was there, too. The subtle smell of smoke from the wood-burning stove lingered in the sofa's olive-green fabric. I sipped a warm mug of cocoa and read one of my school books. Dad tamped the tobacco in his pipe, set it in the china dish on the end table next to him, and turned on the lamp.

He cleared his throat, adjusted the pillow behind his back and turned to face me. "Lill, I never talked to you about your mother. . ." Dad cleared his throat again. ". . . because I thought you were too young to keep the things involving her...in perspective. But I've come to realize there are some things you to should know. The most important thing for you to understand is her belief in *Machawi-shaitani* goes against all God's teachings and against everything I believe."

"She's dead, Dad. It's okay, I saw her soul light. It doesn't matter anymore."

"Lill, you only think you saw a light. It wasn't real. Everything you think you remember was caused by the leopard attacking you or some witchdoctor's tricks. You were scared, as you should have been but those other things, they didn't happen."

"So what do witchdoctors have to do with my mother?"

"That's what I'm trying to tell you. First and foremost, you need to understand that there are people who call themselves witchdoctors, but they're fakes. No black magic, either. It's all African mumbo-jumbo...smoke and mirrors, smoke and mirrors. Voodoo doesn't exist in the real world. Your mother thought she was...never mind, it's no longer important what she thought. What she was...was wishful. And I'm afraid you've become a little wishful, too. It's impossible to see souls, Lill. When we die our souls go to heaven; they don't float around on earth as balls of light, spirits, ghosts, or anything else."

"But Nanta and Senento both said...Dad, I really did see—"

"You thought you saw," he corrected. "Nanta and Senento still believe in voodoo, it is engrained in their very fiber. I tried to teach them the truth. They pretended to believe but it seems I didn't succeed." He paused, combed his fingers through his hair, searching for the right words. "Lill, you have to believe me when I tell you, you just imagined you saw a soul. The light was never really there.

"Your mother wanted to be able to do magical things. It was hard for her to behave normally so she pretended to be...no, that's not right either. She persuaded the natives she had special powers, and it seems Nanta was her most ardent believer.

"Your mother believed her voodoo god was more powerful than our Christian God. She thought her god—her witchdoctor god—gave her magic abilities. When it became obvious she was not going to survive your birth, she told me a fanciful story. She said on your tenth birthday you would be tested to see if you had the same voodoo magic she had. Lill, I tried to reason with her, but she was dying. She became hysterical, so to calm her I promised to take you to Mbali when you turned ten. It was an easy promise. I knew her voodoo magic didn't exist. She didn't believe my promise and demanded I put my hand on the Bible and swear. She knew I would never break a promise I made to God. I gave her my oath in the name of our Lord, and it was done."

Dad flexed and clenched his fingers nervously then continued. "I didn't tell her for me to make such a promise wasn't all that hard. I didn't believe in her witchdoctor voodoo magic, it wasn't real. There was nothing to be afraid of in taking you to Mbali—nothing at all. I loved Africa and teaching Ndogo's people the word of God, so we stayed. And why not take you to Mbali on your birthday? For a leopard to attack you, it was unusual, and I thank God every day you lived through it. But it was God that protected you from the cat. God saved your life, nothing else nothing more."

I watched him knead his hands and twist his fingers as he explained how, when the wind snapped the branch off the tree, he pushed me out of harm's way. Dad said that's how we had become separated. And when the wind died down, the thickest green fog he'd ever seen covered the ground and made it impossible for Semoi, Senento and him to find me.

"Lill, it took hours for the fog to lift, and we were frantic the whole time. We called out, but it was as if the mist caught our words and held them hostage. You couldn't hear us. We could barely hear ourselves. We had no choice but to wait. I was crazy with worry the whole time." Dad pushed his fingers through his hair. "The three of us got on our knees and prayed we would find you alive. When the fog thinned we started searching for you. We looked everywhere and finally we found you. You were unconscious, behind some bushes, less than a quarter of a mile from the Jeep. The leopard must have carried you there. You were scratched and bruised but you were alive. God had answered our prayers, you were alive." He pulled on his lower lip then rubbed his nose, "The things you remember, Lill, all of it is from the trauma of the leopard's attack. Even the doctor said so. We were blessed you survived. It was God's greatness that saved you from the cat." Dad took both my hands in his. His face became somber, "This is the last time we will talk about any of this, to each other, or to anyone else. Understand?"

"Yes, I understand," I mumbled. Then he made me promise, with my hand on the Bible, that I would never go back to Africa. It saddened me to make such a promise. At the same time I felt safer knowing I couldn't. I wouldn't ever break a promise to dad. I wasn't sure if what I remembered about Ona was real or not, but I knew I was never going back to Africa to find out.

Dad settled back into the sofa. He lifted his pipe from the china dish and lit it then picked up his Bible and began to read. We never talked about the trip to Mbali or the leopard ever again.

I rubbed the scar on my palm. It was faint but still there. I could have cut it on anything or the leopard's claw could have scratched it and maybe it didn't magically heal itself after I cut it on a leaf. My necklace was gone. Ripped off by the cat and lost forever in the black earth of Ona. If dad was right, maybe I was never in Ona. Maybe I was just a short distance from them the whole time. And the soul light? Well, maybe he was right about that, too; perhaps I didn't see that either.

Dad gave a sermon every Sunday for the rest of his life to a right-wing congregation of wealthy Baptists. His church was the old brick one on 65th Street. It was a busy street in the center of Sacramento. Each Sabbath morning, the church's heavy wood doors were flung wide and welcoming as a maiden aunt's arms. Dad greeted each parishioner with a two-handed handclasp and a blessing. He no longer dressed in black; his robes were blue, purple, and white. His sermons were joyful.

When the service was over, I stood dutifully at dad's side on the top step of the old church. Dad smiled, patted the men on their backs and shook their hands. He nodded his head and smiled at their wives. The older women kissed him on the cheek and invited him to come to dinner and meet to their unmarried daughters. He kissed their hands and told them how lovely they looked. These women returned the compliment by telling dad how pretty I was. I stood there in my Sunday shoes and dress and listened to them talk. They weren't afraid of my eyes; no one was. My eyes were brown with just a hint of blue. Maybe dad was right; maybe our lives were going to be normal.

As the church continued to empty, dad offered encour-agement as needed, and I continued to smile until the last member of his congregation was gone and the doors were closed. After a month or two, I realized I wasn't afraid of God any more.

I was amazed how many white people filled the pews of dad's church. Until we moved to California I had never seen so many white people in one place at one time. Where were all the African American members of this church? These Sacramentoans were very stern looking and for the most part grumpy. As I watched them leave church on Sundays, I often asked myself—if going to church made them so unhappy, why bother coming?

In Ndogo, after dad had given the final blessing, I remembered the natives sitting in the church pews, their big white teeth smiling out of their dark faces, smiling at Jesus' promise of salvation. They had happy teeth. They were happy people. I missed Ndogo, I missed Nanta, but most of all I missed Africa and the animals. We had moved to Sacramento because of me, but Africa still tugged my heart.

As the years passed, I noticed a pattern. I felt restless and nervous each year on my birthday. It wasn't something I dwelled on, but I did worry about Nanta's whispered prediction that every ten years I would be tested, and I wondered what would happen when I turned 20. However, now that I was in California, I didn't see how anything bad could happen.

The gold dagger-shaped lights in my eyes were gone, but another type of light found a place in my vision. I saw shimmering colors of green, blue, yellow, red and purple around plants. I noticed these lights shortly after we arrived in Sacramento. I didn't mention them to dad. Had he known about them, he would have poo-pooed them away as not being real or my being wishful. Or worse, he'd say they had something to do with the devil, kiss me on the forehead, mark the spot with the sign of the cross, and refuse to talk about it again. So I went to the library and found out these lights were called auras. I memorized what the different colors meant and learned that other people could see auras, too. Some saw auras around people; I was only able to see auras around trees, bushes and flowers. But knowing other people could see auras gave me some comfort; knowing that there were others out there like me made me feel normal.

Early on, I found out that being able to see auras had its drawbacks. I sobbed out of control when dad took me with him

THE WHITE ELEPHANT KNEELS   47

to cut down a Christmas tree. Our first Christmas in Sacramento was to be special he said, so off to the Christmas tree farm we went. I watched in horror as the tree's aura changed from green to a painful shade of red the second the tree's trunk was severed from its roots. I couldn't tell dad what I had seen, but I refused to decorate that tree.

"It's a stupid tradition," I told him. "Why should we kill trees to celebrate the birth of Jesus? It's not right to take a life; even a tree's." But then I would think back to Senento, or whoever it was I had killed, or thought I'd killed, in Ona. Boy, talk about being self-righteous.

I woke up nervous on my twentieth birthday. An apprehensive glance at the clock on my nightstand told me it was 7 a.m. I took a calming breath and watched as it ticked to 7:01. One hour and 46 minutes after the time of my birth...and I was okay. I'd been 20 for over an hour and, so far, nothing bad had happened. Still, my hands shook when I ran my fingers through my hair and I couldn't get warm, even in the shower. My heartbeat was as erratic as a newborn gazelle trying to dodge a lion. Four times I'd gone to open my bedroom door to head downstairs and join Dad for breakfast and four times I had walked back to check my eyes in the mirror. The gold daggers stayed hidden; my eyes were mostly brown, normal.

We were at the kitchen counter talking. At six feet, dad was five inches taller than me and his red hair had begun to turn gray. He tucked his chin close to his chest and gave me a sheepish grin, then stuck a white birthday candle in an orange, from the bowl on the counter. He lit it and sang the sour-noted, happy birthday song. I made a wish, about what I don't remember, and blew the flame out. He removed the candle and cut that orange and one other into four thick wedges each. We stood in the kitchen eating oranges with loud slurping noises and laughing. While he slurped in the juice of his orange, it reminded me of the morning of my tenth birthday and I felt a little flutter of fear. I glanced at the kitchen clock and shrugged it off, another hour had passed. We avoided talking about the past, but it hung between us like a naughty child waiting to be forgiven. We talked instead about my plans to become a veterinarian and dad's plans to add an evening Bible study class at church.

Dad glanced at the clock on the wall and smiled, self-assured, knowing he was right and we had nothing to worry about. "Twenty years old; my little girl is 20 years old today. Happy birthday, Lill." He smiled, glanced at the clock again, and then the smile slid off his face.

That was the first time I saw a human aura.

A freezing black vapor cut between us like a curtain then vanished. My heart quickened. I watched in disbelief as a pulse of red light wrapped itself around dad's chest and squeezed.

"Dad!" I screamed. The red aura spiked out the top of his head, and the air smelled scorched. His blue eyes registered pain and questioned mine. The ominous black veil returned and nailed itself to his heart. His clenched fist knocked the orange slices off the counter as he crashed down onto the cold linoleum. The blackness untangled itself from his body, blurred then snaked in front my eyes and dissolved.

The room became unbearably silent. Dad's sightless eyes were open and stared at nothing. One of the orange slices rocked back and forth like a tiny rocking horse next to his face. The juice that clung to the corners of his mouth was no longer sweet. The juice in my own mouth had become bitter.

Crying, I knelt beside him and touched his face. My trembling fingers closed his lids and I sobbed. With my thumb I made the sign of the cross on his forehead..."Got to keep you safe, Dad..." I choked back tears..."got to keep you safe."

My thumb was still pressed against his cooling flesh when a whisper of white light spun, funnel shaped, out of the center of his heart. I watched in amazement as the light grew brighter and more iridescent. Dad's soul floated in jubilant translucent newness inches above his cooling body. Bright pink, like a newborn baby, his soul collected itself into a rose-colored sphere. It stayed perfectly still for perhaps half a minute then shrugged and hovered in close to my eyes, spinning in a soft flesh-colored glow.

I had the feeling dad's soul was waiting for me to set it free. I didn't want his soul to leave me, so soon but I knew the choice wasn't mine to make. His soul and I faced each other; I knew what it was asking. I spoke softly to his spirit. "Dad...I promised you I wouldn't go back to Africa, and I won't."

His soul hesitated. I dried my eyes and smiled as big as I could. "I swear to God, I won't ever go back."

I kissed my fingertips and placed them into the center of his iridescent light—they tingled with little shocks of electricity and then his soul was gone. He and his God had important things to talk about, no doubt. I envied dad's belief in God. As wonderful and beautiful as it was to see his soul, I knew my being able to see it was connected to Africa and I didn't think it had anything to do with the God he believed in.

A twinge of fear seized my heart, and I recalled Nanta's warning, "Every ten years."

I remembered dad saying, "He'll have to take me first." My fear increased.

Later, I listened to the doctor tell me, "He died of a heart attack." I convinced myself he must be right, he had to be; we were no longer in Africa.

After his death, I continued to live in our house. But I didn't stand at the kitchen counter and eat oranges cut into wedges for breakfast anymore. I ate bowls of cereal at the kitchen table.

I didn't have to wait for another 10 years to pass for dad's pronouncement of "our lives will be normal now" to be proven wrong. A week after his death, I noticed I could no longer see auras. It was as if seeing his soul had wiped them out. However, a different light, a more disturbing light, appeared.

Behind my closed lids, I saw a wash of blue haze. When I looked at my eyes in the mirror I noticed the blue pie-shaped wedges were back, wider than ever; the gold daggers appeared to be gone for good. My eyes were still brown, but when the light hit them just right the wedges seemed to spread and they looked blue. I suspected this change was somehow connected to my mother and wondered if the gold in her eyes had ever gone away and changed to blue, too.

I stopped going to church. I told myself it was because it was too painful without dad, and it was. I missed him more than I thought I possibly could. To fill the void I studied even harder.

Two years after dad's death, I graduated from college and sold the house to pay for veterinary school at UC Davis. During the packing up and moving out, I discovered a thin book 8 inches tall by 5 inches wide. It was on a high ledge spun with spider webs and dust, hidden behind the old cross that used to hang above my bed in Africa. The cross was nailed to a wood beam, high up, in a dusky corner of the attic, waiting to be found. The book was buttoned up like a coat on an undercover agent, cloaked and mysterious, concealed under a facade of black cloth, each layer a muffled shroud bound together by time-yellowed tape. The tape cracked into fragments when I slipped my fingers between it and the dark coat. I pushed the wrap aside, letting it fall to the floor, exposing a shiny pink and white book.

My hands turned icy—a premonition? I blew them warm, as I walked with apprehension past the moving boxes and discarded furniture to the single light bulb hanging from the ceiling in the center of the attic. I held the unsoiled book under the light.

My name, Lillian Kathleen Drake, was written across the cover in bold blue calligraphy. I didn't recognize the handwriting but I knew for certain that it wasn't dad's.

Surrounding my name were faded stars and hearts. Some of the hearts had little tails with curlicues that looped into smaller hearts.

Pushing the boxes aside, I sat on the floor directly under the bulb and nestled the book in my lap. I opened the cover and turned one blank page after another, until in the middle of the book I came across a curl of baby-fine hair. It was auburn in color and held together by the tail hair of an elephant. The long thick strand was twisted around and around the lock of hair and pulled together tight as a corset. A force beyond my own made me pick up the ringlet and smell it. Mute shades of lavender and aqua wafted a ghostly perfume and hinted at memories lost. I closed my eyes trying to recall those memories and was startled when the blue wash of color brush between my eyes and lid and turned the curl of baby hair into a hazy-blue X-ray—and I understood its truth. This baby hair was mine. When I opened my eyes, the image was gone.

I turned the page. My heart thumped.

Three pictures. The pictures were of me; I was maybe a week old. In one photo, dad held me high above his head, his profile and mine, our noses touching. My big baby-diapered self was clothed in a pink romper. In the second picture, I'm in a crib a fluffy stuffed white elephant lay next to me. The elephant and I stared bug-eyed at the camera. Red-flash dots filled both of our eyes. In the third photo, I was being held by a woman. The top of the picture, where her head should have been, had been torn off. Her arms cradled me next to her heart. Who was she? Not Nanta. This woman's arms were not as skinny as my old nanny's.

Lodged in the crease of the next page I found a piece of paper. It was folded twice, then twice again. I unfolded the fragile document and carefully smoothed it open on top of the photos. My birth certificate? Dad had written the birth certificates for all the babies born in Ndogo. Mine was no exception. But this one was different than the one he'd given me when we came to Sacramento, and I needed proof of my birth to get into school. This birth certificate had a second signature on it...my mother's.

In the same blue ink that was on the cover of the book and in the same beautiful writing above the line asking for my mother's signature, the name Hata was signed. *Hata* in Swahili means "until." Neither Nanta nor dad had ever mentioned my mother's name to me, and I never asked. If Hata was her first name why hadn't she signed, Hata Drake? Why just Hata? Had my dad not married her? I touched the ink that spelled her name. My mother had to have been alive to sign it. The time and date of my birth matched what I'd overheard, but her signature was dated three days later.

Dad and Nanta had both told me my mother died on the day I was born. Yet, if this paper told the truth, it appeared she did not die in childbirth, holding me in her arms when she took her last breath. Why had Nanta lied? More important, why had dad kept the truth hidden from me?

Were the arms holding me in the photograph, my mother? Was she the woman whose head was missing from the picture? If so, why save the picture and not let me see her face. If my mother was alive after I was born, was the whole story about my birth and her death a lie? My heart tumbled...was she still alive? If she is alive, then whose soul did I see in Ona? My brain twisted in knots of confusion.

On the birth certificate dad presented to the school, written above the line asking for the mother's name and signature, he had written "died in childbirth." I looked at the signature on this birth certificate again. It astounded and terrified me. My heart hammered blood to my head, bringing a million questions with it. Why had dad gone to all the trouble to remove her existence from my life? What was he so afraid of? What truth was he too frightened of to tell? It was a sin to lie, dad taught me, but what lesson was he teaching me now?

I folded the birth certificate and put it back in the book. I took special care to press the cover tight so not to lose it. Then I searched through all the open and unopened boxes in the attic. I looked through the rafters and the spider webs two more times. I searched the pockets of his old clothes hanging on racks and not worn since we left Africa. On the floor, I found *The Book of Sermons* and leafed through its pages but found no more secrets. No more hidden away pictures of my mother or dad or of me. I found nothing. By late that evening, I was physically and emotionally exhausted, more from disappointment than actual work.

Convinced there was nothing else hidden in the attic, I picked up the baby book and opened it. I touched each of the pictures, hoping to somehow extract the secrets they held but got nothing. I opened each and every page of the book and pressed them flat and smooth before I moved on to the next. On the last page I found a note from my father:

Lill, I'm sorry. It was easier to tell you your mother died giving birth to you than to tell you the truth. Forgive me if you can. The truth can only be the work of the devil and I wanted to spare you from it as long as I could. I've written this knowing if you found it, it's because I've gone to heaven to live with God. However, there are some things you must know about your mother now that I am no longer here to protect you.

From the first moment I saw her, she captivated me with her beauty and spirit. Looking back on our relationship, I would have to say that it was her spirit that captured me. We married, but my God was not part of the ceremony. I lied to you, Lill, I'm sorry. I had always hoped you wouldn't need to know the truth.

Your mother was a machawi, a powerful voodoo sorceress, but her powers were not strong enough to stop what happened. Ten days after you were born, the Devil, the people who practice voodoo call him Bayamchawi. He came for her and for you. You were both to die that day. Your mixed blood was the only thing that saved you. Your mother made a deal with this voodoo devil to spare your life. She convinced him that your tainted blood would strip you of any supernatural powers and to let you live. He agreed as long as you were taken to Mbali on your tenth birthday to find out if you could see souls, a sign that you were a sorceress—a test she assured him you would fail.

You are your mother's daughter, but you are also my daughter and I love you beyond my life. What you need to know is Bayamchawi's powers are not strong enough to harm you as long as you stay away from Africa.

Your mother mentioned something before she was taken. It sounded strange when she said it but perhaps it will be important for you to know now that I am gone; she said you should know that you and the elephant are connected.

Lill, as sure as I am that there is a God in heaven, I know your life will be in danger if you ever go back to Africa. Trust in God, Lill. Trust only in our God and no other. Honor your promise, your life depends on it.

I love you,

Dad

I folded the letter and put it back in the book. Unanswered questions sat on my lips with no one to ask. The answers, like dad, were to remain eternally speechless. But the scar on my hand and the blue and gold lights in my eyes told me that I was more like my mother than he wanted me to be; Ona and what I saw in the Mbali Jungle were real. How this would impact my life I didn't have a clue. So I did what I always did when I was afraid and had questions I didn't have the answers to—I studied.

Chapter 5
Nine Years Later

I've been working at L.A.A.S., Land Animal and Aquatic Sanctuary, for the last two and a half years and I love every minute and every day of it. It affords me certain freedoms I didn't have in vet school. Without my old professor, Dr. Moyoulaya, watching my every move, I no longer have to explain how I'm able to diagnose an animal's illness so quickly and so accurately. My secret? I simply focus on the animal, close my eyes, and right through my lids watch as a watery blue veil falls over the sick patient and presto, I can "see" what's wrong and order whatever tests are needed to confirm the diagnosis. The people I work with think I'm gifted. I have a skill, an intuition, a knack. Every day, every single day, I try not to dwell on the fact that it's my voodoo roots that provide the blue haze. Instead I concentrate on the animals' lives I'm saving because of it. Each night while brushing my teeth, I check my eyes in the mirror and worry what will happen if I lose the blue haze the way I lost the ability to see auras. How will I explain losing "the gift" to the people at the animal park?

Nine years and one month ago, dad died. The doctor said it was a heart attack. Maybe it wasn't. Maybe dad died because Bayamchawi blamed him for taking me from Africa and wants me back. Well, he's going to be disappointed when he finds out there's no one keeping me here but me, and I'm not going anywhere close to Ndogo. As curious as I am about my mother's magical powers and what they have to do with me, nothing...absolutely nothing could make me return to Africa or take me away from the animals at L.A.A.S.

I glance at my watch. It's half past midnight. The air is freezing and soaked with heavy dew. I stomp my feet to keep the circulation going and push aside the recurring thoughts of birthdays and Africa that invade my consciousness whenever I have too much time on my hands.

Five of us—four elephant trainers and me—are waiting outside the elephant barn. Our bodies are pressed tight against the barn's weathered redwood walls, our hands are jammed in our jacket pockets trying to keep them warm. Overhead, the green glow from the halogen lights holds the mist captive against a starless sky. Underneath the light's eerie shadow, we are lined up like pins in a bowling alley, wearing white ball caps, blue jeans, denim shirts zipped under navy-blue nylon jackets. The park logo is silk-screened on the left breast of the jackets in white ink—a dolphin and elephant in profile with L.A.A.S. stenciled underneath. The logo is duplicated in blue across our caps.

Jimmy Nwosu, the night security guard, steps out of the guardhouse. We turn our heads in unison and watch him pull the hood of his thick winter coat over his head. Jimmy fishes for his gloves in the coats pockets, puts them on then strolls toward the cargo gates. He's a large African American man with tinges of white hair at his temples. The 10-foot chain-link gates hangs on posts fitted with sturdy steel hinges and open and close on hard rubber wheels. Jimmy removes a glove, unlocks the gate and pushes one section and then the other across the asphalt drive. Then he motions the driver of the eighteen-wheeler to drive through. Seconds after the semi's taillights have cleared the gate, Jimmy brings the two sections back together, hooks the shank of the lock through two chain loops, clicks the padlock secure, and heads back to the heated guardhouse. We stay glued to the barn and out of the way as the driver inches his rig toward us.

When the semi's air brakes make their final *sspitt-sspitt*, and the rig comes to a stop, we pull ourselves loose from the barn wall like chewing gum from the bottom of a shoe. I remove my hands from my pockets, grab my medical bag from between my feet, and shuffle along with the trainers to the cab of the truck where we wait, with our faces turned up, anxious. The engine is turned off, and the cab rattles, shakes and settles. The pungent odor of diesel fuel gloms onto the fog-damp tips of our noses then quickly vanishes.

"Morning," the driver barks as he jumps from the cab, tennis shoes smacking the pavement like wet tennis balls. He struggles into his bright orange ski jacket then hurries to the side door of his rig, tugging on his zipper the whole way, straining to close it over his large belly. The five of us scamper behind him, our muscles tense and twitching with anticipation. We rub our hands together to warm them and to quiet our nerves and watch with unblinking eyes as he unhooks the steel handle on the door, yanks it down and shoves it sideways with a tap. With an easy push, he opens the wide door, and the pungent smell of days-old straw and elephant pour out to greet us. The cold is forgotten, as we move in close to take a look. The trailer's bed is just about eye level. Inside the box, the interior is lightless. The only things we manage to see are the bits of loose straw that tumble toward us and spill onto the asphalt.

"You okay in there, Doc?" the driver shouts into the dark transport trailer then moves us aside with a brush of his hand. He jumps up on the trailer's bed, bounces to his feet and disappears, sending breath-white steam spiraling out behind him. It flows into the lamplight, mixing the ethereal mist from the *Dzanga-Bai* elephant sanctuary in Africa with our California fog. The halogen lights capture the mist and fog, spinning them into long green tendrils like the arms of an octopus. David Cutter, D.V.M., steps into the doorway, transforming the coiling vapor into riptides of froth.

He looks every bit a ship's captain, lean and rugged. His

khaki shirt and pants, like his sandy brown hair, are disheveled. His right hand is cupped over sleep-deprived blue-green eyes, shielding them from the halogen lights. The light's greenish rays play with the creases on his handsome face making him look older than his 33 years. He smiles. It's his smile that sets his face right in the lamp's light, and an unexplainable beat catches my heart. Without saying a word, he turns and steps back into the darkness of the trailer, reappearing a few seconds later with the driver at his side. The driver stops briefly in the open door to shake Dr. Cutter's hand then hops down. On the ground he turns and reaches up. Dr. Cutter hands him a large duffle bag.

"Ask Jimmy at the back gate to take you to the guest quarters," Dr. Cutter instructs. "Get some sleep, Art. And thanks, it was a smooth ride. You did a great job getting us here in one piece."

"My pleasure, Doc. She's a beauty. I wouldn't have missed this trip for the world." Art turns to us and nods. If he'd had a hat, I'm sure he would have tipped it. He walks to the cab of his rig, grabs his iPad and heads toward the back gate.

"You guys look bright-eyed and ready to go to work. What do you say we get this show on the road?" Dr. Cutter's gentle voice prods.

The four elephant trainers scatter toward the barn. Tim, the head trainer, gives the barn door a hefty shove. The sound of metal wheels rolling across steel tracks and concrete is drowned out by the noise of seven female elephants squealing and trumpeting with excitement. Their talk quiets when the trainers enter the barn. However, the elephants continue to whisper amongst themselves in their own deep-throated language as the trainers double check our earlier preparations. In a short while, we'll move the young elephant from the confines of her shipping crate in the trailer to the comforts of a secure and much larger enclosure we've had built for her in the far corner of the barn.

I pick up my veterinary bag and hand it up to Dr. Cutter. "I'm Dr. Lillian Drake. We've talked on the phone. Please, call me Lill."

"Okay, Lill it is. And, likewise, call me David."

Dr. Cutter is the senior veterinarian at our wild animal park and has been in Africa for over three years working at Dzanga-Bai, our sister park. Seven months ago we received the first of many emails and phone calls from him, saying he had acquired information he hoped would lead him to the mysterious and elusive white elephant, an elephant which up to that point had been nothing more than a rumor. No longer a myth or question mark, she is finally here.

"Lill, hand that up." He bends and reaches out for my medical bag then sets it aside just inside the door. He extends his callused hand again, and I reach up. His fingers grasp my hand and wrist. A blush heats my face, and I'm thankful for the dark. With little effort he pulls me into the trailer. Our hands stay together a moment longer before we let go.

The dim light from outside the semi's trailer leaks in behind me and finds its way to the front wall. As my eyes adjust, I think about this small white puzzle that has come all the way from central Africa to LAX and to the doors of our wild animal park. Her journey and ours is just beginning. We don't know her exact age, we're guessing a little over a year, but she's already six-feet at the shoulder. She is an unearthly white bundle, with large African ears flapping white and defiant, sending soft currents of mistrust in our direction. She stops long enough to pick up a trunk-tip of straw and fling it in our direction. Seemingly pleased with herself, a small *hoot-toot-squeak* escapes from her, and with that little bit of noise I have fallen in love.

I lift my bag and walk beside David across thick inches of straw to get a closer look. Halfway between the open door and this ghost-like creature, we stop. Our shadows bravely stretch out in front of us, melting in distorted images on her ivory hide.

She's breathtaking.

She is a rare creature, one of a kind, but not a freak of nature. No. She is a true white elephant, not an albino. She's bewitching. Her eyes are a deep chocolate brown. Her lashes are long and dark drawing attention to her eyes, outlining them in black. She's real, not a myth or an aberration.

L.A.A.S. is being allowed to keep her and train her and show her to the public, until sometime in the far-distant future when she'll be returned to Africa to be bred. More specifically she will be taken to the Dzanga-Keita Forest Reserve—a privately owned and protected elephant habitat—where, hopefully, she will give birth to a white offspring like herself.

This adorable puff of white elephant eyes us from the confines of her sturdy steel-framed crate. Its wood walls have been taken down and are stacked off to the side. A wide circle of white rings her dark pupils. White-eyed with rebellion, not fear, I think. It's then I notice a flickering translucent gold and silver globe in the right corner of the trailer, behind her head. This light looks like what? The soul-light I saw in Ona? My mother's soul? Or another's?

Even after reading dad's note, I still don't know for certain if my mother is alive or dead. No matter what he said about not trusting the lights, I do. They're too beautiful to be anything but good and after seeing his soul being born, I'm positive. I glance sidewise at David.

"Notice anything strange?"

"Ah, no. Want to give me a clue?" He grins.

"No clues, just curious." I turn my attention back to the elephant.

I'm not surprised he didn't see the translucent orb, but I'm curious what this luminous soul has to do with our new arrival. If she's connected to light I saw in Ona, could she be connected to my upcoming thirtieth birthday, the third ten? Fear tightens my lungs; less than a year to go.

Soft silver and gold sparks caress the baby elephant's cheek then gathers together in a misty spinning ball. Violent black air splashes up like a wave between the elephant's front legs and a horrid flash of hazel-green eyes crests above the inky vapor. A silver beam of light lashes out from the orb, hits the blackish backwash and engulfs it. And both are gone. I cast my gaze to the elephant's face, trying to swallow the terror rising in my throat and working hard not to think about my upcoming birthday.

"Less than a year," my voice croaks, not meaning to speak aloud.

"What?"

"Nothing, ah, just thinking out loud. I was just saying we have years, lots of years to get her ready for...for...everything she needs to know."

"We have plenty of time, Lill." His voice is low and surprisingly seductive.

"Right...plenty of time," I stammer, trying to shake off the hidden message I've imagined from the tone of his voice. "So..." Somewhat flustered, I change the subject, "will she let you get close to her?"

"Sadly no, but I'm working on it." His head tilts sheepishly and the corners of lips turn up.

My body tingles.

"We have an arrangement, she and I," he continues. "I can't touch her, but she'll let me get close enough to take an apple out of my hand. Once the apple is in her mouth, she'll reach out and tap my fingers. She's been through a lot. I'm more than willing to do things her way..." his pause is definitely flirtatious, "and at her own pace. I'll do whatever it takes to win her over."

For a lack of anything better to say I sputter, "Good idea," and move a foot closer to the elephant and a foot away from David. He steps in right beside me almost touching my shoulder. Neither of us says a word; we just watch her.

I can't help but imagine the terror she must have endured when she was separated from her mother. My heart tugs at my own life, growing up without a mother. I hoped her mother hadn't been hurt or, worse, killed during her capture.

"What happened to her mother?" I ask, breaking the silence between us and thinking in my entire life nobody has ever asked that question when talking about me.

Not taking his eyes from the elephant, David answers, "Strange, she didn't seem to have a mother. It's as if she came out of nowhere." He squats, resting his elbow on one knee and rubbing the days-old stubble on his face. I crouch in the straw beside him and wait for him to continue, twirling pieces of straw into circles with my fingers.

"Once we located her and her family unit, we watched them for weeks. There seemed to be a lot of aunties taking care of her, but not one of them claimed her for their own." He twists on the balls of his feet, placing his fingertips on the floor for balance and faces me. Our eyes lock and hold. I draw in a quick breath.

His lips press together in a crooked smile as if he knows something I don't then his eyes saddened. "If her mother was white, she's probably dead. Her hide would be worth a lot of money. If her skin was gray, maybe ivory poachers killed her. Even in a protected area and with a thick forest to hide in, it's hard to keep them 100% safe."

It is something I already know, and I nod at the truth of his statement. I also know it was a way for us to rationalize stealing her from her homeland and taking away her freedom; we were saving her.

David, we, the animal park, all of us had done it, removed her from Africa, brought her here, for her own protection...and, if I was being honest...for profit.

David's full attention has refocused on the baby elephant. His face tells me that he, too, is mesmerized by her.

"There's this voodoo legend about a white elephant," he began without looking away from her. "Nah, forget about it. A little over three years in Africa and you'd think I had lived there my whole life. But you know how it is, it's Africa; there is a voodoo story for every unexplainable thing that happens." He chuckles, stands and rubs his chin then stretches out his hand and helps me up. "You have to take all that weird stuff you hear, that witchdoctor jambo-jambo stuff, you have to take it with a grain of salt. That's the problem with their voodoo witchdoctor stories. Good stories but no proof."

At this point, David didn't know I was born in Africa—it hadn't seemed important to mention it during our communications to bring the white elephant stateside. And to be honest, it's not something I share with just anyone. I'd have to get to know him a whole lot better before I told him what I've told no one else; that I'd experienced firsthand Africa's witchdoctor "jambo-jambo stuff." And that this "stuff" he refers to has enough meat on its bones to be heavily salted.

The white elephant's uneasy rumble demands our attention. We need to get going and transport her from the semi to the barn and introduce her to the park's herd of African elephants: a group affectionately known as "The Magnificent Seven."

I hope she won't be as frightened tonight as she must have been when she was captured. I'll use a blowgun to sedate her. A quick quiet slumber, not the loud dart-filled shotgun Dr. Cutter and most veterinarians use. The blowgun is better, I tell myself. Either way, I know she will fight the effects of the drug. The silent dart won't take away the fear she'll feel. For the second time in her short life, at the hands of humans, she will think she is dying. I wish I could explain it to her. I wish I could let her know how much I, how much we, already love her. I wish I could whisper in her ear and have her simply follow me out of the trailer, down the ramp, and into the barn. But I can't. Once she is sedated, we'll rebuild the sides of her crate and move her, with the help of a fork lift, into her pen inside the barn. I open my bag and begin to prepare the tranquilizer dart for the blowgun. While I'm loading the dart into the shaft I think about the elephant necklace I lost in Mbali and the white elephant in its center. I touch my throat remembering the feel of it then take a breath and aim.

Chapter 6

We named her Penda. *Penda* is Swahili for love. She is lying on her side, sleeping a drugged induced sleep on a thick bed of straw. The overhead lights cast soft yellow shadows in her corner of the barn; it's two in the morning. I'm sitting next to her watching her breath and stroking her head. David is kneeling beside her, his stethoscope pressed tight to her chest, listening to each beat of her heart. He looks over at me and nods. I inject the antidote. He continues to monitor her vitals as I pack up my medical supplies.

Penda's eyes flutter. We gather up our bags and quickly scramble to the outside of her pen, knowing she won't be happy if we stay. She rubs her face across the straw a couple of times, lifts her trunk and tastes the air with its tip. She sniffs out one of the apples we placed close to her and snatches it up. Holding it curled in her trunk she snorts, kicks her legs in the air and rights herself in one swift move. Up on all four feet she surveys her surroundings and shakes her head to clear it. Penda puts the apple in her mouth, crunches down and trumpets. The Magnificent Seven, confined in their night enclosure in the center of the barn, bellow, trumpet, squeal, and rumble in return. Penda squeaks with delight and pops one apple after another in her mouth.

All four of the elephant trainers applaud, as if waking up and eating apples was unique to Penda and Penda alone. And just as silly, David and I exchange triumphant smiles and high fives as if we were the ones who taught her to do it.

"She seems okay with all this." I glance at David to see if he agrees.

"I think you're right. Having other elephants to talk to seems to help."

I turn to the trainers, "Looks like she is going to fit in nicely with the girls. Why don't you go home and get some rest? It's going to be a busy day tomorrow."

There's a lot of shuffling of feet and protesting from tired voices. Everyone is willing to stay.

"Guys, we'll need you in the morning. Go home. Sleep," David insisted.

Reluctantly, Tim nods and motions the others toward the door. Tim's the last one out. He waves and slides the door shut behind him leaving David and I alone.

"Hey," he points to my sleeping bag, "mind if I join you? I'm sort of used to sleeping with her."

"You're the boss. Besides, I'd like the company."

"Great, my sleeping bag is still in the semi. I'll get it and be right back."

About nine o'clock last night, I brought sandwiches and sodas to the barn getting ready to spend the night and this morning with Penda. The thought of sharing them with David makes my pulse tumble recklessly. What have I gotten myself into? We've just met but the chemistry between us is undeniable.

I get busy, getting ready, grabbing sacks of food and drink from the mini-frig then start turning off the switches to the bright-white ceiling lamps. One by one, three banks of lights, three switches each. Pink-shaded shadows from the overhead heat lamps take over and fall in waves across the pale straw leading me back to Penda. A small sliver of rosy light blushes her white skin and I fall in love all over again. She seems unconcerned when I lean against the rail of her pen to watch her eat.

"Candlelight? Dr. Drake, you shouldn't have." David pulls the door closed behind him and walks toward Penda and me.

My breath catches at the sight of him. This stranger is my

soul mate. I now know what Dad meant when he said it was my mother's spirit that captured him. David's has captured me.

Sitting cross-legged on the straw outside her pen, I watch Penda and mindlessly start unpacking food. David stands over me, unties his bedroll, snaps it open and spreads it flat between us like a picnic blanket. The smell of fresh straw swirls up then tumbles down over me. Nothing has ever smelled so sweet.

David reaches for the battery-operated lantern hanging on a nearby hook and switches it on. His eyes crease at the edges. He folds his legs and sits opposite me and places the lantern on the blanket between us. I set out the sandwiches, potato chips, and sodas.

"So, Lill, do you want to tell me about this special talent of yours I've heard so much about?"

"Talent?" I gulp, not looking up, instead choosing to concentrate on unwrapping a sandwich. "Tuna," I hold it out to him. "I hope you like tuna."

"I do. Thanks." David reaches for it. "So tell me. Even while I was in Africa I heard about your uncanny ability to diagnose an animal's illness. How do you do it?" His eyes sparkle with playful delight as he takes a bite of the sandwich. "Umm, this is good. I was hungry." He takes another bite then lifts a can of Coke, opens it, and drinks half before he asks, "Well?"

"My talent, as you call it, is not easy to explain, nor is it something I'm comfortable talking about. Would you accept luck?"

"No. I also heard you were born in Ndogo, close to the Mbali jungle."

"Whoever your source of information is, they are pretty good."

"Yep. Your professor in vet school, Dr. Moyoulaya, he and I went to college together. I don't think he ever told you, but he was born in Africa, too. In fact it was his brother who helped me track Penda. Moyoulaya was the one who told me about your uncanny ability to diagnose animal illnesses." David smiles. "I understand there's voodoo in Mbali."

"Some people think so," I say as matter-of-factly as I can.

"Couldn't help but notice your eyes. What I said earlier about voodoo jambo-jambo, well, I'm not saying I believe it, and I'm not saying I don't, but I heard stories about eyes that can see souls...there was this one witchdoctor who came with us and he..."

My heart rate quickens. "David, stop." What will he think if I tell him even just part of it? "It's a hard story to tell when I don't know what's true and what isn't." I finish the last of my sandwich followed by a long drink of diet 7-Up, stalling for time and gathering my thoughts.

"It's okay, Lill. I won't judge. Start at the beginning. It'll be our little secret. I promise, I won't tell a soul." He winks and smiles with his lips pressed together. "What else are we going to talk about until the sun comes up? *Jua*, that's what they call the sun in Swahili, isn't it. When I look in your eyes, when the light hits them just right I see these tiny bits of gold sparks hiding behind the blue wedges. They remind me of little sparks of sunrise."

My heart does a double thump-thump. The gold light weren't there when I checked in the mirror this morning. But he did say tiny. I blink, my eyes don't feel warm. He must have seen something else, the lights can't be back.

David brushes my cheek with the back of his fingers then kisses the corner of my mouth. Penda settles down on her back knees and the moment ends, our full attention focused on her. She inches her front legs out in front of her then slowly lays on her side. Our eyes study her every move, like proud parents we watch her squirm in the straw and kick her legs, getting comfortable. She lets out a long sigh and a soft *toot-squeak*. The other elephants answer with a rumbling so deep that the floor vibrates under us. She toots again and closes her eyes.

"We should let her sleep." David switches off the lantern. We are once again awash in the warm pink glow of the heaters hanging overhead. We get busy gathering up sandwich wrappers and empty cans and stash them safely out of Penda's reach. David folds his sleeping bag then places it on the straw along the wall next to her pen. He sits down on half of it, stretches his legs out in front of him then pats the other half of the blanket, inviting me to join him. I sit down, careful to keep a space between us; I'll need it. I have decided to tell him everything that happened and everything I imagined happened to me while I was in Africa. If he thinks I'm crazy and needs to run, he should do it now.

I explain about dad being a minster and never talking or answering any questions about my mother or what he thought was the devil's voodoo. I tell him about Nanta raising me because my mother died shortly after I was born, maybe. I talk in uncertain innuendos about the number ten and explain about thinking I saw my mother's soul light in a mysterious city called Ona, and how later, I really did see dad's soul as it formed and left his body.

"What do they look like, these souls of yours?" he asks.

"Both were the size of a human heart, translucent as a wish, and to me they looked like small round angels. They are beautiful."

When I tell him about the leopard attack, I keep my eyes downcast, busy watching my fingers break little pieces of straw in half. When I finish, I looked up and met his surprised eyes.

"A leopard?" he asks.

"I think so. Senento, Nanta's son, he was the first person I heard call the leopard by the name Bayamchawi. Semoi, her other son, said the leopard was devil voodoo. But, David, it couldn't have been voodoo. I felt the weight of the leopard on top of me. I smelled his breath. The leopard was real."

"Leopards are nasty animals. You're lucky you survived. How

big was he?"

"Huge, twice the size of the ones we have here at the park."

"Lill..." David scoots close. Our shoulders touch and a warm current flows through me. He takes my hand. "Lill..." His voice is soft and filled with concern. "...I've heard about this devil the natives call Bayamchawi."

"You have?"

He kisses my fingers then releases them, "Yeah, I have, and I believe the leopard that attacked you was evil. For the sake of argument, let just say the leopard was Bayamchawi. Do you know why he wanted to kill you?"

"No. Sometimes I think it would help if I knew, other times I think knowing would be worse. But I think it has everything to do with who my mother was."

"Well, regardless, I think your dad was right; you need to stay as far from Africa as you can. So..." He smiles, trying to lighten the mood. "...does all this voodoo stuff somehow fit in with your special talent to diagnose animals?"

"Yeah, I think it might. When I look at an animal—"

"Come here," he interrupts and leans my back against his chest. His arms encircle me. He kisses the top of my head and with him holding me, I think about my mother and wonder if she really did hold me as she took her last breath.

"David..." My heartbeat slows to match his. I breathe in the warmth and the smell of him. It collides with a passion I had no idea I longed for until he stepped out of the back of the semi-trailer, walked into the lamplight and captured my heart. I close my eyes and tell him how the blue-haze spreads over an animal and how it pinpoints the area that needs treatment.

"I'm jealous."

"Don't be, it's connected to my mother, to what she was...and what I might be. My eyes have always frightened me."

He hugs me tighter. "The color of your eyes is amazing. The little gold sparks are gone, but the blue is still there. Lill, I could look at your eyes forever."

We sit quietly for several minutes, each with our own thoughts. David slowly turns me to face him. A moment passes between us then he gently kisses my lips. He pulls back, our lips moist and wanting more.

He kisses me again before he speaks. "It was meant to be, Lill. We fit perfectly, the three of us. I have no family and the same can be said for Penda and you. The three of us were destined to be together.

"David, tell me about you."

"Compared to you, my life is kind of boring. My parents never expected to have a child. They'd been told it would be impossible. My mother was 42 when I was born. I was their miracle baby. She died before I was twenty. My father died three years later. Cancer took them both."

He leans over and kisses my temple, then looks deep into my eyes. "I think your eyes are beyond beautiful. I know this thing between us is happening too fast, but I don't want to stop it. Lill, I'm falling in love with you."

"David," I whisper and melt into his arms.

"I wish I could see these souls of yours. I know your dad didn't think so, but I think your ability to see souls has got to be a gift from God. How else could it be possible? Still, I want you to promise me, like you promised him, that you'll never go back to Africa. I've just found you, and I don't want to lose you any time soon. As long as you stay close to Penda and me, I promise you, you'll be safe."

"I hope you're right." This time I kiss him. Never once did he doubt the things in Africa hadn't happened, or weren't real and this makes me love him all the more.

"Lill, I only lived in Africa for a short while, but I spent a great deal of my time in the bush with the natives and I listened to a lot of stories dealing with voodoo and witchdoctors. I didn't believe any of it at first, just like I hadn't believed I'd ever find a white elephant, and then we found Penda."

David kisses my forehead, holds my face in his hands and looks deep into my eyes, "If Penda's possible...anything's possible...and that worries me. Penda's existence opens all the doors—white magic, black magic, voodoo, the blue haze that lets you save a sick animals, and a God in heaven that lets you see souls. Lill, I want you to know...I promise...now that you and I are part of each other's lives, I will never let anything bad happen to you ever again. You have my word. No more black magic in your life..." He kisses my lips. "...only white."

*****

With Penda in our lives, everything seems to have shifted into fast forward. She has changed us both. It's just three months after her arrival, and David and I are getting married today. And the elephant barn is the most perfect place to hold it, the most perfect place on earth.

The wedding music is from the movie *Hatari*. It's being played on the old boom box we keep in the nursery to keep the newborn animals company at night. Jan, my assistant, turns up the volume when I enter the barn and everyone stands. David and I chose the theme song "Elephant Walk" for my walk down the aisle because we thought it fit the three of us perfectly. I am barefoot and wearing a simple white dress that brushes across the top of my feet as I walk. My hair is pulled back in a French braid with small white lilies tucked in-between each plait. The path to David is a thick layer of animal bedding and smells of pine. The Magnificent Seven are quiet and watch from inside their night time enclosure. Penda is the most important "person" at our wedding. She's a foot taller than when she first arrived and stands at David's side. She is his "best man," and has a black bowtie tied around each front leg, just above her toes. David wears his black suit and a white shirt with no tie. He and Penda are waiting between makeshift pillars made of white, 50-pound bags of monkey-chow stacked seven feet tall. Vases of white roses and lilies are balanced on top of each one. Instead of flowers, I carry a bouquet of carrots wrapped in red leaf lettuce, green kale and cilantro. The pews for our small gathering of guests are bales of straw.

Miles Turay is marrying us. He lived in Africa for a while and ran Dzanga-Bai before he moved back to the states and became director of L.A.S.S. A savvy businessman, he was the mastermind behind sending David to Africa in pursuit of our elusive white elephant. He got a one-day license via the Internet and is the perfect person for the job. His deeply accented African voice and his ebony skin lend a stately presence to our otherwise casual ceremony.

We say our vows in whispers, our love too private to share. When we kiss, Penda trumpets, as if on cue. The Magnificent Seven join in. There is not a dry eye in the house, mine and David's included. Penda walks between us as we leave our makeshift church. When we reach the end of the path I turn and toss my bouquet to the elephants. Taatee catches it with her trunk and flings it back. Penda snatches it from the air then shoves the whole vegie-bouquet in her mouth. She trumpets and everyone applauds. Instead of rice, our friends throw sweet grain and peanuts over our heads.

In the following months, Penda continues to grow, and she is doing it at lightning speed. She seems to grow inches overnight and is maturing in other ways, too. We take blood tests and worry. I close my eyes and watch while the blue haze washes over her and find nothing wrong. We take X-rays to make sure her bones can support her weight and rapid growth. We confer and share the results of our tests with veterinarians from around the world; they all agree the speed at which she is growing is unusual. They don't offer an explanation, but they all agree she's healthy. Time rushes by and everyday Penda grows taller. David's promises to keep me safe become more and more frequent as my thirtieth birthday approaches.

Chapter 7

One last click of the mouse, and I'm finished. All necessary emails have been answered and sent. The invoices have been filed, and I've forwarded the ones needing to be paid to accounting. Beside my utilitarian desk, Rita's knobby gray Macaw feet are wrapped tightly around a eucalyptus branch acting as a perch inside her super large bird cage. Her scarlet plumage is relaxed and her yellow beak is busy pushing aside and selecting the perfect tidbit from her food dish. Having Rita quiet is the next best thing to winning the lottery or having a wish granted.

Five o'clock and it is time to go home. The temperature inside and out is warm, which isn't helping my headache, a headache that's threatening to become a migraine. Little flash dots are hip-hop dancing in my right eye. My allergies, like the smog outside, are in full bloom—you have to love summer time in Sacramento. Add to this, a day that has been insanely busy gathering notes and slides for David, Miles and Mike our head primate trainer, for their trip to Florida. It's no wonder my head is throbbing. The guys left this afternoon from San Francisco International Airport to attend a conference, in Tampa, on "The Physical and Mental Care of Animals in Captivity." Both David and Mike are guest speakers. Miles is tagging along to bask in the afterglow and drum up business, typical of Miles, he's all business. Everything for him comes down to money, that's all he thinks about. When I'm around Miles, I'm thankful I can't see 'the blue haze' when I look at humans. If I could, I'm positive he would be awash in a turbulent sea of blue dollar signs, rough enough to make me seasick.

With David gone, I've planned a sleepover with the girls. Lots of giggles (elephants do have a sense of humor) and fattening food. It will be picnic style on the floor of the barn—elephants don't afford any other choice; table and chairs are not an option. Penda, as do all of our elephants, loves French fries. Fries are the party item on their snack menu tonight.

Standing and stretching, I reach above my desk for Rita's nighttime blanket. It is folded neatly on top of a stack of veterinary medicine books on the shelf above the computer. The fish on the screen have already started chasing bubbles and their mindless parade will continue long after I've gone. Sitting next to the screen is a picture David, Penda and me—our wedding picture. I tap the glass with my finger, missing David already. I turn my attention to Rita.

"Goodnight, Rita."

"Hi boss, good morning! *Squawk!*"

"No Rita, it's not morning, it's time to say goodnight." I fluff the blanket over her cage and let it drop, covering the sides. My head continues to pound. I need food and a Benadryl.

"*Squawk!* Lights out, boss. *Squawk.* Lights out."

At the office door, I switch off the lights, turn right and walk down the dimly lit hallway. In the background I can hear Rita singing a farewell lullaby.

"*Squawk!* Goodnight, Irene, goodnight, Irene . . ." Rita spent most of her life in a tavern in Old Town Sacramento, and this is her favorite song. Her voice fades as I close the door behind me and lock it.

The vet clinic's golf cart is parked next to the back door. I reach down and ease the plug out of the socket, hop in and whiz down the service road toward home. L.A.A.S. has given David and me a cute little house to live in, a two-bedroom ranch house situated just outside the park's perimeter fencing. A moat and a tall wood fence separate our house from the simulated African veldt behind it. Our whole yard, front and back, is fenced and safe enough for the occasional recuperating animal to roam in. It's a win-win. We get free housing, and they get 24-hour veterinary care.

Thirty minutes after leaving the house, I've circled the parking lot at Jack-in-the-Box twice before finding a space to park my Chevy truck. I'm not surprised to find the inside crowded with after work folks, tired moms, and cranky kids. After waiting in line a short five minutes, I place an order for nine super-size bags of French fries, one for each of us, and a Sirloin Swiss Burger with onion for me. With David gone, I don't bother to hold the onions.

By the time I return to the animal park, it's almost seven. It's a little later than I wanted, but I stopped at the house to get the golf cart and pick up provisions: a sleeping bag and pillow, and a canvas bag to dump my Kindle, toothpaste, toothbrush, and a hair brush in. I also took a little extra time to change out of my scrubs and into jeans, a lightweight pullover and cowboy boots.

At the barn door, I grab the food and leave everything else on the seat of the cart. I'm starving and looking forward to chomping into that burger. I shove the massive barn door open just wide enough to squeeze through.

And there it is—the sound of heaven on earth—eight elephants saying hello. Next to David, these girls are my family and Penda is the daughter I've yet to have. Don't get me wrong, I love all the animals at the wild animal park, but elephants are special.

As the girls cluster together, I set our dinner on top of the small mini-fridge under the panel of light switches by the door, then un-wrap my burger, take a quick bite and flip three of the switches on. The overhead lights blink to life in the center of the barn, creating a soft spotlight on the straw-covered floor. The elephants' pen has been enlarged since Penda's arrival and looks like a very, very large boxing ring. It's about a quarter the size of a football field and is defined by 8-inch round steel pipes, standing five feet tall, each driven five feet into the ground and spaced six feet apart. These posts are filled with concrete for added strength. Three rows of horizontal steel pipes are welded to the posts, keeping the elephants and barn walls safe. The floor is asphalt, soft enough to have some give under their massive tonnage and easy to clean.

I take another bite of my burger, gather up the sack filled with the boxes of fries, and walk over to the pen. I say a quick hello, duck between the rails and step inside. Instantly I am encased in a sea of trumping elephants. The barn and my ears are filled with the jubilant noise of elephant. My headache is gone, blasted away by the percussion of their enthusiasm. I have to chuckle when Lu and Taatee squeal and shake their giant heads in a circular rotation, at the same time flipping their trunks in smaller circles and sniffing the bag filled with fries.

Surrounded by seven gray behemoth friends and one white one, I start handing out the boxes of fries. Elephants are super intelligent and they know not to eat the boxes. After they each have a box, I lean against the rails, eating my own French fries and watching the girls eat theirs. Each of the elephants eats their fries differently. Bandi blows the straw with the tip of her trunk exposing the asphalt, dumps the fries on the cleared spot, then smashes them with her foot and sucks them up like they were mashed, which, after stomping on them, they are. Lu sets the box upright on the floor and daintily picks out one fry at a time. Taatee slams the box and the fries in her mouth all at one time. She works her huge pink tongue around until she has eaten all the fries then spits the box out on the floor; "Amazing," is all I can think. Penda empties her fries onto the floor, tosses the box aside and eats them in small bunches. While the elephants are munching away, I go outside to get the rest of the things I've brought for tonight's sleepover.

Back inside, I drop my sleeping bag and canvas carryall by the door and head straight for the feed room. It takes up a quarter of the barn interior and holds alfalfa, grass-hay, straw for bedding, and salt blocks. There is also a small sink and toilet tucked into a cubby in back. The room is dark and turning on the lights brings a scurrying of quick feet. The center aisle is kept clear and is wide enough for a forklift and mice to run across if you catch them unaware.

Climbing up a short stack of straw, I push four bales to the floor and climb down, sink a hay hook into one, and begin dragging them one at a time into the center of the elephant pen. I place three of the bales side by side, long ways and stack the forth bale on top, at one end. I now have a chair and bed all in one.

I head back to the refrigerator and take a moment to wolf down the rest of my burger, something I don't want to share with the girls. Then I turn off the lights. Overhead, the red security bulb remains on and weaves a dim pink glow onto the straw. Snatching up my sleeping bag and Kindle, I head for my makeshift chair. It's story time.

Yawning, I unzip the sleeping bag and spread it out on the bales. As I climb on top, the girls start to move in, ready for a story. I cross my left leg on top of my right knee and remove my cowboy boot and rub my toes. Taatee sniffs my foot and blows hot damp elephant air over it and flips her trunk with a quick snap against my foot. Then she opens her mouth and sticks out her tongue like she's going to gag.

"Taatee, stop that. My foot does not smell."

She shakes her head up and down, flaps her ears, and rumbles.

I laugh. "No it doesn't."

Ignoring her continued rumblings, I remove the other boot and pull the sleeping bag up to my waist. The straw bales make a perfect bed for a sleepover. "Okay girls, are you ready for a story?" I turn on the Kindle, repress a second yawn and start to read "Dumbo the Flying Elephant."

As I'm reading, the elephants begin to get comfortable. Koni and Motsi are the first to lie down. Rra and Kutsi lean against each other, trunks entwined, rocking from side to side as if they are intent on hearing every word. Penda folds her body gracefully to the floor and scoots around until her head is touching the side of my straw bed. She stretches out and sighs then reaches her trunk over the edge of the bale and sniffs my arm. She curls it down as I start to read.

"'Dumbo, what's the matter with your ears? Mouse asks.'"

Three-quarters of the way through the book, Penda swishes her tail in the straw and smacks it with a cushioned thump. I stop reading and look up. A disorienting swell of black mist catches my eye. It boils out of the darkest corner of the barn and mixes with the pink glow of the safety lamp. The hairs on my arms rise as an incomplete figure forms in the vapor. Dread catches in the back of my throat. I shut off the light to the Kindle, blinking to readjust my focus. My heart races, but whatever it was is gone. I look around at the elephants; not one of them is acting spooked or anxious. If someone or something was anywhere in the barn, I tell myself, they would have trumpeted a warning but my heart beats faster than normal.

"Hello, is someone here?" I ask, feeling foolish. I suck in a deep breath filling my lungs, hold the air in then slowly let it out hoping to calm my jumpy nerves. The smell of the elephants reminds me of the words I read in Dad's note—"Your mother wanted you to know you're connected to the elephant."

Penda's trunk taps my hand. "Okay, okay, you're right," I say to her, "we all need to get some sleep. I'll finish the story another time."

The dry grass smell of hay bales hugs my pillow as I wiggle down into my bedroll. In an effort to push the image of the tumbling black mist out of my mind, I turn onto my side, ease my arm over the edge and rest my hand on Penda's cheek. We are connected, she and I; and I feel safe.

"Good night, Penda."

Penda rumbles, a low-throated reply telling me not to worry, she and the other elephants will protect me.

I dream of mice. I've had more than my share crawl into my sleeping bag while I've slept on the floor taking care of a sick animal. It scares the hell out of you, not to mention that you've got to get out of the bag without killing the little critter or, worse, get bitten.

I wake up to the sound of elephants peeing. The aroma is so pungent it makes my eyes water. This is when, and only when, I question my love for my giant friends. I untangle myself from the sleeping bag and shake it out, happy not to find any mice.

Stretching out the kinks, I greet Penda first and then the rest of the elephants with sour morning-breath kisses and start putting things away. On my last trip to the feed room, I brush my teeth, comb my unruly hair, and twist it up with a clip in the tiny bathroom. On the way out of the barn, I kiss Penda one last time.

The ride down the back road to the clinic is a quick one. The morning is crisp with the smell of wet dirt from an overnight rain. In my office I tap the computer keyboard, bringing the screen to life, and hit mail. While it's waking up, I go to the small kitchen area in the nursery and set Mr. Coffee to brew then head back to the office where I exchange my boots and jeans for scrubs and tennis shoes. I keep a change of clothes in my locker just in case I don't have time to go home or need fresh ones.

I look through the email. There is a note from David saying he misses me and loves me. Then one from Kevin, the night keeper: *Angela gave birth at four-thirty this morning. Mother and baby seem to be doing fine. Haven't been able to get close enough to tell if it's a boy or girl.*

Angela is a twenty-six-year-old chimp, and she's waited a long time for this baby. It's her first. At twenty-six, Angela is well over 100 pounds and stronger than most men. It's a good thing the public doesn't understand how strong chimpanzees really are. If they did, they wouldn't think they were so cute, much to Miles' chagrin. Angela lives in the park's nature habitat with a clan of eight other chimps. She was hand raised, but more wild than she is friendly. She won't let anyone get close to her except Mike and sometimes, Kevin.

"*Squawk.*"

Knowing what's coming, I take a moment, then remove the blanket covering Rita's cage.

"Twist and shout. Morning's about. *Squawk!* Over hill, over dale, *squawk!* Ride'em down the dusty trail," Rita shrieks.

"Hi, Boss," Jan shouts over Rita's morning medley, entering the office with two cups of coffee, one in each hand. Jan is ten years older than me and is my other right hand. She's the best vet tech on the planet and in my eyes there's nothing she can't do. Born on a working ranch and raised with cows and horses, large animals don't frighten her. Having two older brothers doesn't hurt either. She's one tough lady.

"How's yesterday's headache?" she asks, handing me a cup and glancing from me to Rita and back, her bushbaby brown eyes, magnified behind the thick lenses of her glasses.

"Gone." I take a sip.

"Good, because I saw Kevin this morning. He looked beat. He was on his way home, seems he pulled an all-nighter and then some. He sent you an email about Angela's baby. You got the message, right?"

"Yeah, great news."

"Not so great. He asked me to tell you, the baby died." She glances at her watch. "About fifteen minutes ago."

"No. Darn it."

"More than darn it."

"Damn it?"

"Worse. A big damn it. Angela won't let anyone get near her. She's not giving that baby up, not to Kevin anyway, and next to

Mike he's the best chance we've got."

"Call over to chimp housing and ask Liam and his team keep her isolated in the night housing area and have them let the other chimps into the public viewing area. I know it's early to put them out, but we need to get her separated, ASAP. You had breakfast?"

"Yep."

"Good. Tell them I'll be over as soon as I toast a couple of Pop-Tarts."

"You got it. Pop-Tarts? Oh, right. How was the sleepover last night?"

"No mice in my sleeping bag."

"Doesn't get any better than that."

"No, it doesn't."

"With Mike in Florida, do you want me to call Kevin back in?"

"Let's see what we're up against first. Kevin's got to be exhausted. Let him sleep for now."

"What happens if you need to go in with Angela to get the baby? You know you don't like chimps."

"It's not that I don't like chimps. I don't like getting bitten by chimps; there's a difference. It's just not right for an animal to have human teeth, that's all."

"If you say so." Jan drains the last bit of coffee from her cup and tosses me a I-don't-believe-you smile before she waltzes to the door where she stops and turns, adding, "I'll meet you at the chimp house as soon as I finish feeding the tiger cubs."

With one raspberry Pot-Tart eaten and the other in my hand, I step out the clinic's back door. Plopping myself and my medical bag in the golf cart, I back out, change gears, pull forward and take a quick left over the bridge leading into the park and to the chimp house. As I drive through the park, I go over all the things that can possibly go wrong in an attempt to get Angela to give up her dead baby. It's a good thing to do, running over the worst-case scenarios, but I keep getting stuck on the image of chimp teeth chomping down on my body parts.

The park is getting ready to open at nine and the smell of fresh popcorn winds its way through the air in tempting clumps of melted butter and salt. Maybe I'll get a bag on the way back, assuming I still have my fingers.

I zip the cart up to the front of the chimpanzee nature exhibit, apply the brake and start counting. All the chimps are here except for Angela and her baby. Good. It seems the keepers were successful in containing her to the night housing area. My toe taps the pedal, and I'm off to the side entrance of the exhibit, to see what Angela is up to.

I park by the door, grab my medical bag, key the door and let myself in. The warehouse size room is awash with the aroma of animal bedding, fresh produce and Downey fabric softener. I can hear the dryer running in the background. "Hello," I shout into the cavernous space and head for the large cage in back.

"Lill," Liam calls and waves a hand as he and Sandy, his assistant, walk to meet me.

"We got one unhappy chimp in there. Come have a look," Sandy says and motions me to follow her and Liam to the cage. Liam is as Irish looking as his name implies; thin, tall and good looking. Sandy is the opposite in every way. On the way we pass bags of chimp food, stacked neatly next to boxes of assorted fruits, bananas, vegetables and bread. A fresh supply of blankets for the sleeping platforms fills the shelves above a washing machine and dryer. A well-used desk and a computer sit close by.

Sandy, Liam and I pause outside the chain-link door of the chimpanzees' night enclosure. Standing shoulder to shoulder, we keep an eye on Angela as she screams and beats her feet on the highest and most inaccessible sleeping platform in the cage.

"Nice." I smile sarcastically.

Sandy sighs. "I've never seen her like this. She's always standoffish, but she's never been this aggressive."

The chimp's sleeping quarters, their bedroom, is a thirty-foot-by-thirty-foot chain-link cage twenty feet tall. It has a chain-link top and a cement floor. Inside the cage there are large faux trees made of concrete. The sleeping shelves attached to them, are at varying heights and widths, cut from thick plywood. The whole thing is designed to be functional and easy to clean, but it's not very pretty.

Angela continues to shriek and shake her fists at us, so Sandy, Liam, and I ease back and let her vent while we talk about what we are going to do. After a few minutes, Angela grows quiet, hugs the tiny chimp against her body and swings down to the lowest sleeping platform. Apparently she has decided she wants to show us the baby. Her brown eyes watch us watching her the whole time. When she's comfortably situated on the shelf she lifts the baby up, tilts her head and pokes at the baby's little lips with her finger. She looks at us, dark eyes blinking and sad. A keening wail spills from her mouth, begging us to fix her baby. I take a tentative step forward. She grabs the dead chimp to her breast, jumps up to a higher platform, screaming and baring her teeth, warning me not to get any closer, and then ups the noise level. I didn't think it was possible.

I cover my ears and step back. Angela drops her baby on the platform and lunges for me. In a split second she has grabbed hold of the chain-link and is shaking it with both hands and feet in a gorilla-size rage of desperation then she somersaults off the chain-link, picks up her baby in one arm and races to the door that leads to the chimpanzee habitat outside. Angela pounds on the door with her free hand, hitting it with everything she's got. She wants to be with her chimpanzee family, and she wants to be with them now. Angela continues to alternate between screams, pounding, crying and punching the locked door for another five minutes. Finally exhausted, she sits on the floor and holds the baby up to her face and shakes it like a broken toy, trying to restart it. The baby's head flops back and forth. Angela turns her body to face us, her eyes sad. She howls in anguish and lays the chimps little body across her lap. It's a girl. She reaches for the baby's hand and slaps it against her own in an effort to wake it up. The three of us move closer. She stares at us with suspicion then turns and stomps away. We follow her down the length of the cage as she drags the baby by a single leg behind her.

When she stops, she crouches down and leans her head and shoulder against the chain-link. Her eyes blink, her nostrils flare and her lips quiver. Angela picks at the baby's eyes with a long black finger nail, in an effort to wake her up. I dare to edge close. Angela's sad eyes look up and question mine. Chimps can't cry; they have no tear ducts, but she might as well have been crying.

"Angela, I'm so sorry."

She cradles the tiny chimp in her arms and lovingly strokes the hair on top of her little girl's head.

A half hour later, I've had to rule out tranquilizing her because of her thinness. She had a rough pregnancy. She was sick a lot. We've tried everything we could think of to get her to let go of her baby. She wouldn't even give it up for a peanut butter and jelly sandwich, her favorite food. It seems I have no choice but to go in the cage and somehow take it from her—it's important to do a necropsy as soon after death as possible and too much time has passed already. We call Kevin but he doesn't answer, so we leave a message.

Upon arriving, Jan fills a syringe with xylazine. I'll use it to knock Angela out only as a last resort, to save myself from being bitten or worse. When Jan has finished, she marches to my side and drops the pink-capped syringe into the shirt pocket of my scrubs and makes a show of placing a second syringe in her own pocket.

"Don't do anything stupid, okay?" she instructs.

"Stupid? *Moi*?"

"*Vous.*"

"Look," Liam says, pointing at Angela.

Angela appears to have fallen asleep. She has crawled up on one of the lower platforms, her head resting on the cement tree trunk. Her face is slack, her eyes are closed, her breathing shallow. The baby is hidden from our view, tucked protectively in her arms.

"It's now or never. Maybe I can slip in and snatch the baby before she wakes up." I roll my eyes, knowing that's never going to happen. Then add, "Hey, she was raised by humans. I'm betting she'll come around when she sees my smiling face."

Jan rolls her eyes, mocking me. "I wouldn't count on that fairy tale coming true."

"Let's hope you're wrong. If I can't have the fairy tale I'll need a miracle. Other than darting her, this may be the only chance I'm ever going to get."

The four of us move to the cage door. Angela screams and violently smacks her feet on the platform. If she was sleeping, she just woke up. My stomach churns. I try and blame it on the coffee and Pop-Tarts, but even I don't believe it.

"Lill?" Jan voice is filled with concern.

"I'll be careful, but I have to try. Guys, unless I'm bleeding or hurt, keep absolutely quiet. Once I'm inside she's going to feel threatened, so stay back. Let's keep the threats to a minimum. "

"You sure you want to go in there?" Sandy asks.

"I don't like this," Jan murmurs.

"We'll do whatever it takes to keep you safe, Lill. That's all I'm going to promise," Liam states and stays put. "Doc would have my ass if I let anything happen to you."

"Jan, once I'm in, lock the door."

"Lill, that's not the best idea you've ever had. If you need to get out in a hurry, the seconds it would take to unlock it wouldn't be worth it."

"Chimps have thumbs. She could have the door open before we ever got the chance sedate her, and then we'd have a much bigger problem."

Reluctantly, Jan turns the key in the lock. It opens with a loud click. Angela raises her head and pulls the baby to her breasts. This is not going to be easy. I enter the cage with my back facing her and my head down but my eyes remain vigilant. Angela draws her lips back, exposing her teeth, and she's not smiling. This is the first time since she's given birth that I've had a clear view of her. With no chain-link blocking my sight I close my lids and let the blue haze wash over her. She's sick; she needs to be treated for toxoplasmosis, and she underweight. I don't want to jeopardize her health further by darting her if I don't have to.

I want Angela to think I'm not interested in her, so I nibble on a make believe leaf and slowly ease toward her. Hopefully my submissive body language is telling her I'm not a threat. A few feet in I stop, giving her a chance to get used to me being in her space. Taking great care not to upset her, I pretend to be more intent on finding an imaginary bug on my shoulder than her. When it feels safe, I sneak a glance. Angela's brown eyes lock onto mine. I quickly look down, praying she studied from the same text book I did—Chimp Behavior 101—and knows by my downcast eyes that I'm inferior. To be honest, right now I am.

Ever so carefully, I inch another foot closer. I stop and scratch my head chimp-style, at the same time stealing a quick look from under my arm. Angela imitates me by putting her own hand on top of her head and stares back. Creepy. She slides off the platform. Holding her baby in the crook of her arm, she shuffles toward me. I lower my hand and pick nonexistent bugs off my wrist, indicating I'm unconcerned with her movements. Hoping to further convince her of my disinterest, I settle onto the floor, slump my shoulders forward and rest my hands nonchalantly in my lap while my heart ticks to overdrive. Out of the corner of my eye, I watch as she draws nearer, knuckle-walking, flexed posture, weight pressed down. Angela approaches as if she doesn't have a care in the world. When she's just a few feet away, she suddenly stops. Her eyes dart left, then right, then return back on me, questioning my intentions. She stands up straight, arches her back, raises a fist over her head and screams. The hairs on her neck, shoulders and back flare. Not a good sign. Angela is challenging me, chimp style.

Sneaking a glance at Jan, Sandy and Liam, I warn them with a quick wiggle of my finger not to move. In preparation for an attack, I bring my arms up to my chest, cross my wrists and take the syringe out of my pocket all at the same time. I slide my knees up, shrinking my body into a tight ball. While I'm doing this, I uncap the syringe, exposing the needle. My thumb finds the plunger and stays there. A burning sensation travels along the old scar on my palm. I rub it with a free finger and wait for Angela's assault.

Nothing happens. So I wait. And wait.

I hear a shuffle.

With as little movement as possible I glance up. Angela is no longer standing she's sitting on the floor picking at her arm. I give it a second then cautiously, and perhaps unwisely, unwind my body. Angela ignores me. Okay, I tell myself, this is good. She's getting used to me. I inch forward on my butt. Angela pays no attention, so I scoot another inch closer. She stretches her legs out in front of her and places the baby across them and begins to pick at her stomach. I copy her movements, straighten my legs and pick at my stomach, too. The scar on my palm warms.

Angela sneezes. My head jerks up too fast. Angela's panicked eyes flash into mine. I hold my breath. She snaps the dead chimp under her arm and rises to her feet. I release my breath. My thumb is ready on the syringe. Angela screams an earsplitting warning and shakes a fist at me. I press my chin against my chest to protect my face but keep my eyes on her. Fear and knowledge hold me stone still while I wait for the attack.

"Ooooo," she sniffles, looks at her baby's lifeless face then squats on her haunches.

I eke out an unsure, "Ooooo?" Imitating her as best I can and hoping I haven't made a horrible and possibly life-ending mistake.

Angela brings the tiny chimp to her face and moves her lips softly over its head, eyes, arms and neck. She lowers the baby to her side with one hand then lunges.

She punches me on the shoulder with hard knuckles, hard enough to knock me over. I curl into the fetal position and cover my head with an arm, defensive, needle ready, protecting myself from the blows sure to follow. She jumps up and down, screaming and hitting the back of me then screaming some more. I don't move. She leans over me. I ease the syringe out to the side. She sniffs my hair. I get ready to roll, ready to plunge the needle into her. Angela's stiff finger pokes my head. Her warm breath crosses my neck then she sits down next to me. It's a strain to keep my breathing shallow. We are close, maybe too close.

"Lill?" Jan's worried voice whispers.

I don't dare answer. A minute drags by, then another. Another minute passes and still nothing happens. One of us will have to make the first move, and it feels like that someone is going to be me.

It's risky, but I have to do something. I inch my arm from over my eyes a look at Angela, then I close them and let the blue haze wash over her a second time. The haze gathers into a darker shade of blue around her heart . . . she's not angry anymore, she's just heartbroken. I take a breath, hoping I haven't misread or misjudged her. Keeping my movements as small as possible I uncoil into a sitting position. I don't look at her face instead I focus on her midsection. Angela's baby dangles limply against her swollen breast. Tentatively, and I hope not foolishly, I transfer the needle to my left hand then reach over with my right and brush my fingers across the baby's lifeless foot. Angela tenses, her eyes blink-blink, then she sighs and taps her baby's chest. I risk crossing my legs in front of me and opening my hands in a gesture of friendship. Angela pokes the baby's foot where I touched it, flips her wrist in circles, then looks at me and chatters. The scar on my right hand pulsates. My left hand tightens around the syringe ready to jab her, if I need to.

"Ooooo," I coo sympathetically and stroke the baby's tiny foot with the back of my open hand. The scar turns bright red and Angela lets the baby slip from her arm and on to her outstretched legs. My heart breaks. Taking a calculated risk, I reach over and lay my hand gently on the baby's stomach. I look up at Angela. Her dark, almost black eyes melt into mine and my eyes fill with tears.

Angela's eyelids open and close.

I blink my eyes at her in a Morse code of understanding.

Angela picks the baby up and holds it to her face. She sniffs its eyes and nose then lets out a mournful, "Ooooo, oooo." She brushes her lips across her baby girl's mouth and puffs out a breath of air and another sad, "Ooooo, oooo."

It's over. We are just two females who understand loss. I remove my hand from the baby and rest it on Angela's shoulder. She reaches over and touches my forehead and hair with soft fingertips. I brush her cheek with my thumb. She places the baby on the floor next to her. Then, one leg and one arm at a time, she crawls into my lap. My hand slides down her back and around her waist. I set the syringe on the floor and wrap my other arm across her chest.

"Ooooo, oooo," Angela exhales and lays her head against my

shoulder.

"Ooooo, oooo," I answer and hold her tight, as we begin to rock.

Chapter 8

The Mayans believe the number ten is the number of life and death. Tomorrow, three tens will be added together; the month of October, the first ten. The day I was born, the fifth day, and the hour, five o'clock, add up to the second ten. And lastly the minutes, fifty-five, the third ten. Today is the day before I turn thirty. What will I be tomorrow?

Hunched forward at my desk, I stare brain dead at the goldfish on the computer screen watching them swim in repetitive motion eating air bubbles. I tap a key and bring the computer to life. Habit slides my lower lip between my upper and lower teeth while I check email. I release it every now and then to chew the fingernail on my left thumb. The coffee in my cup is cold. Behind me, on the opposite wall, David's desk is scattered with clumps of messy paper, stacked books and a candy jar half full with M&M's. His chair is empty. It's not yet 7:30 a.m. The sun is struggling to rise, but what I've seen of it so far does not impress me; it's sullen and dull. The lamp on my desk provides a dim circle of light on the keyboard, nothing more. The overhead fluorescents are waiting for me to throw the switch but I'm not yet ready to have the day begin. Next to my desk Rita sleeps, her cage still hooded in cloth. I hope she won't wake until I lift it off.

My right hand trembles on the mouse. A simple click is all I ask of it, not a difficult task, but I'm having a problem controlling the curser. It won't stay put. My heart pounds and skips two beats, pounds then skips another. I press my hand against my chest—my imagination—it's beating normally but then I check my pulse; it's way too fast. My eyes are having trouble focusing on the print displayed across the screen. I turn and look at David's desk, to clear them. He was called away on an animal emergency at U.C. Davis at six this morning. He will be gone all day. I tell myself I can handle today; it's tomorrow I'm worried about.

Nothing is going on at the park today. No medical emergencies, so far. Not a cough or sneeze, no cuts, bites or broken bones that need my attention. Just routine check-ups on the schedule and paperwork, nothing that Jan and the techs can't handle. I need something to do. I close my eyes for the umpteenth time to check the blue haze; it's still there.

Swiveling around, I push myself up from the chair and walk out of the office, careful to close the door softly, not wanting to wake Rita. I turn right and shuffle down the corridor to the animal supply room. Once inside, I open the door to the large walk-in refrigerator, take a small paper bag from the shelf above the 25-pound bag of apples and start counting out apples. One, two, three...filling the bag slowly, one apple at a time, until I have eight. Back in the hallway I remove my jacket from the hook on the wall, put it on and step outside. The electric cart is charged and ready but I decide to walk, trying to slow time down.

The back road, heading in the direction of the elephant barn, is just now coming to life. Animal keepers zip along in flat-bed golf carts filled with breakfast for both land and sea animals. To my left, a wide bridge spans the width of the moat connecting the public area to the road. Staff and animal keepers wave as they drive by. I keep my lips fastened when I smile, nodding and giving, quick shoulder high hand waves; afraid speech will kick-start the day and send it speeding toward tomorrow.

Hungry seals bark in the distance, wanting breakfast. The seagulls flying overhead cry for handouts, "me first, me first," they seem to beg. Silos filled with grain and hoof stock pellets stand tall and shiny on the right side of the road. Dozens of pigeons rush around on spindly pink legs, busy clearing up the spilled kernels underneath. Empty wood pallets are stacked haphazardly against rusting chain-link fencing and posts. A forklift scurries in and adds another half-dozen pallets to the pile, then hurries away. The road is wide enough for large trucks and safe enough for groups of school children coming to visit the vet clinic wanting to know what it takes to become a veterinarian.

"Hey, Lill, got a minute?" Melissa's shout comes from the bird mews and breaks my self-imposed solitude. I look in her direction. A large golden eagle sits on her gloved arm. She beckons me over with her free hand.

I hold up the bag of apples, "Elephants, I'm on my way to the barn." These are the first words I've spoken since David left for U.C. Davis. I glance at my watch. It's 7:48 a.m., less than 24 hours until my birthday.

"Birds okay?" I query without moving towards her.

"They're all good I just wanted to wish you a happy birthday, in case I don't see you tomorrow." Melissa's eyes squint into the morning sun.

"Thanks," I give her a fake cheery smile and continue on to the elephant barn. There it was, she said it—happy birthday. I take a deep breath, working to push the what-if game out of my head, and remember dad dying in our kitchen and seeing his newly-birthed pink soul. That's good parts of this voodoo stuff, seeing souls. And if I am to believe anything in dad's note, it's that I am connected to the elephants. I know it might sound...dad would say wishful, but I feel the elephants and I share a secret language; we understand each other. Perhaps they will be able to calm my fears.

The elephant barn is empty when I reach it. They have been turned out into what we call "the playpen." It's an acre of land connected to the back of the barn. It has a swimming pond large enough for them to splash in and lots and lots of dirt and sand. This morning all eight are giving themselves a dust bath.

Dust and dirt is flying everywhere. Two of the elephants, Rah and Taatee, are on their sides kicking up their legs, having a grand time covering every inch of their bodies in sand. I have to laugh at Penda; she has blobs and blotches of dirt and dust sticking to her in a haphazard design, her own version of elephant camouflage. Unlocking the security gate I ease inside, avoiding as much of the dust as I can. Seeing me, Taatee and Rah give their tonnage a big heave-ho and swing their bulky bodies onto all fours. They rush to join the other elephants, sticking their trunks into their ears to trumpet a hello. The whole herd comes to a stop in a crescent shape in front of me, reaching out with their trunks to sniff the paper bag in my hand. I'm sure there must be an old proverb written somewhere that states: "If your bag is paper, you can't hide apple from elephant."

Elephants are very polite, so they wait for me to hand out each apple individually. I start with Taatee as she is the oldest and the matriarch of the herd and end with Penda the youngest. Penda takes the apple with the dainty fingertip of her trunk and quickly hands it back. Fear flashes my mind back to Ona and the apple I found in my sweater. Coldness stabs my heart when I think of Senento and the black leopard. Determined not to let these memories get the best of me, I hold the apple out a second time. Penda takes it and pops it in her mouth with a crunch. The smell of apple juice and the sounds of the elephant's rumblings ease my fears. I touch each of their faces before I go, getting ready to face the day. Elephant therapy is the best homeopathic remedy I know. I'd stay and visit longer but unless I want to join them in a dust bath, there's nothing for me to do.

"Hey, you ladies have fun today, okay?" Penda opens her mouth and exposes her tongue. She wants it scratched. Not one to ever refuse an elephant's request, especially Penda's, I reach in and scratch it, then kiss her trunk and say good-by.

The rest of day goes painfully slow. Rita's endless squawking and jabbering was driving me crazy so Jan took her to the nursery. Then it's the quiet that sets my nerves on edge. I play solitaire on the computer and lose. Thankfully, David gets back to the clinic earlier than I expected. He enters the office carrying a big bouquet of white lilies and a huge smile.

"Lilies for my bride Lillian, a.k.a. Lill. No more work for you today, my dear wife. We're going out." He hands me the flowers with a flourish then takes my face in his hands and gives me a long kiss.

"I didn't work today; I worried."

"Enough with the worrying, it's time to go out and celebrate. I'm taking you to dinner."

"Dinner?"

"Yep. We go home, we change, and we drive to Caruso's. We eat. You drink. You laugh. You forget about turning thirty. Okay?" He leans in, scrutinizing my head with his eyes and fingers, "Nope, nothing to worry about, no gray hairs, yet."

"It's not about gray hairs, David."

"Lill, I know. I know it's not about that. But I'm going to be with you from this moment on and all day tomorrow. I am not going to leave your side, not for one single second. You gotta trust me."

*****

Caruso's is our favorite restaurant. It's on the wharf in Old Town Sacramento. David and I don't drink but we always look at the wine list and dream about the day when we can. It's important to us that we stay sober, in case there's an animal emergency at the park.

The waiter looks like he's seen too many *Godfather* movies. His dark hair is slicked back and jelled in place. His shirt is bright white and his pants are sharply creased and black. His knee-length apron is starched and has a pocket holding pens and a pad of paper. The only thing missing from his, "Good evening, my name is Rocco, I'll be your waiter tonight," is an Italian accent. The décor is an Italian restaurant cliché, red-and-white checkered table cloths. Chianti bottles with straw wrappers dripping old wax and newly lit red candles. Baskets of hot crusty bread smelling of yeast and garlic are carried through the restaurant and placed at tables with each new arrival. The restaurant is only half full but overflowing with laughter and clinking glasses. The night outside the windows is interrupted, intermittently, by cheerful boat lights blinking off the water. Most of the boats are commercial fishing boats tied to the long dock, washed clean, restocked, and waiting for the dawn to start fishing all over again.

David and I seem to be playing a part in a Godfather movie, too. I'm wearing a short red dress, red high heels and red lipstick. My hair is up and flirty. David is handsome in his suit, black and cut to fit. The collar of his white shirt is open and stirs up little butterflies of passion that I can't wait to let fly.

Rocco seats us at a table by the window. He hands us each a menu and begins to recite tonight's specials when David holds up his hand and stops him. "My wife's birthday is tomorrow, but we're celebrating tonight. I don't care what it costs. I want the best bottle of champagne you've got."

"Not a problem, sir, I'll be right back."

"So here's how this is going to work. We're going to toast you, not your birthday, just wonderful, very special, and very beautiful you."

"But if they need us..."

"One little sip is all I'm going to have. You, on the other hand, are going to get blotto. Drunk as a skunk. Loose and sexy. The sexy part is for me, I admit. I plan to take you home and ravage every inch of your body. After all, I promised to keep you close. And, hard as it might get, double entendre intended, a promise is a promise."

"This is starting to sound good."

"You think it sounds good now? You have no idea. I plan to have my way with you, in ways you never dreamed of. I'm sticking very close to you, my love, and I mean that literally. I'll be right next to you long after the sun comes up tomorrow morning and all the rest of the day. Nothing will get between us. Nothing. Okay?"

"Ummm. Dr. Cutter, you are very persuasive and, might I add, a very sexy man."

"Sir," the waiter interrupts, showing David a bottle of *2005 Roederer Lewis Cristal*. David nods and Rocco pops the cork and pours.

"To us and a long and happy life together," David clinks his glass to mine.

"I love you." I raise my glass to him and take a bigger sip.

David sets his glass down and reaches across the table. He takes my hand in his and kisses my fingertips.

*****

I am alone. It's dark. The elephants are screaming. Fog engulfs me. It is wet and freezing cold. I can't move. A thick shackle of fog cinches my feet to the ground. My toes dig into the cold rocky soil. Ribbons of gray muck wrap around my body, soaking my green hospital scrubs to my skin. Visibility is zero. I can't see the elephants, but I can hear their distant cries for help.

"Don't be afraid. I'm coming!" I shout, but they can't hear my muffled promise. My voice is unable to penetrate the layers of fog. Frantic trumpets cut into my heart as the elephants' pleas grow more urgent, more desperate and louder.

"Hang on, girls. I'll find you." A huge gust of wind suddenly blows me backwards and out of the fog. It sends me rolling and stumbling like a tumbleweed across trampled dry earth, then scoops me up like a plastic produce bag and shoots me through the air.

The scene changes. I'm clinging to a tree. The wind pelts my back, neck, and head with debris—the velocity of each blast stronger than the last. I will myself to hang on and silently pray to a God I don't know if I trust, to help me. I end my prayer with an Amen. And the wind stops. Just like that.

A coincidence, I tell myself, blinking in rapid succession at my new surroundings. I'm standing at the edge of a deep canyon holding onto the low branch of a baobab tree. I look up, the cross isn't there. I'm not in Mbali. The sky is a hot cloudless blue. The earth is barren and dry. Perched on the opposite side of the gorge is a large barn. It looks like the elephant barn from our wild animal park but instead of weathered redwood walls, stacks of splintered wood and chains hold it together. The roof is gone. A rank wind whips up a dust devil and rips the barns massive doors wide open. Inside, the elephants scream and struggle against the chains that bind their feet to the earth. A bolt of lightning flashes black and dark red down the center of the ravine. The barn doors bang shut and I am sucked off the cliff, spinning inside a dark tube filled with the sound of screaming elephants.

Then I'm outside the barn. Above my head a fist size padlock is looped through the handles of the doors. I grab it and pull. It's locked tight. The elephants' screams grow more frantic. A black-red bolt of light crashes against the doors and sends the barn speeding away from me. It grows smaller and smaller until it dissolves to a pinprick and vanishes. The lock remains in my hands, pulsating like a heartbeat. The elephants—the elephants' cries can no longer be heard—I've lost them.

Kooee-kooee, outside our bedroom window an eagle repeats. *Kooee-kooee*. The cry shatters the nightmare.

Still feeling the effects of the dream, my hands shake as I push sweat damp hair off my face. On the nightstand the green digital numbers of the clock read 4:53 a.m.

Behind the clock the white cotton curtains on the window billow. A surge of cold air runs over the top of our bed and sends a warning tremor through my heart; we closed and latched the window before we went to bed.

It's the wind. It's always the wind that brings back memories of Africa and my tenth birthday; memories of *Machawi-shaitani*, witchdoctors, the black leopard and darts shooting from my eyes.

Hoping to quell my childhood fears, I look away from the curtains and watch David sleeping peacefully beside me. I inhale the scent of him. His deep unconcerned breathing does little to ease the foreboding I feel. Rolling out of bed, the touch of the cold floor on my feet heightens the sense of urgency and sends adrenaline surging through my veins.

"David, wake up. We have to go."

I don't wait for him to answer. I rush to the closet and flip on the lights switch. Inside, I grab underwear from the wire basket and pull a pair of jeans and a sweater off the shelf. I stick my head out of the closet as I dress.

"David!" I snap.

"Huh?" he mumbles, turning over and focusing his eyes on me.

"We have to go. Seriously, David, we need to check on the elephants, and we need to do it now."

David flops on his back and squints over at the clock, "Lill, it's not even five. Your birthday's more than an hour away. Come back to bed. Come on, I promised to hold you until after the sun came up, and I will."

"I don't care what time it is." Sitting on the end of the bed, I toss David's underclothes, jeans and sweatshirt on top of him then tug on my socks on. "Hurry, maybe it was just a bad dream, but it feels like something wrong."

"Okay. Okay, I just need to wake up here." David sits up in the bed, rubs his face with his hands then struggles into his T-shirt.

"You don't have time to wake up." I turn and head for the bathroom.

He shouts after me, "Nothing bad is going to happen; I won't let it!"

When I walk back in the room, David's pulling on his pants. "Lill, nothing bad, I promise." He smiles and flutters his eyes at me trying to lighten my mood, set on the bed, pulls his socks on then yanks his sweatshirt on over his head and flutters his eyes again.

"David, you know I'm scared as hell about today. So stop kidding around. Humor me, okay."

"Got it." He gives me a quick kiss on the cheek, takes his keys off the nightstand, and heads out of the room singing, "Head'm up-n-move'm out, Rawhide," as I race after him.

He pauses in the mud room long enough to slip into his barn boots and waits while I pull on mine, then he opens the back door.

I scoot past him onto the porch and stop. "Shit."

"Lill?"

"Fog. Oh my God, David, it's the fog. It's how the nightmare started."

Chapter 9
The Third Ten

'Calm down, Lill. We're just a few minutes away." David's voice soaks into the fog as he steps off the porch and into the carport.

I jog past him, too worried to wait for him to start the vet cart, "I'll get the gate." My boots and knees disappear in the low lying cloud as I run down the driveway.

Tense and fearful, I push the gate too hard. It bounces open and bangs against the steel fencepost, then settles. When David reaches me he slows just long enough for me to jump in beside him, then he jams the pedal to the floor. The batteries engage and we lunge forward at full speed—five miles an hour. As we travel the twisting path toward the elephant barn, thin columns of air circle around the lamp posts, cut into the fog and tie it in knots. Anxious and apprehensive, uneasy, I glance at David. He looks over, takes hold of my hand and kisses it.

We come to a stop at the security gate. The light inside Jimmy's hut is off. He isn't here. He's probably making rounds, checking locks and doors. I reach for the keys attached to the belt loop on my pants, they are not there. In the rush to get out of the house, I forgot to clip them on.

"David, I need your keys." I bound out of the cart heading for the gate before he has a chance to hand them to me. I hold the lock in my hand and turn toward him. He tosses the keys in a smooth arch; an easy catch. My hands are surprisingly steady while I unlock the padlock, push the gate wide enough for David to drive through, lock up, and leap in. Seconds later, the cart skids to a stop on the damp asphalt in front of the barn.

We jump out at the same time but I'm closest to the door and reach it first. Scared, I hesitate, too terrified to push the door open. We shoot each other concerned looks. David's thinking what I'm thinking; the elephants are too quiet. Dark rivulets of ice-cold fear run through my blood, my hand frozen on the door.

"Go ahead, Lill, open it," David prods. "They're okay," he reassures. But I can tell by the tone of his voice he is trying to convince us both.

"They're never this quiet, never. They know the sound of the cart. They always trumpet when they hear it."

David reaches over and slides the barn door open.

Eight elephants trumpet our arrival. Earsplitting squeals of delight greet us with non-stop noise. Eight trunks wave in the air like flags on a pole. Tears leak from my eyes, and David closes the door behind us. They're safe. The red glow from the overhead heaters lead us to the steel rails of their pen. I brush back my tears and smile.

I ease into David's arms and kiss him, saying, "They're okay. It was just a nightmare." I smile wider, jokingly, punching him on the shoulder. "A stupid nightmare."

"Didn't I tell you not to worry?" He kisses me on top of my head then we slip between the rails and are swallowed up by the herd elephants; the tips of trunks moving over every inch of our clothes, hands and face. We hug each of the elephants in turn. This is the perfect way to start my birthday.

I peek at my watch. David catches my glance and raises a questioning brow.

"Five-fifty five," I whisper and we both watch as the time ticks to five-fifty six.

"And look, you're okay. Didn't I tell you I wouldn't let anything bad happen to you? Didn't I? That's it, you're safe. No more witchdoctor voodoo. Happy birthday, Lill." David's kiss is long and passionate. He's right—nothing bad happened...so far.

While we kiss, the elephants' voices change to a deep-throated rumble. David and I lean apart; confused by the change in their pitch. The girls shuffle, gathering Penda into the middle of the herd then inch away from us. Their heads and trunks are down. On guard. Wary. Their brown eyes are open wide and ringed in white. Nervous.

"David, what's going on?"

"I don't know, but I'm not letting go of you." He holds me tighter.

A surge of wind whistles against the barn and rattles the metal roof overhead. An unfathomable sense of dread overwhelms me when I feel the vibration gathering under my feet.

"David, do you feel that?" My voice is pitched high with fear. The shaking increases. My eyes question his and my heart bangs against my lungs. The shaking stops. We look at each other with guarded relief.

"An earthquake, Lill, that's all it was." David kisses each of my cheeks. "No wonder the girls were acting scared. They probably sensed it coming before we felt it. It was just a California earthquake, a little rock-n-roll." He grins. Then the shaking starts again, stronger and more violent this time. The asphalt cracks and split open in front of us. The straw spills aside. David pulls me back.

A red-black vapor rolls out of the ground, and we take another step back. David's eyes dart from the froth spilling out of the crack then to me, back and forth, not understanding or believing what he's seeing; we keep inching backwards.

"Lill?" He questions, his eyes never leaving the abomination coming from the earth.

The thick fog billows and churns a foot high. "Noooo!" I scream, but it's too late. The leopard's huge head rises above the fog. His shoulders quiver as he muscles the asphalt further apart. The cat's eyes lock onto mine. He continues to climb out of the abyss, every movement calculated and deadly. The elephants are strangely silent.

"Lill, what is going on?"

"I'm...Oh my God, David. It's happening again. What does he want with me?"

The cat crouches, all four feet on the barn floor. His tail whips from side to side with eager anticipation. David guides me behind his back with a strong arm then confronts the cat.

"C'mon, sucker, give it your best shot." David signals the hellish black feline with his fingers, baiting him, "Bring it on, buddy." David risks a glance over his shoulder. I'm right behind him. "Damn it, Lill, get back." His voice is stern. He glances at the cat then pushes me aside with superhuman strength. I stumble backwards, twist my ankle, and end up hitting the ground hard, and when I try to breathe, I can't. I curl into a ball, waiting for my breath to catch. All I can do is watch.

The unholy cat snarls. His ears flatten against his head. He flashes deadly white teeth and his tongue licks the air, savoring the tastes of the terror that fills the barn. The red light from the heat lamps tangles with the cat's black body, cutting lines in his fur like waves of blood. A second snarl sends frightful droplets of red tinted saliva somersaulting in David's direction. The leopard rotates his evil head slowly to the right, checking the elephants then he turns back and targets his eyes on David. His ebony lids compress his eyes into sinister green slits. His wet nostrils flare one quick second before he leaps.

Ready, David balls his hand into a fist and shoves it down the cat's snarling mouth, just like we were trained to do: "better to lose an arm than your life." I watch horrified and helpless as the leopard jaws climb, undeterred, up David's arm. The beast drives him backwards. David falls to his knees. The cat's teeth rack across his flesh, then he bits down and shatters David's arm.

"Aaagh!" David screams.

The leopard unclenches his jaws and steps back. David's bloodied arm hangs broken and useless at his side. He struggles to stand. The leopard shows him no mercy and slams his head and the full weight of his body into his chest. David crumples lifeless atop the straw.

The leopard slowly turns his head and trains his eyes on me. They flash red, and his evil body quivers with delight. My breath regained, I roll to my knees, push off on the balls of my feet and run. The leopard's quick claws hook my foot and drag me back. I flip on my side and kick his face, punching him as hard as I can. He snares that foot, too. He's got me. His claws pierce through my jeans and dig into my flesh. Twisted on my side I dare to look at him, he tilts his wicked face up at the rafters and snarls his victory. The elephants watch from the far side of the barn.

His growls and howls reverberate across the ceiling. The overhead heaters blink off and on like spasmodic red disco balls, the light crisscrossing the elephants' hides in a hellish dance of pink. The leopard's lowers his head and delivers a satanic hiss. Bits of David's torn flesh hit my face, and the leopard leans in. His rough tongue runs over his muzzle, tasting David's blood, tormenting me. He leans closer and his black whiskers slice across my cheek. I turn my head away from the cat's rancid breath and look over at David. He's still slumped on his side, not moving. I close my eyes. The blue haze covers him. He is alive but barely.

Beyond David, Penda and the Magnificent Seven have formed a line; three elephants on Penda's right, four on her left. They stand shoulder to shoulder, like offensive linemen, readying themselves for battle. Penda stomps one foot on the floor and then the other. The seven elephants follow her lead and the ground convulses in an insistent drumbeat. The leopard's eyes leave mine and shift in their direction. The slow pounding of their feet intensifies with each step forward; their voices remain silent. The leopard's claws pull back into their sheaths and release me. He spins to face them. The elephants charge. The earth bucks with the weight of them. The leopard springs into the air and into the line of attacking elephants. Penda's trunk snatches the cat in mid-air and slings him back, sending him skidding across the asphalt. Straw flies. He tumbles to a stop a few feet from David. Unscathed, the cat shakes off the assault. The elephants hold their line but Penda moves forward, wanting the kill for herself. The cat's deadly eyes dart to David. My eyes follow. Horrified, I watch David's soul spin from his heart. A vortex of evil vapor pours from the leopard and spews its black-death shroud over David's soul. Then the leopard turns his hateful eyes on me.

Behind the leopard, Penda moves in. He doesn't even glance in her direction, his full focus on me. The cat's eyes cut into mine. He snarls and dissolves into a black vapor and is gone. Penda tilts her head to the rafters. Her angry scream consumes the air. She wanted this battle.

Penda inches pensively to David's side. She taps his chest with her trunk then her brown eyes follow me as I crawl to David.

Stillness clings to the sorrow of death trapped inside the barn. The girls push gently against David's hips, legs, arms with their trunks, trying to wake him. I cradle David's face against my chest and lean on Penda's front legs for support. A faint smell of something burning clings to David but there are no signs of the fight anywhere on his body. No blood, no torn flesh or broken arm. The floor isn't cracked. It is as if none of it had ever happened. I beg for David's soul to return, hoping that is also part of the illusion. I close my eyes. The blue haze behind them is gone. I rub and close my eyes and try again, nothing.

The big barn doors are pushed open. The red glow of the safety lamp is fractured as shadowed pre-dawn light crashes in. Tim and Jimmy, seeing us on the floor, rush to my side. Penda's trunk touches my wrist. I glance at my watch...the glass is shattered, the hands have returned to 5:55.

*****

Dust thou art, and unto dust shalt thou return. Genesis 3:19. Dad's truth, not mine. A morning and a day have come and gone since David's death. The doctor told me David died from a heart attack—a heart attack, just like Dad. There was no reason to protest the diagnosis, nobody would believe me if I told them otherwise. I can hear David's voice saying, "That's the trouble with their witchdoctor jambo-jambo, there's no proof."

Death's darkness is collapsing in clusters of messy emptiness all around me. Our friends and co-workers bring food to the house. I eat, feeling neither hungry nor not hungry. They cluster awkwardly together in small groups, talking softly and sipping coffee and juice.

Miles stops at my side, touches my elbow and leans in close. His breath smells of shrimp.

"I'm so sorry, Lill." He wipes his lips with a paper napkin and continues. "There are some things we need to talk about." My ears stop listening. Business, I think. Important, I think. He adds, "We'll talk later."

I walk away, leaving him standing with the others speaking in hushed voices about happier times. Before they go, they kiss my cheek and leave their tears behind.

After everyone has left, I find myself relieved to be released from their good intentions. Alone, I can indulge myself in self-pity as my swollen puffy eyes search the emptiness of our house for David's soul. I light a candle and place it on the mantel in the living room. The softness of its glow tries as desperately as my own heart to soften the loss of the man I love. The flame's tender light labors to still the tears that fall unashamed from my eyes, but nothing can stop them. I have lost my soul mate, my husband, my lover. Souls linger for as long as you need them. No one has to tell me this, I just know. It is a truth that

God's good book doesn't mention.

"I need to see your soul, David. Please, just let me know you made it." I beg the empty wall in front of me. "I need you."

David's name crashes against my heart like a lost wave in a wild sea. Gloom deepens into weariness, yawning into depression; both refusing to give life to his name.

"David." To speak his name is so painful I want to follow it into death.

Gathering a blanket off our bed, I pull it behind me like a toddler across the floor into the living room. I can't stand the thought of sleeping in our bed without him. I lie down on the sofa, knees to chest under the spread trying to find the warmth that left me when he died.

Time passes uncounted and counted.

Something flutters on the other side of my makeshift cocoon. I push the cover off my face. A gathering together of translucent lights float above me. David? My hearts beats like a bass drum. I watch the in-n-out soul beat with the same rhythm as my heart. The empty feeling eases.

"David?" I whisper, hopeful.

The light stops its rhythmic pulsing. No, it's not his soul. Gold and silver sparks flash at the edges of this celestial orb. It is the soul from Ona.

"What do you want with me? What does Bayamchawi want?" I beg as bright gold specks shoot off the orb and spin away, leaving no answers to my questions. The candle's flame flickers and goes out. The smell of cooling wax sticks to the inside of my nostrils in a waxy puddle of discontinued time.

Shattered, I bury my head back under the blanket.

Mjane is the Swahili word for widow.

Chapter 10

J immy waves from inside the guardhouse. It takes a moment for me to get my bearings. I don't remember driving here. He moves to the door and steps outside, the clock that was behind his head, now visible, reads half past midnight. He taps the bill of his cap with an easy salute and walks to the gate. He unlocks it and pushes back on one side, wide enough for the vet cart to drive through. He raises his hand as I start to inch forward, Jimmy wants to talk. I stop and cross one hand on top of the other and tighten my fingers on the steering wheel. A cold breeze circles me and I blow a warm breath into my cupped hands then return them to the wheel. I'm wearing David's sweater. I should have worn a jacket.

Jimmy places a fatherly hand on top of mine and crouches down so we are eye to eye. I can smell the spice of his aftershave and the mint of his chewing gum as he tucks it beside his cheek.

"Sorry about Doc." I hear the catch in his voice and watch his cap dip, sending an uninvited tear away. I rub the back of his hand with one finger and nod.

"Me, too..." My throat tightens.

"He's still here, you know. Look at the moon. Look at the halo around it. That's his light up there; he's watching over you..." Jimmy's finger draws a circle on the back of my hand then squeezes it before he lets go and stands. "The moon doesn't lie. Doc's up there. You have my word on it."

I press my lips together and look into his eyes unable to speak then I tap the pedal and drive to the elephant barn. I coast to a stop opposite the barn door. I'm not ready to go inside. The door blurs out of focus as tears flood into my eyes. I blink them away and look up at the moon. It's full. Unlike me, it's whole. The halo of mellow white light has grown wider; a ghost shadow, a prediction of rain or, according to Jimmy, David's halo of light watching over me.

I want more.

I want David back.

I push my hair away from my face, gather it up, twist it into a rope then tie it into a knot at the back of my head, getting ready. My shoes tap softly on the asphalt surface of the road as I walk to the barn. When I reach the door, I rest my arms against it and press my face into David's wool sweater. It smells of him. Above me, the pigeons stir. Some *coo-coo* noting my arrival, others fly to the roof and start a pigeon *tick-tick-tap* dance on the metal. I slide the door open and squeeze inside. The elephants' voices rumble low...reverently. They are mourning David's death, too. I close the door behind me and lean against it, drinking in the enchantment of the elephants. As I ease toward them, their voices swell into a rhapsody of intoxicating euphoria and happy memories of David. The memories crash with crushing pain into grief. My throat bolts them down; one year of memories isn't enough.

The elephant's guttural bass notes caress the earth beneath my feet, beckoning me forward. When I slip between the rails and join them, their greeting softens to a song, and then shifts to a whisper. Each hushed undertone bathes me in a gentle elephant lullaby and rocks me like the mother I never had.

Elephant trunks reach out and stroke my arms, in an effort to comfort me. Their concerned rumbles work overtime to lessen the sorrow lodged in my heart. This is why I hesitated outside the barn. I didn't want to feel the loss of David so profusely. My body shudders with the truth-telling honesty of his death and cuts my heart into unrepairable sorrow. I stroke and hug each elephant, one after the other. Their trunks support me as I move in hesitant steps among them. My sobbing becomes threadbare and raw, the loss of David unfathomable. At Penda's side, I stop and wrap my arms around her thick white trunk. I crumple down her rough leg to the straw covered floor; my heart is broken. Gently, gently, she lays her trunk across my shoulders and holds me.

"Penda, I think Bayamchawi took David's soul." My throat swells and gagging sobs overtake me. Penda trunk tightens more.

A sound so very sad and one I've never heard before cries out from deep within her. Penda is wailing. She presses the velvety tip of her trunk against my ear and blows a whisper of silky moist breath inside, telling me a secret or perhaps a truth I don't know or can't understand.

*****

A stirring among the elephants wakes me at the same time I hear the scraping of the barn door being pushed across its steel track. Laughter and the smell of coffee interrupt my unplanned sleepover. Penda has tucked me safely between her front legs, my face resting on her foot. Still groggy, I stretch my back and neck to loosen the kinks caused by sleeping on the floor. Then I hold my right hand high above my head. Penda wraps her trunk around my wrist and pulls me to my feet. I hurry to brush off the straw clinging to my clothes and hair. When I have finished, Penda opens her mouth and I automatically reach in and scratch her tongue while waiting for the morning crew of elephant handlers and trainers to notice me.

"Dr. Drake." John Tillman's brassy voice sounds surprised when he sees me. Fresh out of college and taking a year off before going to grad school, John is the newest and youngest of the elephant handlers and still calls me Dr. Drake. I'll give him maybe two more weeks before he slides into the casual Lill that everyone else uses.

"Hi, John." I give him a weak smile then remove my hand from Penda's mouth and wave a silent hello to the others. As they approach, I wipe my hand dry on Penda's cheek.

"You be a good girl today. I'll see you later, okay?" I kiss her trunk then dip between the rails to join the crew.

Rose, our only female elephant trainer mumbles, "Ah, sorry about Doc," opens her arms, pulls me into an awkward hug then quickly lets go.

"So am I," I say dry-eyed but my voice breaks with fresh sorrow.

"Lill," Don calls out as he enters the barn. Don is one of the best hoof stock wranglers we have at the park. He is a short, powerfully-built, thick-legged man from Nebraska.

"Rose," he smiles when he reaches us, then turns his attention to me. "Lill, I, ah, I kinda expected to find you in here, actually I was hopin' to. We got us a situation out on the veldt. One of them zebras, well, he's gone and got himself tangled up with somethin-or-another and is limpin' around on three legs. He's not wantin' to use his left hind leg. There's puss and blood's runnin' from a gash by his hip. I got the herd closed off in the old wood corral in the corner, but they ain't happy about being shut up in there. No, Ma'am, they ain't happy at all. By the way," his voice falters, "I'm truly sorry about Doc; he was a good man. I hope I'm not out of line here, asking you to help, so soon after."

"That's what I'm here for. It's what I do. What I need to do, especially today. Give me a minute to go to the office and get my bag and blow gun and I'll meet you at the west gate."

"Jan's got your bag and she's waitin' for us in the Jeep right outside the door. We're ready if you are."

When we step outside, Jan's weak smile questions me from behind the wheel. I'm okay, I mouth silently. Her smile widens and she tosses me one of the spare jackets from the clinic then revs the engine, anxious to get going.

"You positive?" Jan asks, when I reach the passenger side door. "I can ask Dr. Dennis to come over and help."

"Dr. Dennis is a great vet, but I need to keep busy. Besides I don't know how comfortable he'd be. He's used to working with sea mammals. I'm afraid our zebra might be a little too "earthy" for him." I wiggle my arms into the coat then grab hold of the roll bar and pull myself into the seat next to her. Don swings into the seat behind us.

Six minutes later, Jan snugs the Jeep next to the west gate and turns off the engine. We step to the gate and rest our arms over the top rail, scanning the three acres of simulated African grassland. In the distant, the wood corral made of weathered pine poles holds our herd of Burchell zebra. Inside, the injured zebra and a dozen of his striped friends move in anxious erratic circles.

In between us and the corral a pair of Blesbok rams mark their territory by rubbing their faces in dung. When they are finished they trot their small family of twenty females as far away from us as they can get. Eight Nyala—medium-sized antelope—ten yards to our left are curious but unwilling to venture from the fresh piles of morning hay. I close my eyes to check on their health but see nothing. The blue haze remains missing.

"Okay, I'm ready when you are," I say brightly. But my gut twists as I return to the Jeep, knowing I'm going to have to rely solely on my veterinary training to determine what's wrong with our hoofed friend.

With practiced repetition, Jan and I set to work. I lift my medical bag off the Jeep floor and head to the back to join her. On my way, I grab Don's lariat and toss it to him. At the open tailgate Jan untethers the metal supply box and pulls it to her. With quick efficiency she snaps the case open and takes out the supplies I might need: scalpels, needles, sutures, gauze, packets and bottles of antibiotics, and puts them all in my bag. Jan hands me a bottle of Xylazine, the drug I'll use to sedate the zebra, then she passes me two syringes. I fill one syringe with the drug, snap it into the dart and place the dart in my jacket pocket. I hand the second syringe back to her. I have a theory about loading more than one syringe; you usually get only one shot at an animal, if you load two syringes you've just admitted you're going to miss on the first, and missing can compromise an already taxing situation. This bravado of mine was easy when David was alive. He always loaded a backup and kept it ready in the chamber of his rifle. But now without him, I wonder for the first time in a year, what I'll do if my smugness backfires and I get someone or something hurt.

"Jan, you be my backup today, okay? Go ahead and load the rifle..." I force a grin. "Just in case."

Jan's brown eyes widen behind the thick lenses of her glasses. "You sure?"

"Positive,"

"Great. Thanks," and hands me a loaded syringe of Yohimbine—the antidote to wake the zebra when we've finished. I drop it in my other pocket, then tap them both; Xylazine in the right and the Yohimbine in the left. I'm good to go.

Don keys the lock, unclips the worn chin holding the gate closed and pushes it open. Inside, he clips the gate shut and puts the padlock in his jacket pocket. He'll lock up when we are finished. The three of us stride across the veldt, in a wide straight line, like gunslingers walking down Main Street in some old cowboy movie. The only thing missing is the jingle of spurs and cowboy hats.

On the way the to the corral the nyala become nervous and stomp their hooves repeatedly before darting to the farthest edge of the veldt, where they stop, stretch their necks and eyeball us with cautious curiosity.

The flight of the nyala spooked the zebras and they have picked up their pace, moving in ever-tightening circles and kicking up short tumbleweed-sized balls of dust. Their heads jerk up and down and their eyes grow, more wild the closer we get. In the middle, the injured stripe tries to hide.

"I'm always amazed how the animals know which one we're lookin for," Don says as we continue our slow walk to the corral.

"It's kind of strange," Jan agrees.

"Every time we do this I wish we had a good cutting dog," I wink at Don, repeating something David must have told him at least a hundred times.

"Doc said the same," Don acknowledges keeping his face stern then glances at me with questioning eyes.

I nod. "Doc did."

The relief that fills his face is so big I can almost hear the Nebraska accent in it. I knew he was hesitant to talk about David, so soon after his death, I think he is afraid it might make me cry. And it might.

"Is that Hank?" I ask Don when we reach the rails of the corral, but I already know the answer.

"Yep, I was going to tell you when the time was right."

"And that would be now, I'm guessing?"

"Yep."

"Lill," Jan intervenes, "it's okay, you're going to dart him. He'll be out cold. He won't be able to get to us, and right now he's only got three legs that work. How bad can it get?"

"He hates people. You know it, I know it, and Hank knows it."

"He's got a mean streak in him, I'll grant you that," Don says.

"Think the leg's broken?" Jan asks.

"I don't think so, but I won't know for certain, until I get inside and take a closer look." I don't bother to close my eyes. The blue haze is gone and I'm pretty sure it's not coming back.

"You ready to do this?" Don taps his lariat against his leg and lifts his chin in the direction of the zebras.

"It's now or never," I tell him. "Jan, you work the gate. Stay on the outside and be ready with the rifle if I need you."

I set my bag in the dirt, take out the blow gun, shove the two black tubes together then tap each pocket, double checking.

"Jan, when I get the herd separated from Hank, I'll send them to you; all you have to do is open the gate and let'm out," Don instructs then thumbs the clip open, slips it from the link and lets the chain drop, dangling from a nail in the fence post. Jan reclips it once we are inside.

The zebras scatter to the far corner, press their bodies against the wooden rails and glare at us as. The corral gives the herd ample hoof room not to feel too cramped, and gives us enough space to keep from getting trampled. Don cuts his way into the center of the herd, doing a very good imitation of a Queensland Heeler. I stay put and out of the way, admiring his skills.

With one quick smack of the rope against his pant leg and two steps forward, the zebras start to move. Dust tumbles in inch-thick clouds along the ground as the zebras pick up their pace, not sure they want to go where Don is telling them to. Don steps sideways, shakes the lariat in their faces, waves his arms wide and cuts them away from Hank. Jan opens the gate, and Don sends them out—Don's the best cutting dog in the biz. He turns and walks back to the center of the corral, his eyes pinned on Hank the whole time. I move in, coming at Hank from the opposite direction, but still staying close to the rails. Don stops two feet from Hank and faces him head on. Hank hops left. Don hops right, the two still face to face. Don slaps his boot heel with the rope. Hank snorts and takes a short hop to the right. Don matches the move eyeballing Hank the whole time. Hank's withers twitch. He swats his short tail against his rump. Don stares him down. I swear, if Don was a dog he would have picked up his front leg and pointed his tail. Hank's head jerks up, then down. He snorts and flattens his ears. He paws the dirt with his front hoof and blows out hot air and snot. His eyes flare white. Alone and separated from the rest of his buddies, Hank's ready to run or worse, charge. Don shakes the rope over his head. Hank looks up and decides not to move. I glance at Jan to make sure she's ready with the rifle. She nods and I drop the dart of Xylazine into my blowgun.

I suck in a lungful of air then exhale. I take another deep breath and press the blowgun tight against my lips, then lower the tube and nod at Jan to take the shot. She's waited a long time and practiced many hours with David waiting for this day. I signal and mouth, "go ahead." She positively beams as she brings the rifle to her shoulder and gets Hank in her sight.

Don takes his eyes off Hank for one second to give me an approving smile and Jan a thumb's up. Hank gets the break he's been waiting for. He brays, tosses his head up and down, and twists his body in a loop. Don barely has enough time to leap to safety as Hank races for the gate, and he's using his damaged leg to get there. Jan holds the gate shut. Hank stops, spins and runs the rail, looking for another way out. I glance at Jan. She's following Hank with the rifle. She fires. Hank screams and bucks. The dart scarcely misses him then skitters to a halt in the dirt behind him.

Don bolts, his quick-footed boots kicking up their own puffs of dust, running straight for the Hank. I put the blowgun to my lips and hold it there, steady, ready, watching. Hank thunders past me; I lower the tube and wait for a better shot.

Don slaps the rope against his thigh with two sharp smacks then jumps directly in front of Hank, yells, "Whoa!" and raises both arms above his head.

Hank slides to a stop. Dust swells around him as he pivots, snorts and hops back and forth, but he doesn't run. I bring the blowgun to my lips, take a deep breath in and blow out. The dart enters Hank's left shoulder as neat and easy as any shot I've ever made. He squeals then bends his neck and looks at the dart as though he doesn't believe what's just happened. Hank thinks about running but doesn't; instead, he walks, then sways and chooses a three-legged hobble instead. We wait. He stops. His front legs splay out for balance. He stumbles, manages to stay standing but his head droops, his lips almost touching the ground. Don moves in next to him, loops the lariat around Hank's neck and pulls the rope tight. Half heeler and half pit bull, Don leans his body against Hank's shoulder, pulls him in, taking Hank's weight, and guides him to the dirt with a cushioned thud. In less than a minute, the three of us are kneeling next to Hank assessing his wound.

Jan hands me a bottle of hydrogen peroxide and a stack of four inch square gauze. I dump half the liquid into the gash, and start wiping off the layers of dry dirt, puss and blood. As I'm cleaning the mess, Jan whispers, "I'm sorry I missed, I hope you're not..."

"Don't ever be sorry for trying. Next time you won't miss. It wasn't an easy shot. I doubt I could have made it. From now on, you always carry the rifle, let's make it routine. Okay?"

Smiling, Jan hands me another stack of clean gauze and I pour on more peroxide. Minutes later Hank is scrubbed up and clean. It looks as if one of his zebra buddies took a bite out of him and it got infected.

"You want penicillin powder?" Jan asks, handing me the packet, already open, knowing I will.

"Thanks." I pour half of the antibiotic directly into the wound. Jan hands me two syringes, one empty and one already filled with more antibiotics, I inject the medicine then reach for the Yohimbine in my pocked, fill the second syringe and shoot the antidote into Hank's muscle. I toss both empty syringes in my bag, break down the blowgun and toss that in, too. Don removes the rope and together the three of us back out of the corral. It shouldn't take long for Hank to come around. Don clips the gate open so Hank can join his friends when he feels up to it.

Jan and I take a moment, standing next to each other, watching Hank's breathing to make sure he's okay. "You and Don, head to the Jeep. Give me a few more seconds here, just in case something goes wrong."

"You sure you don't want us to wait with you?" Don said.

"No, I'm good. Soon as his eyes open, I'm gone." I wave them off. Hank moves his head and I start walking backwards, checking my patient and feeling confident that I'll be safely in the Jeep by the time he's awake enough to walk.

I'm about halfway to the west gate, still watching Hank, when his head snaps up. He doesn't even think about struggling to stand, he bounces up on all four legs like a spring colt, shakes his head to clear it and shoots me a deranged look. Ungrateful for our medical services, Hank charges like the devil has got hold of his balls, and I take off running. Unwisely, I turn to see how much distance is left between Hank and me. Not enough! I clutch my medical bag to my chest and run faster, but sensing he's gaining on me I foolishly chance a second look. Hank's neck is stretched long and his teeth are snapping the air. I will my legs to move faster—the bastard is trying to bite me.

"Lill, watch out," Don and Jan shout in unison when I'm almost at the gate.

Hank's hoof clips the heel of my boot. My medical bag goes flying. I stumble forward but Hank's teeth manage to grab hold of my pants pocket, bouncing my face in the dirt. He lifts his head and shakes; flipping me like a flapjack. The last flip tears the pocket off my pants and spins me loose. My head ricochets off the metal fence post next to the gate. Hank's hooves rise over me. I tuck in as best I can. Hank dances across my chest but misses my face.

Don smacks Hank in the face with his lariat, to back him off before he can do more damage, but it only makes Hank madder. He bucks, twists and kicks. His back hoofs connect with Don, shooting him into the side of the Jeep. Hank lowers his head, his teeth are snapping, he is determined for this day to be my last. I raise my arms over my face in a feeble attempt to protect myself.

My chest tightens. I can't breathe. I have no air. A cutting pain burns through my eyes and a blast of blinding white light explodes between Hank and me. It slashes across his striped face in arcs of noiseless lightning. He snorts. His mouth opens wide, screaming in shock. His thick tongue curls into rolling knots. His eyes pop open then freeze in a stop-motion moment of fear.

Chapter 11

'Lill, you fixed him up to good. Lill? Can you open your eyes for me?" Jan's worried voice pushes like slow sludge through my consciousness.

Wanting to please her, I battle my eyelids, pleading for them to open. Thin slits are all I can manage. I have better luck on the second attempt, but instead of Jan, I end up staring at an inspirational poster tacked on the wall at the end of the couch. It's a picture of a lion licking his paw, with a quote by James Russell Lowell—*One thorn of experience is worth a whole wilderness of warning*—fitting. The letters start to spin and nausea hits. Jan holds a small bucket in front of my mouth. Undignified, I lean over and vomit. When I've finished, Jan eases me back on the sofa's pillow. We're in the break room next to the nursery. I'm thankful to be here and not on a stretcher in the hospital emergency room.

"Welcome back to the land of the living." Jan hands me a wet cloth, and I wipe my mouth and face. I hand it back to her. She folds it in quarters and drapes it across my forehead.

My body hurts but my head feels worse. I reach up to feel the top of my head—bad choice—even my fingernails hurt and instead of a lump, I find an icepack.

"Leave it alone," Jan barks and lifts my hand away.

"Okay." I'm too weak to argue. "Don, you here?" I ask through closed eyes.

"Of course."

"You teach Hank to do the cowboy two-step like that? Or was that something he learned on his own?"

"Wasn't me, Lill. You must have inspired him."

"Inspirational, that's me." Keeping my eyes closed and more

determined this time I grab the ice-pack and hand it to Jan and feel the knot on my head. "Bigger than I thought it would be. Jan, I need to sit up."

"Okay, you're the boss, but let me help." She places a hand behind my back and lifts me forward then shoves a pillow behind my back. I'm leaning more than sitting against the back of the sofa. I'm still nauseous, but more pressing I have to pee.

"Jan, I have to go to the bathroom."

"Considering what you've been through, you don't look too bad. I think we can manage that." Jan tries too hard to sound chipper, "You don't look too bad...for a woman your age."

My eyes spring open with that remark. Motivation is everything. Jan's grinning face is directly in front of mine, not an inch away. She flashes a pin light first in my right eye, then my left.

"Lill, something strange is going on with your eyes."

"Strange?" Fear seizes every inch of me. I wipe my eyes and look at Jan. She's not smiling anymore. "I can see you okay."

"Don, take a look at her eyes, will you?"

"Whoa, I'm not playing doctor with the two of you. That's a lose-lose situation," Don tucks his head to his chest and slinks out of the room.

"Chicken," Jan mutters loud enough for Don to hear.

"I heard that," Don pokes his head in the doorway, smiles then backs out.

"Lill." Jan holds up a hand mirror in front of my face, "You should take a look; I don't want to alarm you but your eyes look kind of funny." I take the mirror but hold it in my lap, afraid of what I might see.

"Please," Jan begs, "I'm worried. I couldn't stand losing you, too."

I lift the mirror to my eyes. The gold daggers have returned and around the pupils a tiny ring of silver has been added. I'm starting to suspect the flash of light that saved me from Hank wasn't anyone's soul; it was something else altogether. Mbali and its voodoo still haunt me.

"Jan, you're not going to lose me, I promise, and my eyes, it's no big deal. I had these gold things in there since I was a kid. Getting knocked around must have shaken them loose. They'll probably go away in a couple of days." I manage to crack a small smile, while not believing anything I just said.

Jan starts to cry. She's a strong woman, and this is unusual for her. "It's so hard to stay upbeat with Doc dying and all and then…" She removes her glasses and wipes her eyes…"You…" She puts her glasses on and looks at me. "There was this flash of light, and Hank just stopped. Don said it must…"

"You saw a light?"

"Don said it must have been the sun catching the side mirror on the Jeep. I guess he's right…but it was strange. It seemed too bright to be the sun. It sort of freaked us out. We were both worried about you, and when we brought you back here and you didn't wake up right away, we…" She sniffles. "How do you stand it? How do you stand losing someone you love?" Jan breaks down, relinquishing herself to a steady stream of tears.

"I have to stand it. I didn't die." My own tears gush out. After a couple minutes of shared crying, Jan and I sniff, wipe our eyes dry and smile cherry fake smiles at each other.

"Jan, I really do have to pee. Please, would you help me stand? And I'm pretty sure I could use a shower." Jan takes my hand, and with her help I manage to get up. I start to teeter but Jan grabs my waist.

"You're not okay. I think I should hang on to you, at least till you get to the bathroom. We can reassess when we get there. "

"Let me try it on my own. We'll see how it goes." Jan slips her arm away but like a mother Guinea fowl she stays close all the way to the bathroom door.

"I'll bring you some clean scrubs. And don't close that door. I want to be able to hear if there's a problem."

Leaning against the tan tiles of the shower wall for support, I let the hot water run over my body while trying to figure things out. Before the light flashed it felt like I couldn't breathe. Then there was a sharp pain in my eyes and then nothing. No matter how I work it, the events don't change and they don't make sense. I start to lift my face up to the shower's spray but the best I can do is tilt my head from one side to the other. I let the water fill my ears so I can hear my heartbeat. I lean against the tile and slide down the wet slippery surface till I'm sitting on the shower floor. I miss the sound of David's heartbeat. If not for Penda, I don't think I could go on. An anguished sob leaves my throat and rips my heart apart. My chest tightens around the sound, choking out the pain and keeping it in, at the same time. I bring my knees up under my chin and let the hot water pelt my body.

"Lill, you're pretty quiet in here; are you alright?" Jan asks as she enters the bathroom.

"I'm fine," I stand, sucking in tears, wondering if I'll ever be okay again.

"I'm hanging clean scrubs on the hook next to the towels."

"Thanks."

"Need anything else?" Jan lingers outside the shower and shows no signs of leaving.

"Nope, I'm good." I don't think either one of us believes this.

"If you're sure."

"I'm sure."

"Okay, call if you need anything. I'll leave the door open."

After she's gone, I continue to let the warm water splash over me a minute longer, relishing the solitude. Then I turn off the hot and wait for the cold to take over. I need to wake up, clear my head, to be ready if and when another animal needs my help. The icy water hits. Goosebumps cover my skin but I force myself to stand under the flow for a minute longer then turn it off. Shivering, but awake, I step out of the shower and grab a towel off the hook, rubbing dry the parts of my body that don't hurt and patting dry the ones that do. I dress in the over-laundered scrubs Jan brought in and wrap my hair and the goose-egg on my head in a dry towel. With a steadying hand on the wall, I pick my way down the hallway to my office.

Thankfully, the office is empty of Rita. Knowing I needed quiet, Jan must have taken her to the nursery. I sit down at my desk and touch the glass on our wedding picture. Our smiling faces taunt me. Were we really like that? That whole? That complete? That happy? I pick up the shiny silver frame and take a closer look; there's a shadowy blotch above Penda's ear. I rub the glass with my thumb to wipe it off. The smudge remains. It's underneath the glass. My heart thumps.

Since our wedding I must have looked at the picture a thousand times and I'm positive the spot wasn't there. I flip the frame over, slamming it on the desk and shoving my chair as far away from it as I can get. I stand, ready to run for the door, I'm up for a second, my legs give way and I collapse back into the chair and push myself away from the desk. My stomach cramps, and the nausea returns. Hot beads of fear dot my face and I start to shiver. I lean against the back of the chair, look up at the ceiling, and take deep breaths, to slow the panic.

Gradually the fear lessens and I pull the chair, using my feet, back to the desk. I stare at the back of the frame for a second then turn it over. My hand shakes. Beneath the glass a veil of black smoke blows over David's face. Vomit coils up from my stomach. I bolt up out of the chair and throw the picture against the wall to get rid of the desecration inside. The shattering glass explodes into silence. The room tilts and my head hits the floor with a sickening smack.

I'm in a tunnel. David and Dad are standing under a white spotlight at the end. I reach out for them but blackness engulfs my hands and cold steals what's left of me...

*****

Early Wednesday morning; the air is heavy and the sky cloudy. Rain is predicted for the end of the week. Two days of living with Jan and her family is all I can take. I'm better, but even if I wasn't, I'd lie. How a couple with two teenage daughters and only one bathroom can manage is beyond me.

On the way to work, I stop at the house to pick up a sleeping bag, a couple of days' worth of clean clothes and some toiletries. It's not that I'm afraid of sleeping in the house without David; it's just that I want to be near Penda. Something feels off. Call it women's intuition or perhaps it's the voodoo blood of my mother running through my veins, warning me to watch my back. David's memorial is on Friday, but it's something else, something I can't put my finger on that's causing my anxiety.

When I tap the computer key to check mail, the first message that pops up is from Miles; asking me to stop by his office sometime today. He wants to talk. My mind runs over a quick list of the clinic's expenses. It's always about money with Miles. I'll deal with him later.

Sorry, Miles, not today. Not until I've buried my husband. Maybe then I'll be in the mood to talk business. I type the message with angry fingers, pause and hit delete...it's not worth the attitude. Instead I simply type, *Next week,* and hit the send key.

Jan has replaced the glass in the frame holding our wedding picture. There are no black blotches or smudges anywhere on the photo. She has organized David's desk, too. It doesn't look like him anymore. I wish she'd left it the way it was until after...My throat tightens...his...I press my lips and hold them closed with my fingers to prevent a sob from escaping. I have to start getting control of myself if I'm going to get through David's funeral.

"*Squawk!* Pay attention. Pay attention!" Rita screams.

I am paying attention, I think to myself. I'm thirty and my birthday's over and the test—the third ten, should have ended things. So why am so I worried? Nanta said three tens, not four, not five. "Our lives will be normal now," Dad promised. But even with the third and last ten behind me, my life will never be normal, not without David.

"Rita, please," I beg, reaching for the food dish inside her cage. "Can you be quiet for just a few more minutes?" I fill her dish from the 50-pound bag of parrot mix next to my desk and put it back in her cage.

"Eat your seeds, Rita. I have two days of work to catch up on."

"Eat! *Squawk*. Eat Rita! Seed'em and reap! *Squawk*."

Shaking my head and smiling for the first time in a week, I silently thank her for the comic relief. I watch her and wonder what it must be like to be a bird. Especially a bird that can't fly and has a mouth that, at times, would make a hooker blush. She looks so innocent, sitting on her perch splitting open sunflower seeds. Who would guess she's here because sometimes her raunchy vocabulary isn't rated PG and isn't suitable for the public. A shell from a sunflower seed zings from her beak and splashes into my coffee mug.

"Thanks." I plunge my finger into the warm liquid and retrieve it before it sinks to the bottom.

"Dance with me. Twist and shout. Laaaa, laa, laa, I was born this way. *Squawk!* Oh, baby, oh."

"Rita, please, I have a ton of work..."

"Workin' for the man every night and..." Rita flings another shell into my cup. "All hoop, all hoop, baby," confirming my suspicion that she knows what she's doing.

"That's it, you're outta here."

"You're outta here, *squawk!*"

"Jan, save me," I beg half-heartedly, knowing she's in the nursery feeding the tiger cubs and can't possibly hear me.

"Save me, Jan." Rita screeches then adds, at the top of her voice, "J-a-a-a-n!"

"Rita, honey, please, five minutes."

"Rita! Ha-ha-ha. *Squawk*, you're outta here. Jan, save me!"

I swivel out of my chair, open Rita's cage door ready to take her to the nursery when I'm stopped by the sight of Miles standing in the doorway. His face is pinched with worry.

"Lill, we need to talk."

"I don't have the time right now, Miles, I'm really busy."

"Too busy, Miles, too busy to talk, *squawk!*"

I grab hold of Rita's cage when a wave of dizziness washes over me, reminding me that I am not yet 100 percent. The floor dims then rises up. To keep from falling I sit gracefully, I hope, on the edge of the desk and close my eyes to stop the room from spinning.

"Jan," Miles steps out and shouts down the hall, "we need you in here. Now." He rushes to my side to steady me.

"*Squawk*, I need you, Jan. Now, now, laaa-laaa-laaaaaaa."

"You rang?" Jan's voice precedes her appearance in the office doorway. "Oh, my God, are you alright?" Jan shoves the tiger cub and a half-full bottle of milk into Miles' arms then guides me into my office chair.

"Stay," she scolds and points her finger at me like I'm a dog who's misbehaved.

"I'm fine Jan, just a little dizzy."

"Miles, what happened?"

"I don't know. Her face turned white, she started to fall, and ended up sitting on the desk."

Miles hands the cub and bottle back to Jan while he stares at me, "We still need to talk, Lill. You take care of yourself, but I need to meet with you...sooner than later." He turns and walks briskly out of the office.

"Wonder what he wants to talk to you about?" Jan drapes the cub over her shoulder, patting him on the back to encourage a burp.

"I don't know; money if I had to guess, but right now I don't care. I need to get through David's funeral. I'll deal with whatever Miles wants after that."

Buurrp. The cub bubbles sour milk on Jan's shoulder.

Jan smiles and lifts the baby tiger away from her shirt. Holding him up to her face, she kisses his nose, then straddles him over one arm and tucks him against her body.

Buuurrrp, squawk.

Jan laughs. "Rita, how rude. Lill, you okay to be alone?"

"I'm fine."

Jan screws up her face like she doesn't believe me but lets it go.

"When you're finished feeding the cubs, would you come and take Rita? She's driving me crazy."

We have five tiger cubs in our nursery, all needing breakfast before they are turned over to the keepers, who will take care of their needs for the rest of the day. They will be taken to a public area for picture taking and play, then returned to us when the park closes; well played with, well fed, and ready for sleep.

"I'll do it right now, if you can hold this little guy for a second." Jan hands the cub over to me.

"Rita, you're coming with me." Jan reaches into the cage, Rita hops up onto her arm and together they walk out the door. "I'll be right back," she calls as she speeds down the hall to the nursery.

Squawk!

Chapter 12

Friday. Ten days after David died. It's 1:30 in the afternoon, and the small nondenominational chapel at the cemetery is filled to capacity with close friends, people I know and barely know. One of David's college classmates, Garwood Singer, a blond good-looking man, is here with his wife and three children. David's childhood friend Rick Monotony and his partner Steve are also among the mourners. It's good to see them, but I wish we had, or they had, visited more when David was alive.

A storm blew in last night, adding to the gloom that has overtaken the day. The stained-glass windows in the church shed little light. Heavy clouds block the sun and threaten more rain. Jan is standing on my right, Don on my left, their hands clasping my elbows. Still, I feel isolated and alone as we walk down the aisle together. My eyes are steadfast on David's rosewood casket. The funeral director has placed the flowers David requested on top—on top of the wood, on top of him— white lilies. "Lilies for my wife, Lillian, Lill," David had written in his will.

We are the last to sit and we sit the same as we walked; Jan on my right, Don on my left. Black surrounds me. I am wearing green. David loved me in green with my hair loose. For David, I wear my hair down uncontrolled and free. Today, it's my emotions that are bound and penned up—what is the logic in that? One row back Garwood stands; the noise he generates makes me turn and look. The scent of his aftershave follows him as he moves to the center aisle. I tuck my hair behind my ears and glance at Rick and Steve sitting across from me. I envy Rick when Steve squeezes his hand then rises and joins Garwood.

Sadness fills the little chapel as the two men walk side by side to stand next to David's casket. Nervous coughs interrupt the silence and echo off the walls, bouncing back a reaffirmation to the living that they are the lucky ones. Jimmy, the back gate guard, is here. He's brought his family, his wife and four kids. He smiles and nods when I glance at him. His white teeth remind me of my childhood in Ndogo, and I wish Dad was here to shout *Hallelujah* or *Amen*, or just to hold my hand.

When David's friends speak, they speak in petal soft voices and bring fingers to the corners of their eyes to stop fragile tears. They talk of David and the happy times they shared. I'm glad they liked him, loved him. They attempt to cover the pain of his death and the reality of their own mortality with light-hearted stories and forced laughter. I don't blame them. It feels good to laugh even though it doesn't last and is replaced, too soon, with sorrow. The relived stories go on for too long. I stop listening, filling my ears with imaginary cotton balls to keep their voices muffled. I have my own memories to recall.

After we bow our heads in prayer, Jan and Don walk me outside to a waiting car. It's a short drive to the gravesite. We ride together. We don't speak.

Ominous dark clouds bubble and brew across the sky. A cold wind pushes us forward when we step out of the car, rushing us to David's gravesite. To hurry us even more it starts to rain. Black umbrellas open. Jan and Don hold theirs like crossed fingers wishing for good luck over my head. The raindrops pelt the umbrellas taut cloth with a benumbed death-like cadence and the pressure drops to icy cold beneath them. My lungs are sucked empty of air when David's casket is carried past me. The pallbearer's chins are tucked to their chests trying to keep the rain off their faces.

When the men reach David's grave, they hold his coffin firmly while placing it gently on the rigid straps of the lowering devise. A wide white cloth covers the mounds of freshly dug earth at the gravesite, puckered like hungry lips anxious to swallow David into the pit. The rain stops. The black umbrellas close and fold up with shakes, snaps, and clicks, then are tucked away like wet wings. The wind continues to blow.

The minister recites some Bible verses I refuse to hear, but when he's finished I want to shout—"don't stop!" It's too soon to put my husband, my love, in the ground. But I don't; I stay quiet and David, inside his casket, is lowered into the hole.

Jan and Don steer me to a turned up corner on the cloth. The flowers from the top of David's casket have been placed next to it and the triangle edge of freshly exposed dirt. From on top the grave, the straps are loosened and pulled up. David remains. I bend down and watch my hand scoop up a handful of earth. I do my widow's duty and sprinkle it on top of David's coffin, then pull a single white lily from the bouquet.

"I love you," I whisper and toss that in, too. The white flower tumbles, slowly, over and over until it hits his casket with an anguished tick-tap. The sound crawls back up the earthen walls like the grim reaper's hand and shoves the finality of David's death down my throat. I'm glad David's soul is not here to see or hear this. Death is too painful even for the dead.

It's a little after eight, and I'm finally alone. Exhausted, I wander into our bedroom to change my clothes; exchanging numbness for emptiness but holding on to my broken heart— it's all I have left of us. I trade the green dress for old jeans and an old sweater, high heel shoes for running shoes. I take a jacket from the hook by the back door and head for the elephant barn.

*****

The elephants' greeting is an uneasy low rumble. I breathe in this new sound trying to understand the message. A shiver spreads between my shoulders when I notice how tightly the elephants stand at the rail. Solid, like a wall, stretching their trunks out, not to invite me in but to hold me back; something's wrong. They push against my arms and shoulders as I dip between the rails to join them. Taatee grabs my hand to stop me from going any further. The others elephants fold in around me, refusing to let me pass. Panic clutches my throat.

"Penda." I pull my hand free from Taatee's grip and shove my way between the elephants.

I don't see her. She's gone. "Penda!" I scream. From the rafters overhead a small flock of pigeons swoop down onto the floor of the barn, landing in a circle as if to fill the void of her absence.

I race outside the pen to the emergency phone on the wall and call Miles at his home.

"What have you done with her? Where's Penda?" I shriek.

"They came for her this afternoon. The other day when I—"

"Who came? Where did they take her?"

"Back to Africa. Lill, you need to calm down. You knew she was here on loan. They had every right to take her. She grew so fast. She was ready—"

"Shit, Miles. How could you let them? Why didn't you tell me this was happening?"

"Lill, I tried to tell you. I came to your office. I—"

"You didn't try hard enough. I just buried my husband and now you've taken my child. What freaking rock did you crawl out from under?"

"Take it easy. She's an elephant, Lill. She's not your child."

"I love her. David loved her. You have to get her back!"

"I can't. You wouldn't talk to me. I couldn't stop it. She belongs to them. I know the timing is bad, but—"

"Bad? It sucks. David's dead. Without Penda I have nothing. I can't lose her. I couldn't stand to lose her, too."

"You have other elephants."

"It's not the same, damn it, it's not the same, and you know it. You allowed total strangers to take the only thing I have left away from me. How could you? How do you sleep at night?

Huh, Miles? How the hell do you sleep?"

"Lill, please . . ."

"Go to hell, Miles."

"Lill, think. There was nothing I could do."

"I'm going after Penda. I quit, Miles."

"Lill, you don't mean that. You can't quit. Without David . . . we need you here. The animals need you."

"Don't, Miles. Don't stoop so low as to throw the other animals in my face. You're disgusting. I'm done with you and your self-serving, money-grabbing agenda."

"Take a minute to calm down and think about what you're saying."

"Damn you, Miles. You know why you live alone? No one can stand you; that's why. You're a piece of shit. You've got nothing even close to a heart. All you've got is greed."

"Lill, going after Penda, won't change anything. Think it through. Is this what David, would want you to do?"

"No, Miles, David wouldn't want me to go to Africa. Now, because of you, I have to. You've given me no other choice. What's wrong with you? You don't get it, do you? You don't understand. I didn't get a chance to say goodbye to David. I can't let that happen with Penda. Damn it, Miles. What have you done to me?" My body heaves with anguish. I slump against the wall next to the phone.

Pressing my lips to the receiver I sob, "Miles, what would it have cost you to give me one more day with Penda? You could have grown a heart. You could have changed. If you cared, you could have fought for more time. No, no, I guess you couldn't. There's no money in that, is there? If you were anywhere close to being human, you would have given me a chance to say goodbye."

I crumple to the floor. The receiver bangs against the wall, swinging from its cord, twirling in circles. I pull my knees to my chest and cover my face with my hands; crying for David, crying for Penda, crying for myself. It's only been ten days since David was killed. Ten days. I have no choice. I have to see Penda and tell her goodbye. I have to go to Africa and I'm afraid. I'm afraid of what waits for me there.

The pigeons take flight, returning to the rafters overhead. A thin black-red mist tags after them. A soft glow sparks silver and gold and snuffs out the unholy contrail. Imagined or real, it's time for me to return to Africa and face . . . I have no idea what. Numb, I crawl up off the floor and slip back under the rail to say goodbye to the Magnificent Seven, not knowing if I'll ever see them again.

Chapter 13

Recirculated air hangs stagnant inside United's 787 passenger plane. The tiny fan above my head works hard to create the small breeze that barely reaches my blue T-shirt. Guilt clings to the cotton and holds me hostage. I have abandoned the animals at the park in order to confirm Penda has arrived safely in Africa and to tell her goodbye. I feel bad about leaving the animals. I worry about them and I worry about what I'll find in Africa. Or what might find me.

The fear and uncertainty hidden behind my guilt is palpable. I swallow to keep it from rising to the surface but it won't stay down. The plane's droning engines wrestle, ineffectively, with the consequences I face by returning to Africa. Dad's note said my mother was a *machawi*, and not to trust the lights, your eyes are like your mother's, you are my daughter, too, you must promise to stay out of Africa. Nothing he wrote gives me enough information that will help me now.

I relive the horror of David's death and ask myself how smart it is to come back. But it doesn't matter how smart or how dangerous, I have to see Penda. She has to understand I love her and that bringing her back to Africa this soon wasn't my idea. I will my nervousness to calm and remember, Nanta saying "things" happen every ten years. I remind myself, my turning thirty was the third ten. The last ten. Dad said never, ever return to Africa. I promised him I wouldn't and now I've broken that promise. What have I done?

I lean my aching head against the window. My eyelids grow heavy watching the thatched clouds below. I close my eyes and dream; I am a cloud, waiting, idle, an empty mass of indecision. I need to do something. My cloud divides in half. Conflicted.

What harm could come to me if, after seeing Penda, I went to Mbali? The third ten has come and gone. I should be safe. Dad had to be wrong. I'll bet he didn't even know about the three tens and if he had known he'd be okay with my returning home. If I take the time go to Mbali, perhaps...what? Perhaps I'll find out I'm a witchdoctor? That's nuts. It no longer applies. It's over. My eyes are normal. Well, almost normal. The dagger lights are faint and getting fainter every day. The strange silver ring is gone. It is as if it was never there. You're lying to yourself, Lill, a little voice in my head warns. Think about Senento; you killed him, remember? No, no I didn't; he was alive in the Jeep, I argue with the voice. Dad said it was a dream. David's death wasn't a dream, the voice mocks. Stop bothering me, I tell the voice. But maybe it would be wiser to stick to my original plan, visit Penda and get out of Africa as quickly as possible. That's what David would want me to do, get out while the getting's good. The questions and doubts continue to gather like springtime flies around the entrails of a lionesses' early morning kill. I need answers and I don't know if I have the courage to face them.

"Excuse me, Miss, may I take your cup?" The steward's voice wakes me.

"Yes, thank you," I mumble, fumbling to hand him the plastic cup and return my tray to its upright position.

Miles is right, of course. Going to Africa won't bring Penda back. It's just that, with David's death, it happened at the worst possible time. David and I both thought we'd have Penda for many more years. But she wasn't ours to keep. Once I see her and I'm sure she's safe; once I touch her, I'll be okay. Leaving her in Africa will be difficult, but she deserves to be free. Miles, bless him, wouldn't let me quit, not that I really would have. It was an empty threat spawned by anger. How could I leave the Magnificent Seven and the rest of the animals? Penda's starting a new life and won't need me. She'll be safe and have a new set of friends. Miles arranged for Ken Dennis, the sea mammal veterinarian at the park, to take over in my absence. At the time it was suggested, I admit I envisioned Ken wrestling with some of our four-footed land animals and chuckled. It would be good for him and his oversized ego to get dirty. Now safely belted in my seat I worry, not so much about animals, but about my own ego getting in the way of logic; Ken is an excellent vet.

My planned stay in Africa is to be short, so I've brought just two carry-on bags; clothing and toiletries in one bag and then my medical bag, just in case. In case of what I'm not sure, but it sits on the floor under the seat in front of me, the toes of my tennis shoes touching it. After visiting Penda, and if nothing strange happens, I might make a quick visit to Ndogo to reconnect with Nanta. I have some questions I'd like to ask her about my mother. Then I'll slip out of Africa before *Bayamchawi*, if he stills cares, notices I'm even there. Maybe Nanta will know if my mother's voodoo was white magic or black. Maybe she'll tell me the truth about my eyes...and me. Maybe.

"Ladies and gentlemen, we are making our final descent into Nairobi International Airport," the captain announces.

As we cut through the clouds, the tan and yellow-green tundra of Africa fills my window and beckons me home. I brush a strand of hair from my face and have to smile; you can take the girl out of Africa, but you can't take Africa out of the girl. Even with all the strange things that encompass who and what I am, I can't change this.

"If you'd like to set your watches, it is 2:16 in the afternoon, and the temperature is a warm 85 degrees," the captain tells us.

Penda was flown over on Flying Tiger Airlines. She was taken, by truck, to the Dzanga-Keita Elephant Reserve and arrived just as I was boarding my plane in the states. Dr. Keita sent a text message and a photo of her mingling with a group of twenty elephants, all different ages and sizes. One large bull was standing close by Penda. As fast as she's grown in the short time we had her, I wouldn't be surprised if she was ready to breed. I have chartered a single-engine aircraft to take me directly from the Nairobi airport to the private airstrip at Dzanga-Keita.

The Customs terminal is crowded. Ours is not the only plane arriving and there are people everywhere. Bright sunlight streams in long shafts through the tall windows, making it impossible to see outside. So I settle for watching people rush to the line forming in front of me; this is going to take some time.

Forty-five minutes later I'm still waiting, but I'm next. I have two letters with me to give to Customs. One is from Miles and one from Dr. S. Keita, the biologist who manages and owns the Dzanga-Keita Elephant Reserve. Both letters state that the drugs I'm bringing into the country are legal for me to possess.

A large moon-faced Customs lady motions with her chubby brown fingers for me to approach. Her dark brows knit together as she takes the two letters I hold out for her. She's in no hurry, knowing through years of experience, or perhaps some strange psychic ability, that these letters will cause her grief. She takes her time reading first one then the other. I smile pleasantly when she raises a single eyebrow and glances at me. She waves the letters in the air, like a trader at the stock exchange, to someone behind her. My heart sinks. But I know better than to rush her. I continue to smile as she hands both the letters to the older and much thinner African man who has walked up behind her. As she twist around my sleep deprived eyes fixate on the buttons of her shirt, tugging against the fabric, working overtime to keep her large breasts contained. The man's stern face questions mine. His long black fingers unfold the first letter then the second. When he has finished reading, he folds both letters and hands them back across the counter. They both smile and watch me as I return the letters to my bag.

"Bwana Keita," my agent chirps and nods. Then to my surprise and the surprise of the other passengers in line, she waves me on. Dr. Keita must have some serious influence in this country.

Outside the security checkpoint, I'm stopped by a ruddy-faced white man with messy gray hair, wearing cutoff jeans, a smartly pressed khaki shirt, and a bush hat held primly in his hand. "Dr. Drake?" His accent sounds more Australian than British. His breath is more beer than mint.

"Yes?" I gaze into a pair of alarmingly bloodshot blue eyes squinting out from a mass of wrinkles trapped in a face weathered by too many years in the sun.

"Crane," he says, putting his hat on his head and taking my two bags. "Is this all you have then?" He adds something totally indecipherable and hurries away on quick spindly legs.

"Yes," I answer when I catch up to him.

"I'm your pilot."

With that announcement, he speeds up, heading rapidly in the direction of the terminal's glass doors. Crane is shorter than I am by two inches, but I still have trouble keeping up. His legs are traveling twice as fast as the rest of his body. He reminds me of a Road-Runner cartoon. All he needs is a sign reading "Beep-beep!" floating over the top of his head and the image would be complete. I laugh out loud at the mental image and a man walking past me laughs, too, as if we have just exchanged a private joke.

I push through the airport doors after Crane and the air outside hits me with a lifetime of childhood memories. I take a moment to breathe in Africa and to silently promise David and dad that I'll only stay a day or two. I soon regret this indulgence when I find myself engulfed by a large group of German tourists departing from their bus. They shout instructions to each other, gathering their belongings and pointing to the Lufthansa sign behind my head. They have completely hidden Crane from my view. Anxious, I pick my way through them, smiling and squeezing in and out of short towers of stacked luggage until I reach the other side. Crane is waiting impatiently, tapping his foot like a put upon parent.

"First time t'Africa?" he asks then scurries on ahead, not interested in an answer.

"No, it's not my first time to Africa. I was born here," I shout after him. When he stops I remove my medical bag from his hand with a little more force than I intended. "I should hang onto this just in case we're separated again."

"Suit ya'self." But he doesn't move. Instead he reaches down and opens the passenger door of the rusted old red VW Bug parked at the curb. The door sticks then yields to his demands, and he throws my bag in the back seat with an indifference that irritates the hell out of me. Crane leaves me standing alone as he runs around to the driver's side and gets in. Angry, I climb into his junk of a car without as much as a glance in his direction. Crane doesn't offer any help and I don't ask. I fight my medical bag into the small space between my feet then tug the stubborn door closed.

"Where's your plane?" I ask, trying to keep the tone of my voice civil as his old car shudders out into traffic.

"Not far." He engages the engine and glides away from the curb.

A few minutes later we are parked next to a small airplane hangar at the farthest and most dilapidated end of the airport. Metal barrels, rusted and dented, overflow with weeks of trash. Weeds have claimed the cracks in the asphalt as their own, standing tall and proud at their ability to grow in even the most adverse conditions. In complete contrast, the shiniest little red airplane I've ever seen is peeking out of the open hanger doors. Crane hurries out of the car, grabs my bag from the back seat, slams the door shut leaving me to struggle with my own door and bag as he swaggers to his plane like a rooster to a hen.

"It's beautiful," I say, once I'm inside and standing next to him, astonished that this plane could be his.

"She," he corrects. "Her name is Miss Kitty. I was doing a bit of flying in the U.S. when I saw that Marshall Dillon TV show; named her after the Marshall's lady, Miss Kitty. She's a Cessna 180, a cute little tail dragger, she is." His face positively beams with pride.

Feeling a bit more confident about my pilot, I listen as he tells me to wait while he carefully and gently places both my bags onto the back seat of the airplane. He removes the blocks from the wheels, walks to the back of the plane, pulls out a couple of handles on each side of her slim tail, uses them to lift the back end, then pushes her out of the hanger.

Once we are outside, Crane helps me into the plane. The inside is just as clean and shiny as the outside. I doubt if Crane allows fingerprints to linger for more than a moment and I seriously wonder if he even permits small specks of dust to settle. He runs through an invisible checklist that's tucked somewhere in his mind, flicking this switch and that, mumbling to himself as he checks and re-checks whatever it is that pilots check before they take off. When he's satisfied with the results, he gets clearance from the tower and taxies out onto the empty runway. Within minutes, Miss Kitty lifts off the tarmac and soars gracefully into the sky.

"So ya'was born here, huh?" He shouts over the engines noise, once he has leveled the plane.

"Yes, in a village called Ndogo."

"Ndogo, I've heard of it. When did you leave?"

"Twenty years ago; I left when I was ten."

"Long time. Ndogo, huh? It's by that place, ah, what's it called?"

"Mbali?"

"Mbali, that's right." He nods his head up and down. "You know it?"

"Don't know it personally, but I've heard talk. Mbali's got quite a reputation. Voodoo reputation, that's what it's got; strange things go on in Mbali, so they say. Me personally, I don't believe any of that voodoo nonsense. The missus packed us some lunch. It's in that tote bag in back."

"What kind of strange things?"

"Nothing in particular, just rumors. There's a thermos of coffee in there, too. I'd appreciate it if you'd pour me a cup. Pour two if you want one for yourself; it's loaded with cream-n-sugar. I like it that way, gives me a rush. Nothing's better for a pick-me-up than a little sugar and caffeine, especially after the night I had. Grab yourself a sandwich while you're at it, you look a little peaked. And I hope you don't mind if we keep the chit-chat to a minimum, it's difficult to talk over the noise when we're flying."

"I'll wait on the sandwich but thanks." Undoing the seatbelt, I twist up on my knees and reach into the back. "How long will it take us to get to Dzanga-Keita?" I settle back in my seat and hand him a cup of coffee.

"Should be there in two'n a half hours, give or take a bit. Before dark, need t' have some light t' land. Dr. Keita said he would be waiting for you. The landing strip is a cleared bit of land, extending beyond *Tembo Nymuba*.

"*Tembo Nymuba*? Elephant House?"

"It's what he named his place."

I take a sip of Crane's coffee before putting my seatbelt back on. His coffee tastes like hot chocolate, and it's surprisingly good. Lord knows, I could use something to wake me up, and make me look less peaked.

"I can't wait to see it."

"You won't be disappointed. It's a fitting name."

An hour and a half later, we are following a stream of green water that runs along the east side of the Msito gorge. The water comes from the mountains of Dzanga-Msito, Crane informed me. The cliffs are 200 feet high; the east wall is ablaze with golden light that plays with the green-blue and red-yellow brush, as if it were stitching together a patchwork quilt. Forming the cliff walls, wide plateaus of thick shelves and caves offer the perfect resting dens and observation posts for predators to stalk their prey. Underneath these outcroppings, sheltered in dark shadows, birds fly in and out of their roosts snatching up insects.

The canyon floor is flat and sparse, cut with thin crisscrossing lines from animals traveling along the waterway from one grazing area to the next. The few trees growing here have sunk their roots close to the river's edge and cast late afternoon silhouettes up the bright wall like the lost children of shadow puppets. The opposite wall is doused in fading light and yawns, waiting for morning to bring it back to life. A herd of giraffes run in long-legged lopes below us, their tawny beige and spotted brown hides melting into the dust colored earth and dry grass.

"Ya want t' see what's down there up close, Dr. Drake?"

Startled by Crane's voice after over an hour of silence, I stammer, "I'd love to."

"Okay. I'll buzz Miss Kitty down, and ya can have ya self a proper look."

Crane banks sharply, tipping the wing on his side toward the bottom of the canyon and we're on our way. It's exhilarating. Crane levels Miss Kitty, then gestures, pointing to a wide rock platform up ahead and to the right.

"Look there." He motions at two young lions walking lazily along the sunlit shelf going down for a drink or perhaps an early dinner. Crane guides Miss Kitty in for a closer look. As we fly past, both cats glance up; the angle of the sun reflects flashes of gold in their eyes. They stop to watch us like we are nothing more important than a scrawny bird. The outcroppings become larger and flatter the closer we get, their edges more dangerously jagged, their shelves littered with loose stones and dead brush. The platform ahead of us appears to be long and strong enough to land Miss Kitty on, if we had to. Then, without any warning a mass of black locusts whips out from underneath it and swarm. Instinctively, I raise my hands and duck as hundreds of the hard bodies insects smash against the windshield, break apart then are blown aside.

Hundreds more continue the assault. Miss Kitty gives short coughs. The sound echoes through the cockpit. The propeller blades hesitate. My stomach churns. The blades sputter and start to stall. Miss Kitty coughs again then spits out an engine load of the nasty insects. The blades resume full speed. My eyes question Crane. He shakes off my concern with a no-big-deal-I-can-handle-this grin, but the locusts keep coming.

"Crane?" I push back against the seat and grab hold of my seat cushion, not convinced he's being totally honest.

He doesn't speak, instead he points at the cockpit ceiling, jabs his finger in the air a couple of times, then pulls back on the wheel. Miss Kitty responds with a swift ascent, slamming me into my seat. The swarm of locust hangs with us for as long as they can then slides to the edges of the windshield before spinning away and out of sight.

When we've leveled out, Crane removes his hat, wipes the sweat from his brow and parks the hat back on his head. "Damn locust, shouldn't be out this time of year. We've lost them. Won't happen again." Crane taps the glass of the instrument panel with a fingernail checking the plane's vital signs then takes her back down.

"You sure?" I'm working hard to keep the panic out of my voice.

"Relax, nothing t' worry about. Like I said, it won't happen again. Miss Kitty here knew what to do; she chewed those buggers up and spit them out. Everything's good, they ain't coming back."

"Crane, look!" Below us the canyon floor swells with a massive wave of locusts. Their hostile wings reflecting pinpoints of sunlight as they circle and gather speed. Then they lift in unison and zero in.

"Doc, I don't know what's going on, but it sure as hell's not looking like any locust swarm I've ever seen before. Hold on, this could get rough." Crane banks the plane in an attempt to avoid the onslaught.

The locusts hit the plane with deafening splatters, darkening the windshield so completely that I can barely see Crane.

"Crane, do something!" I shout above the noise. My pulse pounds wildly.

"This ain't normal. If ya never said a prayer in your life, now's the time t' start."

There's a loud thump, the plane dips and the blackness slides off the windshield. Crane and I exchange confused looks. Where did they go? The answer comes a short second later, when a torrent of thick dark smoke billows out from the engine and races along each side of the plane.

"It's *Bayamchawi*, Crane; he's found me."

Crane shoots me a look of alarm. "There's no such thing as black magic, Dr. Drake. Now, tighten ya seat belt. I believe you Yanks have an expression, where there's smoke there's fire. Well, it seems we're going to have us a real barn burner, and it's got nothing to do with any voodoo devil."

The plane drops, and my heart sinks with it. Crane banks Miss Kitty. She starts to climb then suddenly lunges forward. Crane pulls up on the wheel. His hands look strong and forceful, but his knuckles turn white with the strain. A loud bang thunders from the engine and fire bites the windshield. The jolt from the explosion thrusts Miss Kitty sideways toward the rocky ledge of the cliff.

"Crane! We're too close!"

"Cover ya head and tuck tight," Crane yells over the shrill

noise of our descent.

Miss Kitty's right wing clips a boulder hanging out above the ledge. The jolt sends my head to the roof then slams me against the door. Crane screams. In a feeble attempt to save myself, I brace my feet against the floor and grab hold of the seat. The wing hit another rock, cracks and bends up, saving us from a head on crash but sending us skidding along the wide rocky ledge, careening toward the end of the cliff.

Gravity pins me against the passenger side door. Flying stones, dirt, and sand race pass my face. The broken wing catches another outcropping and is torn completely off. My head hits the dash then bounces back. The wing flips over the top of the plane and disintegrates into pieces behind us. Miss Kitty pitches sideways then bucks back, her wheels catching on an old stump and stopping us with a violent jerk in a flood of dust and sparks.

I take a breath and look over at Crane. He's dead. His unlatched door swings open on its hinges. His body hangs from his seatbelt, half outside, half in. Crane's neck is broken. His head is bloody. Gray engine smoke whips his face with thick dark ropes of burning engine oil.

Miss Kitty groans. She falters; the ledge beneath us starts to give way. I press my feet against the dash and hang on.

The engine hacks up molten chunks of metal; Miss Kitty recoils.

The ledge crumbles and lets us go.

Chapter 14

'Lill, open your eyes."

"I can't, David, the light is too bright."

"You have to, Lill. You have to open your eyes."

"I'm hot. Let me sleep."

"You're not sleeping, Lill."

"Umm."

"Dr. Lillian Drake, open your eyes. Look at me. Open your eyes, now!"

I can hear hot sparks of flame biting at the cockpit walls of the plane. I can't see them, but I sure can feel the heat. I'm pinned under my seat, facing up. The seat is protecting me from the fire, but it's also keeping me from escaping. I need to get out of here. A two-inch opening allows me to breathe air that is filled with the smell of oil, flames, smoke and gasoline.

Shit! The plane's leaking gas. I hear a whoosh as gasoline ignites and feel the blast of heat as it invades my air space. The plane is going to explode.

Blinding pain sears through my eyes. Panic makes it difficult to breathe. And just like when the zebra was attacking me, I feel as though I'm suffocating. A lightning flash of white erupts inside my tiny space and sucks out the little oxygen I have left. The seat catapults into the air, taking me with it.

The seat hits the ground first, breaks loose and bounces away, leaving me crumpled in the dirt gulping in air. Seconds later, Miss Kitty explodes. Debris and burning wreckage spew flames and sparks high into the sky. Two more explosions rock the little plane. Each blast sending fire and airplane parts in my direction. A chunk of heavy metal and hot sparks strikes my left leg and bite into my flesh. Another chunk bounces off my head.

Blackness.

When I regain consciousness, the canyon walls and valley floor are draped with the dusky purple light of a missed sunset. I'm cold. My right arm tingles from too many hours of lying in one position. My entire body hurts. An out-of-focus finger wiggles in front of my eyes. Strange, where did that come from? The finger is dirty, the flesh torn and bleeding. The nail is broken. It moves up and down then it scratches my nose. Huh, it must be mine. My eyelids shut, too heavy to stay open.

The earth smells thirsty. I work my mouth; maybe it's me who's thirsty. The night sky is lit by a haunting moon. My face and mouth are crusted with dust and dry grass. I lick my lips and taste the blood and dirt that cling together like old friends. The air feels warm, so why I am so cold? In the distance, I can hear the death knell of Miss Kitty as she continues to burn. Her flames have kept the predators away and kept me safe. I can smell the heat as it mingles with the breeze, but I'm not close enough to feel much of the warmth. An involuntary shiver makes my legs jerk. I hear a splash and feel cold water. A shock of sharp pain stabs through my left leg just below the knee. I've ended up in the stream we saw from the plane. Another spasm of pain shoots up my leg. I'm pretty sure it is broken. The doctor part of my brain takes over; the cold water will help keep the swelling down but I can't stay in it forever; I need to assess the damage. I take a deep breath and count one, two and on three, roll onto my back.

"Aaargh." The pain is much worse than I thought it would be, but I can't stop now. I struggle to sit up but can't. The pain keeps stopping me. Tears of frustration trickle down my face. I wipe them away and glance at the sky thinking, there has got to be a better way to do this.

Mwezi, the moon, has grown full. Its yellow glow fills the canyon and gives me nothing but false hope. The stars hanging around the moon seem unconcerned about my dire situation and even have the nerve to twinkle. Chirping communications from nearby crickets add gay chatter to an otherwise quiet night and like the stars, offer no help. My lower lip quivers with the realization of my hopeless situation. Coming to Africa is starting to feel like a huge mistake. As soon as I see Penda, assuming I get out of here alive, I will tell her goodbye and get on the first plane heading back to California.

Tiny stones dig into my hands and elbows, as I find the strength to ease myself into a sitting position then stare into the water at my legs. The lower part of my left leg is not only broken, it's burned. It's not a compound fracture, so why are there blobs of clotted and oily blood swirling in the water? I lean forward for a closer look. The blood's not coming from me.

I refocus my attention to Miss Kitty, looking for Crane. The little airplane is on her back. Her body is fractured, lifeless and broken. Red coals and crackling flames have replaced her shiny paint with black soot. Her tires are smoking. The smell of burning rubber circles the nearby tree and then wafts its way across the short grass to the shoreline. Crane is just a few yards upstream. Even in the dim light of the moon I can see he is the reason for the blood. Crane's head is missing. His torso collapsed in the water. He is as torn up as Miss Kitty.

Grateful for the flames that are keeping the predators away but not betting on how much longer my luck will hold, I figure I'd better get out of the water and find a place to hide as quick as I can. I press the heel of my good right leg into the rocky-river bottom and push down. My left leg twists with the effort.

"Aaargh! Shit!" Bad mistake. Eventually the pain lessens, freeing my mind to work on plan B: slow and gentle is the way to get out of this situation, I reason.

I breathe in a lung full of air and grit my teeth, dig my palms into the dirt and scoot on my butt, one tiny inch at a time, out of the water. It is not easy, and I'm exhausted by the time my legs are on dry land. However, now I have a bigger problem; I must find a way to set or at least stabilize my broken leg; it is imperative that I find a place to hide and keep safe, until my rescuers arrive. A spasm of pain urges me to start looking for my medical bag. My cell phone was in the outside pouch of the bag and I'm hoping it surviving the crash. I need to call for help. There is also a bottle of Tylenol in the bag, it's not much but if I'm going to try and set my leg, Tylenol is better than nothing. My eyes search the ground between me and the plane, praying the bag got tossed out and isn't trapped inside, burned, or too far away.

A sudden gust of wind fans the burning coals under Miss Kitty and shoots hot cinders into the dry grass. The grass ignite, flames flare up and dance like small mice, merrily hopping to the trunk of a nearby tree. The fire marches up the tree's dry bark and starts to climb. Caught near the top of the tree, wedged in the brittle branches and dry leaves is my medical bag and cellphone, I hope. I'll have to hurry if I'm going to reach them before the fire does. Who am I kidding? In my condition, hurry is not an operative word. I'm exhausted but not yet defeated, so I start to scoot toward the tree.

"Aaagh," the pain in my leg stops me from moving any further. No longer cold, it's starting to throb. I stare at the flames. Beaten, I watch as the fire chews on the bottom of my bag. Fatigue and hopelessness zap the last of my resolve. Frustrated, angry and in pain, I stretch my right hand out in front of me, reaching for a bag that's impossible to reach.

"Damn it, I need you!" My anguished scream punctures the night.

A loud cracking sound splits the tree in half, fire and flames engulf it and swallow it whole. A second later my medical bag is spit up into the air, free from the inferno and tumbling toward me, hopping and jumping like a happy puppy across the dirt. It stops just inches from my side and hacks up a puff of ash. I yank my hand back as if the bag was going to bite.

"Not bad, Lillian, an accident perhaps, but you'll learn," a woman's raspy African voice encourages.

I snap my head to the left. Crouching next to me is a very old and very small aboriginal woman. She looks like she belongs to Africa, but she is unlike any of the women in Ndogo. Her skin is dark gray, not brown or black but gray. I think her unusual color might be because she, like her feet, are covered with dust. The moonlight reflects off her brow and cheekbones, and I realize it might be something else...perhaps tiny specks of feathers? A wave of nausea rolls over me and the figure of the old woman blurs. I blink her back into focus then quickly close my eyes to steady the motion circling her.

A minute passes, and I feel steady enough to look at her and ask, "Who are you? How do you know my name?"

"Kooee-kooee," she trills, "you should call me Ku-Mama." The white tufts of hair on top of her head bristle like porcupine quills and send loose scatterings of pale gold and silver sparks on to her shoulders.

"Grandmother?" Black dots settle in front of my eyes and the old woman's image starts to fade.

"Ah, Lillian, we have waited twenty years for you to come back to Africa, and here you are. Ha-ha, and what a surprise. Even in the air *Bayamchawi* couldn't manage to kill you." She folds her legs and sits down, so close to me I can smell the sweetness of her breath blowing out between the thin lines that form her lips. She places a weightless cold hand on my broken leg and singed skin, its coolness sooths the pain. "Soon you will be our *Machawi-shaitani*. But even now your limited powers can heal your leg."

The ground starts to spin and I grab onto the earth to keep from falling off.

"Lillian?" She pokes my shoulder with a hard finger.

The spinning continues. My mouth turns dry. "It's not Lillian, it's Lill," I mumble before the light fades.

*****

I wake with a start to the whoops and yaps of a pack of hyenas. Their demonic giggles echo through the canyon's gray walls. I look around cautiously for the old woman. She's gone. *Jua* the sun goddess is getting ready to kiss the earth good morning; however, for a moment, steel gray light hides the dawn and the hyenas' nocturnal baying grows louder. They are close—too close—and they aren't singing happy birthday to me or anyone else. I look at the wreckage of Miss Kitty. I've lost hours. I'm lucky the predators didn't find me, but I can't count on that lasting another night now that Miss Kitty's protective flames have burned out. The residual coals beneath her are dull white and the short grass flanking the plane's sides is charred and skeletal. Gray ash exhales in short breaths of air from beneath her and ruffles away like a death sentence. Perhaps mine, if I don't get some help soon.

I sit up slowly and reach for the singed handles of my medical bag with stiff fingers and broken nails. The pouch holding my cell phone and wallet is empty. Panic races my heart; no phone, no help...it's getting difficult to breath. David's smiling face flashes before me; he accused me of being stubborn more than once, and now is not the time to give up. I huff out a determined breath and order myself to get a grip, rationalizing that by now Dr. Keita must have figured something is wrong and has sent someone looking for me. While I'm waiting for my rescuers, I fish around in my medical bag for a roll of gauze. There are no boards to use as a makeshift splint, but I'm going to try and wrap my leg tight enough to keep the break from becoming worse. I dry swallow a couple of Tylenol and start to work.

As I rip off a final strip of surgical tape and secure it to the layers of gauze wound tight around my leg, a warning yap-yap-whoop-whoop from a too close pack of hyenas freezes my hand in place. Their yapping stops and is quickly replaced with satisfied yips and grunts, and the sick cracking of breaking bones. I ease my hand away from my leg, drop the tape and gauze inside and squint into the early morning light. A mother hyena and her four pups stand over Crane's body. Thankfully, for the moment, the hyenas are too busy to notice me. They are gathered around Crane like ghouls around a feast. The mother hyena lifts her head out of Crane's ribcage; a chunk of him dangles from her jaws, she wolfs it down then swings her head in my direction. Bile rises in my throat. I swallow it and force myself to remain absolutely still. She sniffs the air then licks her muzzle with her tongue to clean the odor of Crane's blood off her snout. Her thick nostrils quiver and widen, catching my scent. Our eyes connect. My heart leaps. Her lips inch back in a sinister grin exposing blood stained-teeth. She yaps then surprises me when she looks away and licks each of her pups' faces. Perhaps to whisper to them that another, fresher meal is waiting close by. Me.

A twig snaps. And like joined puppets being pulled by a single string her head and mine turn in unison to look further upstream. Her fat round ears twitch, trying to hear more. I wish mine could. The sound is not repeated. She slides her gaze back to me. Our eyes meet for a second time. I remind myself that brown hyenas are scavengers and don't normally hunt or kill their own prey; however, this mother instinctively knows how vulnerable and weak I am. Her brown-spotted haunches hunker down, her muscles flex, and I'm certain that attacking me is exactly what she has decided to do. Her head moves from side to side, checking each pup, then unexpectedly she inches cautiously out of the stream. Her eyes dart nervously about, scanning the surrounding terrain. She yaps a stern order to her pups. Understanding but unhappy, the pups abandon Crane's body to follow her. A few yards out, the mother hyena stops and directs her eyes back on me. She sniffs the air. Her pups do likewise, and then they turn and trot off across the canyon in search of another meal.

Only a predator could scare a hyena and her pups from an easy snack like Crane. The sound of water being lapped draws my attention to the shoreline by the cliff wall. Large golden eyes flash from between two large boulders, and a young male lion's tawny colored mane bounces against his thin body as he lopes his way through the stream. He stops and flicks the water from his whiskers with a shake of his head and scans the area, looking for a meal. Like most young male lions, he will remain alone and outside a pride until he is strong enough to fight his way into a family unit and establish himself as their new and stronger monarch.

The boy-lion resumes his pursuit, his gait leisurely and aimed for Crane, but his hungry eyes never waver from me; lions prefer to kill their own meals. They like their meat fresh. He has a choice—me or Crane. Natural instinct makes his choice easy: me. My own primitive instincts, and my broken leg, force me to remain still while mentally weighing my options. I have none. When the lion reaches Crane, he hesitates, bats Crane's torso around with his huge front paws, playing with it. My heart sinks when he redirects his attention back to me. I'm the one he wants, and he knows he doesn't have to rush.

His stride is gangly. His front feet slap the wet river bed with soft spauuh, spauuh sounds. His back feet repeat the rhythm. He jogs through the water, toward me, with single-minded purpose. Time slows to a tortuous slow motion assault. I'm numb and beyond feeling fear. I watch his wheat-colored body bend gracefully around the river's rocks. My mind, detached from what is to come, is mesmerized by the beauty of the lion's natural grace. When he is within striking distance, he pushes off with his back feet and leaps.

Electrifying pain surges through my eyes. My chest tightens, making it difficult to breathe, and then a flash-explosion of white-light catches the lion in midair and lifts his body over the top of me. His black-tipped tail grazes my face. He lands shaken and standing less than six feet away. He lowers his head, cocks it to one side and quizzes me with cautious eyes. He is confused by what just happened; so am I. This is the same flash of light that saved me from the zebra and from being burned alive in the plane. I am starting to understand if I can control it, I can use it to my advantage. I concentrate my stare on the lion and knowingly send another bolt of light at his feet. He jumps back a foot, shakes his short mane and then simply turns and jogs in a wide circle around me, heading for Crane's body. At the water's edge, he takes a moment to regain his dignity, then lifts Crane's torso out of the stream as if it were a great prize and one that he intended to win in the first place. His massive jaws close down on what the hyenas have left behind and he carries Crane off to the cliffs and out of sight.

"I am not sure where that white light came from, there is this—"

"Aaargh," Once again, I fix my startled eyes on Ku-Mama.

"There is this old legend..." her ancient voice rasps then fades. Her shoulders twitch as if bothered by a fly.

"How did you get here?"

"Kooee-kooee," she whistles and smiles sweetly sending a sifting of gray dust to settle on the earth around her. She sits facing me, her legs crossed comfortably in front of her. As she breathes in, her full breasts rise up and meet the flat wattles beneath her dark gray chin. Her soft cotton shift is a lighter shade of gray than her skin and has a white panel stitched down the front. It is tied, with a single knot, on her right shoulder. Behind her, the cliffs rise up and cast questioning shadows of doubt on my otherwise logical mind.

"Now where were we, Lillian? Before you fainted we were talking about fixing your leg." She reaches for my right hand and turns it over, palm up. Another dusting of gray air follows.

I pull loose of her grip. "You never answered my question.

How did you get here?"

She laughs and cocks her head, "Some would say voodoo, but let's not talk about that now. It's complicated, and you need to fix your leg before I have to leave." She reaches for my hand again. This time her bony fingers hold it firmly. "Look." I follow her gaze to the scar on my palm.

"Why is it red?" I ask her.

Her fingers trace the length of the scar, "Oh my, look at that." My scar swells and turns crimson. "It seems your father's blood has not weakened you in the least." She sighs, "This would have been so much easier if we had taken you when you turned ten. Twenty years old, not as good as ten, but certainly it would have been better than waiting until now. Thirty, and there is so much to teach you and time is running short." She shakes her head, dislodging her frustration in an explosion of silver and gold sparks that dissolve in poofs of air circling her head. "I will do what I can. Today we must focus on today. Tomorrow we will focus on tomorrow."

"Huh?"

A barely audible *Kooee-kooee* slips from her lips. "Now pay attention, it's time for your first lesson. Let us see how much magic your mother's blood has given you."

"Dad left a note; he said my mother was a *machawi.*"

"She is much more than a sorceress, Lillian—a *Machawi-shaitani*—and soon you will be too. You and Penda are here to help with your mother's soul-crossing. Now listen."

"What? Wait. My mother is alive?" My heart beats frantically, overflowing with hope yet guarded against disappointment and disbelief.

"Yes, of course she's alive."

"Really? She's alive?"

"Yes, of course, why else would you be here? Ha-ha. Then you wouldn't know that because you haven't been here. Ha-ha. Oh well. Now focus, Lillian. Let's take care of your broken leg and then we'll talk about your mother's soul-crossing."

"Soul-crossing? As in crossing over to the other side? Is my mother dying?"

"Death is not something *Msafiri's* do. After you have healed your leg, we'll talk about it. Now please pay attention."

Her long fingers move fast and with feather-light touches, ripping away the tape and gauze. She positions my right hand an inch above the break on my left leg, and then let's go. "Time for you to do your part. Hold your hand still, and keep the scar centered over the break. Keep it there until you can no longer stand the heat."

I wait for more information but Ku-Mama remains silent, never taking her eyes off my hand. A crimson flame whips out of the scar and circles my leg then sucks my hand on top of the break and tightens. A surge of anxiety sends my stare to the old woman's eyes; she looks up but her eyes reveal nothing. Heat surrounds the broken bone and bites into my scorched skin— the temperature grows hotter. I grit my teeth; sweat peppers my brow and upper lip. I struggle, desperate to loosen my fingers from my leg but they refuse to budge.

"Ku-Mama, it's too hot." The old woman's eyes and mine remain locked. "Please," I beg her, "make it stop." She breaks eye contact and tilts her head forward, spilling sparks and gray dust between us, but she says nothing. The heat becomes unbearable. "Stop it!" I demand, and my hand releases my leg and the heat is gone.

"Very good. Your leg is mended."

"It is?" I move my toes and bend my knee. I twist my ankle from side to side. She's right, it's no longer broken.

"We weren't sure how this was going to work with your father's blood being in the mix but it doesn't seem to be a problem. Lesson one; if you control the light, you can trust it. I knew you were the one, even before you turned ten. I knew you were going to be a powerful *Machawi-shaitani.*" Ku-Mama stands and holds her hand out to me. I clasp it and she pulls me to my feet.

"I was a witchdoctor when I was ten?" I ask in a tentative voice while taking a cautious step forward.

"Witchdoctor. Ha! On your tenth birthday, when you knew nothing of your heritage, your powers were beyond any witch-doctor's voodoo. Voodoo is at the core of who we are, but voodoo is very basic. We are sorcerers of white magic not voodoo witchdoctors. You'll learn—you have to—our future and the future of the souls depend on it." Then as if to prove she's a sorcerer, she vanishes in a wave of dusty gray air, sprinkled with tiny white and gold sparks.

Alone, I reflect on what's just happened. I keep running this new information over and over in my brain. The most important being...my mother's alive. The thought of seeing her makes me want to skip and shout and behave nothing like a grown woman. I want to run to her and hold her in my arms. I want her to hold me. But what will I say to her? What will she say when she sees me? Funny, my whole life I've wanted a mother; now that I have one, I'm suddenly afraid to meet her. I'm frightened of so many things, in so many different ways.

I run my fingers through my hair in disbelief; a mother and a sorcerer, how can it be? The possibility of both being true seems to be supported by the fact that dad was so afraid of my mother and the powers she possessed, he went out of his way to keep her existence from me.

I rub the scar on my hand—it is no longer red or pulsating. I squint and strain my eyes but I can't make the white light flash, much less find it. The blue haze remains absent as does my ability to see auras. The only proof I have that any of this is real is my leg—it is no longer broken—and I have to admit, that's a big bunch of proof. Still, I'm having trouble wrapping the logical part of my brain around everything that's happened. One thing is for certain; I'm not as afraid of my eyes as I once was. I'm more frightened of me and what I might be. And I'm terrified of finding out what *Bayamchawi* wants from me.

Chapter 15

The sun lies across the canyon's floor like a tattered gold rug. The predators will be sleeping for hours, waiting for dusk before they start to hunt again. The uncertainty, the scared-to-death coldness that's holding onto my bones, isn't about the animals; it's about not knowing when my next encounter with *Bayamchawi* will be.

My leg is tender but that I'm able to walk on it at all is right up there with some weird science fiction fantasy movie. It's swollen, black and purple in the area of the break and I walk with a slight limp, but that's it. I've circled the remains of Miss Kitty twice. I found and have eaten one of Crane's wife's ham-and-cheese sandwiches. It was squashed flat as paper but tasted wonderful. The thermos of sweet coffee was shattered and undrinkable. I looked for my cell in the scattered wreckage, but I didn't find it. The bag with my clothing must have burned with the plane, I didn't find that either.

Discouraged and still unable to figure a way out of this mess, I walk back to the stream, checking the sky and listening for any sounds of rescue. At the water's edge, I settle on a boulder, wash my hands and face, then cup water in my hands and take a drink. The water is clear now that Crane's body has been taken away by the lion. My brain won't stop thinking about my leg. Some supernatural power that I possess healed it, knitted the bones together and made them whole. The ramifications of this, frightens and confuses the hell out of me. To imagine I have such powers is impossible. I wish David were here so I could show him my leg and say, "See, David, no more jambo-jambo, here is the proof."

"Kooee-kooee, I am proof, too," Ku-Mama chirps.

A scattering of gray dust floats to Ku-Mama's feet. My muscles tighten, still uncomfortable with her ability to appear, apparently out of nowhere.

"Okay, its magic," I sigh, massaging my shoulders to relax them. "I get it, I think? But how do you do it? How do you suddenly appear and disappear?"

"Let's start with the basics." Ku-Mama cranes her neck then settles herself on the large rock next to me. "I was *Machawi-shaitani* before your mother and after many other mothers. Now I am *Msafiri*, and your mother will soon be one, too."

"You were a high priestess of sorcery, and now you're a Traveler?"

"Yes. And you are to be our next high priestess. You are your mother's daughter and the next in line. You will be our *Machawi-shaitani*, and with that title there are going to be some challenges. It will be up to you to keep the gate to the spirit world open. Your mother and I thought, perhaps, we might have to use her niece, my granddaughter to take your place if we were unsuccessful in bringing you back to Africa. Pepo was anxious to assume the role, but she has so little magic. We had to face the reality that she might not have what it take to help with your mother's soul-crossing, much less be the next *Machawi-shaitani*. She wouldn't have stood a chance against *Bayamchwi*. We had to find a way to get you back to Africa. When the white elephant was spotted we knew she was the answer and the way to bring you home. So it was arranged to send Penda to your animal park in California.

"I thought David found her."

"He did. We allowed him to. Still it wasn't an easy decision to bring you back. We knew it would test your yet unproven powers and might get you killed. You know so little, but you are the only one who might be able to defeat *Bayamchawi*. From what little I've seen, I believe your powers to be extraordinary."

She raises her eyebrows, the white hair on her head quivers and shakes, sending a torrent of silver and gold sparks, raining into the water, splashing with hisses, sizzles and sighs.

"If you do not succeed, *Bayamchawi* will seize command of the gate and close it. He will lock the souls inside and let no others enter. Newly born souls will have no place to go. They will die when the body dies. David's soul and the other souls in transition will be trapped in limbo, unable to move on. *Bayamchawi* is beyond evil. He is the dark sorcerer of black magic and reigns over the underworld with fiendish pleasure. He needs to destroy the power of our white magic to fulfill his greatest desire; control and lock the gate. And when he does, *Bayamchawi* will rule both heaven and hell. There will be no limits to the evil he will do and there will be nothing good left on this earth. Lillian, you must take care, *Bayamchawi* will do whatever it takes to prevent your mother's soul-crossing and stop you from becoming the next *Machawi-shaitani*. You have so much to learn and very little time."

She leans in close. "On your tenth birthday, he tried to kill you. I intervened, but ultimately it was the daggers in your eyes and your father's faith in his God that saved you. When you turned twenty, *Bayamchawi* took your father's life, hoping you would no longer honor your promise to stay in the States and instead return to Africa where his powers would be strong enough to kill you. On your thirtieth birthday, David's love stood in *Bayamchawi's* way, so he took him, too."

"Why take David? Why not take me?"

"Penda was there, protecting you."

"Dad mentioned something in his note, he said my mother wanted me to know, the elephant and I were connected. Was she talking about Penda?"

"Your mother will explain the connection when you meet her. It is a story she didn't want Nanta to share with you."

"I overheard Nanta talking about the three tens. I thought when I turned thirty all the strangeness would be over."

"A misunderstanding. Your turning thirty was when everything was set to begin."

"Then why start when I was ten? Why kill dad when I was twenty? And why kill David?"

"I was a way to test your powers, and ultimately it became the way to get you back to Africa. To be honest, had you had no powers at all, you would have been killed on your tenth birthday. Your eyes were the thing that kept you alive and gave us hope. Had you been with your mother you would have embraced the magic.

"You would have learned."

"Ku-Mama, I don't know if I can do it. I don't know if I want to."

"For the souls and for your mother, you must try. David lost his life for this. Do it for him."

"For this? No, he didn't die for this. He didn't know this...existed...he didn't know you or my mother...existed. He didn't know...neither one of us knew or truly believed, voodoo existed. We didn't understand what was going on and I never understood my eyes. David didn't lose his life for this...he lost it because of me. I got him killed."

"Lillian, please..."

"Do you know where David's soul is?"

"When Penda was returned to Africa, David knew you would no longer care what dangers might face you or what promises you had made to him and your father. He suspected you would follow her. His soul is here in Africa."

"David's soul is here?"

"Yes." Her long toes curl and uncurl in the stream. "David's love is strong. He will help you when he can, but his soul is no match for *Bayamchawi*. You must be on guard at all times and not be afraid of your powers. You must learn to use them.

Bayamchawi will become more desperate the closer we come to your mother's soul-crossing. He will do everything in his power to prevent you from reaching Mlango."

"Mlango? Gatehouse?"

"Mlango is the house where your mother lives." Ku-Mama stills my next question with a stern raise of her brow. She remains silent while scratching the crown of white wisps on top of her head with her bony fingers and setting loose a tumble of dust and sparks. Her face softens then she looks into my eyes. "Lillian, I have no doubt you will be a powerful sorcereress, perhaps more powerful than either your mother or me. However, I don't know, no one knows for certain, if you will be able to defeat *Bayamchawi*. This white light that you flash is encouraging, but I'm not sure what it means. There's an old legend, a myth that speaks of *Ya-kale Wachawi*, a great sorcereress and a traveler of light...and there was that...event...when you were a baby." Her eyes shift then refocus on mine. "But that is just a curiosity and has nothing to do with what's happening now. What we must hope for is for your mother's soul-crossing to be successful and for your powers to be strong enough to keep *Bayamchawi* confined to the darkness until the next cross; yours and Penda's. Enough now. Let's concentrate on what you need to know."

"Mine and Penda's? How is Penda part of this?"

"Penda has always been involved. There is a prophecy involving three tens that we believe is connected to you and her, and the time of your birth. The ancient prophet Nabii wrote: *If she heals and the white elephant kneels, the soul-crossing is double-crossed. Two equals one when ten equals thirty and death comes before birth.*"

"What does that mean?"

"We believe the white elephant refers to Penda and 'she heals' refers to you. The rest will explain itself in time."

"There is so much to know and it is difficult to believe any of it. When I see David's soul and meet my mother, maybe then it will start to make sense."

"Seeing David's soul isn't up to you or him. It will happen when there is a need. Seeing your mother and getting to *Mlango* is something you must do without my help, and another test of your powers."

"But, Ku-Mama..."

"These tests will strengthen your powers, embrace them. We have only a few days to get you up to speed. I think that's how they say it in the states. But enough talk. Let me show you a few things that might help. You have always had certain powers. You had the blue haze to help you diagnose your sick animals. You just didn't know you could heal them by using your scar. Now close your eyes."

"Wait. How do you know what happened in the states?"

"I have been with you your whole life, Lillian," she shrugs, tips her head up and stretches her neck, then whistles a high pitched, "Kooee-kooee."

"You're the eagle?"

"Yes, and when the white one arrived, you saw gold and silver sparks and the light of my soul."

"That was your soul? I thought it was my mother's."

"Your mother is still living, so it could not be hers. I understand your confusion; your father told you she was dead."

"But Ku-Mama, you're alive. How could I have seen your soul, if you are not dead?"

"It's all part of who and what we are. You will understand in time. But time is short, we must hurry."

"The green eyes of the leopard were there when Penda arrived, too."

"Yes, *Bayamchawi* was there. My magic was stronger than his, and I was able to overpower him. You are your mother's daughter, Lillian, you have her blood. What's happening to you is your destiny. You must accept this. There are some things in life and in death we have no control over. This is one of those things."

"*Bayamchawi* was the leopard."

"Was and is."

"And the black-red mist? And the swarm of locust, that attacked Miss Kitty?"

"*Bayamchawi* can be many things, as can those who live with him in his lightless underworld. They can shift into many things. We don't know the limits of his black magic, but his evil grows more desperate the closer we get to your mother's soul-crossing. Let me show you something. Close your eyes."

Feeling as though I have no choice, if I am going to get any more answers, I close my eyes.

"What do you see?"

"The haze, the blue haze is back." I open my eyes and smile.

"Yes and the ability to see auras, is there, too. If you learn to..."

The distant *whap-whap-whap* of a helicopter turns my head, and I glance skyward.

"Ah, that will be your rescuers," Ku-Mama said. When I turn to face her, she's gone. All that is left is a circle of gray dust floating downstream.

The insistent staccato of the helicopter grows louder. When it is close, I stand and wave to the pilot behind the glass bubble, then watch anxiously as the fat-bellied craft descends. It lands a few yards away, kicking up a swirl of dust and dry grass. The pilot shuts the chopper's engine down and pops open the door. His thick hiking boots hit the ground with a solid thud. He's wearing a weathered bush hat, sunglasses, a tan T-shirt and tan shorts. His legs and arms are darkly tanned. Suddenly self-conscious, I brush the dirt off my torn and dirty clothes and fumble with the loose strands of my hair, tucking them behind my ears while walking toward him.

"Dr. Drake." The pilot removes his hat and sticks out a hand.

"Larry, Larry Kitchener. Glad to see you're all in one piece. Where's Crane?'"

I grasp his outstretched hand, "Mr. Kitchener, I can't tell you how happy I am to see you. I'm sorry, but Crane didn't make it."

"Man, I didn't want to hear that. He was a goofy little guy. He and Miss Kitty were a good team. It would have broken his heart to see her like that." Larry gestures in the direction of the burned wreckage. "Maybe it was the kindest thing to have happen, taking them together. It won't be the same without Crane. I can tell you that." He stares at the plane then back at me. "Looking at Miss Kitty, I'm surprised you made it out alive." His head pivots from side to side in disbelief. "Anyway, and ain't that a marvel, looking at her, I don't know how you survived a crash like that. But we're sure glad you did, Dr. Drake."

"Ah...I was lucky, I guess. And please call me Lill. So, how did you happen to find me? Africa's a big place."

"Lill it is, and likewise, call me Larry. We had a good idea where to look. Crane always flies this same route to Dzanga-Keita and he loves buzzing down between these cliffs. When you didn't show up yesterday evening, we figured something must have gone wrong. We tried his radio and his cell, when we got no reply we started to get concerned. Glad to see you made it safely through the night. We were worried about the predators but had to wait for daylight before we could start looking for you. Do you know where we can find Crane's body?"

"A male lion took part of it away this morning. I don't know where the rest is; may still be in the plane."

"We'll find what we can. I'll send some men back out this afternoon. We need to get Crane back to his wife so he can have a proper burial. Now let's get you in the bird and to the hospital."

"Hospital?"

"Stewart insisted. He said I'm to take you to the hospital, no matter what, and he's the boss. As soon as the doctor there gives you a thumbs up, I'll take you to Stewart's house, Tembo Nymuba. If your elephant's not there, we'll find her in Dzanga-Keita. Until then, it's the hospital, no arguments."

"Sounds like I'm going to the hospital. You're my only way out of here. No way am I going to mess that up." I flash him a smile. "So, how is Penda? I saw the picture Dr. Keita sent but how is she, really?"

"Stewart said you'd be asking and to tell you she's fine. To tell you the truth, she arrived in much better condition than you. Now let's get moving. We can talk on the way. Is that your only bag?" Larry points at the singed and battered medical bag on the ground.

"Yes, it's my veterinary supplies."

"No clothes?"

"Burned with the plane."

"Okay, I'll get this one," he said, reaching for the bag, "and I'll have my wife do some shopping for some new clothes. I have pen and paper in the chopper; you can write down your sizes and what other things you'll need."

"Thanks, but I won't be able to pay her back right away; my cell phone and wallet are missing, too." I limp after Larry, trying to keep up with his long strides as we head for the helicopter.

"Not a problem. Nancy, my wife, will be using Stewart's credit card. You can discuss reimbursement with him. How bad is your leg?"

"Not bad. A little banged up. A little sore, that's all."

A few hours later, I'm resting in a hospital bed, tired but clean; pillows fluffed, teeth brushed, hair washed. It's a rural hospital. The rooms are small and there aren't many of them, so I'm grateful to have the room all to myself. The shower was wonderful. The soap smelled more like disinfectant than Dove, but the water was warm. I was not surprised when I looked in the mirror to brush my hair and saw the gold daggers and blue pie-shaped lights back in my eyes. The thin band of silver circling my irises was there, too.

A tall and very thin East Indian man enters my room. He grins and walks quickly to my bed. He wears a white lab coat buttoned over a blue dress shirt and tan pants and carries a clipboard. Black-rimmed glasses sit on top of his head and a stethoscope dangles from his neck.

"Dr. Drake. Yes. Yes. Hello. You had a shower, I see. You must feel much better. Quite an ordeal you lived through out there by the cliffs. Larry has told me you are lucky to be alive." He extends his hand and we shake. "I'm Dr. Njuguna. Welcome to my hospital." He looks around the room with pride. "A nurse will be here in a minute to take some blood. It will be easy. She is our very best nurse." He waggles his long dark finger in front of me and then pulls a pen from his pocket and taps it on the clipboard. "Yes, yes. You have a million questions, I know, but you must be starving. So briefly I will answer the obvious ones. You will be staying with us overnight for observation. We are going to give you some antibiotics. I was told you were drinking the water in that stream; we must take precautions."

Dr. Njuguna's lanky thin frame moves with quick steps to the other side of my hospital bed. His intelligent eyes sparkle. "You were very lucky with this leg." He points at my left leg with his pen, "Very lucky indeed. I'm surprised it was not broken. Such bruising. So much swelling. It's a miracle. No magical pygmies out there in the bush to help you, were there?" Dr. Njuguna flashes a wide white smile then winks, laughing at his joke. "You're going to live. Yes, yes. You are going to have a fine life. Now rest and eat, I will be back later with your blood test results and to answer any questions." With that, the distinguished-looking doctor returns the pen to his pocket and leaves the room.

Chapter 16

We arrive in Tembo Nymuba in the late-afternoon the following day. The sun has a few more hours to go before the sky's wispy clouds fold into twilight of pink, orange and gray. Larry circles the helicopter above Dr. Keita's house, skimming the rooftop and the acre of partially-cleared land surrounding it and the long dirt road; the only way in and out of Dr. Keita's jungle oasis. The road widens beyond the house and serves as a landing strip for small airplanes. Then he soars out over the more than one hundred acres of tall trees and bush that make up the rest of the Dzanga-Keita Elephant Reserve.

Larry takes a few extra minutes to hover above the forest so I can search for Penda, but the jungle is too compact to see much of anything. After a few more minutes of not finding her, he guides the helicopter to the front lawn of Dr. Keita's house and sets the chopper down with a gentle back-and-forth roll and a soft thump.

The house and yard are steeped in wide strokes of shade and sunlight. Tall native trees grow close to the house on all four sides, and ferns spill over every walkway and under every tree. Tembo Nymuba would be hard pressed to see full daylight except for when the sun is directly overhead. A dirt driveway cuts off from the main road and leads to the front of the house, ending at the parking pad by the front steps. The porch extends the length of the house and down each side. Vines dripping thin green leaves and white flowers knot themselves up each porch post and cascade off the second story eaves.

Larry clasps the door handle then pauses, "Wait here. I'll help you out."

He jumps from the helicopter and rushes to open my door. Holding out a hand, he helps me onto the lawn. The grass curls over the top of my sandals and splashes against my toes in waves of cool greenness. Larry reaches in behind the passenger seat, grabs my medical bag and hands it over. Then he gathers the four shopping bags filled with new clothes and sundries, and holds onto their handles and stands next to me drinking in the serenity of Tembo Nymuba. In addition to the clothes in the bags, the ones I'm wearing are also from Nancy's shopping spree— white cotton bush pants, white tee, and comfortable sandals.

"Welcome to Elephant House, Lill."

"Thank you. It's quite impressive."

The house itself is two stories and looks like a cross between an old plantation house and a ranch house. It's painted pale gray; a shade of gray that reminds me of freshly scrubbed elephants. I wonder if it was named Elephant House because of its color, or if it was painted this color because of its name? Which came first the chicken or the egg? Dark gray shutters flank windows warmed by soft lighting coming from inside. A two-story tall window to the right of the front door exposes a large chandelier hanging from the high ceiling. Somewhere in the background a generator labors, providing electricity. I'm glad Dr. Keita has invited me to stay here. I couldn't imagine a more beautiful place to be reunited with Penda.

Earlier, Larry relayed a message from Dr. Keita, saying he apologized for not being home for my arrival but to make myself comfortable and he would see me for dinner. I have yet to meet the mystery man who has not only taken in Penda, but me, too.

"Shall we go in then?" Larry's voice is filled with enthusiasm.

"Would you mind if I stayed out here for a while? It's so peaceful, and it smells wonderful, not at all like the hospital."

"Not a problem. I'll take these bags and your medical bag and put them in your room."

"Thanks. You know, this is the first chance I've had to really enjoy being back in Africa." An unexpected shudder of dread spoils the moment, creeping from my toes to the top of my head, tapping my consciousness with the brutal truth of the dangers I face by returning. I shake the feeling off as best I can and focus on my surroundings. "This is quite a bit different then the village I grew up in." I look at the house and yard, "Everything is so green here."

"I'd say it's about the altitude; Nancy would tell you it's more about attitude. Either way, I get where you're coming from. I'll be right back. When you're ready to go inside, your room is on the ground floor. Turn right when you enter the house, go past the staircase, and through the door straight ahead." Larry climbs the wide steps up the front porch and disappears into the house.

Moments later he bounds down and rejoins me.

"I let Kipino know you're here," he says. "She's bringing sweet tea out to the porch, no rush to go inside. If there's anything you need, just let her know. The kitchen is through that screen door. Kipino is usually in there." He takes off his glasses, his hazel eyes puzzle mine. "Interesting; you haven't met Stewart yet, have you?"

"No. Why do you ask?" His knowing gaze makes me wonder what he sees in my eyes.

"Nothing, really, but I think you're in for a pleasant surprise." His smile is mischievous. "Take care of yourself, okay?"

"Thanks, Larry, I will, and thank Nancy for the clothes. Tell her I owe her."

"I'll let her know." His lips close in a knowing grin and I'm curious about the hidden meaning behind it. "I hope you get a lot of quality time with your elephant." He puts his sunglasses back on, walks toward the helicopter shaking his head, and, if I didn't know better, laughing.

When he has gone and the noise of his helicopter has faded, I take a deep breath and drink in the forgotten sounds and feel of Africa. It is much greener and cooler here at Tembo Nymuba than in Ndogo. It's the perfect place for Penda. A warm breeze blows across my face, touching it with happy memories of Dad and Nanta, current mysteries of Ku-Mama and my mother and the uneasy fear of black magic and *Bayamchawi*. I rub my scar and wonder if Nanta is still living in Ndogo and if she is, what will she be willing to tell me about my voodoo roots that Ku-Mama hasn't?

The screen door to the kitchen squeaks open. I glance over expecting to meet Kipino with a glass of sweet tea in her hand. Instead, a white-haired Nanta strides onto the porch and back into my life. Her pink sarong ruffles like flamingo feathers as she hurries toward me, barefoot, along the porch's wood planks. Nanta's face is saturated in joy. So is mine. I reach the bottom of the stairs just as she steps onto the lawn. Her long arms embrace my shoulders and pull me to her. I slip my arms around her waist and cling tight.

Click-click. The familiar sound of her African tongue tickles my ears with both happiness and sadness. So much has happened since we last saw one another and so much of it has been death.

"Nanta," I exhale into the dark creases of her neck.

Click-click. "There, there, Lill." Still tall and unbent after twenty years, her arms hug me close as I hold her tighter. When at last we separate, we keep our arms around each other's waist and walk, side by side, like long-lost sisters, up the steps onto the porch. Between the front door and the kitchen there is a cane table with four wicker-back chairs. Nanta guides me to one, she takes another and we sit facing each other, holding hands across the table. I've missed her. She bobs her head up and down and studies my face, and after all these years her eyes remain guarded and refuse to meet mine. I lean forward, closing the gap between us.

"Nanta, why are you here, at Dr. Keita's house?"

"I came to see you, of course." She squeezes my hands.

I squeeze hers in return, then sit back and soak in the renewed feelings of loving and being loved by Nanta. I had no idea, until now, how much I missed her and how little I appreciated her when I was a child. She had been like a mother to me.

"Nanta, did you know my mother was alive when we lived in Ndogo?"

"Yes, I knew."

"And you never told me? Ku-Mama said—"

"Ku-Mama...I should have known she'd talk to you. You would have been better off not knowing. Your mother is part of the reason I agreed and encouraged your father to take you to the United States; far away from Mbali's voodoo, to a place where you would be safe." She risks a quick glance at my eyes; her eyes blink dark then shy away. She stands with slow purpose.

"I'll get us some tea, then we can talk some more."

My stomach tightens as Nanta walks across the gray-painted boards toward the kitchen. She is still afraid of my eyes. Why? When she pauses to open the screen, I catch a vibration of odd light shifting near her heart. It fades before I have a chance to figure out what it is. I glance at the scar on my hand, it has turned pink.

"I heard about your David's passing." The screen door taps shut behind her.

"Who told you about David?" I ask, but I'd rather hear more about my mother than talk about David's death.

Nanta sets two ice-frosted glasses of tea on the table between us but remains standing. "Dr. Keita told me about David. Did you know Dr. Keita, Miles and David worked together to bring Penda here?" She eases into her chair and leans in. "And now you are here, too."

"David never mentioned anything about Penda coming to Africa. It doesn't make sense. He would have told me." I tap her left hand with my right as if touching her will ease my confusion. The scar begins to itch.

"Penda was meant to be in Africa." Nanta's words are suddenly harsh. "She was ready. She grew fast, and after all, Africa is where she belongs." Her voice softens as she continues, "You on the other hand, you should not have come. You should have stayed away." Nanta looks at our hands on the table, still refusing to meet my eyes, "To lose you again would be..."

"It wasn't supposed to happen this way, this soon...none of it was." I can hear the anguish and anger in my voice rising. The scar starts to pulsate and I worry it with my fingers.

"The drums started beating when you turned thirty. The three tens of your birth set your mother's soul-crossing in motion. They decided it was time to bring you home. They didn't ask me, but I would have told them it was a bad idea. They could have taught Pepo the things she needed to know. They could have made it work. But your mother insisted, she wanted you, and the quickest way to get you here was to have you follow Penda. Miles ran Dzanga-Bai for years. It's not close to Mbali but he heard the stories...he did what he could to help. He didn't know David would die, but when he did, he understood the urgency to bring both of you, you and Penda, back to Africa." Nanta stands. Her back is ramrod straight.

"Miles didn't want me to come, he tried to stop me."

"He knew that was the reaction you would expect from him. He also knew he couldn't stop you. I wish it hadn't come to this. I had hoped your father's blood would have lessened your powers, but it seems it didn't." Nanta edges toward the kitchen. "If you want to see your mother, while she's still alive..." She hesitates at the door. "...you must go to Mbali and find the way to Mlango." The sorrow in her voice trails to a whisper. "Now that you and Penda are here, none of us has a choice." She turns, opens the screen and steps inside. My scar turns crimson. I hold my hand toward the door.

"Nanta come back. We need to talk." The door flies open, taps the side of the house then bangs shut. No Nanta. I rush to the kitchen. Inside my shoulders jerk to a standstill. A startled African woman, with a large knife clutched in her hand, stands by the kitchen counter staring in my direction. Chopped vegetables rest on the cutting board in front of her. She is short, wide, and perhaps forty.

"Kipino?" I ask, at the same time notice a faint sent of burned toast in the air.

"Yes." She lowers the knife and resumes her chopping.

"Sorry, I didn't mean to frighten you, but did you happen to see..."

"Nanta? Yes, I saw her. She ran out the back door. She was in a big hurry."

"Did she say where she was going?"

"No." Kipino turns her stout body toward me. Her black tangle of hair bounces like a lion's mane in a wind storm around her face. Her feet are bare, and she wears a red and orange ankle-length kaftan. "Would you like some more tea?" She points to the half-full pitcher on counter.

"No, thank you. I think I'll just go back outside and enjoy what's left of the day."

An uneasy feeling chills my blood as I lean against the porch rail watching the scar on my palm turn cold and white. I puzzle over Nanta's sudden escape and massage the scar with my thumb, determined to figure out how to make it work. I'm beginning to suspect that my life and possibly Penda's life may depend on it.

Honk-honk. A white Land Rover, covered in dust, swings off the main road and down the driveway. It crunches to a stop by the porch, sending small stones tumbling against the bottom stair. The driver's door yawns open. A slender black man with white sprinkles tucked in his hair stretches out of the front seat, waving his wide hand in my direction. He's wearing bush clothes, tan pants and a long-sleeved khaki shirt, rolled to the elbows. His long-legged stride carries him quickly to the front of the vehicle.

"Jambo, Dr. Drake," his deep voice booms. "Welcome to Tembo Nymuba. Welcome to my home."

He bounds up the stairs and lifts my hand with a firm handshake before I have a chance to utter a word. The scar below his left cheek intrigues me, but it's the heat rising between our hands that make us both look up. An opaque-gold ghost-light shimmers across his dark brown eyes. The heat of our joined hands grows more intense. I am the first to let go.

"Well, well, so you really are the one...it is and it isn't a surprise." He laughs then laughs again.

"Dr. Keita, I don't know what you find so amusing, and right now I really don't care," the chilling tone of my voice stifles his cheerful mood. "I understand before David...before Dav..." My eyes tear up as I struggle to keep my composure. I inhale a breath and fiddle a stray hair from my face and start again. "Before my husband died...you, Miles and, I've been told, David had been conspiring to bring Penda to Africa. It's impossible for me to believe that David was involved. He never would have kept her leaving a secret."

"Aaah, yes, that. David was going to wait until after your 30th birthday to tell you. He said you had other things to worry about. I believe Miles tried to talk to you before Penda was shipped over. He said it would be important for you to tell her goodbye. He actually did try to postpone her trip, out of respect for David's untimely death, but it couldn't wait. Things here have escalated, and the arrangements had already been made, so..." He spread both his hands out in front of him, kind of like saying, there was nothing we could do. "Miles called me after you left and explained the miscommunication about Penda coming to Africa. But after seeing your eyes, I think your being here was unavoidable."

"Dr. Keita..."

"Please call me Stewart, and I will call you Lill. We have much to talk about. I see Kipino has brought you some sweet tea and left a glass for me, too. Please, let's have a seat." He motions with a hand to the chair opposite him but we both remain standing. "It's uncanny how that woman knows almost to the minute, when I'll be home."

"It was Nanta who brought the tea. She was the one who told me about the three of you working together." Stewart reaches out and touches my elbow as his face creases with concern.

"Nanta?" His voice sounds troubled. He lowers his hand and glances at the kitchen door then back at me.

"The woman who raised me when Dad and I lived in Ndogo."

"And you saw her here? At my house?"

"Yes." My jaw closes on the unreasonable fear rising up the back of my throat.

"Hum, I'll speak with Kipino about her visit later. I'm sorry she didn't stay. I would have liked to have talked to her."

I look into his Stewart's eyes, questioning the urgency in his voice, and I'm shocked when I see David's blue-green eyes staring back. I sway, dizzy, and reach for the back of the chair. Stewart grabs my arm.

"Kipino!" he shouts in the direction of the kitchen, "please bring some ice water to Dr. Drake's room."

"I'm alright, really." I dare a second look. David's eyes are no longer there, and I wonder if I saw them at all. Stewart keeps hold of my arm and guides me into the house.

The interior can only be described as elegant. Glowing lights fill the spacious main room. The chandelier hangs with soft light from the second-story ceiling. Wall sconces shine ambient light on the rich-wood walls. Floor lamps next to and behind the sofa and chairs radiate causal sophistication and lend a bit of coziness. Plush dark-green draperies frame the windows, floor to ceiling. Dark rattan furniture upholstered in rich taupe, caramel and green blend together, promising decadent comfort. The stairway leading to a second floor landing flanks the right side of the room. A dozen or more spears, some with sharp metal arrowheads, others with bone-white tips, hang on the wall from the bottom step to the top. Under the staircase there is a mirrored bar, carved from rich dark wood. Two slim lamps sit on top of it, the mirror reflecting sparkling wine glasses and bottles of liquor. Stewart Keita is a wealthy man.

"Your home is lovely."

"Thank you. Now let me take you to your room. About Penda, Lill, I understand her coming here happened at the worst possible time..."

"An understatement." My heart collapses around the loss of David and the loss of Penda to Africa. A catch in my breath gives my grief away. "Tell me about Penda," I ask, forcing a halfhearted smile. "How is she? How was she when she arrived? Is she happy?"

Stewart pauses at the bottom of the staircase. Two exquisite hand-tooled elephant heads adorn each newel post. He motions me in through the open door of the guest bedroom with one hand while still holding onto my arm with the other.

The bedroom is as elegant as the living room and comfortably large. Fabrics of gold and olive blend in delightful harmony with the honey-colored walls. The bags from Nancy's shopping trip are lined up on the bench at the end of the bed. My singed veterinary bag, sit on the floor beside it.

"Penda arrived in splendid condition," Stewart explains, stopping in the center of the room, "and was thrilled her long trip was over, I'm sure." He lets go of my arm and faces me, "You got the photo I sent to your iPhone, yes?"

"Yes. I meant to thank you for that. It was a wonderful surprise."

"As you could see, Penda was easily accepted by our elephant herd, which didn't surprise me. She is a very special elephant. Your medical charts arrived with her; she's grown another half-inch. We haven't seen her for a few days, but now that you're here I'm sure she'll show up. However, your diversion to talk about Penda instead of your dizzy spell did not go unnoticed and does little to change the fact that you need to rest. That plane crash had to have been terrifying, especially with Crane getting killed and all." He clears his throat then changes the subject. "I think you have everything you'll need." He indicates Nancy's shopping bags. "The bathroom is through that door on the left. If there is anything else you want, please ask."

"It's a beautiful room, thank you. It's perfect." Directly in front of me, two French doors open onto the side porch. Looking past them to the green jungle outside I add, "All of it is."

"The sun rises on this side of the house," Stewart gestures to the open doors, "although the jungle doesn't allow much light in until the middle of the day."

"Bwana, Keita." Kipino's thick African accent addresses Stewart.

We both turn. She's holding a silver tray. A glass pitcher of ice water sits in the middle with an empty glass beside it. She walks silently into the room and pauses in front of us. A wide smile parts her lips.

"Thank you, Kipino. I'll take that." Stewart reaches for the tray. Kipino glances over at me; a startled look crosses her face the second our eyes meet. The tray crashes onto the honed-wood floor, breaking the handle off the pitcher and splashing water everywhere.

"I'm sorry," Kipino whispers as she stoops to pick up the tray and the broken glass then hands them to Stewart.

"It's all right, Kipino these things happen. No damage done. Why don't you get some towels from the bathroom, no need for a mop."

Kipino's quick steps take her to the bathroom and back. She drops two bath towels on the puddle, bends and sops up the water then stacks the towels on top of the tray in Stewart's hands. He adds the broken pitcher and glass and Kipino eases out of the room.

Stewart's eyes meld into mine, "It's your eyes, Lill. None of us...ah, we thought it would be Ku-Mama's granddaughter who would be the next *Machawi-shaitani*. We held little hope that you would risk coming to Africa, considering the dangers you'd face. None of us expected Hata's daughter to return."

"You know more about my mother and, I suspect, me... than I do. Care to fill in the blanks?"

"I'll do what I can but it is complicated. Why don't you take a few minutes to freshen up then meet me in the kitchen, I need to speak with Kipino. If you would rather rest, dinner's at seven and we can talk then."

Chapter 17

Before changing clothes, I step through the French doors onto the porch and watch *Jua's* orange fireball slip slowly behind the jungle's tall trees, ending another day. Her fading light tints the clouds rose and the sky is transformed into a multicolor slideshow. In the encroaching twilight the moon grows brighter and, for some reason the scar on my palm radiates heat and turns pink. I haven't a clue why. It will be one of many things I'm going to ask Stewart about.

A half-acre of grass is all that separates my bedroom from the jungle. Evening monkeys and birds chatter happily in the surrounding trees and brush. The smells of a warm day and a cooling forest spin together disputing ancient prophesies and legends I know nothing about. I'll have to ask Stewart about them, too. The scar turns crimson. Unsure of what I'm doing but too curious to wait for Stewart to enlighten me, I aim my scar at the forest.

"Penda, where are you?" Nothing happens. I check my palm. The scar is still red. I try again. "Penda, I need you," my voice is somewhat stronger this time.

Then, like a child playing peek-a-boo, Penda's white head and large ears push timidly through the ever-darkening jungle. She flaps her ears and shakes her head then smashes out of the trees and races toward me trumpeting the whole way.

"Penda!" I shout, stretching my body over the porch rail, reaching out, longing to hold her. Her trumpets grow louder and she flips her trunk in excited circles above her head, sending silver shadows of moon glow streaking across her body. When she reaches the porch she drapes her white trunk across my shoulders, sniffing my neck and hair. I grab the end of her trunk with both hands and hold it close to my face, smelling her damp breath and feeling her inhale the scent of me. Penda's ivory tusks rake against the wood rails. Female African elephants' tusks grow as large as the males, but even so, Penda's are exceptional. Her low-throated rumbling shakes the porch and sends goose bumps skittering down my spine. We are connected. We are one.

"I thought I heard an elephant!" Stewart's voice precedes him through the open bedroom door. Happy, I turn to face him. He cuts off any further conversation when he sees Penda standing behind me. A broad smile creases his face. "Aha, I see you two have found each other. I'll leave you alone." He steps back and closes the door behind him.

Penda rumbles, trumpets and blows warm air through her trunk, filled with happy squeaks and squeals, into the center of her ear. Unable to contain my joy any longer, I climb over the rail and join her on the lawn. Penda lowers her head and kneels. I grab hold of the top edge of her ear and place my left foot firmly on her left leg.

"Foot," I cue, and with a swift lift of her leg, I'm on my way. I do a half twist in mid-air and slide easily onto her neck and tuck my legs snugly behind her ears. She rumbles with delight. Over and over she carries me to the edge of the forest and races back again, like a happy child playing tag. Then she slows and walks the perimeter of Stewart's property. In the glow of the moonlight I begin to tell her everything that has happened in short time I've been in Africa. Every once in a while, she taps my leg with her trunk, reinforcing the fact that we are together. I lean over and hug her head in response. I tell Penda about David's soul being here, and I tell her I have a mother who lives in Mlango. I describe the plane crash, the locusts, and Ku-Mama. I tell her how Ku-Mama said we are both here to help with my mother's soul-crossing, although I haven't been told exactly what that entails. I tell her that I might be the next

Machawi-shaitani and I'm not exactly sure what that means, either. It seems rash and perhaps dangerous to even think about staying but I lean over and whisper in her ear, "I think I'm going to stay in Africa, Penda. Without David, you are all I have."

Dad's warning stills my heart, but what can I do? There is something so profound that connects us, it can't be explained. It can only be felt. I think I always knew the promises to never return to Africa were lies. In the back of my mind I suspected that once I was reunited with Penda, I'd never be able to leave her. And now that I know my mother is alive...how can I leave? I'm anxious to meet my mother and to have her meet Penda. In some small corner of my heart, I've always know Africa is where I belong.

An unexpected surge of apprehension runs under my skin. Will *Bayamchawi* kill me if I stay? I push the thought aside. It matters, but it doesn't. I'm not leaving Penda and I'm not leaving David's soul to be trapped in some sort of voodoo limbo. I'll do whatever I can to help with my mother's soul-crossing and worry about the consequences later.

"Penda," I lay my cheek on her head, "what have I gotten myself into?" She rumbles a soft reply. Strangely, it lightens my mood and makes me smile.

When we are back in front of the French doors I tap my foot gently on Penda's shoulder, cueing her to help me down. She raises her leg. I slide from her neck, plant my feet firmly on top of it, then hop to the ground. I scratch her warm wet tongue and marvel at how wonderful it is to be with her again. My mother was right; I am connected to the elephants, especially Penda. I close my eyes and let the blue haze surround her.

"Oh my God, Penda." My eyes snap open. "You're pregnant!" I wrap my arm around her trunk and start making plans. I'll call Jan and Miles in the morning to let them know Penda's pregnant, and that that makes it impossible for me to leave Africa; it's as if the gods have conspired to keep me in here. I stroke Penda's jaw then worry about *Bayamchawi* harming her to get to me. I silence my fears knowing, she'll be safe once my mother's soul-crossing is over. I've got to talk to Stewart and see what needs to be done.

Somewhere in the house a clock chimes, telling me its 6:30. "Penda, I have to go, but I'll see you tomorrow, okay? Take care of yourself and your baby." The thought of Penda having a baby, plasters a huge grin on my face.

I mash my lips against her trunk and give her a flurry of goodnight kisses. When I've finished, I grab hold of the porch rail, pull myself up, climb over then reach back and give her cheek a quick kiss.

"Love you. Goodnight. See you tomorrow."

Penda trumpets and backs away. Another elephant hidden within the darkness of the trees answers her. She spins and hurries away. I watch until the tip of her white tail disappears into the jungle. I close and lock the French doors with a sigh and a pounding heart. I think I'll keep the decision to stay in Africa to myself for now. I want to hear what Stewart has to say about my mother and what needs to be done for her soul-crossing before I tell him of my plans to remain in Africa.

I take a quick shower. After I've dried off, I clip my hair away from my face then look in the mirror and watch the dagger lights dance in my eyes; I am curious and at the same time terrified to learn what they can do. While I'm thinking about my eyes and the ghost-light in Stewarts, I begin to empty out the four bags of clothes on top of the bed, seeing for the first time all the things Nancy bought. She has included a traditional African kaftan, along with everyday pants, tops, a lightweight jacket, dress and shoes. I choose the short green dress and slip it on over my head. Deciding to leave my feet bare, I hurry out.

Stewart is standing at the bar twisting a cork out a bottle of red wine. He nods over his shoulder when he hears me approach and sets the bottle down then turns and takes my right hand in both of his. This time our hands remain cool.

"Green is your color, Lill, it suits you. Your eyes are quite active this evening, I suspect it has something to do with Penda. You had a nice visit with her?" Stewart releases my hand and resumes opening the bottle.

"She's so happy. It is amazing to see her running free."

The cork makes a little pop sound. "Wine?" Stewart asks, not waiting for response and pouring us each a glass. He hands me one and takes up the other. "I'm not surprised Penda knew you were here and came to see you. It's obvious there's an extraordinary connection between you two." He raises his glass. "Welcome home. Welcome back to Africa." We clink our glasses together, smell the bouquet and take a sip.

"Thank you. Muum, this is good. Cabernet?"

"Yes. Glad you like it."

"Stewart, did you happen to notice Penda being bred?"

His eyes register surprise before he answers, "What? No. Why do you ask?"

"I pretty sure she's pregnant."

"Really?" His face fills with skepticism.

"Women's intuition," I say smugly.

"I think it's more than that. He holds up his glass, "Well, here's to Penda and your intuition." He winks.

"To Penda and her baby," we clink our glasses together, again.

"Come, we shouldn't keep Kipino waiting." He carries the bottle of wine and his glass in his left hand and gently guides me by the elbow with his right.

I hadn't really paid much attention when I followed Nanta into the kitchen earlier, so I'm not surprised when I notice the décor is quaint, in a sophisticated English cottage sort of way. And the smells – chicken, tomato and Italian spices—the aroma stabs my heart; a painful reminder of the dinner David and I shared at Caruso's the night before I turned thirty...the night before he died. My lips tremble. I can feel my eyes and nose turning red. My throat clamps shut.

Noting my distress, Stewart pours more wine into my glass then moves to the pot on the stove and stands next to Kipino, giving me time to pull myself together. "It smells delicious," he announces, dipping a big wooden spoon in the sauce and taking a taste. He grins. "One of your best, Kipino." She grins back. "Chicken cacciatore with an African twist," he directs this in-formation at me but stays by the stove, allowing a little more time for me to collect my emotions. "It's one of my favorite dish-es. I hope you'll like it as much as I do," he says, walking back to the table.

I press my fingers to the corners of my eyes to dry them.

Stewart pulls out my chair, takes my glass, setting it on the table while I sit. "I like to keep it simple. I'm by myself most of the time and eating in the kitchen feels homey. I hope you don't mind."

"It's perfect." I smile across the table as Stewart pulls his chair in but I have to look away when unwanted tears start to flow from my eyes. I pick up my napkin and wipe them away.

"Lill?" Stewart's voice is filled with concern.

"I'm sorry. I don't know what's going on. I don't know why I'm crying so much. It's just that..." My throat catches a sob but my voice lays bare my sorrow. "I miss David. I miss him every single day." I suck back my anguish and stutter a faint, "Sorry." I hide my tear in the napkin.

Stewart is polite enough to remain quiet while I pull myself together. I take a deep breath and tuck my broken heart away and change the subject. "Kipino, the cacciatori...my mouth is watering. This reminds me of my dad. He and I ate our all our meals in the kitchen, too." I brave a weak smile.

"Not something I want to do, remind you of your dad," Stewart states, then suddenly becomes intent on watching Kipino preparing our dinner. I suspect he's lonely and been a bachelor far too long.

"So, where do I start?" I ask, working at sounding cheerful while smoothing the wrinkles from the mess I've twisted into my napkin. My eyes puddle and my chin quivers, giving in to my grief. "It was easier being around people I knew; I had to be the strong one. I don't know...now that I'm here with Penda, it seems so much harder."

"May I ask the first question, then? It's about David." Stewart's eyes soften at the corners.

"Of course," I sniffle back what I hope will be the last of my tears.

Stewart takes his time unfolding his napkin, shaking it out and placing it on his lap, giving me time to change my mind if I want, but I wait him out.

"If you don't want to talk about David, I understand. It's okay. I'm just curious about one thing."

"Please, it's alright, really." I fake a smile and my eyes remain dry.

"Miles said David died of a heart attack."

I take a drink of wine, letting my lips linger on the rim and hiding my face behind the bowl while gathering the courage to answer without crying.

"Lill, are sure you're okay talking about this?"

I lower the glass, "No. Yeah. Yeah, actually, I'd like to talk about it. I have to warn you, though, it might make me cry," my voice falters.

"Okay, if you're sure."

"I'm sure." My throat tightens, but I manage to keep the tears at bay.

"Lill, we can do this later."

"No, no." I use my napkin to blot my eyes. "It's okay, honest. It's just tough."

"I lost someone I loved, too. I understand completely."

"You've lost someone, too? I'm sorry."

"Thank you. And you're right, it is tough. The pain never goes away, but it does get easier."

"I hope so," I sniff.

"Miles said David had a heart attack. I only talked with David on the phone but he sounded healthy. He never mentioned he had a problem. In fact, just the opposite; he said he was training to run a marathon. I was wondering if his death might have had something to do with you."

I chew on my thumbnail while I answer, "I think you know more about that..." I lower my thumb and brave to meet his eyes. "...than I do."

"I was thinking David's death might be connected with you returning to Africa."

"I don't want to think so, but I'm afraid you might be right." Stalling, I take a sip wine before continuing, "It's nice to able to talk about what happened with someone who won't think I'm crazy. And you're right, it wasn't a heart attack. It was *Bayamchawi*."

"I thought he might be involved. *Bayamchawi* will do whatever it takes to stop your mother's soul-crossing. Apparently that includes showing up in the states. But he needed you back in Africa in order to kill you; where his voodoo has enough magic to overpower you. That's why he took your dad's life and David's. He couldn't get to you, so he took them."

Tears fill my eyes as I choke out the words, "Because of me, David and my dad are dead. You know, I promised both of them I wouldn't come back to Africa. And I wouldn't have, if it hadn't have been for Penda and *Bayamchawi* had nothing to do with that. Did he?" I stare into Stewart's eyes, waiting for an answer.

He looks down, breaking contact, choosing his words carefully before he answers. "It's not your fault, Lill. You can't blame yourself. Perhaps, if your dad hadn't hid the truth from you in the beginning, things would have turned out differently."

I struggle to hold back the tears and the guilt I feel, focusing on Kipino at the stove, trying to push the images of their deaths away. She opens the oven. The smell of the fresh baked bread fills the room and breaks through my torment. I glance across the table at Stewart, wipe my eyes and settle my sorrow, as best I can.

"My turn to ask a question?" My voice falters, but I refuse to give in to the pain.

"Only one?"

"The first one, there are a bunch more, I promise. Stewart, when I looked into your eyes earlier today, seeing the fuzzy-gold light flow across them startled me. But what I saw next...what I saw was David's eyes. David's real eyes; they took the place of yours. That's what made me lightheaded."

"Lill, we have different powers, you and I. I'm a *Machawi-saa*, a mediator of sorts. I give souls extra earth time, if they need it; time to communicate with those still living. The eyes you saw were David's. He wanted you to know he's here." Stewart's smile widens.

"Hypothetical. What would happen if I didn't stay?"

"There is no hypothetical. From the moment you set foot on African soil, there was no turning back. You will have to destroy *Bayamchawi* if you want to leave Africa alive.

"And my mother's soul-crossing?"

"*Bayamchawi* must, at all costs, prevent you from becoming *Machawi-shaitani* and to do that he must stop your mother's soul-crossing. If you fail at either, the gate will be closed and locked, and *Bayamchawi's* evil powers will consume everything good on earth. I'll teach you what I can, but there's not much time."

Kipino spoons a heaping serving of cacciatori onto each of our plates then sets a basket of her homemade bread in the middle of the table. While she is doing this she glances at my eyes and this time when our eyes connect, she doesn't drop a thing, she smiles. I notice there are lights in her eyes too; silver-lights, with subtle sparks of gray. Stewart catches this exchange between us.

"Kipino's powers are quite unique." He glances over at her and their eyes exchange a silent message. Worry lines pinch Stewart's brows together. Kipino tilts her head in the direction of the window. He raises and walks swiftly over, then cups his hands on the glass to block the reflection of the kitchen lights.

"Stewart?" I ask, joining him at the window. Kipino joins us, too.

"Kipino?" Stewart asks.

"We need to get ready." Kipino's voice is resolute.

"What's going on?" My heart bangs in my chest.

"It seems a welcoming committee has come to greet you." Stewart hurries out of the kitchen and into the living room.

Kipino and I follow, standing on each side of him and looking out the tall window next to the front door. A thin, thirty-foot line of twisted yellow light burns from a gash cut in the earth at the edge of the jungle. An angry breeze sparks the jagged line and whips a wave of yellow vapor across the road and sends it speeding to the porch, engulfing the vine-wrapped posts. The vile fog pauses, as if inhaling the scent of us then recoils with a backlash of screams into the ruptured earth.

"Lill, keep the scar on your hand concealed. If you show it, it will bring them to us and trust me; that's the last thing we want."

"Them?" My throat tightens.

The acid-colored fissure expands another ten yards then coughs out a blazing tower of yellow flame. The fire-ball explodes into the air. We exchange looks. I rub the heat rising from my scar and try to conceal the fear causing my hands to shake.

"Stewart, what's going on?" I ask, as the heat in my eyes builds and the scar begins to pulsate.

"The daggers in your eyes—use them," he orders then turns away from the window to focus on the spears attached to the stairway wall.

"But I don't know how to make the daggers do anything. I've tried but I can't control them." Kipino and Stewart exchange worried looks.

"The scar, Lill. Touch it to your cheek. It will bring the power of the daggers to your eyes."

Stewart stretches his arm to the wall of spears and opens his hand exposing his own scar. He spreads his fingers wide. Near the top of the stairs a long black spear with a silver tip, strains against its restraints, wrenches free, and sails into Stewart's outstretched hand. He clutches his fingers around the shaft and with deliberate precision he draws the tip of the spear across the ragged scar on his cheek. The point flares red and his scar turns crimson.

"Lill, ready or not, it looks like you're going to have to use your powers tonight." I shoot him a panicked look. My mouth opens but I'm speechless.

The three of us stare back out the window, watching intermittent yellow towers of vapor and flames erupt from the fissure when suddenly, an oscillating wall of flames shoots across the yard. We twist away from the blast of heat when it hits the window then quickly refocus on what is happening outside. A different kind of light, a dull greenish light bubbles out of the earth. It churns and coils, piling up thick-tumbles of flesh that slithers along the edge of the ditch. My skin bristles as the terror spews across the road.

"I have a bad feeling about this. Kipino, Lill. Common, let's go outside and have a real look." Stewart moves to the front door, opens it, and steps onto the porch.

I shoot Kipino a concerned glance. Her eyes reassure me then she tilts her chin upward with steady determination and walks out. I'm hesitant, but right behind her.

Stewart looks over his shoulder, "Kipino, please, we need to know what we are up against."

Kipino moves past Stewart to the edge of the steps. She cups her hands around her eyes, like blinders on a horse. A gray beam of light radiates from her eyes. As she spreads her arms, the beam widens and illuminates everything from the porch to the acid-green vapor and flames at the edge of the jungle.

"Snakes," Stewart says. "Fitting, considering who we're dealing with."

I watch, terrified, as a nightmarish multitude of black mambas slither out of the crack. They are adult, easily six to eight feet long, the largest and most venomous snake in Africa. The olive color of their skins is strangely dull and eerily white in Kipino's gray light. Their open mouths sample the air with wet-black flesh. White fangs bracket their long split-tongues as they search for something or someone to kill.

"Mambas are very bad voodoo," Kipino warns.

Stewart moves to Kipino's left side. He motions with his hand for me to join them on his right. "Lill, use your daggers to kill the mambas and clear a path for me. I have to get the edge of that hole to close it. Kipino will—"

"Stewart, I've never killed an animal. It's not what I do. I'm a veterinarian, I save them."

"*Bayamchawi* sent these mambas here to kill you. And believe me, they are not animals. They are not even alive. Kipino, show her."

Kipino lifts her right hand and holds it up in front of her. As she brings her thumb and finger into a circle the night folds in around it. A sharp beam of concentrated light flows from Kipino's eyes: down her arm, through the circle, and out across the yard. The spotlight settles on the head of one, very large mamba. The snake's body coils in protest then straightens and spews out toxic venom; its black mouth glistens behind deadly fangs. A swooshing sound swells from Kipino's light-beam, magnifying the creature's head and eyes. The viper's eyes are empty.

"That's impossible. How can they be dead? They're moving."

"They are dead, but more poisonous and dangerous than if they were alive, so be extremely careful. Now, let's get rid of the damn things."

Kipino lowers her arm. Once again the yard is awash in the gray light. The black mambas' numbers have grown. They blanket the road, whipping their massive bodies toward the house.

"Lill, until I can close up that trench they will just keep coming. We'll have to move fast, if we're going to stop them."

"Okay," my voice falters, exposing my doubt.

Stewart takes my right hand in his. I can feel our joined scars heat up.

"Do it for your mother and Penda. Do it for David's soul. Do it for all the souls. Believe in yourself and the power of your magic." Stewart lets go, then presses my scar against my cheek. The daggers in my eyes flame. "Good," his voice remains serious.

We step past Kipino and down the steps. The taste of fear sucks my mouth dry as soon as my bare feet touch the earth. I should have worn shoes.

The snakes are knotted and crawling over each other frantic to reach us. They are already to the center of the yard and moving fast. I shoot Stewart a nervous look.

He gives me a reassuring nod. "We can do this."

The mambas lift their bodies and let out a deafening hiss. Daggers shoot from my eyes in staggering numbers as we rush their frontline. Round after round the daggers slice into the snakes, stabbing them with molten flames and sending their charred remains tumbling and falling to the ground. We keep moving but they keep coming. Stewart uses his spear to stab and push aside the mambas within his reach. A slithering body brushes over my feet. Repulsed, my body jerks back, I aim the daggers and miss, too high. The snake coils then rises up, his head mere inches from mine. My resolve falters, the daggers won't fire. I look to Stewart for help but he's fighting his own battle. It's hopeless, the snakes have us surrounded. There is no way we can win. The mamba rears back his head getting ready to strike.

In the second before my death, a searing pain flashes through my eyes. It's hard to breath. A blazing white-bolt of light shoots a deadly charge into the mamba's mouth. The monster screams and the light consumes him and the other snakes that had encircled us.

"Nice touch," Stewart shouts, as more mambas rush in to take their place.

I press the scar against my cheek, and the daggers respond; shooting faster, hotter and farther; they melt, burn, and rip apart the mambas blocking are way. We keep advancing; just another two feet to the edge of the abyss.

"Lill," Stewart warns, "behind you!"

I spin, shooting daggers in a wide spray and killing everything within range.

"Impressive. Keep it up, we're almost there."

The heat from the pit intensifies the closer we get, but I'm determined the dark sorcerer is going to lose this battle, a small payback for David's death. A foot to go and the heat, is almost unbearable. The snakes aren't giving up and neither are we. We keep inching forward.

Smoke, sparks, and the smell of charred snakes saturate the air as dagger after dagger drives the reptiles from our feet. At last Stewart is standing at the edge of the pit. He thrusts the tip of his spear into the acid-yellow flames. He rears back and plunges his spear into the crater a second time.

A raging voice from beneath the flames threatens. "This time you lose, sorcerer."

The sound of *Bayamchawi's* voice momentarily shatters my nerves, but I refocus and keep my daggers trained on the black mambas.

"We'll see about that, *Bayamchawi.* Give up and go back to the hell you came from." Stewart lifts his spear and drags the tip against his cheek. The spear's silver point glows red. He stabs it into torn earth for a third time then begins to turn the handle with both hands. The earth responds and starts to pull together.

"This is not over!" *Bayamchawi* shrieks. The ground rumbles, and hundreds of black mambas are yanked backwards, screaming, into the blackness beneath the dying blaze. The earth erupts with acid smoke. Stewart lifts his spear and drives it into the crater one final time. The abyss closes and the night falls silent.

The scorched earth smolders as tendrils of rocks and stones tumble together over the cooling trench, like a bandage sealing a wound. Stewart transfers the spear to his left hand. The heat along my scar subsides and my eyes cool. Tired and drained from battle, we walk side by side, joining Kipino on the porch.

"Stewart...?" My voice falters, unable to continue.

"Things have accelerated. The drums are beating. We need to get ready for your mother's soul-crossing. You must leave for Mbali at dawn."

Chapter 18

Endless green shadows tap the morning's shoulder as we wait for Larry and his helicopter to arrive. Apprehension and a sleepless night filled with worry and doubt make me vaguely aware of drinking coffee from the tall blue mug in my hand, as I try, again, to comprehend the terror of the snakes...daggers shooting from my eyes, and the sound of *Bayamchawi's* voice.

Larry is flying me to the edge of Mbali this morning, a short hop, where I will slip inside the jungle and find my way to Mlango and my mother. Stewart tells me this will be possible because I am a sorcerer. He warns me to keep the sun at my back and to be very careful. He loans me his backpack, and I fill it with food and water, my blowgun and tranquilizing darts, just in case I need something more than magic. I wear a red T-shirt, long tan cotton pants, hiking boots and thick socks; I'm not taking any chances of being bitten by snakes...dead or alive.

"You're pretty quiet, Lill." Stewart brings his coffee cup to his lips and takes a long drink.

"I have a lot to think about."

"I wish I could go with you, but I can't. You have to find Mlango on your own; you must earn the right to be the next *Machawi-shaitani.*"

Before I have the chance to ask him how I'm supposed to do that, the deafening sounds of Larry's helicopter descends on us and drown out any further conversation.

Larry and I talk very little during the flight to Mbali, and as we land I childishly cross my fingers and make a wish that I will reach my mother in time to help with her soul-crossing.

"Thanks for the ride!" I shout over the noise of the rotor tips,

open the door and lift the backpack off the floor, getting ready
to exit.

"My pleasure. Keep safe, Lill."

"I'll do my best." Hopping from the chopper, I sling the
backpack over one shoulder, give Larry a quick wave and set
out to walk the short distance from the helicopter to the
baobab trees.

The moment the helicopter slips from sight and sound, the air
at the edge of Mbali begins to shimmer in distorted sheets of
transparent green light. Knowing my fate lies within the mist, I
take a deep breath and step beneath the cross nailed to the
center tree; without so much as a ripple of hesitation the mist
swallows me into its own reality. A muffled hiss penetrates my
ears, shifting like sand inside an hourglass and filling them with
silence. Panic beats its way down my spine as the mist
thickens.

I drop the backpack from my shoulder and sit on the ground
next to it. The mist of Mbali is so dense I'm as good as blind,
unable to see more than just a few feet in front of me. I bring my
knees up to my chin and wait impatiently, for the mist to thin. I
check my scar. It's cold and white. I have no other magic that I
know how to use, unless it is killing things with the daggers in
my eyes and right now, that is not the magic I need. I drag my
thumbnail across the scar, as if doing so might wake it up and
make the mist go away; it doesn't. Bored, I wrap my left arm
across my knees, bend forward and mindlessly trace a line in
the dirt outlining my boots, waiting for a brainstorm. Waiting
for the magic Stewart promised. I watch my finger aimlessly
push dirt away from the tips of my shoes then bring it back.
Shoes! That's it. I wasn't wearing shoes when I was in Mbali,
before.

I hastily remove my boots, stuff them and my sock in the
backpack, stand up and wiggle my toes in the soft brown soil;
the earth of Mbali greets them like a found puppy. And the

silence spills out of my ears. A gentle wind blows the mist into a large bubble, sending it skyward, soaring like an untethered balloon beyond the clouds, where it pops and gathers into a hollow circle. A gray bird appears on the other side, shoots through the center of the hole with a velocity I didn't think possible, then tucks its gray wings against its body, barrel rolls, twice, and continues its downward spiral, heading straight for me. I grab my backpack and run! But the eagle is faster, so I dive, in the dirt, like a baseball player sliding into home base and cover my head. The crowned eagle pulls up at the last possible second but the downward thrust of its wings kicks up another round of dust. Even before it settles I push myself on to my forearms, set my chin in my hands, and watch the bird skim across the surface of the earth, give an easy cant to the right, and vanish.

When I lower my hands they hit something hard hidden under the soil. I suck in a breath, shoot backwards, sit on my calves and stare at it. A flash of gold winks beneath the disrupted earth; whatever it is, it's not moving. Never taking my eyes off the object, I reach for the backpack, unclasp it, open the flap and take out half of my blowgun then cautiously shove the dirt away.

My throat tightens and my eyes overflow with tears; the gold elephant necklace Dad gave me on my tenth birthday is coiled in a loop, waiting for me to reclaim it. I reach over to pick it up, but stop. I glance right then left, it could be a trap. The leopard ripped it from my neck in Ona...so how did it ended up in Mbali? I prod it with the tip of the blowgun, then carefully slip the tube under the chain and bring the necklace up to my eyes. The white elephant dangles in the middle. I poke at it with my finger. . . nothing bad happens so I gingerly wrap my fingers over it then clasp it in my hand...no black voodoo vapor...no wind, no leopard, but still my heart pounds. I set the blowgun back in the pack, unclasp the necklace and lay it against my throat. I don't hear or see anything out of the ordinary, the brush and the distant trees are sparse and scattered, it seems safe, nothing lurking behind them...it's a risk, I know...but I go ahead and hook the chain around my neck. A deep chill claims my heart. I lift my pack over my shoulder and ease into a standing position, stroking the ivory elephant with my thumb and never taking my eyes off the ground; expecting *Bayamchawi* to come crawling out of the earth at any moment. The scar remains cool and so do my eyes, and bit-by-bit my fear lessens.

"Okay, Stewart, the necklace is a nice touch, but where is the rest of the magic you promised?" I mumble to no one, twisting my feet in the earth of Mbali and letting the sun rest across my back then start walking. I'd asked Stewart for a compass, but he informed me that a compass would be less than useless, and if I was to be the next *Machawi-shaitani*, I shouldn't need one, anyway. My fingers worry the scar; it itches and turns pink. Perhaps this means Ku-Mama is close by, and I lift my palm to call her.

Chirp-huff-wheeze. I lower my hand. What's that? It sounds like an animal in trouble. When I hear it again I realize the chirping sound, sounds kind of like cheetah; a cheetah that is having trouble breathing. Grabbing my backpack, I move as soundlessly as possible toward the distressed breathing coming from some bushes off to my left. Tucked in and hiding under the branches, a cheetah struggles to lift her head. I close my eyes. The blue haze washes over her. Her lungs and heart are a blur of dark blue. I lift a branch. The look of her tells it all, she's too weak and sick to fight. She is old and waiting for death.

Fearing speech will frighten her, I remain quiet. The scar warms, and I raise it to face her. She blinks and takes a shallow, struggling breath, as the scar's magic begins to calm her.

Only a few minutes elapse until her head twitches and sinks into the dirt and not too long after, her eyes close. I move in and pull her from under the bush then kneel on the ground next to her. I've only healed my own leg, so I'm not exactly sure how this is going to work but I'm willing to give it a try. The scar has turned bright red and seems ready so I place my palm above her heart and lungs. A red flame spreads across her chest and draws my hand down. I press my ear against the back of it and listen as the fluid in her lungs leaves, her breathing eases, and her heartbeat pulses a steady rhythm. I've done all I can. I lean back and lift my hand away, roll off my knees to get comfortable and lift her head into my lap then gently stroke her chest. I feel her heart skip a beat and when it starts up again, it is a little uneven; her heart is tired. Sadly, in a few days, perhaps less, this beautiful creature will be dead. I pick bits of crusty dirt from her beautiful face and touch my palm to her chest every now and then giving her body and heart a much deserved rest, knowing that no amount of magic can repair her.

A strong blast of wind loosens a flurry of leaves from the bushes near us and sends them scattering. The heat in my eyes awakens and my pulse quickens. A twig snaps. My heart jumps. I protect the cheetah, as best as I can, hugging her body to mine.

From behind, a large rough hand clamps over my mouth and pinches my nose shut then jerks me back. The cheetah slumps to the ground as I struggle to rip the hand away. Then I'm yanked to my feet with a brutal tug of my hair and the hand is released from my mouth.

"Let go of me," I demand twisting to kick my assailant. "Senento?" But my heart quickens knowing this isn't my childhood friend, it is the one, *the thing* I killed in *Ona*. I rush to get my hand to my cheek and use the daggers to kill this fake Senento, but he grabs it before I can reach it, then snatches my other. I kick out, but his grip tightens and he holds me at arm's length. Three other men join him as he brings my hands up in front of my eyes.

"Not this time, little girl." A sinister smile slides across his face. "*Kipofa yake!*" He orders.

"What?! What are you going to do?" I demand, as panic rises in my throat, *Kipofa yake* is Swahili for "blind her." One of the men places a coarse cloth over my eyes and knots it tight behind my head. Another tightens a leather strap around my wrists then stuffs my hand inside a cloth pouch and wraps a tie around that, too; the scar's power is useless and so are the daggers.

"Stewart knows where I am; you won't get away with this," I warn him.

"No more talk, little girl." He spins my back toward him and ties a gag around my mouth.

Terror pours too much blood into my heart, ramming it against my ribs. A sharp pain is unleashed behind my lids and it is difficult to breath but with my eyes bound I can't release the white light that would send my attackers away.

"You will not live to help your mother's soul to cross," he warns. "Take her!"

Hands and fingers push and prod me forward away from the cheetah. I have one advantage that they don't know about, though—I have the blue haze and I can see what is happening even through the blindfold. They don't take me far, but when they stop they quickly strap me to a pole and plant me in the earth like a tree. The ground shifts, hot and angry, opening and closing assaulting my toes, torturing me with the knowledge that the dark sorcerer, *Bayamchawi*, is waiting for me somewhere underneath.

The ghostly blue image of the man from *Ona* moves in close, he smells of soot and sweat. "Lill, it's been a long time since we have played together." He pulls the gag down.

"I thought I killed you."

"Confusing, isn't it?" He reaches out and touches a cold finger to my cheek.

I turn my head to the side to be rid of his touch. "Who are

you?"

"They call me Mabaya. Senento is my twin, or perhaps I am his." He laughs, and his sour breath slides down my face.

"What do you want?" I can't hide the fear in my voice, knowing what his answer will be.

"You were always in the way, Lill. Even as a little girl, you had too much power. If you wanted to live you should have kept your promise and not come back to Africa. It is such a waste of time to have to deal with you now." The earth shakes, crumbles and drops us five inches into the dry ground.

"Aaah!" I scream as the soil settles then drops us another half foot. Mabaya steps out of the pit, leaving me alone, causing more dirt to fall in the hole and burying my legs to my knees.

"I could go beneath the earth with you. The darkness is a place I'm used to. But I think *Bayamchawi* wants you to himself."

The ground buckles, not from under me but from on top. Mabaya's head jerks around. The three other men rush to his side shouting, "Tembo, tembo!" and pointing at the stampeding elephant in the distance.

Penda trumpets. The earth shakes with the weight of her and Penda's frantic cries grow louder as she rushes in to save me.

The ground underneath me cracks and the restraint binding me to the pole slips loose, and for a split second I free fall into the fissure. Then suddenly the ground heaves up and pitches me back onto the land. *Bayamchawi* explodes onto the surface with me, his ebony face just inches from my bound eyes.

Bayamachawi's eyes open slowly and fill with red hate as I watch Penda's hazy form pounds to a halt, just ten feet away. His shoulder muscles twitch, and a huge paw swings out and bats me out of his way, getting ready to do battle. Six other elephants join her, three on each side. A soul light lingers above Penda's head then slips behind her ear, as if it's hiding. Ku-Mama? My heart beats hopefully. The elephants lower their heads and emit a menacing rumble. *Bayamchawi* lowers his own head, Mabaya and the three other men stand by his side, fists balled tight.

The elephants stomp their enormous front feet. *Boom. Boom.* The percussion shakes the earth. *Bayamchawi* and his men don't move. The elephants lower their heads another inch and swish their trunks, snake like, across the dirt.

"Chui," *Bayamchawi* growls in Swahili, calling out for a leopard.

The men's bodies twist and jerk. A vile smell leaks out of them and they crack in half. A glowing dark red and black vaporous fog consumes them. Terrifying snarls spit up and split the fog, shattering it like glass; four black leopards, eyes empty and blank, face the elephants.

Bayamchawi, nods his head, the villainous cats stand united and powerful, ready to do his bidding. His nostrils flare. His black skin shines blue in the haze hidden behind my lids. His red eyes target Penda. The four cats crouch, their muscles tense and anxious, two black-coated leopards flanking each side of *Bayamchawi*. He hisses and the four unholy creatures bound out in front of him, ready to block Penda's assault.

Penda and the six elephants remain stationary, then all seven stomp the earth with a threatening front foot. *Boom!* Undeterred, the murderous black cats vibrate with anticipation, their haunches bunch and coil, ready to attack. The elephants hold their line; their feet beating the ground at a faster and faster pace, like horses at a racetrack waiting for the gate to open. The leopards snap their deadly teeth then vault into the air, all four aiming for Penda. *Bayamchawi* doesn't move. He watches.

"Penda, no!" I scream. But the leopards are on her before my words were even a thought.

The other elephants rush to Penda's aid, grabbing one cat and then the next, pulling them off her then smashing them into the ground. The unholy leopards fight and bite their way back to her. She screams as they increase the intensity of their attack, their claws digging in and raking across her thick hide. Twisting, turning and spinning, she battles to shake them off. One of the larger elephants grabs the leopard at Penda's throat, slams it to the earth, and grinds her head into his body, crushing every bone. When she is finished with him, she tosses her head back and bellows in triumph. Penda squeezes her trunk around the neck of another of the hellish black cats, strangles it then with a flick, breaks its neck. She lowers her head and sets her sights on *Bayamchawi*. He's unafraid and doesn't move. Penda charges, but the remaining two cats leap, flipping their bodies upside down and seizing the underside of her throat before she can reach him. Her tough hide affords her some protection...but not enough. The cats' fangs and back claws cut and rip into her skin.

Two elephants pull the leopards off her and slam them to the ground. One elephant stomps her prize to death. Two other elephants tear the last leopard into pieces then stand their ground and face *Bayamchawi.* He lifts his head and snarls then twists his body, pounces and straddles me. The heat of his body drips hate and his rancid breath gags my nose and lips. Penda whips her head back and forth then lowers it, appraising the situation. *Bayamchawi* presses his mouth against my ear, his whiskers slice across my cheek.

"You die before your elephant reaches us," and *Bayamchawi's* teeth sink deep into my throat.

Penda and the six elephants charge. She rips the leopard off me and thrusts him out of the way, then pulls the bag off my hands with her trunk. *Bayamchawi* snarls. She turns to face him. She and the other elephants surround him. Blood flows from my throat. I use my teeth, working the knot to unbind my hands, fighting not to lose consciousness and to stay alive long enough to use the scar to heal the wound. Tortuous seconds pass and I'm still able to untie my hands. I glance over at Penda, hoping she can help. She and her friends close in on *Bayamchawi*, as I twist my wrists in a desperate attempt to free them.

The four hellish leopards crawl out of the earth, whole, and rejoin him. The elephants lower their heads ready to do battle, again.

I'm losing consciousness. The blood continues to flow from my throat and without Penda's help there is no way to save myself. I listen to the fading sound of the elephants doing battle, too weak to fight the ties around my wrists.

A bright blue light shines on the other side of the blindfold then floats to my hands and settles on top of them. Heat radiates from my palm and draws my freed hand to my throat. My other hand finds the cloth covering my eyes and rips it off, *Bayamchawi's* treacherous glare stares into them. Somehow, he has escaped the elephants and before I have a chance to unleash the daggers, *Bayamchawi* slinks below the blackness under the earth. Angry, Penda and the elephants slam the ground with their trunks repeatedly. Then slowly the six elephants back away, leaving Penda and me alone. She taps the tip of her trunk against my throat and toots. I hold up my hand, she eases her trunk around it, helping me to stand then she softly taps my cheek with her trunk. I kiss the tip of it.

"It's okay Penda, you and your friends saved my life. Without your help I would have died. I guess I'm not much of a witchdoctor, after all, am I? How would I survive without you?" I lean against Penda and start to cry, frustrated and not knowing what else to do.

"You are a fighter Lill, that's how you'd do it," David's voice whispers.

Penda holds her large white ears straight out; she heard him, too. My stomach churns with hope and then dread, not knowing if this is David or *Bayamchwi's* voodoo magic imitating his voice. A translucent aqua-marine fog shimmers into a small orb behind Penda, the same soul that arrived with her and freed my hands.

It's not Ku-Mama's soul. I hold my breath. The soul stretches away from Penda's and hovers in front of me. White dots wink on and off. And in waves of diffused pale-blue mist an image forms.

"David." Tears flood my eyes. Looking at him is like looking through a gauze filtered lens of a camera; he is here but not quite. My heart beats wildly. I tighten my grip on Penda's ear, afraid to move too close, afraid a shift in the air might blow him away. "David? It's really you?"

"Don't get too excited, Lill; I can't stay." The transparency of the pixels spread farther and farther apart and I see less of him.

"David, it was you that freed my hands. You and Penda saved my life...again."

"It was different this time. Last time Bayamchawi was after me. I didn't stand a chance. Whatever you do, Lill, don't blame yourself for my dying. You have important things to accomplish here in Africa...very important things."

"David, I miss you." His blue-green eyes shine brighter than the rest of him.

Penda trumpets a happy hello and blows a squeal of delight into the air above her head.

"She can hear you, too?"

"She can." David's faint smile widens into a grin. His image wavers, becoming fainter as the scent of him tilts my heart and brings tears of longing to my eyes. "Lill, I came to tell you to trust the lights." His image dims, he becomes less. "But you can't stay in this place any longer, it's too dangerous. You must leave for Mlango at once."

"I've been looking for a path or something to tell me how to find it, but I don't know where to look."

"Your scar, Lill, use your scar."

"But the scar only brings things together. It can't take me anywhere."

"Does it really matter? Either way, you end up in the same place. Use your powers, Lill."

"David, stay and help me."

"Lill, I can't. I'm not like you and Penda, and...this is something you must do on your own."

Penda strokes my arm with her trunk. "Please David, just a little longer." Tears stream down my cheeks.

Penda caresses my face with her trunk then slowly turns and walks away. She trumpets. Waiting for her in the distance, the six elephants answer her back. Penda glances over her shoulder and toots and continues toward them. David's likeness spins into a bright-blue soul with a smattering of aqua sparks and is gone.

"Lill, I will always love you," his soft voice echoes from beyond and I have never felt so alone or so lost.

Chapter 19

D avid said to trust the light. Father said not to trust the
light. Stewart said to trust that I am a sorcerer. Ku-
Mama said I just need to learn how to use my powers.

"Backpack, I need you." And just like that, the backpack
drops next to my foot with a thud. Amazing. I smile to myself,
thinking I could get use to this. Then I think about what David
said before his soul slipped away; something about, it doesn't
matter if it comes to me or if I go to it, either way I end up in
the same place. I harness the backpack and point the scar, once
again, at the sky then square my shoulders, take a determined
breath and yell, "Mlango, I need you."

And a drum is struck. Other drums join in, and as their tempo
increases it resets the beating of my heart to match the rhythm.
The drumbeat grows unbearably fast and my hands slash
angrily at the driving tempo. Like a conductor of a runaway
orchestra, I struggle to synchronize the beat, to slow it, to quiet
my frantic heart. A single drumbeat strikes louder than the rest
and the cadence eases, then softens and slows, and returns my
heart rate to normal. And the whisper of a single drumbeat ends
it all.

The moon yawns, delivering indigo light through the dense
jungle trees, around the low lying bushes and across the noble
jungle floor. Nocturnal birds sing love songs in the warm night
air, hoping to attract a mate. Purple raindrops cling with self-
importance to thick leaves, each drop a wet jewel precisely cut
with the pomp-and-circumstance of legends and prophecies.
The rich soil embraces my toes and holds me spellbound as a
crowned eagle swoops down on a breath of silent wings and
alights a few feet away from me. The bird flutters and folds her

wings with graceful elegance against her body. She ruffles the gray feathers on her back, and preens the white crest of down on her breast with a sharp yellow beak. Her gold eyes blink, and she cocks her head to one side then turns and hops, on large nubby feet a short distance away, twists her neck in a half circle, shakes the white crown of pinfeathers on top of her head, dusting the ground with gold and silver sparks, then she unfolds her wings and flies off with a loud screech, "Kooee-kooee."

"Ku-Mama?" I gasp, too late but wonder what it was about this bird that made me call out my grandmother's name. I shake my head and mutter, "Ridiculous."

The crowned eagle whistles and tilts her wings against the backdrop of a distant mountain; its flat top wavers under clouds of deep-purple. A two-story stone house with a pitched roof sits quiet, in the vastness in-between. A soft ivory light spills out from a window near the top and as I approach the house the white curtains are spread apart and the window is opened. Above, the eagle circles the roof top on extended wings then effortlessly glides through the window, tumbling curtains in billows of lace.

When I reach the stairs leading to the front door, I hesitate, swallow, and just stare at the door...what will my mother think when she see me? And what will I feel when I see her? The door, tucked in an alcove looms above me, only the moon gives it light and the ten stone steps leading to it. They are all that separate me from her. I puff out a breath and brush back loose strands of hair with a nervous hand...the back of my throat tightens and I put a foot on the first step. Ancient vines, with wide trunks grow up the brown and gray stone walls and climb with me all the way to the top stair. The thick wood door is old, aged and blackened by time. A cross has been carved in the middle of it, and in the center of the cross a circle is cut, even deeper. The vertical arm of the cross is washed white; pointing the pathway to the spirit worlds, heaven and hell. The brass plaque on the door reads "MLANGO." My heart stutters and fills with anticipation, and I'm a little scared. I fill my lungs, curl my fingers into my palm, rest my thumb over the top of them and slowly raise my hand...

The door opens before it touches the wood, "Hello, Lillian." Ku-Mama's happy voice chirps as she steps back, inviting me in.

Inside, the foyer is cramped and dark, too small to close the door without moving further into the house, but Ku-Mama stays put. The single candle, burning in the soot-blackened sconce behind her head, flares. And her lips turn up as if they are holding in a secret she can't wait to share.

"Ku-Mama, are you...were you...I feel foolish asking such an absurd question. "Ku-Mama are—"

"Yes. The crowned eagle's soul and mine have crossed."

"Crossed? You're crossed with a bird? I thought the soul-crossing was about dying and going to heaven, like crossing-over. And you're not dead, so—"

"That is something we need to talk about, but now is not the time. Your mother is anxious to see you." Ku-Mama has changed her clothes since I saw her at the crash site. She wears traditional African clothing, a blouse and long skirt, and like before her skin is dark gray. The blouse has a white panel sewn on the front that starts just under her chin and stops at the hem resting on her hips.

My grandmother eases past me. Her gentle fingers touch my arm and linger there while she closes and locks the door then she lets her fingers slide away and faces me. The candle smoke clings to the mahogany walls and begins to fill the tiny vestibule.

A low growl or perhaps a labored breath prickles my skin and a cold breeze blows a warning over my ears.

"Lillian," Ku-Mama's lips compress into a hard line, then

widens, "I'd like you to meet my son." Her eyes focus behind me.

I wheel around, and the coldest eyes I have ever seen stare down at me. His hazel-dark eyes erupt from nothing, his body and face hidden in the dark shadows of the cramped space.

"Giza," his African voice introduces, barbaric and savage. He extends a hand, and when his cold hard fingers touch mine, my skin recoils and I ease my own fingers closed, refusing to clasp his hand. He moves back an inch, and the candle sparks. I steal a quick glance at his feet. They are shoeless and human. Foolish, had I thought they would be the feet of the black leopard, *Bayamchawi*? *Giza* in Swahili means darkness, and the name suits him.

"Welcome to Mlango, niece. We have been waiting for you for a very long time." Giza's wide white smile breaks the threating sound of his voice, but like a crack in thin ice the smile only lasts a few second before it, and Giza are gone.

"Come, Lillian, your mother is waiting." Ku-Mama hurries past. "Follow me." She heads up the flight of stairs to the right of the hall. Only two candles light the stairway, one at the bottom and one at the top. Her feet move effortlessly up each dark tread, weightless, as though she were hopping.

Halfway up, in the darkest area of the stairs, a hot breath of air slithers across my shoulders; the elephant necklace around my neck turns cold. I grab hold of the ivory elephant and lift the chain from my skin then turn around and look down the stairs. It's empty. I stand there a second and listen.

"Lillian?"

"Yes, Ku-Mama, I'm right here, right behind you." I turn and follow after her. As we step into the hallway at the top, I remember part of a poem I read a long time ago, by Mary Mcleod Bethune: *For I am my mother's daughter and the drums of Africa still beat in my heart. They will not let me rest…*And tonight, for me, nothing has ever been truer.

Ku-Mama stops outside the first door. There's a second door halfway down the hall and a third one at the end. Brass sconces hold a single candle to the right of each one, casting dim pools of yellow light on the doors and floor. I ease the backpack from my shoulders and set it against the wall, by my feet. Ku-Mama places her hand on the doorknob and my heart races, then she lets go and reaches for the candle above her head. She removes it from the sconce and holds it steady, just inches from my eyes. My eyes question hers.

"Your eyes are not exactly like Hata's."

"Hata...it's a strange name, it means, 'until.'"

"Yes. Until...it was a promise I made to her while she was still in my womb. I still call her Hata, after all I am her mother. But the others...for a short while longer, they will continue to call her, *Machawi-shaitani*." She moves the flame from one eye to the other. "Your eyes...the silver circle around the edge...it is something I have never seen." She pulls the candle away and replaces it in the sconce then twists the knob and opens the door, my heart pounds.

As much as Mbali was cloaked in an emerald green mist, this room is filled with a brilliant crystalline white light. Dozens of ivory candles burn inside small crystal bowls attached to the walls and to the four dark wood posts of her bed. The veiled glow of candlelight creates a surreal image of the frail African woman resting in the bed. She is awake and a serene smile spreads across her face as I move to the end of the bed. I am able to smile, and tears stream down my face, but I am speechless.

She rests on three plump white pillows stacked against the dark headboard. Her gown is white. The bedding is ivory. On the nightstand next to her a crystal vase overflows with white lilies, saturating the air with the scent of ancient mysteries and voodoo traditions. Her black hair is pulled from her face; wound and knotted at the side of her neck with gold ribbon cascading gracefully over her right shoulder. Her dark eyes watch me, but she has yet to speak. Is she as scared as I am? Her aura pulses purple around her head and hands and seeps up through the silk covers outlining her frail body. An inch above the purple nimbus a thin line of lime-green light ripples in a disconnected layer of fog. I don't need to close my eyes and use the blue haze to know that my mother is dying.

Her eyes flash gold sparks as she slips her slim frame from under the bed covers and stands with her arms outstretched.

I step around the bed and into her open arms. "Mother." All other words are lost, and not needed, as tears spill from her eyes, too.

When our weeping has eased, she gently rocks me back and wipes the tears from my cheeks, "Lillian," she whispers.

And I hear my mother speaks my name for the first time. I gaze into her eyes; she has the dagger-lights, too.

"My baby," she adds, holding my face in her hands and letting her eyes meld into mine. "You have finally come home. I should never have let you go, but I thought allowing your father to take you to the States would spare you from having to face *Bayamchawi.* I was afraid you wouldn't have enough power to defeat him when my time to cross came. Letting you go was so difficult, it was the hardest thing I have ever done." She kisses each side of my mouth and folds me back into her arms, hold me for a long moment then, never letting go of my hands, steps back.

"With your father's blood being half of who you are, I was positive you weren't meant for this life. I'm afraid I've done you more harm than good. You're here in Africa and you know so little of our ways. My decision to let you go may have put your life in jeopardy and may have made it impossible for you, for us, to succeed."

"Mother, I don't care about that, right now, I just want to hold you, and..." I breathe deep, sobbing. "...and have you hold me."

She wraps her arms around me. "Oh, Lillian, I love you so much."

I unwind from her embrace, "The worst part...nobody would talk to me about you. I wanted to know where you were from ...where you were buried...why everything about you was such a secret. Dad and Nanta, they wouldn't tell me anything. They never even told me your name." We separate further, taking in the sight of each other, and I ask the one question I still need an answer to. "Why...if you weren't dead, why did you leave me? Why didn't you ever come back?"

She squeezes her bone thin fingers around my hands and kisses them, "It was the wrong decision, Lillian. I made a wrong decision. I hope you can forgive me. Your eyes, they're so beautiful and they hold so much power, but when you were a baby they were blue...I swear to you they were blue, only blue, like your father's...I didn't know. Every day without you, my heart broke just a little more, but when you were taken to the United States, it broke in half. I thought I would die. I thought I would never see you again."

A slight tremor of pain leaches through her body, "Mother, what's wrong?"

"No need to worry but I should go back to bed. It is hard for me to stand for very long. My earthly body is weak." She wraps her arm around my waist, "Help me into bed, and we'll talk some more."

"I'll leave you two." Ku-Mama's voice surprises me. I had forgotten she was in the room. The door closes after her.

I sit on the edge of the bed holding my mother's hand and the thing I have never had, but have always wanted, is mine...my mother. She lifts her hand and strokes my hair, trying to make everything all right...because she loves me.

"Lillian, your father's religion believes in an afterlife. We believe in an afterlife, too; the only difference is that we can see the afterlife. We can see the souls. Seeing the souls of the dead was one of the things that frightened your father. The powers given to the Machawi-shaitani come with the greatest responsibly of all, keeping the gate to the spirit world open. When the Machawi-shaitani crosses over and becomes a Msafiri, a Traveler, she'll share her soul with an animal...like Ku-Mama shares her soul with the crowned eagle." She reaches for the elephant necklace and fingers the white elephant in the center.

"Ku-Mama is dead?"

"We don't really ever die, do we?" Remember, even your father's Christian God promised a life ever after." She lets go of my necklace, "I see you found it. Bayamchawi tossed it aside when he realized it held no magical powers for him." She looks into my eyes before she continues; a faint question lingers in her gaze then she blinks it away. "Lillian, we have so much to teach you." She sighs. "It was wrong to let you go. I hope I can make it right, I'll try." She smiles and the scar warms across my palm. She lays open her hand and I hold mine next to it. Both our scars have turned ruby-red. She has two other scars, but they remain cold.

"This scar is the mark of our power," she tells me.

She kisses my palm, rubs the scar with her thumb, then settles back against her pillows, briefly closing her eyes.

"Mother, what's wrong with you? Have you seen a doctor?"

"Doctors can't help. It's time for my soul to cross and all the medicine in the world can't change that. Now that you are here, there is no reason to linger any longer."

I gasp. "Yes, there is. We've just gotten together, we need more time. I need..."

"Don't worry, Lillian. We will meet again. When I'm on the other side of the soul-crossing we will have longer than an earthly lifetime to be together." Mother covers a yawn with the back of her hand; it trembles with fatigue and illness.

"Lillian, come closer so I can kiss you goodnight. You've had a long day and so have I. It's late. We will talk some more in the morning."

I lean over and shyly kiss her cheek.

"Lillian, I love you," she takes my face in her hands and kisses me on the lips then leans back. "If you can defeat *Bayamchawi*, this will be our beginning."

"Mother, what if I can't?"

Her cool hands embrace mine as she stares deeply into my eyes, draws in a quick breath, and glances away with a shudder.

"Mother?"

"It's nothing, Lillian, nothing...a small pain, that's all." She tries to convince me, but I don't believe she is telling me the whole truth. She looks behind me then her lips turn up and she nods her head, once.

"Lillian," Ku-Mama whispers.

I glance over my shoulder and see Ku-Mama standing at the open bedroom door. I hadn't heard her enter.

"Come with me, I'll show you your room."

"Mother, dad left me a note, he said you wanted him to tell me that the elephants and I were connected, you were right, Penda and her friends saved my life today. David's soul helped, too." I eased off the bed, regretting I have to leave so soon.

"You have always been connected to the elephants, dear. The white one, your Penda, she is closer to you than you can possibly imagine. Now go to bed. We both need to rest."

At the door I look across the room, "Goodnight, Mother." Saying it sounds so odd. I smile. "I love you."

Ku-Mama walks me to the bedroom at the end of the hall.

"Get a good sleep, dear. Tomorrow and the day after will be busy, for all of us." She turns, closing the door behind her.

The bedroom is lit only by candlelight; long and narrow, the room has three windows. I walk over to each one and look out. My backpack is on the floor beside the bed under the window on the same side of the house as the front door. On the night-stand next to it is there is a lantern holding with a single candle, one of two in the room. Also on the nightstand is a bowl of fruit, and a clear glass filled with water. A wax stopper with a string in the center seals the top. I pull out the plug and take a long drink. When I've finished, I grab a red plantain (an African banana) and a slice of sweet bread and head to the open window overlooking the backyard. I sit on the window's ledge and lean against the frame, pull my legs up and peel the banana, breath in the warm night air and watch the moon and the stars. I can't help but smile, overwhelmed with happiness. I'm here with my mother in her house, and we have held each other...she is real. I sigh, eat my banana then take a bite of bread and look down at the curved stone walkway leading from the house to a small building that must be the outhouse, at the side of the yard. Beyond it a man, who is apparently in a great hurry, strides silent and barefoot along the path. He rushes past the building, heading straight for the back of the house.

A sudden gust of wind snaps a small branch off a nearby tree, whips it through the air so it hits the ledge of the windowsill below me. I flinch, my feet hit the floor, and my chest thumps. I catch my breath then lean over the sill and look out. The yard is empty, the man is gone, but the dagger lights in my eyes have warmed. I quickly close the window and wonder if I should be worried. I touch my eyes; they have already cooled. Maybe the whole thing was just my imagination.

Sitting on top of a wooden chest of drawers is a pale-blue porcelain water pitcher and a matching basin. Beside it, a short fat candle burns in the other lantern. On the wall behind the basin is a large mirror, framed with the same type of wood as the dresser. It hangs from an oversized copper knob. This is the first time I've had a chance to inspect the damage done by the leopard. I move the lantern closer to the mirror and lean close. I can hear David's voice saying, once again, "That's the problem, Lill, there is never any proof," and there isn't. Not one spot of blood, not a single scratch anywhere on my neck or face. I study my eyes. They look the same to me.

I pour surprisingly warm water into the washbowl and wet the washcloth then start to clean my face and neck. Deciding what I really need is a bath I take off all of my clothes and give my body a good scrub. When I've finished, I fold my dirty clothes, putting the damp cloth on top, and stack them on top the bureau, then crawl tired, confused, strangely content, and happy...I have met my mother...into bed.

The strike of a drum pops my eyes open and I sit straight up in bed. A door opens in the hallway. I toss the light cover aside and silently cross the floor and press my ear to my bedroom door. Whispering voices speak urgently to each other then abruptly stop. Ku-Mama and Giza? Footsteps hurry down the stairs. A door on the first floor is snapped shut and the house falls silent. I'll have to ask Ku-Mama about it in the morning.

Chapter 20

I toss the blanket off me, roll onto my side and end up looking at the floor. I have to pee, but the chamber pot staring back at me isn't an option. I need to get dressed and get to the outhouse, soon. At the dresser, the clothes I left last night have been washed, folded and placed in the top drawer, along with the extra clothing from my backpack and toiletries. The blow-gun and darts, syringes, needles, and ampules filled with inject-able drugs are lined up neatly and fill the rest of the space. I look on the floor for my boots and don't see them. I am not a heavy sleeper, so I'm surprised the noise from whoever came into the room didn't wake me. Either I was really tired or they were very, very quiet, and I find the thought of someone rum-maging around in my things unsettling. I'll have to ask Ku-Mam about it, but the pangs of bladder pressure makes me hurry.

I grab my underwear and long pants and scramble into them, then take the white tank top from the drawer and pull it over my head as I rush from the room, run past my mother's door, down the stairs, though the dark parlor, into the kitchen and out the back door then run like a rabbit to the outhouse.

The privy door bangs shut behind me. I am no longer in a hurry, so I take my time back to the house. The chirps from a family of white-fronted bee-eaters tempt me off the path and draw me to the tulip tree, among its wide branches the birds hop and flutter from limb to limb flying off every now and then to catch a bee and bring it back, pluck out its stinger and eat it.

"Hey, guys. Guess what? I met my mother last night and I'm having breakfast with her this morning." They ignore me completely, continuing their quest for food.

"And she's waiting for you, niece." Giza's graveled voice

dampens my lighthearted mood.

My back stiffens, and I quickly crouch to gaze among the bushes at a small group of blue-headed little birds scratching in the dirt looking for seeds; I really don't want to see his eyes. "Thank you, Giza." I continue my preoccupation with the birds and wait for Gaza to take the hint and leave. Instead, he moves closer. His bare feet and the bottom of his black trousers invade my space and scare the birds, sending them under another and more distance bush.

"It is so beautiful out here, I think I'll stay a little longer." My voice is unable to hide the fear I feel with him so near. I touch a pink blossom with trembling fingers, snap it off, pretending to be more interested in the flower and how it smells than him.

"You should not keep your mother waiting too long," his icy voice warns. "It is not wise." The tightness in his voice is unmistakably threatening.

His shoeless feet pivot and as he strolls away the little blue-headed birds come forward and return to the business of finding food. Still crouched, I twist, allowing my eyes follow him as he heads for the house. His long-sleeved shirt is black, American looking, expensive and tapered at the waist. As he nears the door I realize I can't see any aura around him. After he's stepped inside, I turn back to the birds and wonder if he has some sort of magic power that helps him hide it, and if he doesn't, without an aura can a human-being have a soul?

The little blue-headed bird chirps, "So what do you think, my little feathered friends, does he have a soul or not?"

"A soul is a strange thing, Lillian. It can do many things," a masculine voice offers a partial answer. An African man, heavy but not soft, weaves his way toward me across the lawn from the front of the house. He is well over six feet tall and barefoot. He wears black pants, a long-sleeved shirt and a traditional *kofia* (hat) on his head. The hat is also black, embroidered with copper and teal-blue threads in designs of crosses and circles.

"Jambo," I stand, facing him and smile.

"Jambo." He extends his right hand, opened it flat and facing skyward. A scar runs from the base of his middle finger to the center of his palm, exactly like mine.

I take his hand but don't shake it. Instead, I turn it so I can more clearly see his scar then place my palm next to his. I question his brown eyes with a raised brow. He returns my gaze; he has gold daggers in his eyes, too.

"I am your half-brother, Geoffrey." An easy smile widens across his ebony face as his two hands clasp mine with warm affection.

"Half-brother? No one told me I had a half-brother. It seems my family is growing. A mother, grandmother, uncle and now you, a half-brother. Is there a family dog I should know about?"

He lets go of my hand, "No, no. No dog. Come with me, Lill. Let's get something to eat and say good morning to our mother." As we amble to the back door, he continues, "She is anxious to see you again. She has such a small amount of time and so much she wants to teach you." Geoffrey holds the door open and waves me through, "After breakfast, when she retires for her nap, you and I will talk." He steps into the kitchen behind me, "You can tell me about your childhood and I will tell you about mine. We will share our secrets." His laugh is rich and deep.

Three middle-aged African women clustered at the long kitchen counter look up. They avoid making eye contact with me but smile broadly at Geoffrey, then quickly resume their work, rinsing fruit in buckets of water, drying them with small white towels then slicing them onto trays. Two teenage girls, one tall enough to be Maasai, squeeze juice from passion fruit and mangos into a clear glass pitcher at a center island. All five women are dressed in white and in traditional African clothes—a blouse or *buba*, a long skirt, and a *gele* sometimes called a head-tie. An old man with nimble black fingers arranges breads, bowls of honey and jam on a copper platter next to the woodstove. He is dressed in black pants and shirt. All are barefoot. Fresh baked bread fills the kitchen with the smell of nutmeg and banana. My mouth waters with hunger.

"Jambo," I greet them as we walk through the kitchen. They dip their heads shyly, concentrate more intently on the preparation of breakfast and remain quiet.

"That was weird," I whisper, when we've passed into the parlor. I look up at Geoffrey for confirmation then glance around the room.

"Not really. You are a bit of a celebrity," Geoffrey remarks. "After all, you are the next *Machawi-shaitani*."

I had run through the parlor in my rush to get to the outhouse. Still, I don't know how I could have missed seeing the drums. My mouth drops, and I place a hand on Geoffrey's arm, astonished by their size. Three of the largest *songba* drums I have ever seen, they must be at last three feet tall, are resting six inches off the floor in sturdy wooden cradles. Drumsticks made of hard wood lie dormant on top of their taut cowhide skins. The drums are lined up in front of a stunning ivory tapestry that hangs from braided copper ropes attached to two massive wall hooks near the ceiling. Stitched into the tapestry in fat layers of gold, copper, blue, and silver threads is the emblem of a cross, whose center spotlights a circle, sewn with deep-blue thread. The cloth is about six feet tall and four foot wide. There is a ten-inch wide panel of fabric running down each side of it like sleeves, tarnished with brown stains that look like dried blood. On the wall next to the cloth are two elephant tusks, one on each side, each about six feet long. The base of the tusks rests on the floor and the tips are strapped to the wall with leather ties. However, the most intriguing part of the tapestry floats, unattached, in front of it. It is a tiny crystal orb, tiny enough to fit in a cupped hand and captured inside the globe, a pin-point-spark of light; brighter than any Fourth of

July sparkler I've ever seen.

"The tapestry is to carry our mother to the mountain top of Kesho. The cloth will be suspended between the two tusks and one of the tusks will hold the soul that will cross with our mothers."

"And the crystal orb?"

"It is our destiny and our past. Without the spark of the guiding star's light, we lose the power of the lights in our eyes."

"Is it safe to keep it out in the open like this? Couldn't *Bayamchawi* and his black magic steal it?"

"No. That little spark of starlight is more powerful than any of *Bayamchawi's* magic. Only a *Machawi-shaitani* can touch it. It will destroy anyone else, anyone or anything. Even you and me."

"How can it float in the air like that?"

"The magic of sorcery, of course."

"Of course. And the drums?"

"They call the souls from the spirit world. When the moon's center is covered by the shadow of the earth, the soul-crossing begins, and the drum-song, the *Ngoma-wimbo*, will sound until our mother's soul has crossed with the other. She will no longer be *Machawi-shaitani*. She will be an *Msafiri*, a traveler, and you will be the *Machawi-shaitani*." Geoffrey takes my hand and leads me from the room. "We shouldn't linger any longer; they are waiting for you."

My mother sits matriarchal at the head of the long narrow table in the dining room. The morning light washes in from a large window behind her, providing the only light in the room and backlighting her in an angelic haze. Her hair is completely covered this morning, by a white head-tie that blossoms around her head like the tight bud of a flower. Her white brocade blouse hangs loosely on her thin shoulders.

A white cloth runs down the center of the table. A huge arrangement of white lilies placed in the middle spill out of a large copper bowl, drenching the room with their scent.

"Lillian, you noticed the flowers." This seems to please her. "They are the reason I named you Lillian. On the day you were born, your father placed a bouquet of white lilies by my bed. Your skin was light brown, not white, but light enough. And to name you Lillian, after the flower, well, your father and I agreed it suited you. Now, come sit here beside me." She pats the table on her right side. Tilting her head to the left she adds, "Geoffrey, why don't you sit over there this morning?" She point to the chair on her left.

He hesitates, but when he sees me watching, he pulls out the chair then stops and watches as Giza strides to the head of the table, places his large hands on the back of Mother's chair, and stands over her. Geoffrey watches him closely as he folds his large frame into the chair and sits down.

"Good morning, dearest sister," Giza leans over and kisses Mother's cheek. "Geoffrey," He nods at my brother then moves to the chair next to him and stares across the table at me. "Lillian, I see you made it...with Geoffrey's help. He flashes me a tight lipped grin, sits then makes a show of shaking out the cloth napkin and placing it in his lap. "You became bored with the little birds?"

The two young girls from the kitchen enter the room, saving me from having to respond to Giza's sharp tongue. They stand at the right side of Mother, between her and me. The tall girl is holding the crystal pitcher of juice close to her stomach. The shorter one is holding a single glass at the same height. The tall one lifts the pitcher and pours an inch of the liquid into the glass.

The shorter girl puts the glass to her lips and drinks it. When she is finished, she takes a tiny hourglass out of her pocket and places it on the table. We watch in complete silence, three minutes, until the sand runs out. She picks it up, returns it to her pocket and steps away from the table as the taller girl begins filling our glasses with juice.

"We cannot be too careful," Mother tells me, then glances at Geoffrey.

"That girl tested your juice for poison?" I ask.

"Your juice too, Lillian."

"She could have died." Disbelief and horror fill my voice with the knowledge that my mother would let this young girl die without a twinge of remorse.

"Death, we don't believe in it, however she is not a sorcerer, so..." She waves her hand to clear the thought. "Lillian, you must remember, only her body will die. Like your David her soul will live on. After all, that's the most important part, isn't it? I believe you've seen David's soul once or twice, since you've come home to Africa. We don't really lose anybody, do we? Unless," she pats Geoffrey's hand while she continues to look at me. "Unless..." She squeezes his fingers before letting them go.

"I have seen more than David's soul, I've seen him. How is it possible for him to be more than a soul?"

"It is a temporary thing. For the moment, he has attained a higher plane."

"Sister, after breakfast I will take you to Kesho Mountain and on the way I will explain," Geoffrey adds.

"Lillian." My mother clears her throat. "David is in a very special place; he gets to see and experience our realities and in the end he will have his heaven and as *Machawi-shaitani* you will be able to visit his soul whenever you want." The old man from the kitchen steps forward and offers mother the platter of bread and honey. She chooses a small slice of banana bread, ignoring the honey, and takes a bite before she motions for him to serve the rest of us.

"Now indulge your mother and tell me about your life after your father took you away. I need to hear your voice. Later, when you return from your visit with Geoffrey, we will talk some more, and I will answer any of your unanswered questions." She lifts my hand to her lips and kisses it. Her kiss is cool and soft. I love her with all my heart.

We eat and talk or I should say I talk. Mother asks about my life in California and about my being a veterinarian. She wants to know if I use my magic to heal the animals, so I tell her about the blue haze and how it works. I answer her questions about David and Penda. I talk until my back is stiff and I'm bored with the sound of my own voice.

When I finish my stories, the two girls from the kitchen are summoned, and they gently help mother from her chair. She leans heavily on them, pauses, smiles and looks longingly in my direction.

"Lillian, spend this time with your brother wisely and heed what he tells you. It will help you understand our history and our beliefs. Now, my sweet girl, I need to lie down. And when I'm asleep, I will dream only of you." Her eyes sparkle.

After she has gone, an awkward silence weighs heavily over the three of us. Geoffrey and Giza break the silence, stretching themselves from their chair, glaring at each other the whole time, posturing like two male lions. Then Giza nods his head at me and quickly leaves the dining room without saying a word.

"Well, I guess we should go." Geoffrey places his napkin on the table. "Give me a couple of minutes, little sister. I'll meet you at the well by the big tree at the west side of the yard. You can't miss it. And, sister, don't drink the water," his voice warns but his face creases in a smile.

"I can't find my boots. I'll need to borrow some shoes."

"We don't wear shoes here. It is not a good idea if you want to hear what the earth is saying."

A wooden bucket, filled with water, sits silhouetted in sunlight on the rocky-ledge of the well. I dip my hand into the pail and scoop up a handful, mindful not to drink the water, then lean over the opening and let it trickle though my fingers, listening to the water splashing down and echoing up peaceful k-plunks and k-plinks. When I look up, Geoffrey is watching me from the opposite side, his smiling white teeth framed in his African face. My brother's skin is much darker than mine but I can see the similarities, we look like brother and sister.

"Geoffrey, you know about my dad. Tell me about yours"

Geoffrey motions for me to step beside him on the foot-path leading away from the house. "My father was a sorcerer, not as powerful as our mother, but a sorcerer nonetheless."

Geoffrey scoots ahead of me, confronting two heavily-leafed tree branches crisscrossing the path and blocking our way, their interlocking green limbs held together like fingers in prayer. Geoffrey raises his right hand, holds his palm out, and without a word, the limbs unfurl, their leaves rustling and shaking then settling when the path is cleared.

"Your scar opens things," I said, stating the obvious as we walk past the branches.

"It opens and pushes things apart; yours closes and brings things together," Geoffrey tells me as the branches return and once again hide the path.

"How do you know what my scar does?" I search his eyes with suspicion. The gold lights in them are bright but calm.

"We are brother and sister. We complement each other like Chinese Yin and Yang."

"And the lights in your eyes, what do they do?"

"In that we are alike. They fight *Bayamchwi* and his black magic." Geoffrey sweeps his hand in front of him. "Welcome to Kesho," he announces with pride.

The contrast between Mlango and this land is astounding. Golden grass with tall amber stalks blow in the warm breeze like stiff gilded ribbons, all the way to the base of the mountain. The smell of sweet ripe-grass brings back memories of the elephant barn in Sacramento...it seems a lifetime ago. The soft-green mountain of Kesho towers above the tawny sea of grass and waits for us against a crystal blue sky; the mountain's flat top, not tall enough to reach the clouds overhead.

"Kesho, the mountain is named Tomorrow?"

"Yes, it is the mountain where our mother's tomorrow—and yours—will begin. It is where her soul-crossing will take place."

"Huh." I nod, at a loss for words, then stammer, "Ah, and does your father live here, in the valley, or does he live up there, on the mountain?"

"My father was killed, poisoned by *Bayamchawi*." Geoffrey's words are tinged with hatred. "His soul is damned, held captive in the darkness of *Bayamchawi's* hell, below the earth. It is why we don't take chances when it comes to drinking liquids."

"Why did *Bayamchwi* kill your father?"

"To undermine our mother's power."

"How'd he get your father soul?"

"He snatched it as it was leaving his body."

"And there's no way to get it back?"

"No. Even if *Bayamchawi* is destroyed we don't know how to open the gate into his hell, and we fear it may be too dangerous to try."

"Where was mother when your father was killed? Surely she could have prevented it."

"She was with him. It was their wedding night, the night I was conceived. *Bayamchawi* poisoned the water and both he and mother drank it. My father was a strong sorcerer; unfortunately he was not powerful enough to save himself. Mother survived, but when she regained consciousness my father's soul was gone. She saw the black soot of *Bayamchwi's* evil on his chest, but she refused to believe *Bayamchawi* had taken his soul. Heartbroken and pregnant, she went to Mlango to live with Ku-Mama.

Ku-Mama hadn't yet crossed. She was the *Machawi-shaitani* and our mother pleaded with her to use the powers of *Rudiana*, to reunite her with my father's soul. Ku-Mama tried but she couldn't find it."

"Geoffrey, I'm so sorry."

"It was foretold by the prophet Nabii; one day a person would come and release the souls taken into the darkness. Now that you have returned and the white elephant is with you...there may be hope."

"Penda and me?" I stammer.

"You and the white elephant might be...I've gotten ahead of myself and I'm confusing you." He takes a deep breath then continues.

"A month after I was born, Mother went to Ona hoping to find Father's soul. Not knowing how long it would take, she left me with Nanta and Ku-Mama. They were to raise me until she returned. When she didn't find my father's soul in Ona, she suspected *Bayamchwi* had taken it, but she refused to give up and kept looking. Even at Ku-Mama's insistence she refused to come home and began searching Mbali and beyond. After more than a year had passed, she was found wandering aimlessly in the jungle close to your village of Ndogo. She was half-starved and some said she had gone mad. Slowly and with the help of your father and his Christian God she began to heal. She came to believe your father and his God had rescued her from the madness. Eventually, she fell in love with him and you were born."

A soft wind blows the drying grass, rustling the kernels clinging to the top of each stalk like castanets in a Latino dance and whispering in the tiniest of voices the word *home*. It's silly to think I heard such a thing and I cast it aside as nothing more than the wind playing a trick on my ears and direct my attention to Geoffrey. "When our mother returned to Mlango, Ku-Mama sent Nanta, Mother's older sister to Ndogo, to raise you."

"What! Nanta is mother's sister? Nanta never told me. Nobody told me."

"Ku-Mama thought it best you didn't know. On your tenth birthday, after what transpired in Ona, it became clear you had certain powers...Ku-Mama and Mother worried that your lack of education would eventually cost you your life. Mother thought you should be brought to Mlango immediately and taught our ways.

However, your encounter with the black leopard caused your father to insist taking you the States would be the only thing that would save you. Nanta, without consulting Ku-Mama or mother, agreed and encouraged him to leave at once and hurried your departure. After you were gone, Nanta returned to Mlango with the news. She and mother had a terrible argument; the whole house shook with their shouting. Mother thought Nanta should have brought you back here, because of your powers, but Nanta disagreed. More than anything Nanta told her, because she loved you and knew you better than her own mother, she wanted you to be safe and you would only be safe if you stayed out of Africa, far away from *Bayamchwi*. Mother banished Nanta from Mlango that very night and we never saw her again."

"I saw her at Tembo Nymuba."

"You saw Nanta at Stewart's house?"

"Yes. We spoke."

"Mother will want to know, although, I think it's best we don't tell Ku-Mama. We should let Mother tell her. Now let's concentrate on your education. Listen."   Geoffrey points a finger at his ear.

"To what?"

"Shush, listen and you'll hear them. This is one of the reasons we don't wear shoes. You must be connected to Mother Earth to be aware of her many voices."

The tall-grass has grown thick and butterflies brush their wings like soft kisses against my face and arms. Watching them, I contemplate how different our lives are, my brother's and mine. He embracing the ability to see souls and auras, listening to the earth speak and knowing how to use his magic. Me afraid and silent, not understanding the voodoo mambo-jumbo that's haunted me my entire life.

"Sit in the grass with me," Geoffrey said, taking my hand and pulling me down.

"What are we doing?" I ask, sitting next to him.

"Shush, listen to them, listen to butterflies," my half-brother instructs playfully. "Close your eyes and listen with your heart...and your soul."

Whispered voices fill my ears with a single note of their sweet song, "Home."

"Who's singing, that? Geoffrey?"

"Shush, Lill. It's not me, it's them," Geoffrey spreads a wide hand at the butterflies above our heads. "Now close your eyes."

"I don't believe you."

"I am a big man. How could I sing in such a tiny voice?"

"Well, I'm keeping my eyes open and watching your lips and they had better not move," I tease. Geoffrey's eyes crinkle, full of mischief. Here we are, two grown adults behaving like children, sitting in the middle of Africa's grassland listening for the butterflies to sing. I feel like giggling and rolling in the grass.

"Home, home, home." Thousands of velvety notes saturate the air and flood my ears. Geoffrey's lips don't move.

"Geoffrey, I can hear them," I whisper in stunned disbelief.

"Of course you can." His lips part and he sings with the butterflies, "Home, you are home, home, home." He grins with playful eyes.

My heart swells. He tilts his head and raises his eyebrows, encouraging me to join him and the butterflies in song.

Timid, I sing, "H-ho-home."

Geoffrey laughs and shouts, "Louder, sister! The butterflies cannot hear you." He laughs again.

So I sing, "Home, home, home...I am home."

Since David's death I had doubted this kind of happiness could ever be mine again. But for the moment, it has returned. I lie on my back in the tall grass and sing with the butterflies, to the blue sky, to David and to the joy of having a mother. We spend a few more minutes singing, then Geoffrey helps me to my feet and we continue our walk to his village.

When this journey is over, I promise to take more time to roll in the grass and sing. And wouldn't it be wonderful if David could share his soul with an elephant and come and play with me and Penda in the tall tawny stalks? And if he were an elephant, I could ride on his back and we could sing with the butterflies all day.

Geoffrey's village lies beneath the shadow of Kesho Mountain like a sleepy lion resting under a shade tree, all tan and full. The huts look very much like the huts in Ndogo, dark hard-packed mud walls and sun-bleached thatched roofs. A small herd of noisy milking goats are enclosed in a pen built from long tree branches with twisted limbs. Brown-spotted chickens skitter and scurry between their legs, dodging certain death, to reach the child-high coop to lay their eggs.

A dozen or so villagers have come out to greet us; teeth shining white against their happy faces. The women wear long-skirted sarongs splashed with bright colors and sleeveless tops. The men are clothed in shorts or long pants, some with shirts, some without. Everyone wears a necklace of beads and pounded metal. The children are a reflection of their parents and are impossibly cute. A healthy little girl, perhaps five, slips out from under the arm of a fat old woman, comes forward, and tugs on my pant leg. She grins up at me. Her two front teeth are missing; her eyes are dark-brown and delightful.

"Hello, Lillian." Her English is so perfect it surprises me. I wonder how she knows my name, but then the resemblance to Geoffrey becomes obvious and I bend down and shake her small outstretched hand.

"Well, hello to you, too. And you must call me Lill. What is your name?"

"Pia." She giggles, letting go of my hand and covering her mouth shyly.

"Pia, where is your mother?" Geoffrey asks.

"She's in the garden, Papa."

Geoffrey fondly strokes the top of her head before turning to me. "Lill, come, follow me I want you to meet my wife."

"Lill?" Pia pats my leg with the palm of her hand to get my attention.

"Yes?" I look down.

"When will you kill the animal for my grandmother's soul-crossing?"

Shocked by her question, my head snaps in Geoffrey's direction and my eyes bore into his; the daggers in his eyes flash a warning that I don't understand. It frightens me.

"What is she talking about?" I demand.

His eyes narrow, sending a cautionary look at his daughter. "Pia, not now. Lill and I have not discussed it." Geoffrey's hand grips my elbow and he leads me from his daughter's inquisitive eyes.

Away from Pia, I ask, "What's she talking about? Kill what animal?"

"You need to understand how the soul-crossing is done before you worry too much about it."

"Father." A very beautiful young woman interrupts as she hurries forward, her face hard-set and determined. I feel strangely ill at ease when she looks past me to speak directly to Geoffrey, "This is Lillian then," she states, without even glancing in my direction. "She is willing to help with *Machawi-shaitani's* soul-crossing?" Her voice snaps against her sharp lips.

"*Machawi-shaitani* is her mother; it will be her honor to help with her cross, Pepo. And it is rude for you to ask such a question in her presence."

"That would have been my honor if she had not returned." She shoots me a hateful look then purposely bumps my shoulder with hers and stomps off.

"My oldest daughter," Geoffrey offers apologetically with a shake of his head.

"Her name is Pepo, Spirit?"

"Yes. With you no longer in Africa, we assumed she would be the next *Machawi-shaitani.*"

"Lillian, you are here at last," a robust woman shouts, charging towards us in a flowing orange and green sarong. Her arms are open and when she's standing in front of me she pulls me into a hug.

"I am Geoffrey's wife, Nan." She releases her hold and glances at Geoffrey. "Ku-Mama is on her way. You must hurry to the mountain. Lill, we will talk when you get back."

"Our daughter is not happy. Will you talk to her?" Geoffrey said.

"Of course, but she will get over the anger when she witnesses your mother's soul-crossing."

Geoffrey guides us through a shortcut up the rocky mountain path and our journey to the top takes less than a half hour. On the rim a gentle breeze blows a wild strand of hair across my eyes, I quickly tuck it behind my ear then gaze down on the shallow valley of short green grass that stretches to a backdrop of Meza trees. They grow so close together they look like a stiff brown curtain, and the wide branches perched above them stretch out like a green panama hat. A small dot of a bird wings over the treetops and grows larger as she glides towards us on an invisible current of wind. The crown eagle circles once then follows, over our heads as we continue down to a circle of dark grass in the center of the valley floor. When we are at the edge of the circle, she swoops between Geoffrey and me; tilting her right wing to the ground, then lands with a hop, hop, hop, right in front of us. She folds her impressive wings against her body and digs her talons into the ground. Geoffrey points at the area across from her. I shoot him a glance. He nods, folds his legs and pats the grass for me to join him.

"Lill, this will be a little strange the first time you see it," he tells me as I settle next to him, "but this is what the soul-crossing is all about."

The eagle ruffles and fluffs her feathers. Her golden eyes close and vanish under round gray lids. She tucks her large head into the white downy feathers of her breast and remains still for half a minute then spreads her wings. With a slow flap, she lifts up, and her talons change into human feet before they touch the ground. And by the time I look from Geoffrey and back to her, Ku-Mama is standing before us and wearing the same dress she wore when she first appeared to me in the Msito gorge.

"Taa-Taa!" She holds out her arms as if she were taking a bow. "Kooee-kooee," Ku-Mama whistles with delight. "Not a bad trick for an old bird, huh, Lillian?" Gray dust sifts in waves from her outstretched arms and somersaults to her feet as she joins us in the grass.

"Impressive. I had my suspicions on how the transformation would take place but that was way beyond anything I could have imagined. When mother dies, will she share her soul with a bird, too?" I look from Ku-Mama to Geoffrey.

"We don't know. When it's time, the animal she is to soul-cross with will come to Mbali and stand under the cross in the center of the baobab trees. But you really must stop thinking of her soul-crossing as dying."

"I wonder what dad and his God would say about people not dying."

Ku-Mama and Geoffrey exchange looks. Ku-Mama's sigh is deep and long. "Lillian, there is really no difference. Your father's God promised life after death, and a heaven and a hell. Did you believe him when he told you this?"

"Yes, of course I believed him."

"Yet you have no real proof of it happening. You can't see or touch this heaven or hell. You have seen the souls from the spirit world; proof of a life after death...heaven. And you have had contact with *Bayamchawi*, proof of a hell. Why is it so hard to believe in our after life when you can see it, hear it, and touch it? There is only one God; your father knew it and so do we. The thing that bothered him the most was *Binti*."

"*Binti*? Binti means daughter."

"Yes, God's daughter."

"God's daughter. So now you're telling me God has a daughter?"

"Yes." She shakes her head from side to side, sending a cascade of silver and gold sparks into the air then shoots Geoffrey a look and rolls her eyes. "Geoffrey, we have so much to teach her." She turns her attention back to me. "Lillian, we are a very old people, direct descendants of *Binti*. We share her blood. Her blood gives us, and you, the power of white magic and sorcery."

"She only has half her blood," Geoffrey corrects.

"Yes, Geoffrey, of course, half her blood. Lillian, we are *Binti*'s children. She is our heavenly mother. Her blood binds us to the promise she made to her father: to always keep the door to the spirit world open. Once you have killed the animal..."

"Ku-Mama, I have had to put animals down, to relieve their suffering, but that was different. I don't know if I could kill a healthy animal."

"The animal doesn't mind; it is a great honor. You must kill it to capture its soul and to get its blood; it is the only way."

"And why do I need its blood? And how am I to capture the poor animal's soul?" My voice is colored with sarcasm.

A silent communication takes place between Ku-Mama and Geoffrey. He nods in agreement then stands and looks down at me.

"Sister, the soul-crossing must happen as Binti has ordained,"

Geoffrey scolds. "Ku-Mama, if Lill can't or won't do it, Pepo will." His face hardens then he turns and walks in the direction of the Meza trees.

"Don't fret, Lillian." Her hand sweeps a slow loop above her head and the grass around us pulls back into a twenty foot wide circle of blood-red gemstones. Ku-Mama crosses her legs, like Buddha on a mountain top in Tibet.

"Things are clearer inside the circle. It will help you see the soul-crossing differently." She pats the crimson stones. "*Binti's* birth took place right here. The same star that guided the wise men to God's son brought our people to *Binti*. Her skin was as dark as the darkest night sky, her eyes the deepest brown. She caught the guiding star's light in her eyes and was bestowed with its sacred magic. Through her blood she has passed that magic down to her daughters. It is her blood that binds the souls of animals with the souls of humans. Drinking the animal's blood seals it.

Her thin lips stretch into a birdlike grin. "And remember, your daughter will someday do the same for you."

"I don't have a daughter."

"Not yet, but you will. After you become *Machawi-shaitani*, you, your daughter, and Penda will grow old together and then it will be time for your soul-crossing."

"I still don't understand how Penda is involved in all this."

"Lillian, Lillian, what are we to do with you? Now listen carefully. Listen with your soul, not your ears. *Binti's* instructions are clear. In order for the door to the spirit world to remain open, they must be followed exactly."

Ku-Mama's body twitches. Her shoulders jerk and her arms flatten. Her skin becomes a darker shade of gray as feathers begin to gather on her arms.

"Tonight, you will meet your brother and uncle in Mbali, underneath the three baobab trees. The elders and Stewart will be there, too. Stewart will bring the spear you are to use to end the animals earthly life."

I shake my head from side to side, "Ku-Mama, I don't know if —"

"The animal your mother's soul is to cross with will be waiting for you under the wooden cross. Use your scar, it will help guide the spear into the animal heart. It will cause only temporary pain.

"There has to be another way," I sigh, frustrated with the whole soul-crossing ritual but desperate to help my mother soul to cross.

"There isn't. Do you remember seeing your father's soul when it left his body? And seeing David's soul here in Africa? Life doesn't end when the heart stops beating."

I nod, silently acknowledging the overpowering feeling of hope I felt when I saw David's and my dad's souls.

"They had to give up their earthly bodies to set their souls free. It is our souls, Lillian. It is our souls that give us everlasting life. Not our flesh."

I run my fingers through my hair and shake it loose but I'm unable to shake free the feeling of being backed into a corner.

"For the soul-crossing to be accomplished you must release the animal's soul at the exact second your mother's soul leaves her body."

My mouth springs open in astonishment, "How is that even possible?"

Ku-Mama takes an exasperated breath. White downy feathers ruffle across the front of her breast. She is becoming more birdlike with each passing minute.

"Geoffrey and the elders will have brought with them to Mbali one of the elephant tusks from the parlor. After you have killed the animal, you will use your scar to call the soul inside the tusk. When you have captured it, the open end of the tusk will be sealed with wax. It will remain sealed until Hata's soul is ready to cross."

"And what about the animal's blood mother's to drink?"

"Once the tusk is sealed, Giza will hand you a knife and a chalice. You will immediately draw the knife across the animal's throat and fill the cup with its blood."

I rub my temples in a vain attempt to push the mental image of such an unthinkable act away. Unconcerned with my discomfort, Ku-Mama lifts her arms, stretches them out to her side where they quiver and shake until they become wings. Gray dust falls into the circle, sizzles and is gone in a tiny puff of smoke.

"When the center of the moon turns black, your mother will be carried from her bed on the tapestry. The two elephant tusks will be slid into its sleeves and she will be brought here, to Kesho Mountain, and placed in the center of the circle. Resting between her breasts will be the crystal orb holding the guiding star's light. The three *Songba* drums will be struck and centuries of souls will soar down from the spirit world to witness your mother's crossing."

Ku-Mama's legs shorten.

"You will join your mother in the circle. The soul-crossing will begin when the orb lifts and spins above her heart. It is then you will give her the animal's blood to drink. As the orb spins faster, you will release the soul from the tusk and it will join with hers, they will become one."

"Ku-Mama, there is so much to remember."

"I will be there to guide you, if you need. But when the crystal orb leaves your mother's heart, be watchful. During the spinning, the spark of the star's light cannot be seen and we lose our powers. It is during this time that *Bayamchawi's* evil powers will be strong enough to prevent the cross, and to kill you.

When the souls have joined, the orb will float into your hand. From that point you are the new *Machawi-shaitani*. The gate to the spirit world will remain open, and the souls will be safe,

safe until your own soul-crossing."

Ku-Mama's hair shifts, gray and white feathers cover her ears and slid down her face. Her newly hooded eyes blink gold, round and birdlike.

"The red circle will explode into crimson dust and shoot sparks into the night sky. And a silver halo will spin rings around the moon. The drums will beat ten times and the red circle will close. The drums will beat ten more times and we will greet the soul of Msafiri. Msafiri's soul will..." She stops abruptly.

Ku-Mama's bird eyes widen. The heat in my eyes flares as Geoffrey runs towards us.

"*Machawi-shaitani* has fallen," he announces. "You must go to Mlango." Geoffrey's panic is directed at Ku-Mama. "We'll get there as soon as we can." His voice is tight with worry.

Ku-Mama's body twitches, gray dust flies, gold and silver sparks scatter everywhere and her body shifts into that of a crowned eagle, then she spreads her wings and soars into the sky.

"If we hurry we can be at Mlango within the hour," Geoffrey tells me.

"I think I can get us there sooner." I take his left hand in mine and hold out my right. "Mlango, I need you."

Geoffrey and I dust off the chalk-dry fog that is fighting with the afternoon sun along the stone path leading to front door of Mlango.

"I like the way you travel, little sister." The corners of Geoffrey's eyes crinkle then soften. A loud screech from the crowned eagle above grabs our attention and sends us dashing inside the house.

My mother's room is bathed in filtered light, the curtains blowing in the breeze of the open window. Ku-Mama is leaning over her, stroking her forehead with the back of her hand and touching her face with unsteady fingertips. She turns to acknowledge our presence then resumes comforting her daughter.

"Lill," Geoffrey whispers. "You and Mother have much to talk about and not a lot time." He leaves, closing the door softly behind him.

Ku-Mama kisses her daughter's hand and faces me. "She is alright. It was not a bad fall, just enough to scare us. Lillian, I hope you have come to grips with what needs to be done for her soul-crossing."

"You are a foolish old bird; of course she will help my soul to cross," Mother's strained voice coughs, then adds, "now that she has returned to us, it is her destiny."

Ku-Mama's glance challenges me to disagree, "I'll leave you two to discuss it," she says sternly and shoots me a sharp warning then suddenly sparks of gold and silver explode around her head. Her human body shifts, replaced by the incandescent light of her soul.

"Kooee-kooee," Ku-Mama's soul mimics the voice of the crown eagle as her soul-light zooms within an inch of my eyes. They hold me spellbound. Her soul spins, sprinkling sparks of light in my face then speeds out the open window.

"Lillian." mother calls me to her bedside and breaking the spell Ku-Mama's soul has cast on me.

"Yes, Mother?" It's wonderful to actually say the word *Mother* out loud.

"Ku-Mama has explained what is necessary for my soul-crossing? It will happen tonight when the earth's shadow hides the center of the moon. You are prepared?"

I sit on the edge of her bed, nervous and filled with doubt. "I love you and I want you to live forever but I still don't know if I can kill an animal to make it happen. If the animal was sick and was going to die anyway..." My eyes question hers; my heart torn into small pieces. Conflicted and filled with indecision, I offer another possibility.

"Ku-Mama said the last half of the prophecy said something about a double-cross. I was wondering if it may have something to do with Geoffrey's daughter? She really wants to be *Machawi-shaitani* and I think Geoffrey wants it, too."

"Pepo's a sweet girl. She and Geoffrey both wanted her to be the *Machawi-shaitani*, even if she had enough magic your return makes it impossible."

"I never would have come to Africa if it hadn't been for Penda. You would have had to use Pepo."

"Yes, but I suspect *Binti* had something to do with *Nabii's* prophecy and us needing you and Penda in Africa, together."

"I don't understand. How could Penda be part of—"

"On the first Sunday after you were born, your father left the house for an evening christening. You were just five days old when I carried you into the jungle that night. I walked for over an hour then placed you on top of your blanket under a tree, far away from the magic and the mist of Mbali. Ku-Mama was crossed with the crowned eagle and watched from a branch overhead, protecting your life if it was needed. Still, to leave you there alone, it was harder than I had imagined but it had to be done. We had to know if you had enough magic to summon the souls outside the magic of Ona and Mbali. I wept and worried all the way back to Ndogo."

"What happened?"

"When your father came home and found you missing, he went crazy. I assured him you were safe, but I couldn't tell him how I knew or about Ku-Mama. He accused me, over and over again, of being a witchdoctor possessed with the power of black magic and voodoo. As he ranted, I knew I had a decision to make. He wore me down, and agreed to take him to you, to prove to him my magic would never harm you. We took two Jeeps, your father and me in one, and four men from the village in the other. Your father and the men were all carrying guns.

There were no souls to be seen when we reached you; however, there was a young female elephant standing over you. At the time I didn't understand why, but I though it meant you had no magic and would be of no interest to *Bayamchawi*, and in a way I was glad. The elephant trumpeted and swung her trunk in the air. Your father misinterpreted the elephants' actions, and fearing the elephant would harm you, he ordered the men to shoot her. All five rifles were raised and the men took aim. Ignoring them and afraid you might be injured, I ran to the elephant and plucked you from between her legs. Your father and the men shot the elephant anyway.

Desperate, I did something I had never done before. I grabbed his arm with my right hand and held the scar tight against his skin. He was confused as he witnessed the elephant's soul light spinning from her silenced heart. He watched in disbelief as it quivered and shifted into the soft glowing form of a baby white elephant. Then it vanished. It was a message from *Binti*; the white elephant and you would always be connected.

After seeing, what your father called a ghost, he was more positive than ever that I was in possession of some evil voodoo, black magic. I didn't know it then but I would only have you for five more days." Mother reaches for my hand, kisses it and continues.

"When Penda was found I had no doubt you and she belonged together, and it had something to do with Nabii's prophecy. Your destiny was sealed, and so was mine."

"Mother, if the soul-crossing doesn't work...would it be such a bad thing to live in Heaven with God?"

"No, dear it wouldn't. But there is more at stake than just my soul-crossing. The gate to the spirit world will be closed if the cross doesn't take place. Your father's soul and all the souls will be locked inside forever. No souls will get in, and none will get out. And David's soul will be lost in a void. If you are not successful, when people die their souls will die with them, and the reality of a life everlasting will also die."

I ease off the bed, my heart paralyzed by the hopelessness of the situation. I stare at my mother, cementing to memory her beauty, not wanting to leave but knowing staying won't give me the answers I so desperately need. It's impossible to say goodbye. I hold up the palm of my right hand to her. She raises hers to me. My scar begins to burn. The scar on her palm turns crimson. My throat unlatches a single wrenching sob, and I run from the room.

"Go to Penda and talk with Stewart; they will help you." My mother's words trail behind me as I close my bedroom door.

I lean against it, breathing hard and sobbing, watching dust particles tick away time on shafts of dim light traveling from the window to the bed as I gather my thoughts, thinking about what I need to do next. I cross the room and sit on the bed. Mother's right, I need to see Penda. And then what? Dad's words flood my mind: "Our lives will be normal now." And I wonder if that will ever be possible, for me, again. Sudden determination propels me off the bed but doubt and confusion sit me back down; they have become my best friends and my worst enemies. They hang together like heavy bags of sand tugging my heart under an airless sea of unanswered questions. I walk to the window to take one last look into the yard, fingering the elephant necklace and thinking about what my life was like before returning to Africa. I touch each link of the chain—links to my childhood, links to my future. I finger the ivory elephant in the center and take a minute to dream about the perfect life I had when David, Penda, and I were a family.

A vacuum of silence deafens my ears and forces me back to the present. The birds in the yard are acting oddly. None of them are singing or eating, or hopping from tree to tree. They are perfectly still. Their little heads tilted up, watching an ominous black cloud slide across the sun. The smell of damp earth and lifeless air raises the hairs at the nap of my neck.

"Lill?" David's voice calls from somewhere downstairs, breaking the feeling of loss.

"Lill, I'm in the parlor." David's voice implores.

I cock my ear to catch more. When I don't hear anything, I take quiet steps, still listening, across the room to the dresser and open the draw. I take out a syringe, a needle and an ampule of Suomulose, a euthanasia drug for large animals, then move to the door. Unsure if it is really David's voice or a trap, I open the door an inch.

"Lill, come to the drums." My heart leaps, hopeful.

Throwing caution aside I hurry down the hall, slowing for the smallest of seconds outside my mother's room to press my scar to her door. Guilt plays a card—the queen of hearts—tempting me to slip inside and...I shake the thought loose from my head, I don't have the time and scurry down the stairs to the parlor.

In the doorway, I am halted by the image of David floating in the air like an effervescent hallucination. The drums behind him are shimmering in the blue light that is a part him.

"David," my throat catches as I ease toward him, sending a wave of ghostly blue vapor over the drums.

"Lill, I haven't long."

"David. I need your help with my mother's soul-crossing. What am I to do? I don't want to kill an animal, but..." His image begins to fade.

"You're smart, Lill, you'll figure it out. I wanted you to know I love you and if the cross doesn't happen...just in case...I wanted to say goodbye." David's soul gathers into a circle of light until only his face remains.

"My father's God promised an afterlife. If I fail, there has to be something else, there just has to be." David's face fades and his image is gone.

"Ask Stewart about the legend."

"David, please don't leave me, not yet."

"Lill, I love you." And he's gone.

The parlor is empty. The drums and the ivory tapestry taunt

me. And the damn crystal orb winks the guiding star's light from *Binti's* eye right into mine.

The scar on my hand pulsates. I hold it out in front of me.

"Tembo Nymuba."

Chapter 21

S tewart's front yard is falling into darkness and the jungle is nearly invisible. In the sky above, the earth casts a half shadow across the moon. A warm glow from inside the house lingers at the windows, teasing my heavy heart with hope. I have maybe two hours to figure a way to complete my mother's soul-crossing and keep the door to the spirit world open...without killing an animal. My head aches.

The front door opens and a shy puddle of light splashes onto the porch and I am aware of Stewart watching me as I climb the steps, waiting for me to speak. He is wearing ceremonial tribal clothes; the soft red fabric hangs to mid-calf and is belted at his waist with a supple leather belt. There are three leather straps, adorned with ivory circles, crossing his bare chest—also secured by the belt. A red scarf drapes off his left shoulder, it has a white cross and circle stitched in the center. Painted on his forehead is a silver, quarter-sized, dot.

"Hi," my voice weak with the pressure of what is expected of me. "Nice look."

"Traditional dress for a *Machawi-shaitani* soul-crossing," Stewart informs me.

I nod. "I spoke with David..."

"And what did David say?" He cocks his head, listening for my answer.

"He said I should ask you about an old legend."

"I think I know the one he is referring to, it is the legend of, *Ya-Kale Wachawi.* She was an ancient traveler of light; she spoke of a white circle: *"White light circles when the door threatens to close/what travels nowhere changes time when death comes before birth.* She also mentioned something about being double crossed.

"Double crossed? Someone besides *Bayamchawi*?"

"Come inside, we have a lot to talk about."

Ten minutes later, Stewart and I stand by the stairs facing the wall of spears. He has explained the story of *Ya-Kale Wachawi* and the possibility of her ancient prediction involving me.

"Choose your spear," Stewart encourages, sweeping his hand in front of the wall.

"All I want is a sharp knife and it has to be small. These are too big."

"Go ahead and ask. Let's see what you end up with."

I raise my palm, not believing there is anything on the wall that will work, but for Stewart's sake, I'm willing to give it a try. "I need a small sharp knife." The scar on my palm heats and a tattered spear near the bottom makes a loud popping noise, followed by a series of smaller pops then the wood shaft splits and shakes violently. The steel blade breaks free, shoots straight up, ricochets off the ceiling timbers then speeds down into my outstretched hand.

"Shit." I flick my hand, sending the blade to the floor with a resounding ping. Stewart grabs my hand to assess the wound. We watch as the horizontal gash closes and seals itself. I now have two scars on my palm; a vertical one and a horizontal one. They form a cross.

"That's interesting," Stewart touches my palm then lifts his eyes to meet mine. "Well, you did ask for it to be sharp." He grins, picks the spear head off the floor and hands it to me.

"Be careful what you wish for, right?" I say, tucking the blade into the back pocket of my pants. "Are you ready?"

"As soon as I get this." Stewart lifts his hand to the wall, "Spear-of-souls," he intones with a forceful voice.

A solid spear carved from an elephant's tusk breaks free from its restraints and shoots into his outstretched hand.

"You won't need that," I announce, my confidence shaky but determined.

"Are you sure you don't want me to bring it?

"You said I'll need to use my magic if I'm going to help Mother's soul to cross." I shrug and purse my lips. "Might as well start now."

"Okay." Reluctantly he leans the spear against the stair rail. "You're right. We'll do it your way. I have to start trusting the power of your magic, too."

At the front door Stewart pauses, "Remember you'll be safe until the crystal orb of starlight starts to spin. There will be too many sorcerers at the soul-crossing for *Bayamchawi* to attempt an attack before then, but once the spin begins we won't be able to help you until the orb is safely in your hands."

"If I wasn't worried before, I am now. Thanks for the pep talk," I smile weakly.

"Be brave, Lill. You are going be the next *Machawi-shaitani*; it is why you're here." Stewart grins. "Okay, let's get going."

"Where's Kipino? Isn't she coming with us?"

"She already left for Mlango, it's just the three of us," he nods, and we step outside.

Penda is waiting at the bottom of the steps. She is rocking from side to side and slapping the ground with her trunk, sending hollow clapping sounds into the surrounding blackness. There is a faint aura shimmering around her body that catches my eye; it's unusual yet somewhat familiar. I get a queasy feeling and close my eyes to check on Penda's unborn calf. The blue haze isn't as clear as it usually is...the aura is blocking it in some way, and I can barely make out her calf. My uneasiness grows.

A bright arc of light flies off the moon and draws our eyes skyward. Silver flames explode from the exposed edge, shooting sparks into the dark sky. Penda holds her gaze on *Mwezis*, the moon, a bit longer than I do, then looks me. Silver-light circles the rim of her brown eyes. A searing pain circles my own and my chest tightens.

"It's now or never," I glance at Stewart. He nods. I face the moon, forming an allegiance with her. The moon's silver ring sears through the earth's shadow, spinning to the surface like a merry-go-round gone wild—*white light circles and travels nowhere*. The circle's speed increases until it lets go of the moon, shooting a blinding silver vortex of moonbeams down to earth and on top of us. The air flashes white—*changing time*—and sends us away from Tembo Nymuba in an explosion of sterling sparks that erupt...into utter silence.

Penda leeks out a little squeal and Stewart and I look over at the baobab trees; she is standing beneath the cross. A cheetah sits between her front legs as regal as a sphinx. I close my eyes and let the blue haze spill over her. It's the cheetah I saved in the bush; her old heart is barely beating, she has only hours to live. My old scar and the new one both throb as the green mist of Mbali gathers at their feet. My mind churns on the edge of panic, why is Penda under the cross with the cat? The mist rises quickly and hides the cheetah and starts to crawl up Penda's legs, too. Terror invades every inch of me.

"Why is Penda standing there with her?" My voice cracks. My eyes frantic, searching Stewart's for an answer to my question.

"I don't know. The cheetah's here, that's good."

"Yeah, but—"

"—But this isn't right." Gold light cloud Stewart's troubled eyes. "I don't know...something's off. Giza and Geoffrey aren't here, nor the elders. We have no tusk to capture the cheetah's soul and no chalice for her blood. Lill, something is terribly, terribly wrong."

Penda lifts her eyes skyward and bellows. The mist fades from around the cheetah, she falters, struggling to remain standing. Stewart and I rush to her aid and as he lifts her into his arms the green-mist of Mbali swirls and takes us.

Fingers point at the cheetah Stewart is holding when we

step out of the jungle. And the natives take a collective gasp when they see Penda. Hundreds have gathered outside Mlango to witness *Machawi-shaitani's* soul-crossing. I recognize some from my trip to Kesho Mountain with Geoffrey. I catch a glimpse of Senento and Semoi and look to see if Nanta is near but I don't see her. Villager's from Ndogo and members of dad's church, all older, are here, too. Some are astonished to see me, a few, give me a knowing smile.

Everyone is dressed in ceremonial clothing, the colors and styles vary depending on the region they come from. Twelve sorcerers greet us, six men and six women. Kipino is among them. The men are dressed identical to Stewart. The only difference in the women's clothing is that they are wearing sleeveless blouses, tied at their waists.

Anxious whispers saturate the night and 200-plus torches are lifted high as we move forward. When Penda draws close, the natives grow quiet. Some reach out with shy fingers to touch her, most step back, others stay put and lower their eyes, respectful.

Heads suddenly snap in the direction of the jungle we've just left, listening to the distant sound of breaking tree limbs and bushes being flattened under heavy feet. The noise escalates to a frightening level as the threat draws nearer. Eyes stare, hearts pound, ears strain to hear and feet get nervous. We have also turned to see what's causing the disruption.

"By the sound of things," Stewart points, "I don't think Penda is doing this alone."

And they appear, elephants, one, two, and three at a time, charging out into the open. The natives scatter out of the elephants' way; it seems they're not stopping until they reach Penda. Stewart and I huddle close to her for protection, but they ignore us, intent only on Penda, and they cluster near her, greeting her with squeals, rumbles, toots and trumpets. When they have said their hellos and have settled; ten gray elephants and one white are standing in a circle.

I finger the elephant chain at my throat grasping the ivory one in the center with affection. "Penda knows something we don't, and I have a feeling these elephants are coming to Kesho Mountain with us," I tell Stewart.

Penda moves to my right side, Stewart stay on my left and ten elephants gather in behind. Seeing this many elephants this close causes the natives to give us and them a wide berth as we proceed to Mother's house. The natives move their torches up and down when we walk past, mumbling and whispering, *eupe tempo*, white elephant, and *kumi tempo*, ten elephants, the excitement carried in their voices is everywhere. They speak of *duma*, cheetah, when Stewart passes, but their voices quickly return to exclamations of *eupe tempo*.

We pause at the front steps of Mlango. The ten gray elephants spread out in a straight line facing the door. Penda remains between Stewart and me, then without making a sound Penda and the ten elephants reach their trunks up toward the open window of Mother's bedroom. The light coming from inside pulsates purple and a breeze that can't be felt ripples the curtains in waves of divine expectations.

Heated shouts leak from the back yard to the front and everyone's gaze traces the sound to the edge of the house, even the elephants turn their heads to listen. The yelling belongs to Giza and Ku-Mama. Their voices bite the air with outrage and accusations but their words cannot be understood. The shouting stops, a moment intervenes then the backdoor slams shut. Seconds later, the crowned eagle soars out of Mother's bedroom window and the birds loud *Kooee-kooee* pierces the air and gets lost in the night sky

Giza bursts out the front door and strides with agitated steps straight for us. He too, is dressed in ceremonial clothing. However, the scarf over his left shoulder is white and the cross and circle, are stitched with red beads, the silver dot on his forehead, dulled with irritation. When he is close, I can see the gold-dagger flashing in his eyes and wonder if their warning is meant for me.

"Lillian, Geoffrey and I couldn't meet you in Mbali because *Bayamchawi* has destroyed the tusks for *Machawi-shaitani's* soul-crossing; we have no way to contain the soul." His concerned eyes dart from me to Stewart but they stop on Penda. "Is your Penda, your white elephant, is she the animal for my sister's soul-crossing?"

"The cheetah's soul is to cross with Mother's."

Giza's focuses on the cheetah in Stewart's arms, then states, "She's ill."

"Yes. I'll release her soul in the circle when it's time, we won't need the tusks to contain it," my voice sounds more confident, than I feel.

"We still need the tusks to carry my sister...to carry *Machawi-shaitani* to Kesho Mountain. How will you fix that?" Giza's voice is shattered with concern.

"Penda will carry her." I announce, then reach over and take hold of one of her long tusks.

Giza stares at Penda and shakes his head, "I pray this works, Lillian. If it doesn't, all will be lost." He tips his head toward the house. "The elders are waiting," Then he pushes his way through the crowd and stomps away.

"I'll stay with Penda. Go to your mother, Lill," Stewart's steadfast eyes fill mine with reassurance.

Inside, the foyer is dark. The candle in the sconce has not been lit and the little room is cold.

Boom! Three drumsticks strike the taut hides of the *Songba* drums at the exact same time. A spasm of uncertainty clenches my shoulders and sends me hurrying to the parlor. The faint white-light filling the room comes from inside the drums. A reed-thin man stands behind each drum, their chests bare and glistening with silver dust and an ivory cloth covers them from their waists to their knees. Their heads are shaved and a silver dot has been painted in the middle of their foreheads. Stern-faced, they stare straight ahead, never once glancing in my direction. The tapestry and crystal orb holding the guiding star's light are missing, and the two elephant tusks are scattered in pieces on the floor. I run for the stairs and mother.

Outside her door a haunting chant stops me from rushing in, the women's voices strangely soothing. I don't know exactly what is going to happen at the cross, but I'm being drawn into it by a force far greater than my own. I settle my resolve, twist the knob and step inside.

The room falls silent. A dozen white candles burn in crystal vases on the wall above Mother's head, their amethyst light surreal. Nan and Pepo are standing at the foot of her bed, holding hands. Their clothing is tribal, ceremonial; Nan in red, Pepo in pink and when I walk past them, their eyes never stray from mother. At her bedside I stop and stare at her face, spellbound, and the four elder women resume their chant.

Mother's head-wrap is tied close to her face. Crystal jewels, on strands of white ribbons, cascade down the right side of it. Other jewels have been braided into the long rows of hair spilling out from underneath. Her gown, an ivory sheath, lays smooth on top her frail body, her feet are bare. She holds the crystal orb of the guiding star's light in her hands resting at her waist. Embroidered on her gown, over her heart, is a crimson-red circle and cross and painted on her forehead, a dot of white. The ivory tapestry from the parlor is folded and waiting at the foot of her bed. Her aura pulsates with the same rhythmic beat of the women's angelic chanting and its purple glow is intertwined with lime green coils that circle her unhealthy body. I close my eyes. The blue haze is blocked by the aura, but I don't need it to see it to know that she is dying. Dying is my word...I remind myself...not hers.

The elders are dressed in simple white sheaths and have identical silver dots painted on their foreheads. Their heads have been shaved and they stand, hands clasped at their waists, on each side of mother's bed; two at the head and two at the base. Their ebony skin shines, not with oil or silver dust but with the radiance of devotion. The elder, at the head of the bed and on my left nods and the chanting stops. I lean over and kiss the circle on mother's forehead.

"The prophecy tells the truth," mother's weak voice whispers as gold daggers flash in her eyes causing the spark inside the orb to flare...they are connected.

"Mother, I love you."

"I love you too, Lillian, but you must hurry. The time for my soul to cross is soon." She closes her eyes. "Nan and Pepo will help you dress."

Nan leads me away from mother's bedside and she and Pepo guide me behind a screen in the corner of the room. Neither of them speaks as they dress me in a simple ivory sheath, knotted at my left shoulder. A wide white cloth is draped around my waist and hips then tied in front. My hair is combed to one side and with Pepo's practiced fingers, plaited together with long strands of white beads and crystal jewels. A head tie is wrapped then fastened with a bow just below my ear. On my forehead, Nan paints a small white circle. The last of the ritual clothing is secured to the knot on my left shoulder with a jeweled clasp; a white scarf embroidered with red beads and the sign of the cross and circle. When they have finished, Nan and Pepo step outside, giving me a moment by myself. I take the spear head from the pocket of my pants and wedge it securely inside the shoulder knot. The syringe filled with the euthanasia drug Suomulose is sheathed and ready. I tuck it into the tie at my waist and pray my plan works.

I step from behind the screen and the chanting stops. The eldest of the four women moves to mother's side and lifts her off the bed, cradling her in her arms and carrying her past the foot of the bed, to the center of the room, where she waits. The remaining elders, move to the right side of the bed and unfold the tapestry. The sleeves have a break in the middle, giving them four openings, and the three women slide their arms in. Pepo shoots a hostile look in my direction, then steps forward and slips her arm inside the fourth, and last, opening. They step back and stretch the tapestry taut and move in close to Mother. The *Machawi-shaitani*, the high priestess of sorcery and white magic, my Mother, is laid gently on top. The elder who was holding Mother trades places with Pepo and the chanting resumes. And with no words exchanged, I follow them as mother is carried out of the room. Nan and Pepo step in behind me.

At the bottom of the stairs the *Songba* drums are struck. *Boom!* The floor trembles with the percussion and the front door is opened. The drummer's thumbs rap the stretched hides with the rhythm of an ancient heartbeat.

"*Machawi-shaitani*," the crowd cheers when they step outside.

Hundreds of flaming torches move up and down in unison to the cadence of the muffled drumbeats. The night stars sparkle bright against a darkened sky and the earth's shadow covers three-quarters of the moon.

The drummers march down the steps in single file. At the bottom they rotate and wait, spreading out, three abreast. They hush their drums still further, brushing the skins with flattened hands.

"*Machawi-shaitani!*" the villagers shout when mother is carried down the steps. The drummers turn toward her and rest their hands until all four of the elder's feet have touched the earth. Then...

Boom! Their drumsticks strike the hide.

The elders continue on toward Penda and the drummers step in behind. Ten elephants stand opposite Penda on the other side of the path. The native's burning torches twist the air with strands of smoke, circling the drummer's sticks as they raise them high above their heads.

I step forward and lay my right palm on Penda's cheek and the drummers bring their sticks down with great force.

Boom!

Then the *Songba* drums are struck again.

Boom!

And the tribal drums of the natives take up their own slow beat.

I take a sideway glimpse of Stewart. His hand strokes the cheetah's face. He nods and his lips answer my unasked question, "She's still alive." The elders bring mother forward, Stewart's gaze follows her. I touch the bridge of Penda's trunk with my palm and the heat of the scar warms against her hide. The drums hush to a whisper but continue a steady beat.

Stewart, the cheetah in his arms, and twelve sorcerers inch in closer. The ten elephants close in too, their trunks reaching out and touching Penda. The villagers form a cautious circle around us and for the first time I notice the witchdoctors. There must be three dozen, dressed in animal skins, hemp-skirts, long spears and sticks, their faces painted fiercely in multi-colors. They too have drums and their fingers tap them with the same beat.

Giza and Geoffrey shoulder their way up to me.

Penda's eyes widen, their sudden appearance has startled her. Her ears flap, she snorts and spins in a tight circle. Everyone, including the elders carrying my mother, inhale and step back, giving her room. I step in to calm her down. Penda's eyes are wild and showing too much white, she looks as if she is ready to run. The villagers draw further back, giving her an even wider berth. I grab her by the ear to steady her and whisper, "Easy." The sorcerers stand their ground, their eyes bright with gold lights ready to defend *Machawi-shaitani* from Penda, if necessary. Everyone is watching, everyone is waiting for me to make a mistake, or to prove myself worthy enough to take her place.

Penda raises her trunk, trumpets then lowers her head. I place my forehead against hers.

"Penda, it's okay. You know I would never let anything bad happen to you, I promise."

Penda swings her head up to the moon, swishes her ears back and forth and bellows.

Stewart's eyes flash to mine—the cheetah is failing.

The drummers take up a flat-handed beat and increase the tempo. Penda drops her trunk and kneels. The drums stop. The elders exchange cautious glances with each other, then with me.

"It's all right," I tell them. "She's ready."

Carefully they guide the sleeves onto Penda's tusks, past the break, to the front of the tapestry. When they have finished, they back away and Penda rises.

The crowd cheers, "*Machawi-shaitani*," and the drumbeats resume.

"Lillian," mother calls to me in a soft voice.

I step to her side, "Yes, Mother?"

"I see you found the soul I am to cross with. I don't know what you have planned, but her soul is ready to join with mine...I can feel it."

The sorcerers raise their hands and their scars emit pulsating red lines of light, caressing *Machawi-shaitani*'s body. The crowd inhales. The witchdoctors raise their spears, time and time again.

"Rah, rah, rah," the crowd chants in loud voices.

Penda rumbles her own response then slowly turns and faces Kesho Mountain. Stewart and the cheetah move in beside me. We stand united on the right side of Mother. The four elder women step in behind us, and the sorcerers' join in behind them. Penda walks away from Mlango on the last earthly journey Mother will take.

The three *Songba* drums are struck with a forceful boom.

The ten elephants rest their trunks, rumble then step in line. The native drummers rap their drums with a steady beat, clothing the night in a soft embrace. Hundreds of torches dance a slow dance of expectations and the natives begin to hum; the sweet melody coming from the depth of their African souls.

When we reach the tawny field of the tall grass the drums quiet to a whisper, their tempo matching that of the butterflies as they sing, "Home, you are coming home, home, home."

Chapter 22

I have managed the first part of the soul-crossing, having *Machawi-shaitani* carried to Kesho Mountain on the tusks of an elephant. I look at the cheetah and close my eyes; she is so close to death, I pray she can hang on just a little longer. How much longer? I'm not sure. I glance at Mother and remember her telling me that the crossing of two souls has to happen at the same moment, and I shake my head at the probability of that happening. My odds are not good. It's like putting two dogs in the down stay position; one of them is always going to want to get up before the other. I glance at the moon, only a small crescent remains; time is running out.

The two scars on my palm pulsate to the beat of the drums. What does it mean . . . the newly formed cross? Is it proof I'm more than a sorceress? Or does the horizontal line cut the vertical line to the spirit world, in half, and make me less?

We stop on the flat ridge at the top of Kesho Mountain and the singing stops, too. The torchlights send long shadows down the slope ahead of us. And the *Songba* drums are struck, Boom! Penda rumbles and overhead the crowned eagle swoops low, skimming inches above her head, leading the way.

"Kooee-kooee, kooee-kooee," her insistent, plea for us to hurry slices the midnight air as sharply as her wings cut through it. The circle opens and turns red and my heart pounds; the journey Mother's soul is about to take is up to me.

"Penda," I stroke her face when we reach its edge of the circle on the valley floor, "I need you to carry mother into the middle." Penda flaps her ears and answers with a muted trumpet of understanding. I take hold of her ear and guide her in. The crimson stones come to life with each step we take, their cool red sparks rising up against our legs and changing the ivory tapestry to the color of molten lava. In the center, I back away from Penda and mother, leaving them alone.

When I'm once again standing next to Stewart, the sorcerers cheer, "*Machawi-shaitani*," then spread out around the circle, to guard it. The elephants separate and stand in between them, for added protection. The sorcerers lift their right hands. The elephants curl their trunks and the gemstones flash.

Under an increasingly dark moon my eyes follow the crowned eagle as she flies over mother and Penda, scattering translucent gold and silver sparks on top them, then skimming across the circle and landing next to me. She ruffles her feathers and shifts into Ku-Mama.

"Lillian." Her eyes connect with mine. "Your mother is waiting."

Tonight Ku-Mama's gray dress shimmers silver and the white swath on her breasts carries the emblem of the cross and circle stitched in red beads. Her head is adorned in a cloud of wispy white vapor that wiggle and flow in curls and loops all the way to the ground where it puddles and hides her feet. A silver dot kisses her forehead. The distant voice of my dad invades my ears, "Got to keep you sweet, Lill." And I wish he were here with me.

Ku-Mama lifts her right arm. The moon's silver edge flashes a stunning whiplash of lightening and thunders its horizontal strike across the sky. Ku-Mama lifts her left arm and a vertical strike explodes straight down to the earth. With an ear-splitting thunderbolt, a round gate is formed and shines with brilliant starlight against the backdrop of the black sky, and Ku-Mama lowers her arms.

"*Machawi-shaitani*," the crowd chants over and over again.

The drums beat. The sorcerers and elders take up the driving chant. The drums' tempo increases and the chant scrambles apart giving way to nervous expectations. The natives move about, uneasy, restless; scanning the night sky . . . searching. The last bit of the earth's shadow covers the heart of the moon and it goes dark. The drums stop beating and the voices go quiet.

The silver gate in the sky catches fire. Everyone gasps.

Three drumsticks beat the *Songba* drum's taut hide, growing louder and faster consuming the valley with their deafening beat.

The fire in the sky explodes.

The gate opens.

The *Songba* go quiet.

Silver and white sparks catapult through the portal and a round of thunder rolls out with them. Thousands upon thousands of jubilant spirits zoom through the gate, filling the sky with the light of their multicolored souls; all here to witness *Machawi-shaitani's* soul-crossing. Dad's heaven could not possibly be more beautiful than this. Perhaps this is his Heaven and perhaps one of these souls is his.

The souls congregate in a polychromatic array of lights above us; the pounding of their celestial heartbeats hypnotic and electrifying. Ku-Mama raises her right hand to me. I raise mine to her and a glowing ribbon of red light connects us. The sorcerers raise their hands and red beams of crimson crisscross over *Machawi-shaitani* and Penda.

Ku-Mama closes her fingers over her palm and the beams are extinguished.

Three *Songba* drums are struck in unison. Boom.

"Lill, it's time," Giza's rough voice cuts the magic as he elbows up next to me. "*Machawi-shaitani* must drink the cheetah's blood, now. You have delayed long enough. It is time for you to kill the animal. They . . ." Giza sweeps his hand around the circle. "They think your magic willed the white elephant to carry your mother here. But what will they think if you are unable to kill the cheetah to obtain its soul?" Giza's question is unmistakably a dare. Geoffrey and Pepo step in beside him.

"I doubt even you can make the beast bleed without cutting her." Geoffrey emphasizes the word "bleed." He takes his daughter's hand and holds the handle of his sword out to me with the other. Pepo's eyes dart from mine to her fathers. I'm beginning to suspect Geoffrey wants her to be the next *Machawi-shaitani* as much, or perhaps more, than she does. Geoffrey's arm remains ridged, his gaze offering the same challenge he holds in his hand.

"Lill," Stewart's voice is urgent, "you must hurry."

I grab the sword from Geoffrey, clasping it firmly in my hand. Stewart's eyes question my intent. I raise the sword high.

"*Machawi-shaitani.*" Hundreds of voices shout. The soul-lights over our heads spin, shooting a kaleidoscopic of sparks in all directions. I lock eyes with Geoffrey then slam the blade into the ground.

The crowd gasps. Their confusion and questions rifle through the air.

"Giza," I avert my eyes, still afraid of the darkness that surrounds him, "I'll need the chalice for her blood." I extend my hand.

He removes the cup from the folds of fabric at his waist and hands it over, a precious offering. And, like Geoffrey, he thrusts the handle of his sword toward me then pulls it close to his side and leans in, his lips whisper against my ear, "You have misjudged me, niece. There is another, besides *Bayamchawi*, who wants you to fail." He backs off and Stewart shoots him, and then me, a questioning look.

I take the chalice and secure it beneath the knot tied at my waist then take Giza's sword and thrust it into the ground next to Geoffrey's. There is another quick gasp of breath. Panic pounds across my heart like frantic footsteps with the uncertainty of the decision I've made. I glance at Penda, the cheetah, and mother. The crystal orb resting close to mother's heart remains still. But I have been warned. Once it begins to rise, the sorcerers and I will lose the white magic with which to fight *Bayamchawi*.

"Lill." Stewart's eyes are worried. "Your mother's soul . . ." He tilts his chin in her direction.

My eyes dart back to the orb, it's rising. Mother takes a deep breath and it settles.

"Lill," Stewart's voice is urgent, "You must move quickly. *Bayamchawi* is close; the strength of his black magic is increasing," then he places the cheetah in my arms. Murmur of doubt spread through the crowd.

"What are you doing?" Giza pulls his sword from the earth and thrusts the hilt at me again. "Kill the cheetah, Lillian. Do your job." Giza grabs my arm with his free hand and twists me to face him, "Kill her," he demands.

Stewart fingers grab my uncle's hand and forcibly remove it, "Keep your hands off her, Giza."

"I don't need the sword..." I look directly in his eyes. "...to do my job." My voice is filled with rage.

Boom!

The drums are struck and I take a breath and step into the crimson-jewels with the cheetah in my arms.

Boom!

The drums are struck again and the torches are snuffed out. The souls above us spin in counterclockwise rotation, casting a mystical gossamer glow down on the earth.

"Mother." I lay the cheetah on its side next to her. "Mother, this is the soul you will cross with. This will work . . . it has to. I love you."

"Lillian . . . be prepared; *Bayamchawi* is here—I can sense his evil," Mother warns.

I look up at Penda. She gives me an encouraging rumble and the ten elephants guarding the outside ring snap their trunks on the earth in response.

The crystal orb wobbles and lifts higher and the crowd draws in a sharp breath. Then, once again, it rests; giving me the precious time I need. I remove the blade from the knot at my shoulder then ease the chalice from the cloth at my waist and transfer both to my left hand. With my right, I stroke the cheetah's sweet face then grab hold of her leg, press the scar against it and squeeze. The scar pulsates to the beat of her unhealthy heart.

"I need her blood."

The vein swells under the scar. I lift my hand and take the blade in my right hand and cut deep, then hold the chalice underneath and watch her blood fill the small bowl. Sensing a soul is near, the crystal orb rises higher above Mother's heart; her soul is ready to leave and join with the cheetahs. I quickly reach into the folds of cloth at my waist, store the blade, and remove the syringe, unsheathe it and ease the needle into the cheetah's vein. Her death will come soon. The crystal orb hovers higher and begins to spin. Binti's spark winks out. The lights in my eyes and those of the sorcerer's grow cold.

A strong wind blows across the surface of the circle, red sparks fly in every direction. I shelter the chalice with my hands and press my body tight against Penda's leg.

"Lill," Giza shouts above the howling wind.

I glance up, but before I have a chance to locate him, something hard slams against my legs. I grasp the chalice with both hands, covering the top, as I'm driven into the crimson abyss below. Nanta's face flashes in the red glow then quickly disappears as I fight my way back to the surface. On top, bent and struggling to stand, my eyes lock onto Giza's.

The ground beneath him cracks open and drops him, half in and half out of the hole. He grabs at the edge, fighting to keep from slipping further. Geoffrey and Stewart rush to his aid. Stewart grabs the straps across Giza's shoulder, and Geoffrey takes hold of a hand.

"Stewart, let him go," I shout at the same instant Giza screams and a red-black vapor swells over him. He plummets and topples the two men to their knees—they shoot each other frantic looks, somehow managing to hang on.

"It's a trick! He's *Bayamchawi*, let him go." They can't hear me and stretch out on their stomachs, hook their hands under his arms pits and heave up with all their might then roll back, dragging Giza with them.

Bayamchawi's torturous growl erupts from below. I don't understand! My eyes search Giza's prone body, I thought he was *Bayamchawi*.

The wind stops and a burst of black light flashes from the crack and Nanta's body jolts into shape.

"Nanta!" Panic rides my voice. She leaps into the circle, red gemstones flying as she races toward me with demonic speed, jumps, jettisons sideways, and slams her foot into my ribs, knocking me back. I stagger, struggle to regain my footing and keep the blood contained in the chalice at the same time.

Nanta's eyes bore onto mine. They are consumed with hate.

"Nanta? You're *Bayamchawi*?" I question, bent over, holding the chalice against my aching ribs and breathing hard.

"Shut-up!" Her words spew black saliva.

"Why are you doing this?" I beg, scanning the area behind her looking for someone to help me.

Giza moves this way and that waiting for an opening to toss his sword.

"I loved you, and you loved me," I appeal to Nanta.

Behind her, Giza raises the sword to synchronize his throw.

"Ten years of living with you and your father when I should have been *Machawi-shaitani*. I hated Ku-Mama for sending me to Ndogo. I hated her for choosing Hata over me. And I hated you. I was the oldest. It should have been me, not her."

"Nanta, please," I beg, at the same time risking to transfer the chalice to my left hand and touch the scar to my cheek, its cold, nothing happens.

"Your powers are gone!" Nanta rants. "See," she gestures at Mother.

The crystal orb's rotation has increased. I have to get the cheetah's blood to my mother before her soul is born or her soul and all the other are doomed.

"Daughter." Ku-Mama screams at Nanta, "Stop this, stop this at once!"

Nanta faces her mother, "You did this to me! This is your fault."

"Penda, take mother below the stones and hide," I implore. Penda lowers her head and plunges beneath the surface.

Giza takes this moment to pitch me his sword.

Nanta twists and catches it before it reaches me. Had he meant for her to have it all along?

A white light flashes across my eyes . . . I haven't lost its power, yet. Nanta raises the sword and swings. I shoot a lightning bolt of white light at her feet. It saves me from the blade but the force of it propels me sidewise, loosening my grip on the chalice and sending it into the air. Nanta's sword smashes through the glass, soaking the blade in blood.

Panicked, I look over at Ku-Mama for help, thinking she might have some magic left, "Lillian," she points and shouts, "Geoffrey."

I search him out, our eyes connect and he throws his sword. I catch it just as Nanta raises hers and swings. Our blades clash. A sharp pain sears my eyes, it seems *Bayamchawi's* black magic can't touch this white light, and I send another bolt her way. The arc catches Nanta's sword and frees it from her hands. She reaches in the air to reclaim it, but tips the handle and sends the sword tumbling back over her head.

"No!" Geoffrey screams. Pepo twists to avoid the blow, but the sword plunges deep into her back and she slumps to the ground.

Not giving up, Nanta wraps a black aura around herself, ready to latch it onto me and drag me down into hell with her. I swing Geoffrey's sword and slice a gash across her torso. The white light flashes into the wound and splits her body in half. Nanta screams! Her hands grapple for the aura, clawing at it, trying to pull herself back together. Another pulse of white light ignites and she explodes then vanishes, in a charred cluster of dark stars.

I gaze over at Pepo; she is motionless.

"Penda," I call. She resurfaces, Mother and the cheetah are safe, but the cheetah's soul-saving blood is gone and her soul is leaving her heart. I need more blood, but the drug I used to end the cat's life has tainted it and I don't dare give it to mother. The timings off; I've failed.

Hopelessness fills my heart as I look across to Geoffrey and Nan. They are kneeling at Pepo's side. Geoffrey pulls the blade from her back and turns her over. Nan gathers her daughter in her arms, sobbing. Stewart and Giza stand by their side.

I lay my head against Penda's throat and close my eyes. The blue haze fills my sight as my heart breaks; I have let everyone down. Then my eyes snap open, to be rid of the image I've just seen. I turn away from Penda and look at mother, restful and beautiful, on the tapestry between Penda's tusks. Her breathing is shallow, the crystal orb is spinning but her soul still clings to her heart. The timing, the timing, it might not be wrong.

"Mother, I need your help. I need you to hang onto your soul just a bit longer. I need more time." She's too weak to answer, but I pray she understands.

The cheetah's soul is fully formed. Pepo's soul spins pink above her heart . . . the blood on Nanta's blade might have been enough. With a gentle shove of my hand I send the cheetah's soul over to Pepo. Sparks fly and with a flash of light both souls vanish.

And then I notice mother's soul is rising up from her heart.

Frantic, I grab the crystal orb with my right hand to stop its spinning. The rotation burns my palm but I will myself to hold on, I need another soul and more time to figure things out.

Penda bellows; a silver ring haunts the edges of her pupils, she understands what is about to happen and so do I. I must act now.

A leopard snarls. *Bayamchawi?*

"Lill," Stewart's voice, is urgent. "We need that other soul, and we need it now." He bends and picks up the sword at Geoffrey's feet. My eyes fill with tears as he tosses it to me. My fingers tighten around the shaft, dreading what must come next and my chin trembles with the hopelessness of the situation.

I look at Ku-Mama, and she nods. "Lillian, you have to, there is no other choice."

Bayamchawi's rage ripples the earth at the edge of the circle with his hate-filled snarls. I transfer the sword to my left hand and lean in under Penda ear, "Penda, go back under the stones..." I let go of the orb. "...it will follow mother." I glance at my palm, the orb has left its mark; my scar is now a circle and cross.

"Take them now, Penda."

"Lillian?" Mother's confused cry leeks out as Penda slips beneath the stones.

The crater at the edge of the circle rips apart with distorted fury and acid-vapor oozes from the vile opening. Yellow flames lick the air and reach across the gemstones and snakes, large black mambas, slither up through the abyss. Their white fangs spit venom. Their forked-tongues threaten death.

I chance a glance at the moon; a ceiling of souls is blocking it, something is very wrong; the souls aren't moving. Their lights are dim. They are dying.

There is no hope. It is too late.

Bayamchawi growls then slams his ebony body between the snakes, thrusting them aside with his villainous black shoulders. The leopard's muscles ripple with victory. He sucks in the red glow of the circle and licks the taste from his lips with lustful delight. His savage eyes close into treacherous slits of pure evil. His ears snap flat against his head and stabbing jolts of lost hope slice my heart. His eyes bore into mine and blink red and the power of his black magic springs the sword free from my hand without even touching it.

"Lillian," *Bayamchawi's* cruel growl hisses. "Look around you. Your friends belong to me now."

I turn 360 degrees; the sorcerers' faces are masks of pain, their eyes dark, their noses flattened, joined to their lips and thick gashes of green scabs cover their chests. The elephants are still and hard as gray stone. Ku-Mama, Geoffrey, Giza, the elders, the drummers, all of them – every villager and every witchdoctor – stands frozen behind the demonic dance of thrashing black mambas.

"You think you are being clever, hiding Penda and *Machawi-shaitani* under the stones, but they cannot escape me. The gate to the spirit world is closing, the souls are mine!" His growl turns to a sinister laugh. "I have waited thirty years for this day. It is a shame it is going to be over with so quickly."

The black leopard slinks nearer the gemstones. My eyes grow hot. His back feet unsheathe their claws and dig into dirt. It's hard to breath. He crouches. I unleash the white light. His eyes close then open and he rocks his head back then lowers it to face me head on, "I've seized the power of the white light from your eyes. You have nothing to fight me with."

His tail whips back and forth. He switches his weight to his back legs and lunges into the air, rotating his body, aiming all four feet at me.

His back claws strike my stomach first. Then his front claws dig into my back. But I refuse to let him have me without a fight. I clasp my right hand around his throat and hang on. Together we tumble into the darkness below the red stones. I can feel the weight of him on my chest and I will my hand to squeeze his neck harder.

The mark of *Ya-Kale Wachawi* scorches *Bayamchawi's* throat and flings him out of the abyss and onto the edge of the circle. I shoot up through the gemstones after him. Penda and mother surface with me. Mother's soul is inches above her body, the crystal orb racing back and forth over her heart, searching for the soul that will join with hers.

Bayamchawi catapults from the circle's edge, aiming for me. Penda steps in front and takes the hit, his claws penetrate her hide. Penda can't reach him. Her trunk is useless, trapped behind the ivory tapestry. She screams and spins to rid herself of the devil, but can't. She spins faster and, this time, he is flung loose, tumbling outside the circle.

Bayamchawi's demented screams threaten as he slinks back across the red stones, determined to kill me. I hold out my right hand. The circle and cross respond, the magic of *Ya-Kale Wachawi* is stronger than *Bayamchawi*.

A white light circles my palm, shoots out and consumes *Bayamchawi* . . . *traveling nowhere* but *stopping time*. Vapors of red-black mist hiss and snarl then are strangled into silence inside a circle of white light. And *Bayamchawi's* gone. The snakes disappear and the fissure seals shut.

Penda rumbles and kneels. She lays her ear open and Stewart throws me a sword. I use the tip to cut the vein behind Penda's ear. Her blood fills my hand.

"Mother." I lift her head for her to drink. "I love you."

Red sparks shoot up in every direction. I place the sword next to Penda's throat and lean in against her body. Her skin flinches. My heart fills with anguish. Her body jerks. She screams. My lungs clutch my heart. I close my eyes and the blue haze washes over her. I pull in a breath, open my eyes and hold the point of the sword steady. Mother's cross and the promise of everlasting life depend on two souls crossing in perfect timing. My heart breaks, *death comes before birth*. The gate to the spirit world will remain open, but at what cost? Penda screams again, and a thick white mist erupts from beneath her and a tiny white soul spins free. Penda kneels and the ivory tapestry slides from her tusks, laying *Machawi-shaitani* gently on top the gemstones. The crystal orb spins faster and faster above the soul of the baby elephant. Mother's soul races toward it. The two souls join and Penda and I step from the circle.

Crimson sparks spin clockwise as ribbons of red gemstones shoot into the sky. The souls overhead twinkle with renewed life, rotating counterclockwise, singing out a single haunting note that doesn't end.

The crystal orb holding the light from Binti's eyes finds me and settles softly in my hand.

The crowd shouts, "*Machawi-shaitani*." And my fate is sealed, but there is much to be explained.

A vortex of sterling light pulls a veil of white magic over the circle and lifts it into the night sky. Higher and higher it soars until it touches the moon and erupts in a rapture of a billion stars.

Chapter 23

The shadow of the earth has fallen from the moon and the souls have returned to the spirit world through a gate that will always remain open. The red circle of gemstones is closed and once again covered with green grass and the people of Africa have gone home to their villages. The sorcerers remain to witness the consummation of the cross. The witchdoctors have stayed, too, hoping some of our magical powers will be rub off on them.

Jua, shy as always, teases us and takes her time to rise over the edge of the earth. When at last her golden head shows itself, she coils honey strands of curls through the night clouds and breaks the dawn. *Jua* has chased *usiku*, the night, away. And Kesho, the mountain of tomorrow, is alive with the fulfillment of Binti's promise, to keep the gate open.

Penda leads the herd of ten elephants from the brown curtain of tree trunks, to the flat top of the mountain, where we wait. As the elephants draw near, they trumpet and we see for the first time a tiny white elephant scooting playfully between the legs of her aunties. When they are just a few feet away, Penda, takes her trunk and affectionately guides the baby elephant to my side.

"*Msafiri*," I stroke her white head. "Mother, welcome home."

"Hata." Ku-Mama beams, laying her hand on the baby's back. "Welcome home, daughter."

Giza, Geoffrey, Nan, and Stewart crowd in around *Msafiri*, all of them speaking at once. Penda lays a motherly trunk across the shoulder of the little white calf she miscarried and now shares her soul with Mothers.

Ku-Mama's confused voice stutters, "We thought Penda was

the white elephant ...the prophecy spoke of...Lillian, how did you figure it out?" She asks and shakes loose a smattering of gray dust.

"*Ya-Kale Wachawi*, prophecy spoke of two things, the white elephant part wasn't about Penda it was about her miscarried calf...*death before life*. And the double-cross she mentioned was about a second soul-crossing. The double-cross was about Pepo. Geoffrey, Nan, there is someone here to see you." I reach over and place a hand on Penda's cheek. She flaps her ear, and the radiant pink new soul-light floats from behind it.

"Pepo." I smile and Penda rumbles contently.

Pepo's soul hovers close to the ground, shakes off a tangle of pink and gold sparks then shifts into the cheetah. Nan and Geoffrey collapse to the ground, hugging the cat and kissing her face, "Pepo," Geoffrey smiles and Nan pulls the cheetah onto her lap and begins to rock.

"And you, Lill?" Giza asks.

Stewart holds out my hand for everyone to see. "The legend is written here. She is *Ya-Kale Wachawi*," Stewart explains.

"The Ancient Traveler of Light," Ku-Mama adds knowingly. We don't understand everything, but we do know her magic is white magic and we will not have to worry about the gate to the spirit world ever being closed again." Ku-Mama nods her head and smiles, sending another round of gray dust to the ground as I turn to Giza.

"Giza, I thought you were *Bayamchawi*. I couldn't see your soul and you seemed so angry all the time. Why?"

"Ku-Mama and I suspected Nanta had given her soul to *Bayamchawi* when she left Mlango. We didn't have any proof so we couldn't say anything. The reason I was so guarded was because Nanta was my sister; our blood is the same. I had to be careful of her reading my thoughts and aura. The only way to do that was to hide everything. I'm sorry it caused you not to trust me. I hope you will let me make amends." His grin crinkles his eyes.

"There's nothing to amend, only time to know each other better."

*****

Back at Tembo Nymuba unasked questions sit between Stewart and me like a string of unruly school kids waiting to see the principal. Penda road us home on her back as *Jua* walked up the sky. By noon we are both in our bedrooms, napping...or not.

A late lunch and Kipino's gentle knock on my bedroom door entices me to dress and as I do, I think about everything that has transpired. Things that are undeniably true, things Ku-Mama reminded me, are far greater than voodoo or simple witchcraft and things that I am going to have to live with forever.

Standing in front of the mirror I brush my hair loose and let it fall wild around my face, feeling as free as it is. The teal blue Kafka I have slipped on, brings out the gold lights in my eyes. The lights are there all the time now and I am no longer afraid, but I am aware of the added responsibility that comes with being *Ya-kale-wachawi.* It is still difficult to believe Nanta wanted to kill me; all those years filled with so much hate.

Stewart is waiting on the front porch when I step outside.

"Wine?"

"Please."

The white wine is cold and smooth with subtle hints of berries and lavender and reminds me of Mother. *Msafiri,* I let the word and the wine slide over my tongue. It feels delightfully normal and I wonder when I'll see 'her' again. Ku-mama said it will take a little time for Mother to get comfortable with all three of her new forms. But she promised, soon.

"How long will you be gone?" Stewart asks the question I've been asking myself since we left Kesho Mountain.

"Long enough to settle things at L.A.A.S, but not too long,

what would I do with the magic in the states? They'd lock me up and toss away the key if I even so much as willed a pencil to my desk without touching it."

"If they did lock you up, you could use your powers to break free. I can see the headlines now—Vet escapes, bars couldn't hold her." Stewart's eyes laugh and hold mine a second too long.

Penda's trumpet travels from the jungle seconds before we see her and we walk down the steps to greet her. A man engulfed in shimmering blue light walks beside her.

David.

My breath catches. Stewart takes the wine glass from my hand. My heart hammers out of control.

"I will leave you two to talk." Stewart touches my face with his open palm. His scar flares against my cheek. Our eyes lock, then he breaks contact and slowly walks back to the house.

David's image has become more flesh than soul by the time the three of us come together. The soft green grass caresses my toes as we face each other; Penda remains by David's side.

"Lill." He takes my hand then folds me into his arms. "It is so good to hold you again."

I begin to cry. "How is—"

"—is this possible? It just is, Lill." David kisses my lips then slowly starts to fade, and I can no longer feel his arms around me but his blue-green eyes grow brighter. "Lill, I love you. I always will, but it's time for both of us to move on with our lives." His essence distills into a translucent orb. A refraction of light flashes tilts on its side and David's soul-light is gone.

Hanging onto the tip of Penda's ear, we walk together back to the house and Stewart, content and not doubting for a minute that Africa is where we belong. Stewart sits on the top step; two wine glasses rest by his hip. He stands when Penda and I reach him. He reaches out and strokes Penda's cheek, then steps down and takes my hand in his. The heat from our scars begins to warm and the scar on his face turns red.

I'm going to have to ask him to tell me the story behind that scar; maybe tomorrow, or perhaps the day after, *siku nyuma ya, baada ya*, or the day after that...

About the Author

"The White Elephant Kneels" was inspired by Roxana Gillett's private month-long safari in the 1980s following the migration across the Serengeti-Mara in Africa. Lill's story is based, in part, on Gillett's own experiences, including the 12 years she spent as a wild animal trainer at Marine World Africa USA in California and a three-year stint as an "elephant broad" with Circus Vargas. She has raised and lived with 27 big cats, a mixture of lions and tigers, and one small bobcat with a serious attitude problem.

Gillett taught Creative Writing on an Arts-in-Corrections grant at Mule Creek State Prison in Ione, California, for three years. The class was held on "A-yard" in maximum security. The men were the worst of the worst, all lifers, and most of them in for murder. She found it an interesting challenge, a job she thoroughly enjoyed, and a book yet to be written.

Gillett can be reached at RoxanaGillett@outlook.com.